All the Windwracked Stars

Tor Books by Elizabeth Bear

A Companion to Wolves (with Sarah Monette)

All the Windwracked Stars

Elizabeth Bear

A Tom Doherty Associates Book
New York

ALL THE WINDWRACKED STARS

A Tor Book
Published by Tom Doherty Associates, LLC
175 Fifth Avenue
New York, NY 10010

www.tor-forge.com

Tor® is a registered trademark of Tom Doherty Associates, LLC.

Library of Congress Cataloging-in-Publication Data

Bear, Elizabeth.
All the windwracked stars / by Elizabeth Bear.—1st ed.
        p.   cm. -(the edda of burdens ; [bk.1])
    ISBN-13: 978-0-7653-1882-4
    ISBN-10: 0-7653-1882-2
    1. Magic—Fiction.   I. Title.
  PS3602.E2475 A44 2008
  813'.6—dc22

                                    2008034076

First Edition: November 2008

Printed in the United States of America

0   9   8   7   6   5   4   3   2   1

This novel is for Kat Allen and Pen Hardy,
without whom it never would have been written.

Acknowledgments

I am indebted to my mother, Karen Westerholm, who gave me the passion for language; to Brian Rogers, without whom there would be no Muire; and to Stephen Shipman, without whom there would be no author.

Kudos also go to my loyal first, second, and final readers: especially but not exclusively Larry West, Kathryn Allen, CMS Burrell, Penelope Hardy, Sarah Monette, Jaime Lee Moyer, Leslie Lightfoot, Ruth Nestvold, Stella Evans, Kyri Freeman, and Hannah Wolf Bowen—and to the critters of the Online Writing Workshop for Science Fiction and Fantasy, without whom this book would certainly not exist in the form it does today.

I am also indebted to my editor, the redoubtable Beth Meacham, and my agent, the miraculous Jennifer Jackson.

Contents

1:     Isa (ice)   13

2:     Thurisaz (thorns)   32

3:     Hagalaz (hail)   42

4:     Ansuz (insight)   58

5:     Wunjo (comfort)   68

6:     Mannaz (humankind)   80

7:     Othala (home)   99

8:     Ehwaz (a horse)   114

9:     Jera (the harvest)   127

10:   Dagaz (daylight)   149

11:   Eihwaz (the tree)   159

12:   Tiwaz (the sky)   173

13:   Raidho (the wagon)   192

14:   Gebo (gifts)   203

15:   Fehu (possessions)   215

16:   Berkano (family)   231

17:   Perthro (casting lots)   238

18:   Uruz (tenacity)   256

19:   Sowilo (sun)   268

20:   Nauthiz (want)   283

21:   Ingwaz (growth inward)   304

22:   Laguz (the sea)   318

23:   Algiz (shelter)   334

24:   Kenaz (the pyre)   354

All the Windwracked Stars

Isa (ice)

|

On the Last Day:

> *He was born white, before* she *burned him.*
> *But that wasn't what happened first. Not in the beginning.*
> *In the* beginning *was the end of the world.*

There was snow at the end of the world, and Kasimir was dying in it. Broken wings dragged from his shoulders like defeated banners, disordered feathers hauling crimson streaks through the snow that would not stop falling. The wings were the worst pain, each step grinding bone shards through savaged muscle and lacing his withers with acid ribbons.

The worst pain, but not the only. One foreleg wouldn't bear his weight. His harness dragged askew, girth snapped, stirrups banging his ribs as he hobbled in circles, right head hanging, antlers scraping ice and frozen earth and fouling his remaining foreleg.

But still he walked, limping in tightening circles, bellying through drifts that rose to his chest, blood freezing bright as hawthorn berries on feathers and hide that faded into the mounting snow.

It was cold, and he was dying alone. But somewhere under the snow was Herfjotur, who had been his before she was torn from the saddle. Kasimir was a valraven, the war-steed of a waelcyrge, and they were dead, all dead, every one of them, the waelcyrge and the einherjar, the Choosers of the slain and their immortal warriors.

They were dead. Herfjotur was dead. It was snowing.

And Kasimir would not lie down until he found her.

They had sworn to die singing, and they had done it, every one of them. Ten thousand taken all together, einherjar and waelcyrge and the tarnished, the children of the Light and those fallen to the shadow, together again under the falling snow.

Every one of them, except for Muire.

Now she slogged through thigh-deep snow, returning to the field of battle. She was not dead, though she should have been. She lived because she had fled, because she had broken and run and left her brothers and sisters to fall without her. To fall like stars, and die singing, here on this high place with their backs to the ocean and the snow drifting over their corpses. She stumbled past the great slumped shapes of valravens, the smaller hillocks of her brothers and sisters lying tangled in their silver chain mail and their ice-colored swords and their cloaks of midnight blue, spangled with embroidered stars.

In death they were anonymous. She could not tell the tarnished from the Bright, and she did not pause to uncover their faces. She tried not to see the gaunt black shapes of the sdadown sprawled among them, red tongues lolling in the snow, poison-green eyes sunken and lightless.

And over all of it the blood, and the ice over that.

Muire did not feel the cold. She was a child of the Light, of the North, of the ice and the winter, and no cold could touch her. It could not make the bones in her hands ache or numb and gall her feet. It could not crack her lips and pull the moisture from her skin.

She was a child of the Light, one of the wardens of Valdyrgard. But now she reached out to that Light and touched nothing. No song, and no singing, and no power of the massed will of her brothers and sisters. They were gone, and she was the last, limping through snow on a leg scored by the teeth of a sdada that had charged past her, to join the pack pulling the war-leader apart.

Strifbjorn had died there, eaten alive, borne down under a black wave of sdadown. And Muire had lived, because she ran.

Now she returned. She'd lost her helm somewhere, and her crystal sword, Nathr, was dark as a splinter of glacier in her hand. Ash-colored plaits hung down her back like a pair of rope ladders, snow snagging on stray hairs. She saw other braids vanishing under the snow, smooth golden or flaxen ones without the split ends and sprung bits that always seemed to come of Muire's impatience with the brush.

Snow had drifted over most of the blood, but her boots broke through the crust to ink a red trail behind her. She trudged, head down, and when the brief winter light was failing, she found the place that she had fled from. She sheathed her blade and dropped to her knees in the snow, fresh blood oozing from her ragged wound, and there, with bare hands, she began to dig.

She found Arngeir first, Bergdis lying half over him, as if their mutual slaughter had been the consummation of an embrace. Menglad Brightwing was cold and quiet beside them, her hand cast over her mouth, palm outward, as if expressing surprise. She lay unmarked, except for the blood of her enemies, victim of a tarnished kiss.

And then Muire uncovered Strifbjorn. She hunkered, knees drawn up before her, and bit her fingers and stared and tried to find the courage to lie down in the snow beside him.

He had died bravely, but he hadn't died well. The sdadown had had their way with him, so she would not have known him from his face. But his stature and his silver-white plait told her whose body this was, as did the blade called Alvitr lying unbroken by the remains of his hand.

Behind the storm, night was falling. The long sweet howl of a sdada lifted the hair on her neck, as perfect and mournful as the call of the wolf the monster had once been. Muire pulled her cloak tight to her shoulders and rubbed at icy tears.

She could not stay here. She did not have the strength to bury them. They were frozen in the snow, and there were too many. She dared not even sing them to sleep; a raised voice would lead the hunting sdadown to her.

It would be a fitting way to die, but she looked on what remained of Strifbjorn, and she feared it. And so instead, she reached down, deep, to where the Light should have filled her. Where there should have been an answer, the knowledge of what it willed, a *swanning*. But the Light had no counsel. The brilliance that should have blazed from her hands and eyes and open mouth was nothing but a flicker, the last blue flame crawling over spent fuel before the wind unravels it.

It was only the ghost of strength dying in Muire's breast. The Light did not answer.

———

Kasimir could not find Herfjotur. There were so many under the snow, and the stench of blood and the dead musk of sdada was everywhere. He nosed aside the vile-wolf corpses, and swept snow from bodies with his horned head because the antlered one hung dripping blood from chill nostrils. The wind gusted this way and that, twisting his feathers. The night came on, and he, who had never known the cold, felt it leaching into his bones, pooling in his muscles, puddling in the bottoms of his lungs. It was heavy, that cold. Heavy, and it clawed at him with sharper talons than the sdadown.

Worlds had ended before: he had heard of the fall of Midgard, beyond a sea of space and time, whence the very oldest of creatures had journeyed: the Grey Wolf, his demon sibling, and the World Serpent, who was called the Dweller Within, and also the Bearer of Burdens. There were many tales, and Kasimir had heard them by firesides with his rider, when the Grey Wolf had deigned to speak. Before the Wolf had done what he had done.

Kasimir pushed through another drift, breast deep, hooves scrabbling as he floundered. Sometimes his feet struck frozen flesh under the snow, and each time he stopped and uncovered what he found, cold scents as good as names and faces in the gathering dark. As the sun fell it grew more difficult to tell the texture of flesh from that of stone, but he found Hrolf and Horsa, and Brynhild who had been Zacharij's rider, and the valravens Zacharij and Hryhoriy, more torn than Kasimir. Their feathers fluttered like tattered cloth when he swept the snow from their wings.

Then he found Olrun who had been Herfjotur's spear-sister, Olrun who had gone to the tarnished and whom Kasimir had shattered under his flailing hooves, there at the end of the world. Wings dragging, he paused to remember who she had been, before she had fallen.

But only for a moment. Night was falling, and he would find Herfjotur. He would lie down beside Herfjotur, and that would be good. But first he would rest here, only for a moment, he told himself, as his foreleg failed him and he went to his knees, ice and blood crunching under his settling weight.

Or maybe he would just lie down here. Beside Olrun. He had missed her, after she had tarnished. And surely Herfjotur would not wish her left alone. Surely she would forgive him. It was, in the end, only one more tiny failure.

He let his muzzle rest in the snow. He let his ears sag forward. He would only rest a little.

A sdada howled.

Kasimir, struggling to lift his head, saw a torn light flicker through the snow, and neighed with renewed desperation.

Muire found her feet, pushing against the unaccustomed pain of stiffened joints and the insulted, frozen muscle of her thigh. She grunted and staggered and caught herself with a wince.

The night seemed darker than it should, so Muire knew her waelcyrge's eyesight was also deserting her. But the cry was repeated, a frail, frantic neigh, and she unslung Nathr from her shoulders and used the scabbarded blade as a crutch.

Undignified, and the sword deserved better, but Muire's only other choice was to cast her aside, and she had not yet fallen so low. She comforted herself that even the tarnished had kept their blades, though the act profaned them.

He called again before she found him. Herfjotur's stallion waited with a sagging head, wings draggled like a dying falcon's, the other neck broken and twisted sideways, on his knees in the snow. He snorted, whuffling like a stabled horse when she came into sight, and even through the darkness, Muire could see enough to be cruelly glad she'd kept her sword. He would need its mercy.

"Bright one," she breathed, not daring to reach out and touch his neck. He made the connection for her, nosing her chest hard enough to nearly knock her off her feet. She gasped when her weight rocked onto her injured leg and she caught one spiraled horn to steady herself.

He froze, as white and still as the white drifts around him, and let her cling. And then, in a deep and sonorous voice that would have resonated through her chest if it had been spoken aloud, he said, **Alive? Alive how?**

She let his horn go as if scorched. His great brown eyes were soft and living, but she could see the broken bones jagged through the flesh of his wings, the twisted, back-bent leg. "Cowardice," she said, and leaned on her sword-crutch a moment before she could force the next words out. "I ran."

He turned his head to center her in one eye's vision. **The Light?**

"No more," she answered. She braced herself on her one good leg and raised her sword, her hand clutching the scabbard below the crosspiece. "Bright one—" she did not know his name; none but a valraven's rider knew his name "—I cannot heal you."

She could not even heal herself. Only hours ago, it would have been no more than the matter of a thought. Only hours—

Live, the stallion said, unflinching, and Muire stopped with her blade half skinned from the scabbard.

"We *can't*," she said, as an edgy, grieving howl drifted to her. She swallowed, and it felt as if the crunching ice cut her tender throat from the inside. She finished sliding Nathr's dark blade into her hand.

Ingrained habit made her work the sheath back through her baldric, where it banged her spine when her cloak lifted on the wind. The blood on her tongue when she bit her cheek brought some measure of courage. Somewhere out in the darkness, the sdadown hunted, and Muire jerked her chin. "I will be quicker than they."

The stallion surged up in the snow. **Live**, he demanded, his wings flopping with the sickening violence of landed fishes. Muire fell back, waving her blade well clear, and sprawled in the snow. It crushed down her collar and under her mailshirt, chilling her flesh—another unpleasant, unfamiliar sensation. **Live**, he said again, more softly, as she held the sword foolishly up out of the snow, struggling on her wounded leg. She floundered until the stallion extended his head again, offering his mane for a handle, and then she managed to haul herself up. She leaned against him, gasping, his warmth transmitted through her tunic and chain.

Live. One more time, and this time, no more than a meditative murmur. She stroked his blood-iced forelock from his eyes in time to feel him flinch from another howl, an answering one. She sighed. If only she'd had the sense to stand and die earlier, this would have been over now.

But the stallion, she thought. The stallion would be alone. Perhaps she could make some sort of amends by standing with him.

"As well now, here with you, as later, otherwise."

She whipped her blade on long twinned curves and put her back to the stallion's worse-injured shoulder. He whickered again, ears up, half braced on a leg that would not hold him, and mantled her with shattered wings so her flank was covered.

No such courage in all the world, she thought, and the sdadown came upon them.

It was a small pack, only four, and not the dozen it had taken to pull down Strifbjorn. When they ventured close enough, she saw how their rib cages protruded, how their backbones and tails were knobby and spined. Great splayed paws held them lightly on the snow, and their red maws dripped slaver.

Once, she would have met them singing. Now, it was grim fury, ice and blood and her own silence, and the silence of the beasts. The sdadown hunted like the wolves they had once been—feints and distractions—but they were dead already, and the only way to destroy them was to destroy their hearts.

At first, they circled. Wise monsters, they knew that the valraven and waelcyrge were wounded, that the snow and the cold collected a toll that could not be replenished. Two feinted at the crippled stallion's haunches, and Muire surprised herself, half scrambling and half sliding over the broken wing to meet them, her sword outreached as she lunged.

She pricked one through the throat, but it dragged itself off the blade and retreated. Through what will she did not know, the valraven found the strength to kick out, sending the other sdada tumbling. A living wolf would have yelped, rolled to its feet, and circled, limping. The sdada rose and circled, certainly, but it did it in bitter silence, head sunk between jutting shoulders.

Muire prayed, and went unanswered. And as if they slipped over greased ice, the sdada struck again.

She stepped into it, thrusting, and staggered with the shock as the sdada impaled itself on her blade. The second one, the one she had earlier wounded, hurled itself out of darkness at her throat. She shied back, clinging to Nathr's hilt, and got her arm up as she whipsawed sideways. The first sdada's rib cage offered grating resistance to the blade, the vile-wolf thrashing until it slumped, suddenly, its heart bisected.

Through the hot sting of teeth meeting in the muscle of her off-side arm, she barely noticed. The weight struck her shoulder and chest and she staggered, thumping solidly into the stallion's haunches. Her blade, knocked free of the broken sdada, swung wildly, the ridged brass and iron hilt twisted unready in her hand.

The stallion snorted and stood firm, supporting her, while the sdada gnawed and thrashed. It felt hideous, not hide and hair but warm soft slickness, shadows wrinkled and slippery over the skinned flesh beneath. It had no breath.

It pressed her forearm against her throat, teeth grinding into bone, the pain eye-watering. But the warm hide against her shoulders heaved and surged over living muscle, and she heard the stallion's labored breathing, the sick kitchen sound of ripping flesh. Her own blood wet her face, her feet slipping as she floundered in deep snow. Kasimir surged and snorted, something crunching under his teeth and hooves.

She let the sdada shove her back against the stallion and struggled to right her sword. No blade for a mighty-thewed warrior, Nathr, but a light, quick sword, still long enough that little Muire had to wear it slung between her shoulders rather than at her hip. She was the least of her sisters, small and quiet, a sparrow among falcons.

She still could wield her sword.

Her fingers tightened, the blade's weight pushing her arm down. The sdada scrabbled against her, smelling faintly of loam and rotten meat, dead green eyes glowing behind clouded corneas like a sun behind mist. Its silence offended her.

She grunted as its skull slammed into her face, and hammered its head with her pommel. The teeth loosened incrementally.

A dam burst. Muire shouted, slammed the beast again, let the stallion support her weight as she leaned back and kicked the vile-wolf in the ribs. Her flesh tore under its teeth, nauseating bursts of agony with every blow she delivered. She hit it again, gasping names, prayers—*All-Father, Bright Mother*—and knocked it back, struck it free. She found a breath as it rolled in the snow, tumbled to its feet, crouched and snarled silently.

Fine, she thought. *Die in silence.*

Not me.

She found another breath, and her defiance, and she sang.

Let it bring down every sdada left on the battlefield. Let them come. She had the stallion at her back, and blood trickling from her split lip and broken nose, blood flowing from her savaged forearm. She had death in her right hand and death in her heart. Let them come.

She would welcome them.

She waded forward, the snow numbing her wounded thigh, and swung her ink-black blade, singing between ragged breaths, gasping the words over a broken melody. And Nathr flared blue-white in her hand, bright as a full moon on snow, streaking the drifts with hard-edged deceptive shadows you could fall into, you could cut yourself on.

Muire flinched from the light.

She raised her right hand as if to shield her eyes, angling the blade down. The sdada leaped, thinking her dazzled, and she cut it from the air. Nathr went through it, scattering flesh and shadows and bits of bone, leaving Muire staring at her hand and the undimmed blade as if they were a stranger's.

Muire heard the stallion grunt, felt him lunge forward, uncoiling off powerful haunches. She turned in time to see him catch the fourth vile-wolf by the throat and shake it like a ratting dog shakes vermin. Bones snapped but it still moved, sickly, brokenly. He dropped it to the ground and began tearing out chunks with his teeth.

She stepped forward, around the dragging wing, and finished it with a thrust.

Like a clockwork unwound, she paused there, her blade still transfixing the sdada, her head bowed, plaits and cloak whipping forward as the wind veered behind her. Something stroked her cheek—a tear, already freezing. Her cold fingers numbed on Nathr's hilt.

The stallion nudged her hard with his muzzle and fell back into the snow with a thump. Muire turned, startled, but there was nothing behind her but the wind. She stood for a moment, tottering, her blade gleaming as bright in her hand as if all her brothers and sisters stood beside her. For a brief, cleansing moment she felt the snow in her hair, the presence of the children beside her.

And then there was nothing. She opened her eyes on emptiness, on blowing snow, on the already drifted corpses of the sdadown that she and the dying stallion had killed—two for her, one for him, that last one together—and shook her head.

Wait with me, the stallion said.

It was not so much words as a terrible ache in her breast. She turned, plowed three steps toward him, and propped her sword against her hip while she fought with the bosses of his harness. The cold of the metal went right to the bone, aching, but she struggled frozen leather through stiff buckles and shoved the ruined saddle off his back. There was a corpse in the snow a few steps away—Olrun, tarnished, who had loved swans and the Hall's lean brindled wolfhounds, dead, and neither an ally nor an enemy any longer. She had fallen half wrapped in a tattered banner. Muire dragged the saddle over beside her, covering her with the bloodstained leather and the blanket, a crude sort of crypt.

And then Muire sat down in the crimsoned snow beside the stallion. She leaned against his shoulder and laid her shining, naked blade across her knees. And he in return draped his unbroken neck over her shoulder, his muzzle pressed to her armored chest. She hooked her arm up and reached around, under his throttle, to scratch behind his opposite ear. Frozen blood flaked from his mane.

"I've nowhere else to be," she answered, and tilted her temple against his silken velvet cheek.

Sometime in the night, the snow stopped falling.

Kasimir was not dead by morning, and neither was the waelcyrge. Her oozing wounds sealed, then stopped, the blood freezing or scabbing over them. She breathed against his cheek, her eyes closed, her heart slowing. Was this sleep? Kasimir knew mortals slept, but the children of the Light did not, not unless they were more gravely wounded than his new waelcyrge.

He considered that thought. His.

He did not *have* to take her. There was no law or rule that demanded he do so. He was valraven, and the choice was his.

He knew this one. Her name was Muire. She was the littlest of all Light's children, a poet and a historian and a metalworker rather than a warrior. She had loved Strifbjorn, the war-leader, and the war-leader had been gentle with her but he had not returned her love. Strifbjorn's heart—as Kasimir knew, as all the valraven knew, and never mentioned—had already been given.

She had been very brave, his waelcyrge. He nudged her with his muzzle to wake her, and she blinked and raised her head. **Kasimir**, he whispered.

At first she didn't understand. She scrambled to her feet, limping a little less—not healing like a waelcyrge, but healing. Her sword in her hand, she scanned the brightening horizon for some threat.

There was nothing. The sky arched enamel-blue, the edge of the cliff where the children of the Light had turned at bay visible as a ragged line of white against the steelier blue of the sea, far below. **Kasimir**, he said, again, insistently.

Slowly, she turned, and stared at him. She panted, pain etching shadows under gray eyes that gleamed dimly with starlight for a moment before flickering dark. He stared back, until she lowered the blade and straightened, pressing the flat across her thighs. "You don't have to do that. I will stay with you."

He let his muzzle drop into the snow. **Live**, he said. He felt the raw desire in her as well, chafing at her resignation, her cold certainty that she had betrayed the Light as surely as the tarnished and deserved nothing.

"I cannot—" she said. And then she looked down at the sword in her hands, the sword that still blazed blue-white, dimmer now in daylight, but unmistakable. "Maybe I can."

The Dweller Within never came to our aid, Kasimir said, lifting his head as if he could see more of the ocean. **The Serpent is not dead, but lies dying. That is why there is no Light for you to call on. No Light but your own.**

"Oh," his waelcyrge said, without looking up from her sword. And then she stared at him, her irises transparent pew-

ter, the glow of the rising sun refracted through them behind
ash-pale lashes, and he saw her throat work above the collar of
her mail. She rustled softly, rings chiming on iron rings as she
squared her shoulders. "I could ask for a miracle. I don't even
know if it will work, if the Serpent is dying. But I could ask."

Kasimir paused. There was no promise such a call would be
answered. No reason to believe that the outcome would be an
improvement, if it was. Miracles happened, or they did not, and
were wonderful or awful—or both—without logic or rhythm.
He could find himself healed, remade, destroyed—or ignored,
as they had been ignored as they fell to the tarnished and the
sdadown.

Ask, he said.

The waelcyrge turned her face aside, her knuckles pale on
the hilt of her sword, and closed her dark gray eyes.

The earth heaved under the snowdrifts. The waelcyrge lost
her footing and pitched backward into the snow a second
time, her flailing arms carving angel wings in the white drift
behind her. All around Kasimir, the surface cracked like the crust
of an over-risen loaf; the frozen ground softened beneath him.
He thrashed—whinnying, dragging himself to his feet, tossing
his antelope-horned head, dragging the antlered one—but the
earth bucked again and heaved him to his knees.

He could not stay down. Even a winged horse is terrified of
unstable ground, and Kasimir's wings were shredded hobbles.

His waelcyrge scrambled backward, regaining her feet none
too nimbly, and the earth split wide as the snow around Kasimir's hooves vanished in rushing hiss. Steam billowed around
him, searing, bellying from deep below.

Stand, Kasimir.

It might have been Herfjotur's voice. He couldn't know

over the roaring and the hiss, but he was sure it was not Muire's.

What mattered was that it was a voice he trusted. He locked his three good legs and his broken one, bone grinding, rasping under his weight. He lifted his head and stood his ground, and did not shy as metal oozed glowing from the steaming cracks.

He did not shy. But he screamed, and kept on screaming.

Muire could not go to him. She had been waelcyrge, and fire no more a threat to her than ice. She had been a smith, able to scoop metal from the crucible with her bare hand and pour it palm to palm like mercury. And when the earth yawned open and the white-hot iron smoked through the snow, she could not walk through the fire to Kasimir.

More cowardice. But at least she would not close her eyes.

He screamed while the metal crawled over him, fingerling rivulets broadening into a red-hot weld. It *was* like mercury, like a gold ring dipped in mercury, the quicksilver bonding to the surface. Yet this was no cold quicksilver, but molten metal, rising from the belly of the land in response to Muire's ill-considered prayer. *All-Father, have mercy.*

But mercy, in the end of things, was not what Othinn was for. Not the god who had hung on the world-tree for nine nights and nine days, who had sold his eye for power. And anyway, he had been left behind in Midgard. He had promised he would follow, that he would come to lead them in the new world. But he had not. And they had proven decisively, Muire thought, that they could not do it alone.

———

Somehow, through it all, the stallion stood.

And when it was done, he *shone*.

Impassive now, he straightened slowly. Both heads on their long necks turned to regard Muire, white rings already fading around living brown eyes in sculptured faces. His new skin cooled, his new bones hardened, and his bright steel-blue wings opened and flexed, feather-perfect.

The soft whisper of tiny interlocking barbs on the pinions was like a declaration of war. Steam hissed under pressure as he moved. He shook out his mane, and each hair of it was a single, gleaming wire. The snow sublimated under his footsteps as he came to Muire. He nosed her chain mail–covered breast, not hard, and she gasped at the startling heat. The earth smoldered under his footsteps.

She laid her hand flat against his cheek and jerked it away in a moment, scalded. "What are you?"

Kasimir, he answered. **Metal and meat. Sorcery and steel.**

"What are you?" she asked again.

His eyes were warm and soft. **I am War.**

"No," she choked, before her voice failed. The world was new and empty, changed from the world it had been at the sunset, and the valraven had changed with it.

And Muire would not change, did not wish to change. "What have you become?" She reached out, but snatched back scorched fingers. "You are the future."

I am the world, what the world will need, and what the world will be.

She turned her head, finally allowing herself to look away. "Why did you tell me your name? I am not worthy of you."

I would not choose one unworthy.

"I fled." He graced her with the steady regard of four patient eyes, and she could not lift her chin to meet it. "I fled the sdad-own, and the tarnished, and I hid while our brethren died."

Heat rolled from him; the heat of the forge, the heat of a summer's day: a physical pressure. Her torn arm ached: it was bleeding again. Her thigh felt like knotted and dried rawhide.

"I am a coward. I will bring you pain."

What pain could equal the pain of creation? The ant-lered head ducked with a hiss of hydraulics. He folded his re-made wings neatly and began to vaporize the snow about his hooves with short, sharp nudges of his muzzle—shyly, and so like any horse.

"Kasimir," she said, softly, just to taste it once, to taste the wonder of his offer. "You said it yourself. The Dweller Within is no more. The Light has failed."

The Dweller Within still lingers. We are the Light that remains.

She could not answer. *He* had not broken and run. "No," she said. "Oh, no . . ." And while she still could, she took the first step away.

His wings rattled and rustled. **You will come back to me. I am Kasimir. I am the new Age of the World.**

When you name me, I shall come.

With a masterful leap he was airborne and gone. The splayed feathers of his wingtips wrote a benediction on the snow, and she was blessedly, terribly, finally alone.

She lived because she fled; he lived because she did not let him die.

I would not choose one unworthy.

When he was gone, when her tears were mastered, Muire began to gather the bodies and build over them a cairn. There would be no second miracle; she asked and was not answered, as she would ask and go unanswered for centuries to come.

Her hands cracked and chapped and swelled with chilblains; her nose dripped blood and snot. She grew thin. She grew weary. She grew—as she had never before been—hungry.

There were only a few brothers and sisters missing, all tarnished, and when she had finished with the dead atop the sea-cliff, she scoured the rubble at the base for those that might have fallen. She found her brother Hafgrim there, broken on the rocks, gored by a valraven's antlers.

And there she found also the sword Svanvítr, but no sign of the Grey Wolf, its master.

One thousand years is a long time to go hungry.

The Grey Wolf wears a sun burning under his heart. A gnawed cord cuts his throat with every breath. He has devoured gods and outlasted the endless snow. He has thrown away his sword. He has eaten everything he ever loved.

He is immortal and alone. He is walking south, to a sword-age, a storm-age.

He is the wolf, until world's end.

Any day now.

Thurisaz (thorns)

ᚦ

And so, twenty-three-hundred years pass. Days wear into centuries, but the hunger grows no easier for all that. No easier, but at least no worse. And the world . . .

Well, the world winds down only ponderously.

But every pendulum slows.

Since the breaking of the Light the wolf has been listening to the ticking decay. Worlds, like gods, are a long time dying, and the deathblow dealt the children of the Light did not stop a civilization of mortal men from rising in their place, inventing medicine and philosophy, metallurgy and space flight.

Until they in turn fell, two-hundred-odd years ago, in a Desolation that left all Valdyrgard a salted garden. All of it, that is, except the two cities—Freimarc and Eiledon—that lingered. Life is tenacious. Even on the brink of death, it holds the battlements and snarls.

But now Freimarc—where the wolf has whiled away the end of time—has fallen, and even Eiledon is failing. Now the heart of the world skips, erratic, and the pauses between beats grow long. And as the wolf hesitates in the cold between shadows, the place that smells of char and ice and where the sun has never, in his memory, risen to warm the creaking frost beneath his boots, he hears that rhythm now, the ragged tolling of a stately bell.

He smiles, and keeps walking.

Once he traversed earthly forests, amid the crack of twigs and the rich scent of pine needles. He ran beside his companions of the hunt, wolves and einherjar. He drank in the mead-hall with his shield-brother, Strifbjorn.

Now, he is more often to be found in the icy world—Midgard, or rather its chilled remains, colder now in its final winter even than Niflheim—than Valdyrgard, the living one. Or, to choose his language more precisely, the dying one.

Travel is nearly impossible in Valdyrgard now—the roads nonexistent, the conveyances destroyed, the few remaining mortals huddled into one decaying city. But the wolf has his shadowy paths, and they serve him.

The heart tolls again. The wolf pauses, tilts his head to savor the dying fall. He lifts his face, eyes closed, as if he scented the wind. But the air here is cold and still. His cloak and queue hang unstirring against his shoulders.

The Last Day was nothing, meant nothing. It has become myth only, as Midgard had been myth to the children of the Light. Waelcyrge and einherjar were barely legends now, and human society had flourished very well—had *blossomed*—without them.

Blossomed. And then fallen like the rose to the canker— rotten, slimed, and dead. They did it themselves, the Desolation, created it with their bioweapons and their radiation bombs, with their shoggoth main battle groups and their killer robots and their orbital microwave projectors, their mass projectors and combat sorcerers and laser-guided death curses. Over two centuries past, the fatal bullet.

Worlds are a long time dying, it's true. But the wolf is old and patient. And soon, there will be peace. The peace he's sought since first he betrayed Strifbjorn.

For *now,* however, he's drawn from his still, silent refuge, from just-dead Freimarc and long-dead Midgard and back to dying Valdyrgard. With a task. So he paces through shadows in the cold world, alone in the dark and fearless, until he comes to Eiledon.

He quells his urgency under patience; he is the wolf, the last remaining. He has already waited a long time to see men die. Eiledon is not as it once was. From the shadows, peering from the cracks between that world and this one, he sets out to learn the place again.

Eiledon grows around a curve of the broad, brown, tidal river Naglfar, a dark glittering city that once was bright and fair. It was a great port when there were ships and destinations. Now the river is dead and empty, its chop capped with poisoned foam. Sometimes it burns, and the levees and river-walks that channeled it and made it pleasant once are a soot-stained firebreak now.

Eiledon is an ancient city, a medieval city, a modern city. She wears a dark girdle of ruins. When first he saw this place, it was a city on the south of the river only, hemmed by its walls, well defended. Then she made an uneven enclosure, the river running through chained gates and portcullises into a bailey pierced by eight strong gates. Still later, before the Desolation, she sprawled far beyond her medieval walls, which were kept intact merely for the sake of history.

Now she has contracted again, and her desperate six million live crammed within the gold-green shimmer of the Defile—the Technomancer's guardian wards—which only extend so far as the ancient bulwarks of hand-quarried stone.

Eiledon is bejeweled in its towers and arcologies, glass and steel and chrome, elegant masterpieces of architecture and technomancy. There are citizens who never leave these hothouse spires. Along the riverfront, buildings are older, solid stone and brick, bristling with gargoyles and fantastic with murals and relief carvings and stained glass.

But that is not all. Between the riverfront neighborhoods and the central city, in the shadow of the tallest towers, hangs a great rough-bellied hemisphere, a floating promontory twenty stories above the ground. The river runs through it, climbing the sky and then tumbling down again as if its channel lay undisturbed. That floating island is a university campus, ripped from the earth and hurled aloft, a gesture of flagrant power and defiance made by the immortal Technomancer when she seized control of the city from its Thing more than two hundred years before. Its shadow is the shadow of the Desolation, an endless reminder of the genocidal war that Eiledon fought—and survived.

At the time, the citizens were disinclined to complain. Eiledon blessed its savior's name, and—rare, precious—children are still named after her: Thjierry Thorvaldsdottir, the Technomancer of Eiledon.

Eiledon's inhabitants call her home the Tower, though it is ten or eleven buildings rather than one. Classes—in a particularly Eiledain madness—still take place there: the floating bastion is a functioning university. But it is also the Technomancer's holdfast. She dwells there, far above the city she still protects, amid her truman students and her unman servitors.

In the shadow of the Technomancer's Tower, in the twilight where it never rains, lie the slums.

And that is where the wolf travels. Something he left behind has been taken up again. Something he once owned has been stolen. He is the wolf, and he is einherjar no longer. He does not want it back. But neither will he suffer another to misuse it.

Especially when that ancient magic might strengthen the world's limping heartbeat, buy it a few more years, centuries, millennia of life. It is time—*a wolf-age, a wind-age.* Following a voice that sings only for his ears, the wolf steps from the cold emptiness of a dead world into the bustling street of one that is merely dying fast.

He has outlived two Ragnaroks and a far more human apocalypse. It is time to tear down, shed the husk, leave behind a dead world to see a new world reborn.

Cathoair got these feelings sometimes, and he was having one right now. Specifically, the prickle across his shoulders and up under his hair that had nothing to do with the ring sweat drying on his scalp in the cool night air. He reached up left-handed, because his range of motion wasn't as good on the right, and tugged the thong out of his ponytail as he stepped down out of the kickboxing ring, onto the crowded floor of the Ash & Thorn. Astrid was there, her black hair falling in a wrist-thick braid over her shoulder, smiling under her twice-broken nose.

She never could keep her guard up.

She threw his robe over his shoulders and handed him a towel. "You did good, Cahey," she said. "Real good."

Cathoair dropped his skull back on his shoulders and breathed deep. Rolling his head from side to side gave him an excuse to scan the crowd, looking for the source of that uneasy prickle. Right now, most of them were talking, eating, slurping drinks, placing bets on the next match. Once he'd dropped down to floor level and Hrolfgar had limped out of the back side of the ring, the applause—and whatever attention Cathoair rated—had stopped.

But the prickling sensation hadn't. And when he turned, he saw why.

It wasn't the three women and a man who were eyeing him with the sort of sidelong appreciation he was used to, the admiration that told him they were nerving themselves toward the eventual offer of a drink in the hope or expectation of more. No, it was the second man—neither tall nor heavy boned, sitting with his back to the wall in a shadowed corner behind the ring, out of traffic and away from the dance floor.

Cathoair had seen the man before, occasionally, on nights when he was fighting or covering for Aethelred behind the bar. He mopped his face with the cold towel that Astrid handed him and stole another glance. A craggy, almost ragged face was made more stern by silver-shot dark hair pulled back in a warrior's braid, bound by silver clasps and hanging long over the man's shoulder. His eyes seemed light under graying brows, his left ear pierced at the lobe by a heavy, twisted ring in the old style. His clothes were invisible under a cloak he wore, clasped with heavy silver brooches at the right shoulder.

And he was looking directly at Cathoair, as boldly as if he did not expect to be seen.

Cathoair had never been one to back down from a challenge. He dropped the damp towel back in Astrid's hand and lifted his chin, staring the old man directly in the eyes. He wasn't expecting the watcher to meet him with a close-lipped smile and a shrug that disarrayed his cloak only slightly, or the toast of a drinking bowl carved from what looked like horn, but couldn't be: nobody would bring a precious antique to a public bar where it could be broken or stolen.

"Star, do you know that guy?" Cathoair asked, ducking his head to whisper in Astrid's ear. She was a big girl, rangy, heavy-boned and heavy-muscled, but he topped her by half a head.

She turned and kissed him a quick peck, so as not to spoil his chances with the clientele later, and said, "Guy?"

"At table twenty."

She glanced over her shoulder as if checking the ring, and shrugged. "Nobody there now."

Cathoair lifted his head and blinked. The table was empty, the horn bowl gone along with the silver-brindled occupant. All that remained was the candlefaux and a crumpled note trapped under it, ten kroner in the Technomancer's scrip by the color. "Huh," Cathoair said. "I wonder where he went."

"He'll be back if he's interested," Astrid said. She dabbed at a bruise on Cathoair's sweaty shoulder. "Come on. Let's get you into the sauna and cleaned up so you can mingle."

Blood would have been easier.

If the cobbles had been sticky under Muire's boots, if the blood had runneled between stones and flooded the rain-damp dead-end square between Ark and the Well, it would have been simple. She would have dropped a knee beside the man slumped along the blind, truncated stair that had once led to the university, and she would have tried to breathe for him as long as his heart fought to help her, and when his heart stammered and failed, she would have stood in her blood-daubed armor and made her own way home.

But there was no blood upon the stones. And the man was still breathing. Faintly, shallowly, not a mark on him, surrounded by the lingering traces of bitter, predatory musk.

Muire knelt. Her ancient sword hung heavy between her shoulders and her ceramic armor clicked against the stone steps. Cowled in a cloak of midnight-blue, she bent over the dying man. And there could be no question that he was dying: his last few breaths came shallow, and his lids fluttered over closed and sunken eyes.

There was not a mark on him.

Muire touched his cheek with a gauntleted hand, and closed her eyes, knowing the chill that radiated from his skin before she ever properly felt it. She bent over and breathed for him, knowing it was useless, making the gesture all the same.

He was expensively dressed, too much so for the Well and neither like a student nor a lecturer, which meant that he must have come from the Ark—the Arcologies, the hermetically sealed habitations immediately east of the Broken Stair. He was unarmed and he had rings on his fingers, and he didn't look like much of a warrior with his neatly trimmed hair and his clerk's embroidered robes, his comm clipped, silenced, to his belt along with the other paraphernalia of a white-collar job—a palmtop parser, an audiovid privacy headset folded into compact form and beaded with droplets that had to be rain. He lay close enough to the falls to hear them, but not within the drift of their poisoned mist. His skin was unspotted by radiation or disease, and he showed not so much as a bruise. But a scent hung on him like cold moss on stone, and his skin felt chill. And he was dying, without any good reason for it, despite anything Muire could have done to save him.

It spoke of something she had thought left behind on a cold battlefield, more than two thousand years before.

Muire took his hand in her gauntleted one, and murmured, "Don't be afraid."

When his last breath rattled from his throat, rather than pulling away—as prudence suggested—she permitted it to expire into her mouth and breathed it deep.

So he died there, on the Broken Stair, and the last waelcyrge Chose him. And in the choosing she accepted his death and accepted as well the burden of vengeance that death brought.

Our name was Ingraham Fasoltsen. We were walking—we had been walking—and we had made a delivery for our employer, and the moreau—a cat, an unman female, her fur smoky gray in rosettes—had been there as arranged. We had been walking—home, home to our daughter (precious child, little girl, eight years old), home to our wife (we are fortunate)—and we had heard our name.

Softly spoken, and we had turned to it, and He was there, burning beautiful in all his darkness, eyes alight with the starfire that cannot shine through the Defile, that we know only from old songs old memories old dreams old long-lost dreams. . . .

Oh, he was beautiful, there in the shadows beside the descending stair. The new stair, the stair that leads down where the Broken Stair once led upward, the stair that leads into the Well, the dark neighborhoods under the Tower. Beautiful and ragged, broken as an ancient statue, his braid grizzled over his shoulder and his eyes dark as ice.

And we had gone to him, and he had guided us to our knees, and with the folds of his cloak falling all around us—heavy soft strange and faintly greasy-smelling, like real wool, perhaps, if wool could still be had—within the folds of his cloak he had kissed us.

Kissed us and breathed us in, within.

Kissed us and drank us down.

Ingraham's hands slid from Muire's armored shoulders to fall slack on the riven stone. She tilted her head back reflexively, drinking deep of night air tainted by the unwholesome sweetness of the Well, looking upward as if the stars were there to help her bear the pain.

There were no stars. Through the glassy brilliance of the Defile and the shadows of the rain clouds, she could not even make out the glow of the moon.

It hurt. The death hurt. Even a little death, a mortal death such as this, brought its own measure of pain. It settled into her flesh—mere meat and bone now, no longer the numinous stuff of Light—and sank deep talons in her, demanding *justice,* demanding *vengeance.*

She didn't care about the pain. She welcomed the wrath the dead man brought. She would need his strength as surely as he would need her sword, to see this matter through.

Yrenbend, her favorite brother, had said it to her once: "There are seen hands and unseen hands. I am an angel. We do not believe in coincidences."

This was a seen and an unseen hand at once; the one that had wreaked the deed, and the one that had directed her in its discovery.

The tarnished had returned.

Hagalaz (hail)

The walls of Her office were cinder block and limpid shatter-proof, offering a panoramic view of Eiledon's rooftops and towers. Not the loft of the Arcology, strangely, but the jeweled teeth of the old city and the thick bend of river southwest of the Tower. The enormous room—almost the entire top floor of the library—was dominated by a giant orrery encased within moving crystal spheres; the furniture, while comfortable, was relegated to the edges.

Selene, waiting upon Her attention, stared through the tall glass plates, tail lashing, ears still laid flat, and willed herself to calm. Fear-and-fight were not her friends. They were the animal, the instinct that made her a superlative warrior. But the threat had been left behind on the ground, and Selene was in the Tower, in Her presence. Safe.

The broad windows were new, since the Desolation, giving Eiledon's savior, leader, teacher a sweeping view of Her demesne and the Defile, but the marble floor was original to the University. Once it had been smooth, close-fitted, and the cool blocks were still so tight one could not slip a card between them. But the stone had been worn in intervening centuries, and there were little hollows and valleys that showed where feet had trod those hundreds of years away.

She sat in Her habitual chair—no ostentatious throne but the functional work station of mesh and padding she used when she was not afoot on two crutches, or in Her hover chair—and stared over Her city. Selene knew that She was waiting for Selene to regain control, to find her center.

She was gracious.

Finally, She lifted a hand and beckoned. She wore two thick mismatched sweaters over Her red-brown scholar's robes, the gray and taupe cuffs rolled up around Her bony wrists. She'd let Her hood fall onto Her shoulders, revealing Her cropped gray hair, and the pinched marks of Her spectacles remained on the bridge of Her nose.

Selene stepped forward, tail still twisting, and bowed before Her chair. Her hackles bristled, her fur damp from the drizzle but standing all on end under the farmed leather straps and ceramic plates of her body armor, but she forced herself to calmness as she extended the package in her hand. It was long, bound with wire over a stiff cloth wrapping, and it left a chill, buzzing sensation climbing the bones of Selene's forearm.

She groped for one of Her crutches, rose from Her chair with an effort, and came before Selene. "Good girl," She said, softly, slipping the bundle from Selene's clawed hand and tucking it under Her arm for safekeeping. Selene kept her talons sheathed in the soft flesh of her fingertips throughout, breathing deeply, her whiskers smoothed flat against her muzzle and her toenails pressing slight scratches into the hard marble floor when she couldn't quite manage to gentle *them*.

Selene smelled old woman's flesh, acrid electronics, and

constancy, and it helped drive the dangerous musk from her nostrils. She stroked Selene's ears with a palsied hand and stepped back, but not before Her touch and scent had soothed the moreau.

"Why so upset, Selene?"

"I smelled something," Selene reported. "Something in the dark under the Well. Musky. Hunting."

"A rogue?" She asked sharply.

She was not angry with Selene. She never raised Her voice to Her unmans. She never had to: the moreaux were perfectly obedient to Her will, and they would die before they failed. Since She Herself had constructed them, the only blame for their occasional shortcomings fell on the wizard Herself.

She was a just and a forgiving creator-god.

But sometimes—rarely—a moreau would grow strange, go feral, fail to return. Rogues were dangerous to unmans, trumans, halfmans, and nearmans. She did not tolerate them, and Selene would not tolerate them on Her behalf.

Selene was very skilled at her tasks.

"I do not think it was a rogue," she said, carefully. Her words came sweetly despite needle-sharp teeth, rolling trippingly from a rasp-sharp tongue. "A . . . predator. It smelled not like one of us, though I saw nothing when I met Fasoltsen."

"And you did not touch the weapon?" She lifted the slender bundle in Her hand. It was long, long as Selene's leg from hip to ankle, long as her lashing tail.

Selene rocked her head side to side, an awkward counterfeit of a human shake. "The wrappings were intact."

"Excellent," She said, and spared Selene a smile full of an old woman's crooked yellow teeth. "Go, pretty girl. Rest until morning. You have pleased me."

Selene could not smile. She hadn't the muscles for it. But, turning to go, she felt the warmth of Her approval run down her spine like the stroke of a velvet glove, and stood straighter under her weapons and armor as she strode away.

Muire stood in the ruined square and wiped her hands on her cloak, though nothing stained them. It was dark here, in the shadow of the Tower, dark and chill. This was the truncated end of the Boulevard, the mile-diameter, near-geometric ring road that circumscribed the places where *honest* folk traveled in Eiledon. Anything beyond its compass was as likely to be lawless as not; it all depended on the character of one's neighbors. Where the road was broken, its edges had cracked and melted where the Technomancer had pulled her Tower from the earth, interrupting its symmetry.

A dark undercity had grown beneath that Tower in the intervening centuries. Shielded from the weather, from the sun's unfiltered radiation, the Well cradled Eiledon's more dangerous neighborhoods and also her better bars in an improvised arcology, neither as protected nor as pretty as the sunlit ones. There in the depths, one could find bloodsport, sex for hire, specs and killers. . . . and also, real live music, for a change.

The scent that hung about the dead man's body led Muire down the newer stair, the unbroken one. She descended into the Well, where the light trickled from colored floods, tethered floats, and garish signs, and even the green-gold aurora of the Defile was obscured.

She paused at the halfway point of the stair, her gauntlet scraping on the improvised pipe railing, the stone steps gritty under her boots. Below, a moderate stream of people moved along the beneoned street in seasonless darkness. The atmosphere never brightened here, though in the daytime it would gray, sunlight reflected in by systems of mirrors. The lights were never doused, however.

The denizens of the Well were far more colorful than the trumans who lived above, in Riverside and the Ark, or near Muire's loft and workshop on the long side of downtown, near Dockside and Hangman. The buildings were less makeshift than one might expect: Eiledon had been jammed to bursting with engineers and tradespeople, and the suburbs offered rich scavenging. Buildings of four and five stories were not uncommon. The narrow haphazard streets between them coursed with men and women and the undecided, truman and nearman and halfman and unman, sorcerous and cybernetic and between and neither. The tide of humanity drew Muire like the pulse of the ocean in her blood: the dark, starlit ocean that had brought forth her kind.

The Light had failed and with it its children, but these *other* children—mortal children, candle-flickers—continued, endlessly fighting and dying and returning their blood to the wash of the sorrowful sea. The mortals had a saying, that blood was thicker than water. But to Muire blood *was* water: the water of the ocean, and the force of the Light upon it.

She descended the last few stairs and dropped into the current, following the paling scent-trace of cloak and boot caressing stone, whistling a half-heard melody that lit the killer's footsteps for her eyes alone, so they stood out in the darkness as if brushed with phosphorescent dust.

Her geas—the ghost-hungry memory of Ingraham Fasoltsen—drove her. *Vengeance,* he murmured half heard in her ear. *Justice.* And over and over, a father's seaworn murmur that she could do nothing about at all, *I cannot leave my child.*

Music sloshed from open doorways like the surf, and neon and liquid crystal dazzled, but Muire passed them by, patting the snub shape of the flechette pistol snugged against her waist.

She was walking to her enemy. And in the shadow of the Tower, no rain fell.

The tickling sensation on the back of Cathoair's neck came back when he reentered the bar. He'd steamed and scraped, and cleaned his hair, and wore a soft white shirt that was open at the collar over tight black pants. Hustling clothes, and not at all what he'd be wearing if it were him and Astrid lying out on the roof finding shapes in the lights on the underneath of the tower, drinking hot tea and resting their aches in the cool Well air. He paused by the bar and caught Aethelred's eye, and Aethelred—a gnarled boulder of a man with a Twisted Serpent pendant winking in the hair behind his open collar, the half of his face that wasn't radiation-scarred layered in mirror-bright chrome so you found yourself talking to your own reflection when you tried to look him in the eye—fished Cathoair's bowl out from under the counter and topped it up with something that smelled of artificial fruit.

Cathoair studied the mirror behind the bar while he drank it. He didn't take liquor, as a rule, and Aethelred would keep the synthpunch coming all night if that was what it took. But it was a busy night at the Ash & Thorn, and prospects looked good. Aethelred was taking bets on the next bout—a girl fight, Astrid and Feorag, who had an Islander name like Cathoair but was red-haired white-skinned Eiledain, not the dark-skinned descendant of refugees—and the neon and strobes over the dance floor were twitching, the music loud enough to ring his ears.

And, snakerot, he still had that sensation, as if somebody were trailing cold fingers down between his shoulder blades. The gray man again?

He lifted one hand to signal Aethelred. If it was legitimate interest, he wasn't in a position to mind. And if it wasn't, he could take good care of himself, thank you.

Aethelred filled two more bowls with brandy, accepted and tallied another bet on the chalkboard over the top shelf, and then leaned across the bar so Cathoair could shout into his ear.

"Seen a guy, Aeth? 'Bout so tall, gray cloak, salt and pepper plait?"

Aethelred nodded and shouted back. "Yeah. Couldn't tell you if he was safe, sorry. But I didn't like his eyes—"

Something to take on evidence, when a bartender said it. That, and the way he gave Cathoair that creeping feeling, like he sometimes got, the one that always presaged adventure. "What was he drinking?"

Aethelred's smile rearranged the furrowed scars on the mobile half of his face into deep eloquent valleys. "Mead," he answered, with a shrug. "You'd be a damned sight safer with that one," he suggested, with a jerk of his shoulder toward the stairwell and the door.

Cathoair squeezed Aethelred's wrist once quickly and turned, and caught his first quick glimpse of the girl.

She was little, not much better than child-sized, cheekbones plain under the pale skin of her face, her ash-gold hair bobbed even with her earlobes and her eyes very serious behind the escaped strands that fell across her face. She wore rust-brown ceramor and a navy cloak shot through with threads of gold, and the worn, peace-bound hilt of a sword stood over her shoulder. She was poised statue-still, and from the expression on her face when she turned, she must have been staring at the back of his head like a rabbit staring at a hawk.

He didn't know her. And she looked like a girl playing dress-up in her brother's battle suit. But she licked her lips and startled when he looked her in the eye, and Aethelred was right; she looked a hell of a lot safer than the Man in Gray.

"Put five kroner on Astrid for me, would you, Aeth?" he asked the bartender, and—cupping his refilled bowl in his hand—started through the crowd toward the gray-eyed girl.

She knew him. A shock of recognition like the taste of ice water, and then the tall, elegantly boned young man at the bar turned around and fixed Muire with a contemplative gaze. She'd come down the stairs into this teeming underground as much for the wry neon sign by the stair naming it the "Ash & Thorn" in two runic symbols as for the trace of Grey Wolf. And now, here was this man, who shocked her to recollection like the smell of summer flowers.

He sidestepped through the crowd to reach her (trumans and nearmans here, only—no moreaux, and the cybered landlord behind the bar was the only halfman. Muire could hear his chassis creaking under his skin even through the thump of the music and the excited shouts of the crowd), and her breath felt as if it would rasp a hole in her throat.

Because she didn't. Didn't know him, had never seen him before, with his musculature like a classical statue and his oiled brown-black ringlets bound back in a ponytail not so much darker than the polished warm tone of his skin. The broad handsome features, the sensual lips, the smooth-bridged Islander nose and the pink, proud-fleshed dueling scar disfiguring his right cheek and pulling that corner of his mouth up in a mocking involuntary smirk were foreign to her, as foreign as the black slate tiles of this club and the thumping music swinging bodies across the pillared dance floor.

But the *recognition* didn't care. It was strong enough that it almost shook free her tenuous grasp on her spell, and for a moment she forgot to track her quarry's presence as she watched the young man come toward her.

The last time I saw him, she thought, *his face was ruined, too.* And she wondered for a moment if it was his wyrd now, a punishment for the infamous beauty that had brought them all low, or if it was her punishment for cowardice, to meet him again and again, remembered in a mortal hide, and be powerless to save him.

He moved with an athlete's grace, maybe limping a little, but the smile was all hustler, as was the way he ducked his head to speak into her ear. "Are you lonely tonight, pretty lady?"

Light, Muire thought, and closed her eyes. He looked nothing like Strifbjorn. Nothing at all. His eyes weren't even gray; they were a blue-flecked hazel, though still far too pale for the darkness of his skin.

But the voice resonated in the fallible vaults of memory, and she would have sworn it was the same.

But before she could answer, the presence she'd been following evaporated. She jerked her head around and stepped sharply away. "Damn me," she murmured, and didn't even bother to shake her head at the pretty, scar-faced gigolo as she turned and ran back up the stair without thinking too hard of what she was leaving behind, except in that it explained why the Wolf might have come here.

———

At the top of the stairs from the dark, crowded underground bar, Muire hesitated. She knew she wasn't alone. He had seen her, maybe even known her, when the young man had crossed to her with such haste, drawing eyes. And he was waiting for her here, now, in the darkness of an unlit alley halfway down the block from the intersection of Oak Street and Pleasant.

The Well was full of them—little blind alleys and side streets, crooked ways that went nowhere, fire escapes and roads that skipped over crowded rooftops, almost close enough to the light-laced underbelly of the Tower to scrape dirt from it with your fingernails. Muire unbonded Nathr, drew the earth-dull sword into her hand, and turned south, where the Wolf awaited.

She wondered if the rain was still falling. It couldn't *fall* here, of course, but rivulets gathered to streams, and pools collected in the low places of the city, where pumps labored ceaselessly to lift the water to the river. It had been a pleasant riverfront once, with walks and bridges and pubs built feet-wet in the very canal. Now, the scent of it hung ropy on the moist breeze riffling her hair, and she tugged the hood of her cloak up, picking her way between nighttime strollers and the neon-steeped puddles on the clumsily cobbled road.

A group of Mongrels hung about the entrance to a strip club, interchangeable in their green and black livery, keeping the peace merely by the dangerous weight of their presence. They wore their titanium ID bands on their right wrists, and the oldest couldn't have been twenty. She nodded to Muire as Muire passed, her brows drawn together in a way that suggested she was hoping, maybe, for a little trouble.

"The Technomancer provides," Muire murmured, and the

gang relaxed. Bored or not, they were there to keep the peace, and it wasn't as if she needed a license to go armed. She turned down the alley, made two blind corners, and paused in the darkness to let her eyes adjust.

She did not pause long.

Something thumped wetly on the pavement ahead and rolled a half-turn, mewling weakly. Muire lifted her sword, calling Light. A single dim spark ascended the blade like a raindrop rolling in reverse. It cast little brightness, but enough: the figure was that of a young man in his teens, and Muire felt him dying. With the last of his strength, he turned his head to the guttering light, and Muire stepped back from the reflections in his eyes.

A child, a child, Ingraham whispered in Muire's heart.

Night was all around her, but a denser patch flowed forward, stepping over the dying boy to pause beyond the reach of her blade. *His* eyes were a gray so pale as to be silver, ringed about the iris with a darker band. They glimmered in shadow, cloaked in frantic starlight as an ember is cloaked in rippling heat.

"Name thyself," he demanded.

Muire's fingers tightened on the gridded hilt of her sword. "Muire, child of the Light."

She had forfeited her right to the title, and here, with that sad spark trembling along Nathr's edge, the ridiculousness of it ached all along her bones and in the space between her eyes. So frail to raise the Light up as a shield against *this,* before which it had already quailed.

He inclined his head as if to study the stones beneath her feet, the crass meat of her form. "The Light is dead, little sister."

His name flew from her lips as if on the wings of a swan.

"Mingan." A legendary darkness: the hungry void, given flesh and form in tarnished silver. She'd found his sword, but not his body, and so she had the honesty not to pretend surprise at encountering him again. Still, Nathr's Light stuttered when Muire met his gaze.

Vengeance, whispered the voice of a mortal man. Bitter on her tongue, Muire tasted her fear. The Grey Wolf's nostrils flared; he could smell it.

"I am that." He stepped one step closer on the unbloodied stones. He cast open his grey cloak, revealing a belt naked of weapons, black leather boots and trousers and a charcoal shirt. His hands were gloved. He had not replaced his crystal blade.

A twisted silver ring held his grizzled hair back, and he still wore a ring in his ear of clean white metal. Though she was not close enough to see the detail, she remembered the wolf's heads that clasped the metal tongue locked through his ear, remembered the girl who had crafted them with such care and hope, and she hated him a little more.

It was almost a clean hate, for a moment, untainted by her own failures. She went to meet him. His eyes shone as hungry and dead as a shark's. Tarnished silver—scratch it and it still gleams. Nathr felt light and useless in her hand.

"Little Immortal." He smiled a cruel and beckoning smile. "Hast a long life before thee. Wouldst cast it away?"

Thee her, indeed. The world had moved on without them. She would not play his game of memory. Brilliance flared, radiance spilling from her eyes, her open mouth, drawn as if dragged on wires.

"Candle-flicker. Come into the darkness, and be no more alone." His smile grew tender. "Thou art an avenger, sister. Thy Light has abandoned thee. Avenge thyself."

Her foot lifted and stepped waveringly forward. That craving for vengeance let her understand, for a moment too well, why this her brother might have fallen. The desire was in her. The heat of her sword scorched her hand. She came to him. . . .

She lunged.

And failed again.

Light blazed Nathr's length, filling the alley with a stellar incandescence, so bright it washed everything to stark blue and to shadows, making knife-edged the crags of his face. The Grey Wolf sidestepped, weaponless, sweeping aside the swirl of her weighted cloak and catching her right hand with arrogant ease. He twisted, and her bright blade doused upon the stones as the bones in her wrist and hand cracked and slipped.

Muire choked on a cry. Her knees folded. She fumbled left-handed for the flechette pistol, but the Grey Wolf caught her arm and hauled her up again, drawing her into the shadow of the wall. A fragile halo of numbness wrapped her hand, which she knew would shred into agony the instant she tried to move. Ironically, the pressure of the Grey Wolf's hand was a comfort, stabilizing broken bone.

"Not bad." His voice all seduction, he bent over her. His breath ran hot along her throat, against her ear as he whispered. She had expected his flesh to be cold, cold as a shark's, cold as the grave. But it was wolves' breath: hungry, murderous. A bitter scent clung about him. His body within the clothing was hard as sculpture; his heart beat passionlessly while hers hammered in her chest. His fingers left her shattered wrist and tangled her hair, pinioning her head to bend it back. "Fear not. Thou wilt find pleasure in it."

Desperation flared, overwhelming panic. She knew what he intended. She remembered the tarnished, their perverted kiss, and how their victims, even spared, would return to be taken again. She shook her head against the iron of his grip and found her voice somewhere. "No."

He paused. She stared up into his eyes, unwilling to close her own, as if she could force him to see her. As if she could somehow push back through the years and the savagery and the betrayals and *make him see*—

"Strifbjorn," she said, though the name came up as if on fishhooks. "That's why you came, isn't it? You see it. You *see* it. As you loved him, Mingan, listen to me now. . . ."

"And what wouldst thou know of love, candle-flicker?" His hesitation bent to mockery. "This is as close to an act of love as thou wilt ever taste."

He settled his open mouth on hers.

I do not wish it! She braced herself against the pleasure that must follow, the aching gorgeousness of the tarnished kiss.

But—*As thou wish't,* he whispered in her head, and he let her keep the pain. Past the rush and the roaring of the Light, past the terrible intimacy of that murderous kiss as he swallowed her breath and drank deep . . . there was the pain. He honored her request and did not hold away the pain, and she clung to it, and remained herself to the end.

Surely the soul of an immortal must fill his hunger. Surely it must. *Take my life and make it the last life that you take.*

With that in her heart, she gave herself up to him willingly. A fierce joy grew in her breast; this was why she had been spared so long ago, spared for this sacrifice, this expiation. This redemption.

His hunger made a grave for ten thousand souls. In her arrogance, she fancied hers could fill it. And maybe she could come back, too, and be reborn, as innocent as Strifbjorn.

And then the darkness drew her down, into silence, into warmth, into forgiveness. . . .

No.

She came awake on the stones, aching and numb with immobility and chill. Knees, booted feet, a cloaked figure crouched beside her. Starlight shone from his eyes, the light of hungry, distant suns.

"Live, then," he said, and brushed her cheek with the back of a glove, "and be in the future less innocent."

"You have no problem preying on innocents," she answered, jerking her chin at the corpse of the Mongrel boy. In her ear, Fasoltsen whimpered.

Mingan sighed, stood, turned away, straight-backed under the heavy gray cloak. He still wore his hair in the einherjar style, a shot-silver queue hanging long between his shoulders.

He turned back and smiled. "When has the Light ever been gentle to innocence?"

She realized, for she had forgotten, that he was beautiful. Not lovely to look at; he was not that, with his craggy features and his ridged nose. But full of awful grace and wilderness.

She could not answer. She pushed herself up left-handed, moving with exaggerated caution around the waking agony of her right wrist and hand. The numbness had faded, replaced with a pain that made her want to vomit, or curl around her arm and hide in deepest shadow until the hurting softened.

He came back to her, crouched again and lifted her to her

feet with ease, and brushed her hair back although she flinched away. "Mine ancient enemy," he said, as if it were a benediction.

She winced and looked down, and though her geas hammered at her like the wings of a caged bird at the bars, she did not move to strike at him. *Coward, caitiff, craven.*

I am sorry, Ingraham.

"I will hunt you," she said softly. She made herself lift her chin and meet his gaze though she wobbled with weakness and pain. "I will hunt you. For Herfjotur. For Strifbjorn."

"I will await thee," he answered, and slipped into the dark as if he had never been.

Ansuz (insight)

ᚠ

The boy is a whore. For slightly less than the price of a good meal—food which the wolf has no use for—that wolf could hire his mouth, his hands . . . other things.

He considers it, in the early hours of the morning, his back to the wall in a corner of the Ash & Thorn. If the ragged, uneasy fantasy that nags him when the boy's scent strokes his face could be dignified as *consideration*. He can almost feel it: moist air on his neck in a cold alley, sheltered by the Well, rough brick snagging the wool of his cloak, the filthy trickle of water following the crude granite verge. The boy on his knees, his flesh cool, as everyone's flesh is cool to the wolf's touch.

It's not as if they'd ever had a bed, when they were angels. Squalid stones and unclean drizzle would only be appropriate.

Right now, with the taste of Muire's life hot on his lips, filling him with a restless passion, the temptation is unbearable. In the end the wolf could own them both. Both on the same instant, possess them, prove at last who it was whose weakness brought down the Last Day, and the fall of all that was.

The boy who was Strifbjorn is a whore. It's an irony the wolf should be prepared to savor, before he leaves the boy to his fate. The same fate as everyone else. No need to single out one for special treatment. Whatever he was before, he's but a candle-flicker now. A beautiful one, polished and glossy, all the more perfect for the terrible, disfiguring scar that puckers and knots the right side of his face when he smiles. It doesn't seem to bother the young man's admirers; if anything, the wolf thinks some of them find it erotic. The boy shies away like a startled horse, an animal he will never see, when women and men wonderingly brush the raw-lipped pink line.

He looks nothing like he did. But he is still ruined, and still beautiful. And the wolf has an earring, a gift from an apprentice sorceress, that shows him Truth. He knows who this was, when he was something other than a tall, pretty young whore.

The wolf suspects he might even have known him without it.

Delicious. Delicious irony, that they should come back together at the end of the world. Again. And that the wolf should know all, and the boy know nothing. As he means . . . nothing.

The wolf stalks him anyway, this accidental discovery, this pale-eyed, scar-faced child who was not a child, two thousand years gone by, when the wolf loved him.

It's an addiction. An obsession. It is not safe.

He comes anyway, knowing that Muire could find him, now, if she had the strength to drag herself. If he had not left her spent and helpless on the stones. She might, in fact, anticipate him. Might come here, as if she could protect this child. She knew why he was drawn here. She told him as much—

She was never subtle. If she'd guessed that the fall of Freimarc drove him here, she might easily have let that knowledge slip. He should have killed her. He has never *forced* his kiss upon an angel before.

He licks his lips and watches the boy fight. Watches him sell himself, and return, insouciant, laughing by the bar with the other fighters, the ones who whore and the ones who don't. Considers . . . and considers withdrawing, as well. Delicious to know you could have him. Delicious to know that you could *save* him.

Delicious to know that you can choose not to, and leave him to his fate.

Surely, it's a harmless hobby. A way to pass the time, a little cruel pleasure while the world winds down. Surely it is only the cord binding his neck that makes his breath sting when the child catches his eye and—puzzled—frowns as if he thought he knew him. It's like a gift, a little added joy in the end of every-thing, that Strifbjorn is back for him.

The wolf barely admits it, even to himself. But this time, he considers, they might die together.

He stands, the chair scraping because he does not care to prevent it. He wipes his mouth on the back of his glove, the last sting of liquor fading, and shrugs his shoulders to make the cloak swing free. There's scrip in his pocket; it's easy to come by. He pulls his presence around himself, the stillness of aspect, the conscious smile. The boy still smells like Strifbjorn.

Call.

Muire staggered, cradling her broken hand to her armored breast. Age-rounded stones clutched her boots; she stumbled, but pride stopped her fall. The voice rolled over her like storm air rolling down the flank of a mountain. Not Ingraham's thready memorial plaint, nor the harsh luxuriant purr of the Grey Wolf's flawed seduction. This was as silent, but also resonant, electric. She knew it in her bosom, her throat, her spine.

"Kasimir."

She meant to think it only, but her lips shaped the valraven's name.

Call to me, he chanted.

I'm fine.

His silence was a tolling bell.

"I'm *fine!*"

If you were not arrogant, beloved, he would not have done what he did to you and walked free.

It wasn't arrogance. Muire shook her head, forcing her spine straight when she wanted to cringe protectively over her hand. It wasn't arrogance.

But it would be arrogance to say so.

Together we might match a wolf. He showed her flashing teeth, eyes like furnaces, sdadown shredded in the bloody snow. She glanced down. **There are only us three left in the world—and perhaps one other. Let us be allies again.**

"One other?"

There was the Serpent. He was not yet dead on the Last Day.

"If he's not dead, he's abandoned us." But Kasimir was right. Right also that alone she was not Mingan's equal. The Grey Wolf had always been greater.

This was not the first time Kasimir had spoken to her since they parted among the dead. But it was the first time he'd spoken to her since she *knew* their old grinning nemesis walked the bones of the earth, a silver earring in his ear.

It wasn't arrogance. And it wasn't pride that kept her from the valraven.

And if it wasn't either, she could swallow both to call for help, when duty demanded.

You are wounded. The voice came like the voice of the soul that speaks a true love's name. Muire flinched to hear it. The dawn breathed over Eiledon and the undercity, vampiric, glided toward slumber. Above, where she could not see them, jeweled lights would be twinkling out sudden as falling stars.

A wet, ripe smell rose from the gutters. She bent, wobbling on unsteady knees, and smoothed the hair of the murdered boy.

Rest in my shadow.

That was the joy—and the pain—of the Grey Wolf's offer; to be no more alone. She left the body where it had fallen and walked on, toward the scentless, sterile river.

We are the Light that remains.

She stood in a narrow courtyard overlooking a small quay and watched the water ripple. His silence nagged her like a splinter. "Come," she said, and he did so.

The wind that struck her reeked of the forge and was loud as the rattle of shaken metal. The shroud of his wings scraped the walls on either side, black and glittering. He tossed his antlered head, the heat rolling from his body like a physical blow. But his eyes were calm and moist and alive, and he curved his necks to her. **Is it yours to judge, sister, or yours to carry out judgments?**

"It's my failing that no one's left to make judgment." She pressed her hand to her chest and cradled it there. The tears that streaked her face dripped with light; the stallion hovered close and his heat shocked them to crusts of salt, but he only breathed on her.

"He let me live," she said. "He called me sister."

It implied more than she could bear. A coward—she would accept that judgment. But she was not a monster.

The stallion's exasperation prickled as if it were her own. **Ride**.

His hide would burn her. She could no longer thrust her hand into living flame and cup it like water from palm to palm.

"How, Bright one?" The old epithet no longer suited him.

I am the Light, he said, and gently he opened his shadowy wings. Feathers clattered, each perfect, each cast in something harder than steel. Brightness coalesced about him. It wrapped his chest and withers, and when it faded it left behind a saddle of white leather and a saddle blanket, also white, with a thin, scrolled border of gold. **This will shield you.**

No stirrups. No safety straps.

The valraven's laughter sounded in her heart. **I will not let you fall.**

And so what if she did? He half knelt and she vaulted into the saddle, as best she could; her hand hurt so much it made the bridge of her nose feel pinched. But Kasimir's searing hide was only pleasantly warm through the tack.

He fanned those incredible wings. It seemed impossible that their tips could clear the ground, the walls on either side. And then he leaped into the air as if hurtled from a crossbow, sailing over the river before his wings completed their stroke.

Higher, higher, the rush of air, her gasp blown back in her face. The city gyring below, the lights and the dark patches, the cold breath out of the Well. The twin waterfalls of the north branch of the Naglfar shimmered with the city light reflected through them; the river still flowed through the Tower, as it had when it was only a campus, but now it had to fall forty stories in defiance of gravity to cling to its accustomed bed.

Kasimir burst through the up-fall in a joyous flare of wings and a mad hiss of steam. Carbon flaked from his hide, temperature-shocked, leaving him blue in places. The water evaporated before it could fling like hurled beads from his feathertips.

No water touched Muire; his body sheltered her from the upward fall. She leaned forward and called into Kasimir's ear, forgetting he could hear her across half a world if he chose. "Where are we going?"

Your hand must be seen to, he answered. **And then there is the matter of the widow.**

"Widow?" She flinched. "Oh. How did you know that?"

I have chosen you. You may as well learn to like it.

"It's not—"

—as if there were a lot of choices, he interrupted. **If it soothes your guilt, you may forget that you saved me. And you may assume that I have chosen you only because you were the last one left untarnished.**

If it makes you feel better.

He furled his wings among the gargoyles on the rooftop of a granite building just a few blocks from the place where Muire had stayed for the last hundred-odd years. "A cash clinic?"

Assent from Kasimir. She turned to dismount. But as she lifted her leg over the cantle, the world went edgy and dark and she slid bonelessly down.

Kasimir lifted his hoof out of the way adroitly. Muire's head struck wet tarpaper instead of hot metal. Gasping, she lay on her back and looked up at him, the silhouette of his dark heads.

"You said I wouldn't fall."

You didn't, when it mattered.

Was it bad? He looked . . . hard. Your last one. You were gone a long time."

Cahey turned in the darkness, slid his shoulder under Astrid's lifted head, tucked his arm into the indentation of her waist. "No," he said, shaping his mouth around the word before he said it. "He was gentle. He . . . wanted me to make it last."

Gentle wasn't the right word. Not really. But the man's fingers had cradled Cahey's skull in a tender curve, a touch that was as affectionate as it was uncomfortable. And so very wrong, for a business transaction.

Astrid poked him soundly in the chest. "Ow!"

"Answer the question."

He winced, but admitted: "I didn't hear it."

"I was asking what he wanted. But . . . Cahey. You don't seem okay."

She knew. She didn't know what was wrong, and that was fine. He didn't know what was bothering him either. But he loved her for looking for it, like a thorn to be plucked from his paw.

He kissed her. He'd cleaned his teeth. And Astrid had her own ways of paying the bills; she wasn't squeamish. Whoring was better than working the meat tanks, like his mother had done. "I . . ." He shrugged. She nestled closer, breasts molding to his chest, hair a snake down his shoulder. Honesty compelled him to add, "He paid too much."

"Too much?" *How much?*

He didn't answer. *A lot.*

"So . . . what?"

Cahey pressed his face into her neck, where her skin smelled of soap and the flat metal of stored water, and breathed it in as if it could scour him. He couldn't very well say, his scent. Which was part of it. Not dirty, which Cahey was used to, living in the shadow of the Well where there was neither running water nor rain to fill water towers. But rank, animal, raunchy. Wild.

Her hand cupped his groin. "You're hard."

"That's not for him." It never was. Paid sex rolled off his back like so much greasy rain. If they wanted something he had to get it up for, he thought about Astrid, or Hrothgar, or Aislinn, and shut his eyes. "Are you too tired?"

"Never," she said. She shifted, pulled her arm out from under his shoulders, pushed him onto his back. "Are you?"

His hands slid up her thighs from the knees as she settled over him. "Love, all I want is to make love to somebody who knows my name."

She leaned forward, squinted at him through the darkness, lips almost brushing his nose. "Sure thing," she said. "Now, which one were you again?"

Curled in snow, among the roots of a tree so large whole worlds fruit on its branches, the wolf dreams of clean rain and wakes weeping.

These are not his dreams. He does not dream.

He does not sleep.

Once he dreamed waking; once he moved through the

world as a dream. A wolf-dream, a sword-dream. No longer: there are no wolves nor einherjar to need his dreaming now.

When he rubs his palms across his eyes, all he feels is dust. It's soft.

He reaches out a gloved hand and strokes the root he shelters behind. Something is carved there: a rune, a summoning. The most secret spell of all. One a god gave his life and sight for. The wolf hooks his fingertips into the gap. These are Muire's dreams he is dreaming; this is Muire's sleep he is sleeping. She is frail, worn, ancient. Almost mortal now. She eats, she bleeds, she sleeps, she pisses. Like any animal.

She dreams.

And having devoured her, the Grey Wolf dreams, as well. He dreams of rain but wakes to fire. He is burning, burning still, burning behind his heart, burning along his bones. His bed of snow cannot cool him.

It's the price you pay forever, when you swallow down the sun.

Wunjo (comfort)

ᚹ

In the morning, Muire came home. She took a rickshaw from the clinic on Brightside, dozing in the seat, her animal body desperate for the sleep she begrudged it. Rubber and aluminum wheels rattled over broken stones, the driver jogging through dawn-empty streets, bearing her past the gibbet at Hangman. She cradled her arm, which was immobilized in an inflatable cast, and tried not to blink too much because the insides of her eyelids felt scratchy.

She'd slept in the clinic, pain-hazed, half-conscious. It would have to be enough, for a little. She had the driver drop her off downtown, nearly on her doorstep, and paid him for the return trip too.

What use scrip, to an angel?

Moreso, it turned out, than one might have expected.

She stayed in a courtyard industrial building on the waterfront, which might be said to have been converted to a studio, if one were speaking charitably. The heavy doors of wire-mesh-reinforced glass unlocked to her key and thumbprint; when they swung open, she found herself in a slate-tiled entry. The door beyond led to the workspace.

The foundry.

The glass wall to the courtyard admitted natural light, three stories' worth. Much of the main room had always been open space, high and airy for the absent mill machines. Where it had not been, Muire had torn out the second and third floors, leaving only the support members—beams thick with the memory of such trees as no longer grew on Valdyrgard, notched into the red-brick walls—and a four hundred square foot section of the overseer's office, reached by an iron spiral stair, as her apartment.

For now, the whole space stood empty and full of morning light, the only motion her neighbor in the courtyard, his head down over his watering. She didn't garden, herself, and it seemed a kind of sin to let it go uncultivated.

Within the door, she paused and threw the locks. The evidence of her long tenure was everywhere in her studio. The slate floor was scarred, and splashed metal had congealed in gouges left by the feet of giant machines. She hung Nathr on her hook, stripped off the ruins of her cloak—fumbling one-handed—and left a trail of armor behind her as she staggered toward the shower. And if her neighbor happened to glance up and catch a glimpse of her sexlessly bony frame right now, she couldn't be bothered to care.

The water was hot, at least, the catch basin on the rooftop full after last night's downpour. The pressure dropped occasionally—Sig filling his watering can or rinsing his hands—but Muire didn't care, any more than she cared about the soap and water squelching unpleasantly between her skin and the inflatable cast.

The hot water was strength, at least temporary strength, and she took it, leaning against the wall of the shower, eyes closed, breathing.

Eat.

Her eyes opened. She realized that she had been sliding down the tiles, that bent knees and a braced hand were not enough to keep her from collapsing under the water.

Eat, Kasimir repeated. **Sleep. You will be of no service if you find him and are too weary to make an accounting.**

It was better advice than she was likely to offer herself, though she hated to take it. She rinsed off under colder water, hissing at the sting against her face, awkwardly dried herself with the scraper, and found her robe and a towel for her hair. The stairs were too much to consider; instead, she wandered out into the sun barefoot, wincing.

Her neighbor was crouched under the arbor, hand-pollinating sweet peas.

"Sig," she said.

A cheerful grunt emerged from under his hat. That was her entire image of him; the torn corduroy trousers, the floppy hat with the plaid, frayed fabric band, the mass of keloid scarring along his jaw, his blue eyes bright against the purple-red flesh. "The blackberries are in," he said, and squatted down to hand up a bowl. "And you need to eat some of this squash. It's taking the place over."

"I'll make bread with it," she said, a yawn cracking her jaw. "You know, Blodwyn the Adamant and her men would most likely have fallen because of scurvy when they were holding the pass above Arden, if it had not been for the blackberries. They only had flour and salt, and they hunted rabbits. There wasn't much to a rabbit except protein. But there's thirty milligrams of vitamin C in a cup of blackberries."

"You talk about these people as if you knew them," Sig said, amused.

Muire licked her lips. "I was a historian." When she reached for the bowl of berries, he paused.

"Your hand."

"I had a bad night," she admitted.

He regarded her, the blue inflatable cast, the red and purple plastic bowl. "Go on inside," he said. "I'll come and make you some breakfast in a minute."

"Sig—"

"No argument."

"Do I look helpless?"

He looked her up and down, bare feet and improvised turban and threadbare robe and skinny legs and broken hand. "No," he said. "You look tired and half starved. Go on in."

She went.

When Muire had come to live here, the warehouse had represented an obscene amount of space for one woman. But during the refugee years, her floors had been covered in pallets, and she had been a hero for a little while.

And then she had been the woman on the corner, who had been an artist before the war and was a soldier now. And then she had been the old nearman who some people said had fought for Thjierry Thorvaldsdottir, and who couldn't be a real person, not quite, because she never got any older. And if someone whispered that she was a made-person, a halfman living on her own, unsupervised—some rich man's escaped toy—well, it was the end of the world.

There were fewer rules against freedom.

Now, Eiledon was cramped with people—though fewer, she thought, every year—but much of the riverfront stood empty. It was their only cemetery, and prone to fire. Muire—whose youth had been spent in communal longhouses, the only privacy that of the woods, or the silence inside one's own mind—was grateful that Sig now occupied the other half of the building. It had stood empty for a long while, and she'd hated the blind windows and the echoes.

Because now she was just Muire, who lived beside the riverwalk and who had no visible means of support and who joined in the neighborhood patrols. Muire, who had no last name and therefore wasn't truman and therefore didn't matter to anyone. And that was as she wished it: she was a sparrow by preference, not an eagle.

But now the Grey Wolf had come to her. And now, as in the past, she must become a sparrow hawk.

Sig fed her, as good as his word, and left her alone with the food and a pot of tea. She ate one-handed, bracing the bowl against her cast.

Once she could have willed the injury to mend. Now, she thought she could speed the healing, but not as weary as she was, and not before breakfast.

The past, she decided, as she caught herself thinking *once* once more, had all come tumbling down on her in battalions.

Vengeance, said Ingraham Fasoltsen, as she pushed the bowl away.

"Vengeance," she answered. "I'm working on it."

She stood, and wobbled. The dishes could wait. Her loft was too far away. But Muire was no stranger to discomfort. And it would not, after all, be the first time anyone had slept on her foundry floor.

———

Ingraham Fasoltsen's body was found by a moreaux patrol at the foot of the Broken Stair half an hour after sunrise. Selene was the first lieutenant to arrive, descending with perfect poise on an antigrav skimmer no bigger than a dinner plate. It would have given most trumans fits, but for Selene it was as safe and convenient a passage as descending a stair.

She stepped lightly onto the cobbles and paused, as the patrol lead turned to meet her. Achilles was a hound, silky-eared and alert, tawny fur showing between the strips of his half-gauntlets. Where Selene carried her monofilament whip, he wore two brace of daggers, one set on each thigh. His tail fanned slowly when he saw her; Achilles was an old friend.

They touched noses, and she smelled the worry on him. His nostrils twitched. "She sent you," he said, reading Her scent on Selene as if reading a name signed to a card. "Personally."

"Fasoltsen was Hers," Selene said, and did not tell him about the package.

Fasoltsen lay crumpled by the intersection of the Broken Stair and the undamaged one, his hips twisted to the side, his arms spread wide. Selene wondered how many passersby had picked their way over the delicately cupped hand that lay athwart the stair, and how many of them had taken time to rifle the body.

Achilles turned to invite her into the circle around the body, and gave her a sideways eyeroll. "Your scent was on him." Not an accusation. Not even a suggestion. Just a fact.

If She had sent Selene, then She was not concerned that Selene's scent was on the body. And so Achilles was not concerned, either.

"He made a delivery." She paused, as she came downwind of the body. "No blood."

"No." He sniffed, as the other two unmans—another dog, prick-eared and fuzzy, and a brown-and-white skewbald rat with long nervous hands—fell back. "There's more scent."

"That musk. It's rank." The same she'd caught last night, drifting from the Well.

With an effort, Selene quelled her flehmen response. There were trumans about, observers and some Mongrels. They might mistake it for a snarl.

"Can you smell the others?"

She sniffed, lightly, and sneezed. "We're not all hounds."

But she crouched beside the body nonetheless, balanced on the tough pads of her elongated feet. She placed her elbows on her knees and craned her neck, surveying the scene from closer now. Selene might not be a hound, but even after sunrise this intersection lay in the shadow of Her Tower, and would until afternoon. Hers was the dark-adapted eye.

"Is there rigor?" she asked. She wasn't ready to touch the dead man yet.

She remembered the brush of his hand, the nervousness as he'd handed her the weapon, the determined lift of his jaw.

"And the livor is congealed," Achilles said, referring to the settling of uncirculated blood. His voice had a sonorous, belling quality, even when he spoke softly, and the slow fan of his tail accelerated. It was not friendliness, now: he was on the hunt. "At least four hours."

"And how many came up the stair, or along this road?"

"The scent's under the dew." She looked up at him and he shrugged. "It's strong, but there's a lot of it. Too many to count. I might be able to pick one out individually."

"Mmm," she said. She twisted her head to the side, ears flat, her tail curving for balance. There was, indeed, dew. Enough to soak the fur on the underside of her tail into twisted spikes. "And how many touched the body?"

While Achilles spoke, Selene slowly focused her gaze from one end of Fasoltsen's body to the other.

"Four," he said. "The bottom layer is—"

"That," she supplied, curling her lip.

He whuffed understanding. "And then something else, truman or nearman, female. She touched his hair and kissed him on the mouth."

"Comforted him while he was dying? May I have a light along the body, please?"

The rat moved to oblige.

Achilles whined. "The one who stinks like a predator kissed him, too."

White light, directional, spilled the length of Fasoltsen's corpse. Selene ducked lower, looking for the telltale shine of fiber. She wished the hawk, Diana—the only hawk—were here. "Interesting," she said. "Sexual assault?"

"It was only the two who came later that opened his clothes."

"To search him."

That little noise again. As if to say, *Your speculation, lead.* But not disagreeing with her.

Selene shifted her head, and a bright filament caught her attention. The leather armor on her thighs was sewn with tubular pockets: she slipped a claw into one and hooked forth a set of tweezers, delicately so as not to scratch the metal. Her claws were no longer the horny barbs of her dim recollection, when she had been only a huntress and a mother, before she had become Selene. The claws she wore now could slice bone or gouge metal, and she had learned at painful cost to have a care for them.

There were no instincts to provide for what She had made of Her unmans.

Selene plucked up the hair and had no need to ask for an envelope. The rat was there with one already. Selene collected the evidence, and while she was writing out a tag, Achilles took the unsealed pouch and sniffed lightly. "The woman."

Selene did not nod, not unless talking to trumans. For Achilles, her ears pricked and her whiskers came forward. "Somebody saw something."

"It's a hope. We could canvass."

If anyone in such a neighborhood as this would be willing to come forward. Selene glanced under her arm: the Mongrels were standing around in clumps, keeping the gawkers away from the moreaux while they worked. Nearmans, she guessed, in the ghetto. One or two cybered halfs. Some of them might be trus, like the Mongrels—pure-blood humans, unmutated—but you couldn't tell them from the nears to look at them.

It would be hopeless for moreaux to canvass here. Selene blew through her whiskers. "I'll ask Her to put the Mongrels on it."

Trumans, even those who worked for Her, wouldn't take orders from an un.

Achilles held up the sealed envelope. "Make sure She knows we're looking for a blonde."

"I'll do better than that," Selene said, uncoiling, stretching her spine out as her heels dropped to the cobblestones. "I'll see if there's enough material for Her to run a trace on it."

Achilles wagged, and handed her the envelope back. And

Selene did not finish her thought: *. . . if Her strength will support the effort.*

When Muire awoke, the sun was low through the windows, skipping eye-watering brilliance across the faceted river. She covered her eyes with the cast and groaned, but sat up easily. Sleep was an excrescence.

And she needed to eat—already—again.

It would wait.

Over a life as long as Muire's, objects accumulated. She owned a bed and a reading chair, lamps and end tables, a forge and an anvil. Clutter and memories. A viscreen and a hook to hang her fiddle from.

The fiddle was upstairs, and she fetched it when she went up to change. It was old, pre-Desolation, resonant and red-varnished. It had been given her by a dying man in a railroad town, when there were railroads, when they needed towns. She was tired, she thought, of dying. Dying people, and things, and ways of life.

Dead tired.

The fiddle case was dusty. "Muire, really," she said, and found a cloth to wipe it clean.

Sleep had brought some healing. Her fingers would flex, and so she bent them around the bow. It scraped; painstakingly, she tuned the melody strings and the drones. Her wince was for the instrument, not for the pain in her hand.

Once—that word again, and she wished it would fade back into dusty memory, where she'd meant to abandon it—once, the children of the Light forested a world with their song, voices raised in concert for mighty wreakings. Once they had been the makers of miracles.

Now, she might be able to speed the healing of a shattered bone.

If she were lucky.

The music cascaded through her, pulling energy with it, drawing light. In rivulets and streams, it crept out the tips of her fingers and whispered back into her ears. Her fingers softened, moved more surely, and the tone grew pure, and she closed her eyes and tilted her head back and leaned on the music hard— because, for a moment, she could. She put what she could into it, the wildness and frustration, the fury that scoured her when she remembered the Grey Wolf's touch, his mockery, his grief. The ends of her cropped hair shook about her face as she bent forward.

Oh, how dare he presume to be sorry?

And then the song was done. She stood panting, head bowed, her broken and pinned hand aching. Itching, too, and that was a positive sign. She set the fiddle in its case and closed the latch. She wiped her forehead on the back of her uninjured wrist.

"Vengeance," she said.

The cast had to come off before she could attempt a sculpture of her prey.

Clay, first. And wire. The flea-colored mud—dense and slick under Muire's fingers—marked her nails in purple-brown crescents. She knew his face, the narrow-bridged nose, the furrow to the corners of a thin mouth. She knew the earring and the fold at the corner of his eye.

She made him as perfect as her hands could shape. And

when she had done it, she pressed her nails into her palms—her eyes tearing when she tried to fist the right one—and managed not to smash it flat.

How many can say they got to see the world end twice?

I, said Kasimir's old-iron voice, in the back of her mind.

She could have laughed, but it hurt her throat to think on it. Instead, she opened her viscreen. It chirruped—*Happy birthday!*—in a dead man's voice, as it did each day of the year.

The net always knew her.

She wondered if the man who had written that clever little technomatic virus still would have done so, if he had known he would be breaking her heart for centuries to come.

She imaged the sculpture and burned it to a chip, which she libraried to her reader—*Happy birthday!,* when she fired it up—and then pocketed. When she turned back, the bust stared forward, opaque eyes unreadable.

A cloth lay around its neck, where Muire had draped it. She reached down and pulled it over the sculpture's head.

Vengeance, Ingraham Fasoltsen nagged.

It was more welcome than Kasimir's gentle reminder: **There is still the matter of the widow.**

6

Mannaz (humankind)

ᛗ

Gunther Watsen had been the first person Muire met when she returned to Eiledon. It had been a summery morning near the spring solstice, two hundred and seven years previous to meeting the Grey Wolf in a dark alley under the curve of the Tower. She had walked—she walked a great deal in those days—from Freimarc, and she paused on the shoulder of the green mountain overlooking the valley of the Naglfar, at a place where the trees broke.

Below, an agate-colored river wound seaward, restrained by the topography even as it reinvented it. On its banks the city rose, a sprawl of multicolored glass and faceted metal set in the landscape like a rococo jewel in a verdigrised setting.

The last time she stood on the shoulder of that peak, Eiledon had been a walled cluster of three- and four-story buildings. But it had far outgrown those medieval walls, though she could still detect their presence in the pattern of the streets. A steady procession of aircraft slid down the sky, the foaming wakes of freighters and pleasure craft scarring the placid river. The port was ten miles downriver, in the delta, and the city and its sub-urbs lined the banks the entire way.

Outside the walls, where the city was less crowded, Muire

walked beside a broad avenue bordered by flowering trees. It was not especially well designed for pedestrians; electric cars and at least one ground-effect vehicle blurred past, blowing dust into her eyes. But she walked on, and Eiledon rose up around her.

The population of the metropolitan area crested at twelve million souls: a teeming center of commerce, romance, and artistic endeavor.

Eiledon had eight gates and two river locks. Muire entered through the easternmost, the Wolf Gate, for easy access to the Green and the University. Here, the walking was easier—only electric and human-powered vehicles were permitted within the walls, and bicycles, scooters, and hoverboards outnumbered autos in the knotty cobblestoned alleys.

One long block—ignoring the winding, tunnelish side streets of the Wolfgate neighborhood, with its aura of decayed wealth—brought her to Boulevard, which she crossed. This was the new Old City. The Ark rose on her left until its heights were lost in the haze, a contrast to the government center on her right, with its elaborate lacework stone.

It was noon by the time she reached the Riverside Market, and glossy heads shimmered in the mounting sun. The earthy scents of vegetables and the sweetness of berries saturated the air, but a flower-seller's booth reeked of humid jungle.

Muire breathed deeply, rubbing her hands in the warmth.

She bought a newschip and slid it into her reader. Several people eyed the device: judging by their appearances, she guessed they were wired.

Country cousin, she thought, and tried not to burst out laughing. It was far from the first time.

She could have bought a mapchip, too. But it was just as

easy to turn to a gangling young man buying coffee ice cream from a stand in the tree-shade by the Green and ask.

He looked down on her from a towering height, and smiled in a way that rearranged his features engagingly over the bones. Brown hair, uncut in recent memory, blew across his eyes and into his mouth when he spoke.

Muire thought he might be a little too aware of his own quirky androgynous beauty. But he was nevertheless polite, and at least his teeth were crooked. "Of course. Down Park to University, turn right. The campus is up the hill: there's a stair at University and Boulevard."

"I just crossed Boulevard," she said, as his ice cream dripped over his knuckles.

"It's a circle. It makes a big loop around the Green. You . . . must be new in town?"

"I've been away a long while," Muire answered. The best she could do: waelcyrge did not lie, unless—until—they grew tarnished. "Thank you for your help—"

But he fell into step beside her, twisting his long wrist awkwardly and craning his neck in the opposite direction until he could suck the ice cream off his fingers. "I'm going that way. I'll walk with you," he said, seemingly unperturbed by the dust on her clothes, her greasy plaits, or the rucksack dragging her shoulders down. "Are you a student? Or have you taken a job at the University?"

She should have shut him down, and she knew it. But he was as awkward and eager as a puppy dog, self-conscious to the point of stammering and somehow still seeming entirely genuine.

"No," she said. "Neither. I'm an artist. I have a fellowship."

"Oh," he said. Still waging left-handed war with the melting ice cream, he reached out and pressed an only slightly sticky fingertip to the pad of her reader. It chirped when it had scanned his print, and he said, "Look me up. I'm Gunther Watsen. I'm an assistant to Professor Thorvaldsdottir."

And for some reason, Muire looked at him wiping hair out of his eyes, and said, "I will."

Muire really needed to stop taking in candle-flicker strays. She tried, Light knew: she held herself aloof, didn't place calls, avoided social engagements. She didn't take lovers. She didn't need friends. She especially didn't need friends who would in-evitably break her heart with their fragility, their evanescence, the shadow-quick passing of their mortal lives.

Gunther Watsen appeared at the door of her brand-new, just-rented warehouse studio as if by magic, two days later, carrying a picnic basket and a bottle of wine.

"*An* artist," he said.

Muire had been on her hands and knees, face daubed and hair smeared with tile cement, replacing the broken slates of her floor. She stood holding the glass door open on Gunther, who swung his basket meaningfully and grinned—smirked, really—like a hopeful schoolboy. "I beg your pardon?"

"You said you were an artist."

"I am . . . ?"

"You didn't say you were the sculptor-laureate."

"I said I had a fellowship," she replied, but somehow he'd gotten past her. She turned and watched him wander in slow circles, his head angled back as he took in her distinctly indus-trial space in all its tumult of renovation.

Without looking at her, he continued, "They said you walked from Freimarc."

"Who said?"

"Gossips," he answered, with a disarming grin. And now he looked at her directly. "I brought lunch. Can we eat it?"

Muire opened her mouth to say something along the lines of *don't you think you're presuming a little?* and instead, heard her stomach growl. She glanced down at her hands, scraping her thumbnail against a black bit of cement. "I haven't a table yet."

"You have a courtyard," he said, and led her out into it. Or, more precisely, he exited, and she pursued.

It was a weedy, erratically shaped patch of earth, partly paved in cracked stones, partly carpeted in dandelions, saw grass, and violets. A dead cedar tree stood in one corner, a failing magnolia in the other, its bloom already past.

Gunther plunked himself down on the sun-warmed earth, avoiding piles of broken brick and mortar, and pulled a square of fabric from his basket. "Do you mind eating here?"

Muire opened her mouth. Shut it. Gathered herself, and said, "Mister Watsen—"

"—Gunther. I get enough of that from professors—"

"—I'm afraid I'm a vegetarian."

He paused in the act of laying out napkins, plastic cups, disposable knives. "Well, that's only a small problem," he said. "I hope." He tapped a little heap of wrapped sandwiches. "Two of these are cheese. Is cheese okay?"

"Cheese is fine," she said, surrendering to the inevitable, and plumped herself crosslegged at the edge of the cloth.

He had not only wine but a thermos bottle of tea, redolent of cinnamon and already cloudy with milk.

"You're a student?" she asked, taking the cup he extended,

pressing it to her cheek for the warmth and the scent of the tea while he sorted sandwiches.

"Not exactly. Here, have this one. I'm a postdoc. I work for Professor Thjierry Thorvaldsdottir."

"You said. And she is . . . ?"

"Dean of the School of Technomancy."

Oh. "You're a technomancer?"

"Well, not a very good one." He grinned, and unwrapped another sandwich for himself. The stuffing of this flatbread was the bloody magenta of rare beef.

"Did you know," she said, shifting a buttock to avoid a pointed stone, "that technomancy grew out of the old rune-magic?"

"We still learn the seventeen runes," he said. "As apprentices. We've advanced some since the old days."

"Seventeen? There are eighteen." He was staring at her. She looked down at her hands. "According to the Eddas."

"The eighteenth one is secret," he said. "Nobody knows it. Tell me about walking here from Freimarc."

"Part of it was by ship," she answered by reflex, while he poured the wine: pale gold, too sweet and not cold enough. "I like walking."

It beat thinking.

"How long did it take?"

She shook her head. "Four months? I started in winter."

"Wow." The eyebrows did something expressive, which Muire wasn't entirely sure how to read. His facial expressions were as theatrical as the rest of him. "The University is lucky to have you. Were they reluctant to wait?"

"Is this an interview?"

"Maybe." He rolled a walnut half between his fingers. "You're interesting. When's your birthday?"

"I don't have one."

"Seriously!"

She waved him off. "No day in particular."

He laughed—"So it must be every day."—and ate the nut. "You're very mysterious, you know. There's not much about you on the net."

"Stalker."

His sandwich held in both hands, he examined it as if determining an angle of attack. Muire felt a sort of kinship with that lump of bread and meat. "Sculptor in residence. Did you haul all your equipment here on your back? What do you sculpt, feathers?"

She unwrapped her sandwich and sniffed it: the aroma of sprouts, mustard, and an earthy mushroom smell rose from an envelope of unleavened bread. The sharp scent of aged cheese triggered a pang of hunger. She shoved a corner of the bread into her mouth and then spoke through the food, covering her lips with her hand. "Normally, in a conversation, the parties take turns asking and answering things."

"You forget to eat," he said.

She nodded, swallowed a painfully large lump, and washed it down with wine. Then crammed another mouthful in.

He shook his head. "So does Thjierry. Side effect of genius? No, eat, don't answer that."

Gunther touched the translucent skin on the back of Muire's hand. It was thin over the bones, and she pulled her hand away, uncomfortable with the touch.

He shook his head, seemed to cast about for a safer subject, and failing that took another bite of his own sandwich. He ate with neat decorum. Of course, Muire thought, compared to her right now, wolves ate with neat decorum.

She knocked crumbs from her chin. "Thank you," she said, when she realized that she hadn't already. "Apparently I need a keeper."

"Or at least a feeder." He pushed another sandwich at her. "The other cheese one. Go ahead."

She reached for it, and her braid fell over her shoulder.

"How do you work metal with such long hair?"

"Pin it up," she said, wax paper crinkling as she flattened it. She abandoned the sandwich for a moment and lifted a plait still damp from the morning's washing to where she could study it. It was neither gold nor gleaming, but a threaded shade between brown and blonde. "You should have seen my sisters'. Bright blonde, and down to the floor. Never cut. Mine was thought mousy."

"You have a sister?"

Had. Many. But Muire did not correct him. "I'm orphaned. No family left."

A dead moment of silence weighed the air between them, and then Gunther picked up his tea and drained the cup.

"Well, I'm the king of Foot in Mouth." He set his lunch on the cloth and pushed it out of the way. "I'm sorry. I'm not doing very well at finding safe topics, am I?"

"I'm prickly," Muire answered, after a longer silence. "I'm sorry, I know that."

"Look, Muire . . . I am not . . . I don't have an agenda. I like interesting people. I'm boring myself, but I'm drawn to greatness." He chuckled, with irony, and refilled both drinking bowls. "Can we be friends?"

She ate two more bites of sandwich before she answered,

and this time managed to swallow before she spoke. "I don't know. I can't yet say."

"All right then," he said. "Can we be acquaintances for now?"

"Yes," she said. "That I think I can manage."

She did not quite look down in time to avoid the warmth of his smile.

In the years that followed, Muire was happy in Eiledon, though she feared admitting it—even to herself—even more than she feared the happiness. It was all the evidence of bitter experience, that if you have something to lose, you will lose it.

The first sign of wrong came as a whisper, a murmur of war on a distant wind. A famine. An accidental release of a bioterror weapon. A border skirmish, a too-hot summer. A spill of tech-nomantic effluvia. There was news, images, text and flash-holos and chatter on the nets. A scandal when a main battle shoggoth crushed a student demonstration. But it was four thousand miles away, in another hemisphere.

It might as well have been another world. What could any-body do?

And then Muire started finding the songbirds.

One or two, sparrows and robins, orioles and thrushes. And then more, scattered on the sidewalks, their wings twisted and stiff, while the skies grew silent. Cagebirds and parrots fol-lowed. The ubiquitous city pigeons.

Crows, ravens. Owls and falcons and hawks.

Insects, too. There had been a white-faced wasp nest in the corner of Muire's courtyard. A thriving colony, until the day when she found them scattered, dying, on the broken paving blocks. She knelt down on the stones beside the wasps and lifted one up on her fingertip.

Its wings buzzed faintly, their strong cellophane crumbling. Fuzzy yellow filaments of some invasive fungus protruded from its white-and-black abdomen. It stung her, reflexively, the poison in her finger a searing heat, and she held it while it stung her again.

The tears that choked her breathing weren't from the wasp's futile venom. They came because she could no longer deny that she knew. Cascading catastrophe, the system in failure. It was not Muire's first apocalypse. But then, her kind had always been better at retribution than prevention.

And she knew as if it had been blazoned on a banner, with desperation would come war.

Black sorcery, radiation weapons, nanites, railguns, orbital assault, biotoxins and all the ills the flesh is heir to: Valdyrgard had died its first death in ice. The second was in flames. Mountains were heaved up and pounded flat. Oceans steamed and cities died in silence, suffocated under the falling dust.

Eiledon . . . was spared.

No, spared is the wrong word. Eiledon went to war with all the rest.

But Eiledon had a hero.

In a steep green valley, beside a narrow brook that hopped from stone to stone like a child skipping down steps, Kasimir dwelt alone.

His wings fanned like black blades when he spread them, and he had learned caution early and quickly: have a care where you step, for your hooves can scorch the earth, and a fire grow up about you; have a care where you light, for your weight can crack stone; have a care whom you love, for your touch can burn them flesh from bone.

He did not weather, except to char flat black with soot. He did not rust or stain. He did not weary.

He could not feel the stroke of a hand.

But he could feel his rider. Though she denied him, though she repudiated herself. Though she was his rider in name only, having never sat his back.

Though it was she who had made of him this new thing, flame-hearted and forged in iron.

She never called, but she was there always, just at the edge of his awareness. He knew her despair and her grief. She punished herself. He thought she must not understand how she punished him, as well.

At first, he had approached her. He had tried to speak to her, to cajole her. To make her accept that they two might still have a purpose in the Light, together. "The Light is dead," she answered. "There are no more angels. The world must fend for itself now."

And he persisted. But at first she argued with him, and then she denied him, and then she cursed him, and then—in the fullness of centuries—she would not speak to him at all.

And though she was his, and he hers, a valraven has his pride. He would not trail her like a kicked cur, seeking approval.

And so he found his own tasks, and waited. Someday, she might need him enough to call.

A forlorn hope, in the end. Even the end of the world— another end of the world: in a long life, Kasimir had begun to suspect they happened with distressing regularity—could not move her to seek him.

Muire would not seek him.

But another—did. An accident, except not really.

Kasimir believed in fate, in wyrds and dooms and ordained consequences. It was a problem of having been born and reborn a destroying angel. And so when he found another, a creature such as he had never seen, a made-thing, he did not believe it mere coincidence.

His valley was steep and narrow, removed from human habitations, so when the jays flew up crying *man! man! man!* he lifted his antlered head from the water curiously. The horned head continued drinking, slow swallows to fill his belly and maintain the pressure in his hydraulics. If he were as he had been, before Muire changed him, water might have dribbled from his lips and splashed back into the brook. But now he was a thing of fire and iron, and it wreathed his face in steam, hissing off into the cold morning air.

He would go and see this man, he decided. And because Kasimir lived in hope, he would hope that it was merely a wanderer, and not someone against whom he would have to take measures.

Stealth was not his métier. He did not come silently, did Kasimir, but with the rattle of steel on steel, the hiss of steam, the thump of hooves shaking the ground. Still, he came down along the stream bank cautiously, staying to the shadows, blinking into the light. His lids closed like iron shutters over his moist brown eyes. His lashes made the soft sound of stroked wire-brush when they meshed.

Kasimir had not been for subtlety reborn.

It turned out not to matter.

When he heard the noise of scrambling, he paused behind an outcrop that knocked the stream into a wide curve, craning one neck to peer beyond. Whatever staggered up the rocky bank, scrambling over roots, half erect and half scuttling, was no man. It wore rough tattered brown robes, and its fingers were long and narrow and knotted, the right hand solid black on the palm, furred black on the back, and the left hand blotched with white hair and pink skin. A long whiskered nose twitched on a wedge-shaped head, and the fur here too was spotted, the muzzle divided black and white.

The front of the robe was soaked; it had obviously drunk from the stream, as Kasimir himself had been doing. And the entire animal smelled of injury and filth and machine grease, of malnutrition and illness. It dragged itself along the bank, the scent of blood and pus preceding.

And among all that, Kasimir could also smell the sorcery upon it. Technomancy, which had been in old days the magic of letters and forged things, and was now the magic of words and machines and microscopic knives and wires.

In other words, the new animal was a made-thing. A made-thing, like the sdadown.

Kasimir felt no sting as his tail struck his flank. But he heard the slap of wires on metal, and the rustle of a falling branch where his careless gesture had savaged an alder. And so did the dying new animal.

It cringed, curling in on itself, mismatched hands raised to protect its mismatched head. Kasimir saw the gashes on its bony palms, the blisters, the infection. It didn't speak, but it chittered—a high, distressed sound, frantic and terrible.

A sdada knew no fear. And this creature was terrified.

Kasimir came around the outcrop. He had to step into the stream to do it, and the water boiled around his ankles, hissing. After a moment, it cooled the metal a little, though his hooves still steamed when he lifted them. And down the bank, the little creature—no bigger than a small human, just about the size of Kasimir's rider—huddled into itself and bared chisel teeth under beady mismatched eyes.

It was a rat. A black-and-white rat, made giant and dexterous.

Fear me not, Kasimir said. **For I feel pity.**

It did not know whether to trust him, and he believed—in its fear, too exhausted to flee—that it would hurl itself at him in an instant, and die in futile combat. He had known rats; rats were creatures of the field and stable.

They were not quitters.

Fear me not, Kasimir said, again. **I will not harm you. I will save your life. What is your name, made-creature?**

It chittered once more. And then drew back, head lowered, and made a noise that could have been a word.

Your pardon? the warhorse asked.

And it choked, and repeated, "Cristokos. This one is Cristokos. What is that one?"

My name is my own, Kasimir answered. **Come, follow.** He began to turn away, to lead it at a right angle to the stream. He knew where there was a cave, a dry sandy floor, piles of leaves and pine needles for warmth. If he scraped the earth clean, it would be a safe place to build a ring for fire.

The new animal made a small weary sound of distress, and Kasimir glanced back over his shoulder. **You must follow.**

He thought it would protest, but it pushed itself up on wavering arms and crawled forward, moving by inches. A foot, ten feet.

It fell, and crooned exhaustedly.

It is not far, Kasimir said, waiting. **Come. I cannot carry you. I am not built for giving succor.**

"But that one does anyway," the rat-creature answered, without lifting its head.

We do not always do what we are built for.

"No," it answered. And then while he watched, it somehow got hold of a branch, and pushed itself to its knees and then its feet, its naked pink tail dragging heavily behind it. "One does not always." It paused, breath whistling through its teeth, head lowered. And then it pushed itself up and shuddered. "Go on. Slowly. This one *can* walk. This one *will*."

On a windy, clear day in September, Thjierry Thorvaldsdottir arrived at Muire's studio much as had Gunther Watsen, five years before: unheralded and with an armful of dinner. She came accompanied, however, and not entirely as a stranger. Muire knew her slightly, from University functions and the social circle that surrounded the irrepressible Gunther.

They were cordial enough, in that way that people can be who have nothing in common and little to talk about. Muire was satisfied with the lack of depth in that relationship, even as Thorvaldsdottir's political activism lead her to celebrity and a series of public confrontations and condemnations over the Eiledain Thing's handling of the current crisis.

Muire had never expected *the* Technomancer, as people were beginning to call her, to come to her door.

She took Professor Thorvaldsdottir's wrap, and nodded in acknowledgment when the Technomancer said, "Please, call me Thjierry, as I must call you Muire."

It was rare for a truman to cede the social capital of a real human name to one of the undercastes. "Thank you," Muire said, and would have led them into the workshop, but Thjierry paused by the door. "This sword. Did you make it? Or is it old?"

"Very." Muire stretched her back against the brick wall, joints crackling in several places.

"It's fascinating. May I ask where you came by it?"

"Would you believe on a beach, cast up by the waves?"

"Up North?"

Waelcyrge didn't lie. But they didn't always need to press the truth.

Muire nodded.

"A lot of interesting things are cast out of the sea," Thjierry said, through a smile. "Carved amber and ivory turns up there, too."

"I've heard. Glass beads, bits of old ships."

"Maybe when this is all over the Institute can send an expedition."

Muire shrugged and offered tea, and Thjierry confessed that she had forgotten her bowl. Muire fetched a spare from the kitchen upstairs and filled it, while Gunther cleared off one of the work tables and laid out a repast of cheese spread on crispbread and sliced oranges.

Oranges.

There almost weren't any left by then.

Thjierry was a sturdy woman in her early middle years, with a mechanic's hands and a fondness for neutral colors. She had sallow skin, and her eyelids were beginning to droop in a fashion that emphasized her epicanthic folds: obviously a heritage from her mother's side of the family, given her name. She wore dark-brown hair cropped at the sides, showing a stippling of silver, and long enough to curl at the top.

The oranges were dry, tacky, their best past. Muire licked the bitter aromatic oil of the peel from dry fingers and wondered if she would ever taste it again. And Thjierry eyed her and made small talk at first, but that was not why she had come.

She had come to talk about magic.

And eventually, she took a deep breath. Her eyes—a hazel shade, between brown and green—flickered around Muire's studio, taking in the foundry and the half-finished wrought-iron railing that would, once complete, decorate the stair. And when she let the breath out, she said, "Gunther tells me you're something of a sorceress."

Muire poured more tea, stroking her fingers along the slick blue glaze of the pot. The purple-brown around the rim had been dipped on before the pot was fired so individual runnels slid beneath her fingers with smooth, irregular rise and fall.

"I used to be a poet. A historian. Now I play fiddle," she answered. "And bass."

Those words: so soft, so short and so uninflected. *I used to be a poet.*

And then she had stopped loving history.

She used to be all sorts of things.

"Bass for heavy work?" Thjierry asked. She sipped her drink; Muire nodded.

The Technomancer drained the bowl, and with a smile produced a flask from the pocket of her tan corduroy swing jacket.

She poured herself a measure of something transparent and jewel-gold before holding the little bottle out. Muire held up her bowl, and Thjierry filled it, then did the same for Gunther.

The Technomancer cleared her throat and said, "Galdr, spell-singing. Skaldry's a man's magic, Muire."

"So are the runes," Muire answered. "And the art of the forge and the wire. But the Technomancer of Eiledon is a woman." And because she had it in her to say it, she added, "And the second-wickedest seithr I ever knew was a man, who could drive minds mad and make hearts forgetful of love."

The Grey Wolf had used the rune-magic, too. But Muire did not feel the need to cloud the argument.

Thjierry's face remained impassive as a statue's. Muire could imagine stroking the clay into place along her age-softened cheek, notching her upper lip with the pressure of a thumb.

"Who was the wickedest?"

"History suggests a name," Muire said. She touched the liquor to her lips. It curled soft flame across her palate. "There was Heythe, of course—"

"Mythical monsters don't count," Thjierry said, softly. "So you have never practiced seithr?"

"No," Muire said. "I am not a witch. Nor have I any gift to spae. I am no seeress, no volva. And I have learned to have little love of those who would prophesy. Or claim to know the ancient law."

"How unwomanish," Thjierry said, but she smiled.

Beside Muire, Gunther cleared his throat.

Muire peered over at him. "Your comment?"

He shook his head, eyeing her over the top of his bowl as he sipped the spirits therein. And Thjierry said, "The refugees are coming from Starkhaven."

The city had fallen only days before. Muire closed her eyes and spoke around a heart's denial. "I know."

Across the corner of the table, the Technomancer sipped her liquor and coughed. "I am pressing the Thing to elect a Thane to lead us through the war. They are divided, but there will be a vote. I mean to have a corps of sorcerers—technomancers, seith-wives and seith-men, skalds, seers—behind me when I go to them."

"Implicit support and implied threat. The Thing will not wish to relinquish power."

"No one ever does," Gunther said. His hair had stuck to the corner of his mouth and his lips and cheeks were pink from the alcohol.

"Everyone has a price." Thjierry turned her bowl with her fingertips. "I hope I—we—can find theirs."

Muire wound the end of her braid around her hand, over and over like a ribbon, until her left fist rested against her shoulder. "I hope so too," she said. "You will have my support."

"Good," Thjierry said.

Muire let the braid slide between her fingers, and decided she would cut it as soon as Gunther and Thjierry left. It was a relic, and better gone. "And in case they prove obdurate, we must consider other options."

"We need an army," Thjierry said. "I know."

Othala (home)

The day after her encounter with the Grey Wolf, Muire—dressed now in street clothes rather than armor, Nathr concealed under a draped cloak and her right hand back in a sling—crossed the bridges at Rivereye and made her way north to Ark before the sun went low.

She had argued with herself, and lost. However much Ingraham Fasoltsen's red craving for vengeance picked at her, however swiftly she, herself, burned to see the Grey Wolf made to pay, she first needed to pay her respects to Fasoltsen's widow. Information learned there could be valuable. Even if the Grey Wolf killed indiscriminately—and Muire was not yet certain he did—there might be a pattern. Something about the victim that would show her how Mingan had chosen him, and lead her to where he might strike again.

The weight of Kasimir's opinion had nothing to do with it. And she would keep telling herself that. She would not permit him to bully her.

He just happened to be right this time.

It was easy enough to find the place. Fasoltsen knew his own address; Muire merely followed him home. He resisted her—he was the chosen dead, and all things were consumed in the flame of his desire for vengeance—but in the end Muire prevailed.

His codes gained them entrance to the arcology, and her mockery of his voice called the lift. Not that security systems were of much concern to a child of the Light, but Muire was still walking the border of exhaustion, and a fresh attempt at sorcery wouldn't speed her recuperation.

Instead, knowing it was a shocking thing to do, she disembarked the lift on the 105th floor, walked through the dappled oblongs of watery light that fell through the windows of the lobby, and presented herself at Gjerta Ingrahamswif's door. She considered the announcer, and instead—in the time-honored fashion of bearers of bad news—raised her hand and knocked thrice hard.

The Ark was closed to outsiders by decree, but whatever men could build, men could find a path around. Muire was aware that she was observed and catalogued quite carefully before the door slid open, and if she was not facing automated weapons she would be enormously surprised.

On that topic, Fasoltsen was significantly silent.

But when his wife answered the door, Muire felt his response to the shadows under her eyes, the carelessness of her dress. Over Gjerta's shoulder, Muire glimpsed a glamorous home. Expensive self-aligning furniture scattered at apparent random across a carpet of living violets, under a faux-sky ceiling.

Muire took a deep breath, met Gjerta's gaze, and started to extend her right hand, only to find it restrained by the sling. "Gjerta Ingrahamswif?"

She nodded, wary. Her eyes were a modified green inside bruised-looking circles, her hair cycling through a pattern of pinks and pale reds.

Tasteful.

"Don't be afraid. I'm Muire," she said. "I was the last person to see your husband alive."

Eyes narrowed, Gjerta appraised her. Muire stood, hands at sides, and tried not to look like a con artist or a burglar. "You didn't report the death," she said, at last. "You left him lying in the street."

Muire inclined her head. "He died in my arms," she said. "I—"

"You could have *helped* him," the woman said, bitterly, her body still blocking the door. Behind her, though, Muire saw something that made her stammer in surprise rather than guilt.

There was a moreau in the apartment, a slight beagle-headed creature with blunt, deft hands. It was clearing away the tea things, and it was all Muire could manage not to turn her head and stare.

Only the Technomancer made unmans. And she did not, as a rule, lend their service to any but her closest associates.

Muire hated them, dull-eyed and docile things. She hated remembering animals—real animals, wolves and horses, bulls and cats and hounds—and knowing that this alone remained.

"I did what I could," Muire said. "By the time I arrived, he was already gone."

Gjerta's glower never wavered. Muire counted breaths, though, and after four of them Gjerta nodded and touched the tether, permitting the door to swing wide. "You were afraid of the Mongrels," she said.

"I'm not truman." Muire stepped into the apartment, past its mistress, and allowed herself to be led to the couch. The mobile slouched a little to accommodate her lack of height, warm and just the right blend of soft and firm where it cupped her body. "The Mongrels—"

"I understand," Gjerta said, though Muire noticed she sat down farther away than she might have been about to. "You spoke with him."

"For seconds," Muire said, while Ingraham caroled in her head like a cat. "Only. He failed fast. I do not think there was any pain."

A facile understatement, Muire knew, for the shriveling pleasure Ingraham had known before he died.

Gjerta worked her lower lip back and forth between her teeth. "Did you . . ." She stopped, worrying at her words. *Did you see what happened, do you know who did it. . . .*

"No," Muire said, and as if the words had released her, Gjerta sagged forward, arms crossed over her belly and her elbows on her knees.

"And you came because?"

"He wanted you to know," Muire said, "that his last thoughts were of you. And Brynhilde."

At the child's name, Ingraham reacted with all his passionate, mindless force. Muire might have gasped, even doubled over with the force of his desire to see her, but she had been braced for it. And that request would surely mark her as a predator. Truman children were creched. Protected.

When they grew older, they might earn an education with service in the Mongrels. The boy Mingan had slaughtered had been some household's hope and pride.

"Thank you," Gjerta said. And then she looked down at her hands. "Did he promise a reward?"

Muire shook her head. "No need," she said. "I'm only here because any decent person would be."

Any decent person who left my husband lying in the gutter, said Gjerta's quirked eyebrow and narrowed lips, but she did not make the condemnation patent. "Thank you," she said again, and stood, by which Muire understood the interview to be complete.

"I'm sorry," Muire said again, and allowed herself to be shown the door.

When she emerged into the sunlight, she turned back toward the Well. She walked directly but not too quickly, free hand in her pocket, and could not help but notice the number of Mongrels and unmans on patrol. One group passed very close—two rats and a canine under the command of a Black Silk officer, all pricked ears, smoky eyes, and lashing tail. The cat, a snow leopard by its spots, eyed Muire appraisingly as they passed, but Muire kept her gaze front and walked on, and there was no trouble.

It was no idle supposition: Ingraham Fasoltsen had been in the employ of the Technomancer.

Muire was in it now.

Even at midday, the Well lies in shadow, reflected light cold and amorphous upon its streets. The wolf feels it, the weight of all that earth overhead. It reminds him of a cave, the air moist and unmoving in the belly of a mountain, the sense of pressure and clammy chill.

It amuses him to think that when he walks into the Well, he walks from shadow and into shadow. The lights burn summer and winter, day and night. Power is one resource Eiledon will never want for.

The wolf is on a scent.

One he sniffed from Ingraham Fasoltsen's dying fingers. The scent of a woman who was also a cat. An unman, one of the Technomancer's perversions. She retrieved Svanvitr before Mingan arrived, and vanished within the Technomancer's wards, where the wolf could not follow.

But she'll emerge again, if she hasn't already. And there are certainly enough unmans and Mongrels on the street. So Fasoltsen's death has served: it's brought the wolf's prey within reach. But now, when he should be cool with the hunt, as cold and detached as he has been these long centuries of waiting, he is troubled and wild.

Because he cannot push aside the seething memories of the last time he visited the Well, and even as he slips among the shadows, they threaten to overflow him. He tastes the whore's mouth again, and almost chokes upon his collar when he swallows.

Slut, the wolf rages. *Whore. Strifbjorn would not have—Strifbjorn* never.

It was the wolf who sold himself to the enemy, all those years ago.

And that thought checks him, because it's not the voice of his own mind that says it. *That's a long time to live to go mad at the end,* he thinks. Schizophrenia wasn't invented yet when he broke for the first time: there were only the mad and the sane, and some of the mad had been holy, and some had been dangerous. He has words now he did not have then.

To have a name for it does not change what happened.

But he hears her again—*It was never Strifbjorn that betrayed us*—and this time he knows.

It is the historian who speaks to him so.

Not in her own self, but the ghost of her he's swallowed

down, and the ghost of her he knew, when they were young. He feels as if he might glimpse her at his shoulder, should he turn, and that presence is as much a weight upon him as the mountain of earth and buildings above. He can imagine her in the blue and white of a waelcyrge, her hair in plaits under her helm, her cloak lifted on the wind.

If he turns, she will be there. He's certain of it.

He could put out a hand to raise and drain the mead-horn she would be holding.

"Go from me," he says.

I will not, she says. *You should have killed me. You should have killed me when you killed Rannveig.*

"That was not me—"

When you killed Rannveig, she says. *When we were angels, and we loved. And you should have taken the knife in your own hand, and bled out your life.*

The wind brings a scent to the wolf, and for a moment he thinks it too fell from accusing memory. But it's real, thready and present. The real Muire may not be at his shoulder, but she is not too far distant.

"I should have," he says to his ghost. "I should have died in the ice."

People stare, those few that pass. His vision blurs; he sees her face over each of theirs.

Why didn't you? Why choose to live?

"Thou shouldst have died too," he snarls. "Why didst not thou?"

Whoever had been staring backs away now, pretending they notice nothing as the wolf bends double, gloved hands on his knees. He shuffles until he bumps a wall, pulls away from the lights mounted in sconces on the building. Shadows, and he steps into them, steps through the abandoned realm of Hel where the gates stand wide, pulls the cold and ash and the creaking ice of Midgard close.

He falls to his knees in the dead world.

"Why didst not thou?"

As if her hand touched his cheek, he feels her speaking. "Because I was a coward."

He looks up, and she is crouched before him, knees nearly touching the frozen soil. She shimmers. He can see the stars through her. There is nothing behind her but the cinders rolling in the frigid wind.

It does not stir the loose hairs escaping her plaits, as it does his. No gooseflesh rises: this is Muire the demigoddess, and human frailties cannot touch her.

She rests her elbows on her knees. "I was craven. I was weak. And I was unfit for war. What's your excuse, Suneater?"

He kneels down, lets his palms fall to the earth. It's cold enough to burn even immortal flesh. "I wanted to see the world die."

"Liar." Not mocking, but level. Soft. And all the more mockery for it.

He opens his mouth to curse her. And she smiles at him, gray eyes alight with starlight, snub nose and face made plain by braids too severe for such mild features.

"Vengeance," he says. "I stayed alive for vengeance."

"Upon Strifbjorn? He was dead, Mingan. Your monsters ate him."

"They were not my monsters."

"They were your wolves," she says, and for that he has no answer.

He covers his face in his hands. "Upon a wicked queen," he

answers, and though he cannot see her he knows the ghost of Muire frowns. He feels it as if on his own mouth, and scrubs the glove across his lips. It's not her frown, not precisely. It's another man's, that of another ghost he swallowed.

As he senses his dead love's expression on the lips of the waelcyrge, the wolf recalls himself. Muire is not here; she is not real. She has no power to call him to tribunal. She is only a scrap he's swallowed, half-nothing next to swallowing a sun. If he'd had the sense to kill her, she would by now be long consumed.

"Oh, yes," says the ghost of Muire, who has become the ghost of Strifbjorn, and who stands impassive before him in a cloak made of the pelt of a white bear, hands folded on the hilt of his crystal sword. His face is stern and noble, his hair nearly as pale as ice. His eyes shatter light like faceted diamonds. "Heythe. Why would you seek vengeance against her?"

"She spoke of returning," Mingan says. "At the end, when all is lost. Hers is a conquering heart."

"And you await her in service." Strifbjorn's ghost drips scorn. It is Mingan's own scorn, his own self-loathing. It is only what he imagines Strifbjorn would feel.

The wolf could say that there is no proof that she will return. He could say that she was a liar more than anything, easy in her lies as a human, something no child of the Light could ever be.

But he is arguing with himself, in the form of these ghosts, and he knows it. So instead he says, "I await her in vengeance. I serve her not."

"Would a wolf betray its mistress, whom it loved?"

"I never loved her," Mingan says, and wishes the words did not ring so hollow.

"No," says Strifbjorn, in Muire's voice. "And those were not thy monsters."

𝕸idweek meant bill-paying, which meant rising early. Sponged clean in soap and cold water, dressed in what passed for presentable in the undercity, Cathoair pinned bundled scrip inside his shirt, laced his boots, and made his way through the dank stinking half-light to a hospice on the river's north bank before lunchtime.

He paid, folded his receipt—Aethelred and Astrid, between them, had seen to it that he could figure if he could not read—and walked as softly as he could through the old cut-stone corridors of the sanitarium. It was better than most such places. It didn't stink, except of illness and antiseptic, and the floors and walls were scrubbed.

He could never have afforded a private room, but the wards were tolerable. His mother's had a cheerful purple-and-yellow-painted door, which he nudged open with an elbow. Her bed was the third from the wall.

He had half hoped she would be sleeping. But luck was not with him: she sat up, propped on pillows, her rust-colored robe falling open at the collar. She was absorbed in a game of concentration on her monitor, but when Cahey crossed the floor, boots clicking, she glanced up and paused it with a smile. "Hey," he said, and plunked down on the edge of the bed, careful of whatever might be going on tubewise under the covers.

"I was hoping you would come," she said, and opened her arms.

The bruised smudges under her eyes were like inky fingerprints, darker than her rosewood skin. When he touched her, that skin slipped over her bones like tissue paper wrapping some complex jewelry. No resilience remained.

"Don't I always?"

"Mmm. Nearly always," she said, and he laughed, and touched her cheek again. "The doctors—"

"They showed me the chart," he said. Not out of kindness, but out of selfishness. He might have been sparing her, but even if she wanted to say it, he didn't want to hear it. "I—"

She shrugged. "It's no matter. I'm not getting better, Cathoair."

"No," he said. She covered his hand with hers. He turned his over, and wrapped his fingers around her own. "Whatever I can—"

But she pulled free. Her shoulders were back, her neck stiff. He never had been able to comfort her, or protect her even a little. Any more than she had ever been able to do for him. "It's over," she said. "I won't have you sacrificing yourself for nothing."

"It's not a sacrifice," he said, through gritted teeth. "I'm doing fine."

"Mmm." She looked at him, direct and level, her eyes dark and hard to read. "You're still taking classes? You're still working at that bar, then?"

And Cathoair, without looking down, smiled at his mother and lied.

Some indignities are more palatable than others. Cathoair should have slept when he came back to the Ash & Thorn, but he found himself too restless for his narrow pallet and the small room Aethelred gave to him and Astrid. Astrid was off somewhere—out with Hrothgar, Aethelred said—and although Cahey spent forty minutes working over the heavy bag in the storage room, he didn't have the focus. He emerged from behind the curtain with bruised knuckles and a pout and sulked across to the bar.

Where Aethelred handed him a broom, and said, "Well, then make yourself useful."

It wasn't an unkindness. Cathoair, already stripped to the waist and barefoot, leaned the broom against the bar and drank two tepid glasses of water, then wiped his mouth on his hand and started pushing sawdust and scraps into tidy piles. There wasn't too much of it, but the day was humid. Sweat trickled between his shoulder blades despite the chill of the Well. Hrothgar had propped the door—they were technically open through the afternoon, but most of that time Aethelred just spent polishing glasses—and a faintly desperate breeze found its way down the stairs now and again, sometimes bringing the sounds of the street.

The sawdust was so damp that wind couldn't stir it. But the wind *could* carry the tap-tap of light footsteps as they paused before the door and descended the stair. Aethelred looked up from his brass-polishing and Cahey let the broom still.

He didn't know, in that half-second, what he was waiting for, but his heart skipped a beat and it seemed as if his sinuses filled with the eye-watering musk of the man in the gray wool cloak. Blood roared in his ears. He bit his lip for the focusing pain, anything to slow the thunder of his heart.

Just a trick, Cathoair reprimanded himself. *And why are you getting so hung up on a john, anyway?*

He could ask himself the question, but he couldn't force himself to answer. But he almost swore under his breath in relief when it wasn't the wiry man with the gray-streaked braid who paused at the bottom of the door and glanced around curiously.

It was a woman. *The* woman. Even smaller, pale and fragile-seeming, so that Cahey thought of recordings he had seen, of sparrows. She cocked her head from side to side like a bird, scanning the nearly empty bar, and by that gesture he recollected her. She looked very different, stripped of her armor, in skirts and a blouse.

But she came forward, still blinking as her eyes adjusted to the dimness, and he saw the hilt of her sword over her shoulder, poking from the folds of her wrap. That wrap half concealed it, but her right arm was in a sling, too, the fingers that protruded purple and knotted with bruises. His lips parted, as if to say, "Oh—" but her eyes slid off him and she walked past, spine erect, bootheels clicking a little more aggressively.

Maybe she didn't like whores, he thought, bitterly, and went back to sweeping while she spoke with Aethelred.

Whatever was going on at the bar, money changed hands. Cathoair heard the woman murmur, "No, I'm looking for someone," and Aethelred's demurral. Cathoair almost dropped the broom and intervened when the woman reached across the counter to touch Aeth, but all she did was tap the bowed and rebowed Serpent pendant at the old halfman's neck and ask, "You're a believer?"

Aeth, of course, tipped his head. "Got me through the war," he said. "And you're not?"

Cathoair heard the smile in her voice, even while looking at the back of her head. Or maybe he caught a glimpse in the mirror behind the bar.

"I used to be," she said. "Have you seen this man?"

It was an odd thing: when she pulled her reader out of her pouch and tapped it on, it chirped "Happy birthday!" and she flinched. And then she pressed a button, and a hologram shimmered into existence above it.

An image, if Cathoair was seeing properly, of a clay sculpture. A sculpture that looked right through him, with empty eyes.

His hands tightened on the neck of the broom, as if he could throttle it. He imagined soft hands and flesh too heated to be human, the stroke of a thumb down his throat and fingers spread across his nape to behind his ear.

He gasped, flushed with heat, and turned away.

Too much to hope the woman hadn't noticed. Too much to hope she wouldn't turn around and say—

"You know him, then?"

Oh, fuck it. He swallowed and summoned whatever brass he had left. "Pay for my time," he said, "and maybe I can tell you something."

"Pay you?" she said.

He nodded. "Or maybe there's something else we can do for each other."

She studied him, and he thought an expression of pain narrowed her eyes. "I'm not in the market for a toy."

Hard words, said hardly. She'd meant to sting. Aethelred turned aside, stepping away from the bar. Cathoair looked at the woman steadily, drawing himself up, poised and aware that whatever his face looked like, from the neck down he could turn any heterosexual woman's head.

He had to assume she was an investigator, a vengeance specialist. She must be working for someone, and—

He hardly dared follow the train of thought where it led

him. But her boots and her sword were expensive, and it didn't look like she had to fight, or whore.

"No," he said. "Those aren't the services I'm offering."

She blinked, but finally nodded. "What do you want?"

Aethelred had vanished into the back. Cathoair was on his own. "I want a job," he said. He swallowed the harsh taste of skin, and sweat, and blood. "One with a little dignity."

She looked him up and down, the hologram glowering past her shoulder. And then she nodded slowly, but said, "What makes you think I can help with that?"

"You're a revenger?"

Something about the question made her smile. "Not exactly." A pause, and then she nodded, slowly, and—much to his relief—clicked the holo off. "I'll pay for information."

For now, it would have to do.

"Come on," he said, leaning the broom against a chair. "Sit down."

Ehwaz (a horse)

As Muire and the pretty gigolo sat down, the landlord appeared from his strategic retreat and came to them across the empty bar. He set a pitcher of "lemonade" between them and asked, "Do you want something stronger?"

"What do you have?"

"Gin. Brandy or vodka. Rum. Synthetic wine and mead." The mirrors of his face gleamed all the wrong ways when he smiled.

"What's the difference?" she said, just managing to hold on to her own grin.

"Other end of the bathtub," he admitted, so Muire laughed and said, "Just this."

She dug in her pouch for chits and her bowl, only to have the landlord stay her with a gesture. "It's on the house," he said. "Any friend of Cahey's is a friend of mine."

There was no threat in the words; it was all implied, and softly. Muire put her money away and laid her bowl on the table. Across, the young man did the same.

"Thank you," Muire said, trying to hide her interest in watching the interaction between the young man and the older halfman. She'd assumed the landlord was also a whoremaster, the young people working his establishment more or less chattel. But that wasn't what she saw when the landlord laid his hand on the other man's shoulder before walking away.

She frowned, reassessing.

And then the young man she would not allow herself to think of as Strifbjorn touched her hand, drawing back her attention. Muire extracted herself and poured the lemonade.

"So you're Cathoair," she said, conversationally, and guessed that she only didn't manage to make him choke on the lemonade because he wasn't drinking any.

He recovered faster than she would have expected. "Of course. Aeth called me Cahey."

"And your name is over the board, in the kickboxing standings," she agreed.

"And you claim you're not an investigator."

"Not by trade."

The lemonade had never been closer than fifty years to a lemon, but it was wet and chill. She swallowed it reluctantly, sugar coating her teeth, and noticed that Cathoair still had not touched his own.

Thus proving that death and resurrection could teach even Strifbjorn wisdom. Muire pushed her own bowl away with the tips of her fingers. There was still clay under the nails. Typical, to have failed to notice.

"Why do you fight?" she asked. "Or, if you're going to fight, why do you—"

"Whore?" Coolly, as if to show that nothing she could throw at him would shock. "For the money. Aethelred pays us a cut of the book to fight, and the fighting—" He swallowed, and did reach for his lemonade this time, the motion reminding her uncomfortably that he was still half naked. "—the tricks pay more once they've seen us."

"Seen you fight." She could imagine him in the ring. Yes, people would pay a premium to touch that.

"I'm good at it." He shrugged, rolling his head back on his long neck as if it hurt him.

"You could compete citywide."

She wasn't prepared for his answering laughter. "No, I can't. I'm not truman."

She squinted at him. If he wasn't, he could pass.

"My mom," he elaborated, "caught an engineered flu when she was pregnant. I'm a Mute. Reflexes, eyesight. Strength and muscular coordination. I'm not allowed to fight real people."

He paused, as if expecting her to answer. She couldn't, at first. But in a gesture of solidarity, she tapped the table left-handed and said, "I'm Muire."

"No last name."

"Muire," she answered. "No last name either."

She shook her head, and they grinned at each other. Animals, both of them. With animals' names. Not even really human at all.

"So," she said, "tell me about the Grey Wolf, won't you?"

"That's his *name?*"

"It's his epithet," she said. She wondered if she should be telling him this. But trade for trade. If he ran right back to Mingan with it, then the Wolf would know Muire was hunting him.

And the Wolf had to know that already.

"Mingan," she said, when the candle-flicker stayed silent.

This time, he reacted. Eyes wide, nostrils flaring. "That's not his real name."

"But it is," Muire said, pitching her voice so it would not carry. "You see what you've wandered into?"

"So he calls himself after a devil," Cathoair scoffed. He

scrubbed at his mouth, though, and Muire pitied him his denial. "How very . . . romantic. And overwrought."

She couldn't lie to him, but she didn't have to correct his misapprehension. "Is the beer any better than the lemonade?"

"I don't know," he said. "I don't drink."

She must have looked shocked into disbelief, because he dropped his eyes in embarrassment. "Soap operas and sex are my only vices," he said, and she laughed because she believed he meant it. And then he tilted his chin up. "So ask me your questions, Muire. You're paying for the time."

"Right," she said. It was hard, not staring at the scar that pulled his lip up and the corner of his eye down. It looked like a sword or knife wound, and when it happened must have laid him open to the bone. "What do you know about him, then?"

"He's a client," Cathoair said coldly, trying to make her look away from his stare. But she held the eye contact and he glanced down first. "Well, not exactly."

"No?"

He shook his head and hunched. "All right, exactly. But he's been coming to the Ash & Thorn for . . . not too long. A month? He never touched any of us, though. Not before last night."

"And last night?"

"He wanted me."

"Not any of the others?"

"Me." He swallowed, and poured lemonade, and drank it off the way Strifbjorn would have drunk off mead. "But just sex. Nothing—"

Muire's cheeks stung. She didn't want to think of them, or of Mingan's obscene pleasure in finally having Strifbjorn under orders and biddable. Nor did she wish to think that the Grey

Wolf had gone from hanging his deadly embrace over her, to having his way with this candle-flicker.

Who was *not* Strifbjorn, who did not remember Strifbjorn's failings, who could not be held accountable for Strifbjorn's crimes. But who could be punished for them, it seemed—and if the Grey Wolf had his way, would be.

"He didn't harm you," Muire said.

Cathoair shook his head. "Actually, it was kind of creepy. He was . . . tender."

She watched him, the long hands folded on the table before him, the regulated breathing, the long scars on his right arm that matched the one on his face in age.

She did not know why the Grey Wolf had let her live. But she knew why he had come to Eiledon.

If she took Cathoair on, she would be using him, as surely as Mingan had used him. And with less excuse, because she would not be using him out of some terrible old need, or even the memory of love, but in spite of it. She would be using him to entrap someone he had once died for the love of.

Someone he had loved, when he could not love her.

She held the thought in her hand, and wondered how much of it was seeing the only way to avenge Ingraham, and rid the world of the Grey Wolf forever. And how much of it was her own ancient loathing.

"You're hired," she said at last, though after long moments she still was not certain of the rightness of her answer.

Nothing is ever as easy as it could be.

Kasimir was uniquely suited to appreciate that particular platitude. He flew over devastated country, and it would have been simple if he could flit back to his valley with the same ease by which he could reach his rider's side. Whenever Muire bespoke him, he could be with her instantly, without regard for distance.

Leaving again was less simple.

And so, painstaking wingbeats carried him away from Eiledon. He could have awaited her in the wasteland, just beyond the Defile, but there seemed little value in that. She might not summon him again for weeks, or longer. The Grey Wolf was canny, and Kasimir harbored no illusions about his rider's stubbornness.

He did however husband a bright spark of joy that she had summoned him at all.

Still. Better to fly the afternoon and through the night, to be by Cristokos if Cristokos should need him.

Not that the rat-mage was incapable.

But Kasimir *was* War, and should anything untoward occur, he was more sufficient to it than Cristokos. He passed over furrowed fields, the glint of shattered plastic and fused sand, the bloody smears of rusting machinery. His wings reflected the crawling blue of radiation through the night. In one blasted metropolis, the heaving glisten of a battle-cratered shoggoth came around to track him, gliding on a trail of slime, and locked weapons. But his shadow was fleeting, and either its power, its ammunition, or both were long exhausted.

If one could call it alive, it was the only living thing he saw between Eiledon and the moment when he banked, climbing sharply, riding gusts that pitched him up a high barren slope. As he rose, the land below twisted with eroded gullies, blown snow or ash obscuring the view, gray as grave netting. As he skimmed the sharp crest of a saddleback ridge between two peaks that leaned away from one another as if expressing the aftermath of an argument—not the pass Cristokos had braved, but the one at the high end of the valley—the terrain changed.

Pine and cedars, and the flicker of a mountain sheep's white rear as it plunged away from the silhouette of his wings. There were eagles in Kasimir's valley, still—the last eagles in the world—and an eagle would not scruple to dine on mutton, if the opportunity presented.

Here there was green to trap the sun's warmth, and roots to trap the rain's moisture. High wind-wearied desert gave way to forest and glade, cliffs like stone curtains, water plummeting hundreds of feet to pound deep icy pools at their bases. The slope swept down to a valley floor that, while not level, was partially terraced into fields. Kasimir had labored like a plough-horse to help clear them, and to split and haul the wood for Cristokos's ramshackle cabin with its sagging porch and shading fruit trees.

The rat was on his knees in the garden when Kasimir descended. The valraven, for all his size and weight, cupped air and settled behind Cristokos silently, except the hiss of steam and the creak and tick of metal.

"That one should not go to the city," Cristokos said, without raising his tapered snout from the weeding. "She will notice that one. What She notices, She would possess."

Kasimir snorted, stretching his necks long and low under the weight of his horns and his antlers. **Who can hold such as I? Summoned, I will go to her.**

His *her* was not the same as Cristokos's.

Cristokos laid his whiskers flat against his face. "That one is too loyal."

His own loyalty did not trouble Kasimir, but their disagreement did. Cristokos had only scorn of service, and for those who served, pity. But service was Kasimir's purpose, even when that service was best met through disagreement and argument. His service, however, had always been a chosen one. Cristokos's has been plundered.

But if Kasimir were to say so, Cristokos would answer that Kasimir deluded himself as to the nature of his and his rider's bond. The rat-mage would speak of how Kasimir's rider disregarded him, and that Kasimir martyred himself to his service. And Kasimir, in honesty, could not answer that.

The argument was old. He folded his wings and shook out his mane, letting the wires rasp and rattle. Under his hooves, the grass smoked; he stepped aside, onto the gravel they had laid to prevent unwanted burning. Cristokos still did not turn.

Kasimir suspected the rat-mage was angry with him. So he waited. Patience was cardinal.

And eventually, Cristokos looked up from tucking straw carefully around the roots of his strawberries and turned to him. Black eyes flashed in the variegated face, bright as obsidian. "What does that one desire?" he asked.

Kasimir shook out his manes. **Perhaps your help.**

"And perhaps not?" The rat-mage tilted his head and folded spindly arms. It was not Kasimir alone who made a virtue of obdurance.

Your She.

Cristokos glowered as only a rat can. "What of Her?"

My enemy, and my rider's enemy. He hunts her creatures.

Cristokos stiffened, lips lifted away from chisel teeth. "The moreaux?"

Not that I have seen, though that is no guarantee of truth. The trumans who serve her. The Mongrels and the messengers.

"Then how is that one's enemy not a friend?"

Kasimir flicked his tail against his flank, striking sparks. Cristokos did not flinch, or even appear to notice. **My rider has sworn vengeance against him.**

"And finally called you out of exile, because she can't do it alone. Bright one—"

He is a killer. He is tarnished. Kasimir said it as if it ended discussion. For him, it did.

Cristokos might feel differently.

Kasimir lowered one head and stretched to tear grass in neat bites, falsely idle. With the other head, he regarded Cristokos.

They had known one another for a very long time.

Will you help me?

The rat-mage didn't answer. His black-and-pink-tipped fingers rippled on his upper arm.

Will you tell me about your She, and her creatures?

The stare continued. The dew was burning off the grass, even further from the heat of Kasimir's inner furnace.

Cristokos sighed and turned away, dropping down beside his zucchini. He spoke as if to the plants. "What does that one care to know?"

How is it that you won free of Her control?

When stalking the tiger, set lures. Traditionally, tiger-traps were baited with goats, either bloodily slaughtered or terrified and still bleating.

Muire suspected that the techniques that worked on a tiger would work on a wolf. Mingan had always been impassioned, impetuous. The years might have made him crafty, but Muire hoped the wolf within would not be able to resist his ancient bond with Strifbjorn. Whether Cathoair would feel the same enticement was an open question, and one she did not care to dwell on too deeply.

Still, she would not mislead him.

She hadn't put her reader away; it was still set on the table. Over Cathoair's warning, she ordered bread and cheese and vat-grown apple from the landlord, and tapped the screen to turn the reader on, ignoring the "Happy Birthday, Muire" and Cathoair's quizzical expression. She said, "Do you think he'll come back for you?"

He played with his bowl, rolling it between his fingers. "Depends what he was looking for."

"What's your instinct?"

"Yes," he said, without hesitating, and then looked at her, as if seeking approval or critique. The food came. Muire thanked the landlord and paid, and Cathoair held his peace while she did. The blue flecks in his hazel eyes seemed brighter than the green, momentarily, and Muire glanced down at the platter. "The bread is *fried*."

"Don't say I didn't warn you." He shook his head. "There is literally nothing I can eat here without breaking training."

Without returning her gaze to him, she asked, "Does it happen often?"

That rocked him against the back of the chair. "Does what happen often? Breaking training?"

"That," she said. "Knowing things about people. Whether you can trust them. Which ones you can go down an alley with. Which ones not to let your friends go off with alone."

He blinked.

"Knowing to trust me when I started spouting about myth-ical monsters."

"Okay, you're creepy."

"Yes," she answered, and reached for the pitcher. "I get that a lot. You're not answering my questions."

"You haven't paid me yet," he said, and held out an open hand, pink palm creased in ocher.

Muire stared at it for a moment, then reached into her pouch and started counting chits into his palm, one at a time. He clearly expected her to stop long before she did, because his expression of surprise when she pulled her hand back was quite comical. "I hope that will suffice to ensure your loyalty for a week or two."

"Loyalty is one thing," he said. If she'd meant to shame him, it seemed to roll off like water from slate. He pocketed the money. "Service is another."

"So about your knack for telling if people are trustworthy?"

"I just know," he said. He smoothed a straying lock back into his ponytail. "I've always known. I knew he wasn't going to hurt me. How did *you* know I knew? Er—"

"I've seen it before," she said. "And there's a lot of history, if you know where to look. In five-twenty, I think it was, or maybe five-twenty-two, there was a seith-wife in Ardrath-in-the-Islands, who had the knack of telling truth—"

"What was her name?"

Muire shrugged. "Saibd. According to some versions. Or Berrach. Does it matter?"

He smiled and waved her on.

"She was," Muire said with resolute archness, "very much in demand. As you might imagine. And made a fair living as a soothsayer until a local warlord took offense."

"Occupational hazard? He had her executed?"

"Locked in a tower," Muire answered. "Until she died of old age. A resource like *that*, you don't just waste."

"Nice," Cathoair said. "When you say five-twenty, though . . ."

Muire actually stared at him for a moment in confusion before she realized her error. "Oh, uh. Five-twenty old style. Eighteen hundred ante-Desolation, more or less."

She held her breath for a moment, but he snickered and shook his head and said only, "You read too many old books, don't you?"

"Yes." She waved broadly. "Probably. So, as I see it, we have two angles of investigation."

"You mean to use me as bait."

Muire almost bit her cheek. Whatever this child had from Strifbjorn . . . he was smarter than Strifbjorn had ever shown himself. "That's one way, yes. Although I'm bait too, for what it's worth."

"And the second?"

"We go out looking," Muire said. "I know what he's hunting. It's the Technomancer's people. Trumans, not the unmans. So far. I only wish I understood why."

He sipped his drink, made a thinking noise, and rubbed a spatulate fingertip across his annoyingly well-formed nose. "Well, there are a bunch of possibilities."

She waited.

"First," he said, ticking off on his fingertips, "it's a personal grudge. Second, he works with—or is!—a political enemy. Third . . ." He thought about it for a second. "I had a third a minute ago."

Muire washed down a mouthful of grease. "Third, they're convenient, and he doesn't think she'll care."

"Convenient for?"

"Food. He's tarnished," Muire said. "He eats *souls,* Cathoair. It's where he gets his strength. Fourth, he's her enforcer, and he's getting rid of the ones that annoy her."

"That's the only one I see causing us problems." He reached for a slice of her apple and some of the bread, his gaze a challenge, as if daring her to slap his hand away.

Muire was unlikely to eat it all anyway. She waved him in. "Help yourself. If you really want to contaminate your finely honed system with that stuff."

He snorted and stuffed the impromptu sandwich into his mouth. "Why can't we just pick up his trail?"

Muire bit her lip. "Because he doesn't leave one," she said. "I can trace him—feel him—if I come close enough."

"You've got some knacks of your own."

She chose not to answer, exactly. "The problem being, if I get close enough to scent him—"

"He scents you."

"Exactly." She patted his hand, but wound up jerking her own back sharply, as if the contact sparked. "Get some rest," she said. "We hunt tonight."

"I fight tonight," Cathoair answered.

"Do you fight every night?"

He shrugged that loose-necked shrug of his. "Three or four times a week."

A lot. Muire wondered, not idly, what he needed the money for. She wondered if he'd keep whoring while she was paying him. If he had a drug habit, there were no marks on his arms.

"I'll meet you after," he volunteered.

"I'll pick you up," Muire said. "What time?"

Jera (the harvest)

Muire returned to the Ash & Thorn a few minutes before midnight to find it as crowded as the night before. No trace of Mingan fouled the air. Though shamed by her cowardice, Muire was relieved that the confrontation might be postponed.

Eventually, she was certain, he would come for her, if he did not come for Cathoair.

Cathoair wasn't in the ring, and according to the standing chalked above the bar had yet to fight, so Muire sidled through the crowd to the bar. She'd replaced her ruined gauntlet—for all the good the armor had done her last time—and the new glove, not yet lacquered, shone unsullied white.

The first white she'd worn in two thousand years.

It would have been nice if a stool miraculously opened up just as she arrived, but she wasn't so lucky. She pushed between dedicated drinkers to the scarred granite surface and slid her bowl across to the landlord, Aethelred. She ordered slivovitz, which could under no circumstances ever have been in contact with a real plum, and wondered if it were brewed in the same bathtub as the gin.

The bowl came back to her with a side order of advice. "Be

careful around Cahey," he said, leaning over the bar so its wood creaked under the weight of his chassis.

"Is he dangerous?" Muire didn't mean it to sound mocking. But her tone did something to Aethelred's expression, something almost impossible to read through the scar tissue and the chrome.

"He's been hurt enough, is all I'm saying," Aethelred answered. He took her money and handed her change. "Don't hurt him more."

She picked up her bowl and nodded, turning away so he wouldn't see the confusion of emotions that tugged her face in incompatible directions. Her initial assumptions about Aethelred's relationship with the young people who flocked around his bar seemed to have been less than precise, or—at the very least—lacking in nuanced understanding.

Muire stepped away, letting the barflies seal the gap behind her. She threaded between bodies toward the corner where the fights were, certain she vanished into the crowd in an instant. There were advantages to being the shortest person in the room.

But it also meant she couldn't see the action in the ring, and didn't know what, exactly, had happened as a roar went up around her. She sidled past a tall man, who was distracted by his betting chits, and aimed for a high, vacant stool against a side wall. It was behind a pillar, which was why it was empty, but it was tall enough to offer an obstructed view if she climbed up, and fighting her way to the front was a project that might take half a night.

She availed herself of opportunity, and clambered up the rungs, careful not to spill her slivovitz.

The next fight was two young women, not anyone Muire recognized. Muire cupped her bowl in both hands and watched them carefully, thinking of the holmgang, and when that roped ring would have been a hide staked to bare earth, the weapons axes and swords rather than fists and feet.

In this combat, there were no three shields to be broken. And so the bout lasted three falls, or to first blood.

About seven minutes, in practical terms, and by the end of it both women were sweat-slicked, heaving for air in the hot, close basement. The winner was muscular, straight-shouldered, young enough that it hurt Muire's heart to look at her. Her close-cropped hair had been spiked and stained pewter-bright, almost glistening, before the sweat had dampened it, and her whole body between her trunks and halter, across her shoulders and down to her wrists, was covered in vibrant ink—reds and violets and violent orange, a writhing pattern so complex Muire would have had to walk up to her and stare to pick out any representations.

Muire drew her feet up a rung so she could rest her elbows on her knees. *Vengeance,* Ingraham muttered, and not for the first time, Muire wished she could silence him.

And then felt guilt. For he had already been silenced, by her own enemy. Another failure: lay them all at her door.

Hers, and Mingan's, and Strifbjorn's.

As if thinking the name had summoned him, then, Cathoair passed through the press, tall and lithe. Persons of every and indeterminate gender turned to watch him move, so the crowd folded like a radiant flower around him, and Muire pressed her knuckles to her lips.

So different.

And not different at all.

She would have closed her eyes rather than watch him

climb the elevated platform and step over the ropes into the ring, but even she could not be so craven. Whatever brought the Grey Wolf here, Muire had come to bear witness.

Perhaps she should have been surprised when Cathoair paused in his corner, turned over his shoulder, and smiled directly at her, but she wasn't.

Nothing alike, and everything. She would have known him anywhere.

His opponent was another young man, not as tall, heavier, blue-haired and pale, and with longer arms, Muire thought. She watched them square off and pulled her legs onto the seat, kneeling high to see better. Her armor bit into the flesh below her knees.

She placed a hand on the wall for balance and watched the dance.

Cathoair's style was pantherine, well suited to his long frame. He used the space in the ring and made his opponent pursue him. They were unshod, sure-footed, and they moved fast: Cathoair languid, the opponent—Hrothgar, by the board—blocky and choppy and prone to lightning sallies, rains of jabs and feints that fell away again quickly if they didn't find a mark.

It was savage. Cathoair gave ground, and Hrothgar took it, trying to use his reach to an advantage. He landed more blows, but this wasn't a fight for points: that didn't matter, except in the toll it exacted from his opponent.

But when Cathoair hit, he hit solid, flesh leaping away from the impact of fist or foot or elbow, Hrothgar staggering back finally from a left jab under the solar plexus that lifted him onto his toes.

It was the step back that finished him. Muire expected Cathoair to close the distance and go for the pin. But with perfect timing, instead, as Hrothgar came off the ropes, Cathoair bounced on the ball of his foot and kicked out hard, weight and momentum behind it, sweat flying as he committed, the neon running rivers of color down wet skin.

He struck Hrothgar across the mouth.

Hrothgar went to his knees.

Muire expected him to come up spitting teeth, but he stayed down long moments, both hands pressed to his lips, face clenched, hunched forward.

When he pulled his fingers from his mouth, Muire could see that they were smeared with red.

First blood.

Cathoair reached out, and Hrothgar reached out also. Their hands clasped, and Hrothgar came to his feet, and into Cathoair's arms, and kissed him gingerly.

A warrior might kiss another warrior, a friend kiss a friend. That would not look like this, with tilted heads and possessive hands.

And by their titillated roar, the crowd knew it. And approved.

Muire looked away, mouth dry, face on fire.

Of course.

Oh, she should have known.

In just two days, Selene had had time to experience any number of uncomfortable revelations. The one that nagged at her most was the queasy, exotic sensation of not being the hunter.

It was not bred in her to be quarry. But with tail-lashing certainty, she was being forced to admit that her seeming prey was toying with her. She traced him through dark streets and cold abandoned buildings. Neither a patrol of other unmans nor a pack of Mongrels could have made her safer, and so she went alone, losing the trail, regaining it—cold—by mere chance, blocks farther on.

Chance . . . or because he had laid it for her to recover.

And though she knew she moved silently as smoke (and not always—or even often—at ground level) through the confined city, the predator who had killed Ingraham Fasoltsen was always gone a moment before she arrived. As if he were not *like* smoke, but smoke exactly, scattered on the wind of her arrival.

Selene suspected magic to go with the mockery. She reported in, apprising Her of her suspicions, and was ordered to continue surveillance at a distance. "Engage him if you have the opportunity," She said. "I trust your judgment. Do you require technical support?"

A mage, she meant. "Not yet," Selene said into her headset. "A rat would slow me down, for now. If I know what the prey is doing, I believe I can take countermeasures. However, I would recommend detailing another Black Silk, independently, and having support teams on standby."

"Those are sound recommendations," She said, and Selene basked in the glow of praise. "Helios is available. He'll be on the street within the hour. You may coordinate with him directly as necessary: it remains your lead."

Selene, crouched among gargoyles in a building outside the western edge of the Well, could not stop herself from purring. She liked Helios the lion, but she liked being in charge more. "Thank you," she said, and She dropped the connection.

Not entirely, of course. She would continue to monitor telemetry, and would be there if Selene or Helios required Her. But She had many responsibilities, and could not pay personal attention to them all.

Which was why she had Selene and Helios and the trusted unmans, both the beasts—and the others.

"Gunther," Selene said, and felt the system's attention fall on her. "Can you generate a map for me, coded to time and space, showing where the prey has left traces and what his routes and rates of movement between them must have been?"

"Of course," said the computer. "Anything for my favorite kitty—oh, I see what you're driving at. I don't think this is physically possible."

"He's apparating."

"Technically not supposed to be possible," Gunther replied. His voice wasn't mechanical at all, but human and warm. More flexible than Selene's, which, despite its lightness of tone, could be painful to use at length. "I've never known a sorcerer, wizard, or anything else that could do it. But it's a working theory. Watch your back, kittycat."

"Watch Her back, Gunther," Selene answered. "If he's hunting us, and he can come and go as he pleases—without using the standard approaches to the Tower. . . ."

"I take your point. Are you sure he's hunting us?"

She grimaced, a curl of her lip exposing thick-rooted yellow fangs to the night air's chill. His scent was still there, lingering, scratching the inside of her face until she turned her head and rubbed her wrinkled nose against her armor.

"Yes," she said. "I'm sure."

———

Through keen observation and ruthless opportunism, Muire had managed to secure a table by the time—clean and shaved and dressed, rubbing his knuckles and limping a little—Cathoair threaded through the crowd to join her. He turned away at least two propositions along the way, and Muire bit her bottom lip and watched him do it. *Open your eyes,* she told herself. *This is not Strifbjorn.*

She'd had to defend the other place vigorously, and she was sure she saw more than one disappointed glance when Cathoair dropped into it. He seemed oblivious, however—perhaps intentionally—and more casually dressed than when she'd seen him hustling. He leaned forward on his elbows and said, "Have you been waiting long?"

Maybe a conversational gambit, because she was fairly certain he knew exactly how long she'd been waiting. That uncanny awareness . . . he might not be an einherjar. But he wasn't a mere, dull human, either. A Mute, he called himself. Mutant.

Just another animal, like Muire, like most of the Well.

"Long enough to see you fight," she said. Someone else was coming up behind him, a sturdy dark-haired girl maybe four or six years older. And he knew it: though he didn't turn his head, she saw his eyes flick toward the side.

"Hello, Star," he said, as she set a handled cloth bag on the table. "Star, this is Muire, my new boss. Muire, this is Astrid, my partner."

She levered his head back with a proprietary grip on his ponytail and kissed him, hard. Muire studied the writing on the bag, a line drawing of a rooster. "There's no chair, I'm sorry," Muire said, when Astrid decided she'd sufficiently claimed her prize, and broke off the kiss.

"It's okay," she said. "I'll stand. Cahey, eat."

Obediently, he pulled the bag over, while Astrid held her right hand out to Muire. An X of white tape crossed her nose, and both her eyes were ringed in violet, so it wasn't surprising that she winced when she smiled. But she moved with springy strength, like a small muscular dog. Another one of the fighters, then, a heavily built girl who wore her black hair in a braid the way Muire's sisters used to wear their blonde.

She extended a hand and a smile. Muire accepted both gingerly. She clasped the hand, released it as quickly as possible without exposing her discomfort, and sank back into her chair, wondering if Cathoair was sleeping with *everybody* that he beat up on a regular basis.

"And of the Holmish warriors," Muire said, "it was the doughty women Harald feared most."

Astrid grimaced—it wasn't quite a smile, but it wasn't a frown either—and cocked her head. "Sounds like you're quoting?"

"Sturla Half-wise," she said. "He was a historian of the Arnian conquests who wrote about eleven hundred years ago. Harald was Harald Clawhand, the one who sired only daughters, about twenty of them. His sons-in-law wound up slaughtering each other in civil wars until they had succeeded in carving up the empire between themselves."

"Oh." But Astrid actually sounded interested, even as she found a nearby pillar to lean against. "I hope you know what you're getting into," she said, conversationally, as Cathoair started laying out waxed-paper packages in a row.

Muire wasn't sure which of them she was talking to. "Pardon?"

Astrid nodded sideways at Cathoair. Cathoair threw a

wadded sandwich wrapper at her without even looking, and just as reflexively, she knocked it away. He was staring at Muire as he chewed, a challenging expression, and she found her eyes sliding off of his. She trained her gaze on his scar instead. "That doesn't look like a kickboxing injury."

He touched it as if puzzled. He'd been lucky, or as lucky as anyone might be, to find himself disfigured—the nerves and muscles still worked, and whoever has sewn it for him had matched the edges well. His face twisted around the scar, but it seemed like everything worked. Whether from that, or something else, he lacked the vagueness of feature that young people almost always seemed to have: the thing that made any given holo of a teenager look like a dozen other pictures of completely different children, taken years apart.

His face looked lived in. So did Astrid's.

"It's a sword wound," he said. "Dueling. From when I was young and stupid." Then, as if to stop up any further words, he took a bite of sandwich.

With the air of someone intentionally changing the subject, Astrid reached out and tugged Cathoair's ponytail again. "How's your mum?"

He swallowed a too-large bit and said, "Keeping," with a sideways twist of his head. "You know."

She nodded, frowning, and patted him on the arm. Muire hooked her fingers together under the edge of table, telling herself that the pain under her breastbone was only the bittersweet tenderness of the very, very old for the very, very young. They seemed so incredibly far away. He called her *partner*. Were they lovers? Did the word even apply to such relationships anymore?

Astrid produced a flask and a bowl and poured, sliding the result in front of Cathoair. It smelled fruity, not alcoholic.

"Drink it fast," she said, "or the bubbles will go out of it. Muire, Cahey says you're an investigator? A specialist?"

Vengeance specialist, she meant. A mercenary vigilante.

"After a fashion."

Cathoair apparently attracted caretakers. Muire wondered if he needed them.

Astrid grinned. "You'll keep him out of trouble, I hope."

He started to protest, reaching out to swat her, and she side-stepped nimbly. A cold liquid sensation filled Muire's belly, and in a moment she recognized envy.

Ridiculous. He wasn't a tenth her age.

A child. An innocent. A candle-flicker.

The bait in her trap. *Vengeance.*

Muire all but felt the hot breath of the Wolf at her throat.

Cahey and his new employer had been out for half an hour when she called a pause. Behind the waterfall, where the street-lights lit cobbles and peeling stone buildings slick with spray, Muire balanced on one foot beside the anchor of a lamp float and tugged at the other boot.

"Stone?" Cathoair asked.

She grunted. Her gauntlets seemed to interfere with the removal; she twisted the boot and her hands slipped, and she swore—"Shadows!"

Cahey laughed. He couldn't help himself. "You swear like my grandmother."

"Is your grandmother a stevedore?"

"What's a stevedore? She was a salvage tailor. She's dead now."

"I'm sorry," Muire said, after a long pause. Awkward as the

way she was standing, balanced on one foot. Awkward as if she hadn't expected to hear of a death. As if death weren't everywhere.

Cahey squatted in front of her and pushed her hands aside. "Here. Let me."

She seemed about to hop away, but gathered herself and stood steady, one hand on the lamp cable. He pulled, and she leaned on the cable, and overhead the streetlight swayed. When he was little, Cahey had done that on purpose, to make the shadows dance.

"The street's filthy," she said, as he dropped a knee for balance.

He looked up at her, her face peering at him from across her armor. He had to raise his voice to be heard over the thunder of falling water. The noise was probably why this had become such a rough neighborhood; nobody wanted to live in thunder, and so the buildings were unmaintained squats.

Even he was a little nervous coming to this part of the neighborhood, though he wasn't about to let Muire see it.

"I'm used to it," he said.

Whether he meant to shock her or not—and he wasn't sure, honestly—it worked. She whitened, and twitched hard enough that her helm swung on its strap and knocked against her backplate. He pulled hard, and the boot popped free. A hard shake rattled the pebble loose, and he handed her back the boot.

He was standing before she could look at him again.

"We swear by whatever's most taboo in the cultures we grew up in," she explained, as if to fill up the silence. "Thus, I blaspheme. You . . ." She grinned up at him, and he could see the effort to not make it look forced. She put her foot down and stomped. ". . . don't swear much at all, do you? Which leads me to believe—"

"—that not much is 'taboo to my culture?'" She blinked at him, and Cahey grinned. He was a pretty good mimic, and she was easy, with her formal tones and big vocabulary.

He thought she'd change the subject, and she did, checking the hang of her sword before she said, "Do you always go out unarmed?"

As if she'd just thought of it.

"I can handle myself."

The sword was at last seated to her liking. She shook her head. "You have a death wish, kid. Come on. More walking."

He fell in beside her, matching two strides to every three of hers. She probably could have walked under his outstretched arm.

"I didn't know detective work was so glamorous. Are we just waiting for him to kill again?"

"Or to come to us," she said.

He nodded. "I have a hunch we'll find something soon."

"I'd love to know more about your hunches." She sounded genuinely curious. "We should talk about it. When we're not—"

"Right," he agreed. "It's on the list. Somewhere after serial killers, but before regrouting the bathroom tile."

She laughed. It sounded rusty, every time she did it, but he managed to make her do it fairly often.

Still, when he looked over at her, she was staring straight ahead. "You don't sense him?"

"Not yet. Let's keep moving."

"It pisses me off that he could be killing almost at will. We wouldn't even know about it unless somebody happened to notice a weird death, and one of us happened to stumble across that somebody. I keep thinking there has to be something in the history that will help us. If it's really *him*—"

"It's really him."

"And he's really that old."

Muire hurried in half-steps to catch up. He'd allowed his stride to lengthen, but he checked it when he realized. "I wish I could see the stars," she said, craning her head back.

"I've seen pictures." He shrugged. "They say you can't see them anywhere in Eiledon."

"You've never been out of the Well." Not a question: just a flat statement.

"Where would I go?" he asked, and tried not to notice that she closed her eyes in pity. "Muire, you said you were going to research him—"

Their footfalls squelched in the muck. There wasn't much litter—almost everything useful was put to use, especially here—but that didn't mean the streets were clean.

Muire shrugged. "The sources might have been an enormous help if they didn't contradict each other every step of the way." She kicked a cracked half of a brick lying in the road. "How much of it is legend? How much is direct report?"

Cahey hated to bring up religion, but if you spent time with Aethelred, you got soaked in the stuff. "He's mentioned in the Book of Riddles, isn't he?"

For some reason, Muire chuckled dryly. "Oh, yes," she said. And then after a pause: "Secondhand," and then she quoted from memory.

> *"At the closure of the slaughter, there remained upon the strand/One who fled, one who lived, one who chose not to attend.*

It maybe loses something in translation."

Apparently, Aethelred wasn't the only one. "I didn't think you were a Believer."

"I'm not. I was a historian once. And a poet. And couplets are easy to remember."

"Do you know it all?" He had a good memory, and a lot of what he'd heard had stuck, but it wasn't the same as being able to read it for yourself.

They passed two registered gangsters cleaning anti-Technomancer graffiti off a stained concrete wall. One of them, a darkly glossy gray-eyed girl, turned to check Cathoair out, but after a single glance turned back to the work. He looked after her, shook his head, and caught Muire frowning at him.

His own fault, if she thought he was shallow and conceited.

She said nothing for a moment or two. And then just when he'd given up, she bit the side of her thumb and said, "Hardly, anymore. Some stuck."

"What else does it say about our friend?"

"He's not a friend."

Fiercely enough that he stepped back.

"Sorry."

Her glare wavered. She looked away, started walking again, and beckoned him on with a sweeping hand. "On the Last Day, in the battle between the Children of the Light and the tarnished, he did not fight—betraying both sides, for he had in turn been sworn to each. He preferred to live among men and prey upon them rather than perishing with honor, and so he survived. If you can call what he does surviving."

"For thousands of years," Cathoair breathed. "Wow."

For whatever reason, Muire let that pass without an answer.

But there was something in the quality of her silence that dragged at him. So he quoted at her, two lines of the old poetry that he did remember:

"So the Children singing came all to the slaughter/Stars and shining suns, sons and shining daughters—"

And without hesitation, she picked it up, singing rather than chanting, her voice high and pure and unanticipated, the sound filling his own throat with the urge to sing with her. Nobody wanted to hear his singing, though, so he bit it back.

"And all the windwracked stars are lost and torn upon the night/Like candleflames they flicker, and fail to cast a light./To begin with there was darkness, darkness, Light, and Will/And in the end there's darkness, darkness sure and still."

She choked off, sniffling, and he was struck by the way the single tear she didn't catch in time seemed to collect all of the available light. She cuffed at it clumsily, before he could reach to wipe it away.

"You're good," he said, and when she dismissed the praise with a shrug, said, "I guess you do remember a lot of it."

"I guess I do," she answered.

"Aethelred always talks about the Bearer of Burdens—"

"The Serpent," Muire said. "He's supposed to absorb the suffering of the world—"

"He's not doing a very good job," Cathoair said, and then glanced at her sidelong, hoping she hadn't noticed the bitterness saturating his tone.

But Muire just rubbed at her face with her gauntlet as if feeling the itch of the Wasteland dust that coated everything in Eiledon. She examined her fingertips and grimaced; the tear had smudged a clean trail through the dirt. "Yuck. I want a shower already."

"It's not toxic, once it comes through the Defile," Cahey said, maybe a little too sharply. It wasn't that she was spoiled, he reminded himself. It was—

It was just that she was spoiled.

He found he envied her.

"It's still not something you want on your face." She shook herself, as if chilled, and then lightened her tone and said, "Nice to know I annoy you."

"You pay me," he said, which wasn't entirely true. He needed the money, but—

There was something about her. Something that was in her eyes now, as she turned and frowned, and for a bad moment he thought she was going to ask him about the money, and what he needed it for. Not that it was a secret. Not that he was ashamed. But somehow, he realized, he couldn't bear to have her know his frailties.

So when she said only, "Hey, kid, where did you come from?" he sighed silently in relief.

And then he misdirected, teasing, playing the role he played. "Halla sent. Didn't you know? I'm einherjar."

She stared, face sallow in the streetlights, and bit her lip. "You shouldn't joke like that," she said. "Something might hear you."

He opened his mouth to argue, make some flip comment. Her intensity silenced him. "This block is deserted," he said, instead. "There's nobody here."

"You should have seen it during the Desolation," Muire answered. "Squatters and refugees on every corner. Field hospitals in every courtyard and marketplace."

"I've seen the same films you have," he said. "It's emptier every year. But the Technomancer still keeps the housing aboveground for the ones who can afford it. Trumans. Citizens."

"You can't see the stars from up there either," she said, as if that was what mattered. And then her head snapped around and she spun like a compass needle, sticking southwest instead of north. "Someone's dying—"

"Someone," said a gravelly voice from not far away at all, "is dead. Thou didst sing to me, sister?"

Cathoair knew that voice. He knew the scent that came with it, too, and as he turned to face the Wolf his hands were shaking. Beside him, Muire lifted her helm on its straps and seated it over her hair. A ringing scrape followed as she drew her sword, and Cahey saw to his surprise that the blade was black crystal. And then it flared in her hand, savagely, with a light as cold and sharp as starlight, and he swore he saw the same blaze from her eyes, from her mouth, chopped between her teeth when she spoke.

"Not to thee," Muire said. "Who was it this time, shadow?"

"Candle-flickers," the Grey Wolf answered, and stepped into the light. His cloak swung heavily around his feet, and his hair was slicked back, shining like oil, into its braid. "A girl and a boy, hard upon their labor, garbed all in green."

Sickened, Cahey thought of the Mongrels they'd walked past, scrubbing walls. The Wolf said *singing*. Had Cahey and Muire led him down on them?

"Just try to lay hands on him," Muire said. "Lay hands, and hold on."

"Yes," the Wolf said. "Do try."

Cathoair lunged. He didn't think he'd make contact, not with this first feint, but the Grey Wolf only stood his ground, looking—at best—curious, and at worst amused.

At the last possible moment, Cathoair planted himself, converting his momentum into a spinning side kick. The Wolf leaned aside, though, and Cahey missed cleanly with the first blow. He'd expected to, however, so rather than coming down off-balance and staggering, he managed to continue the arc and clothesline the Wolf, getting a double-fistful of shirt and pulling him to the ground.

They rolled, and it was like wrestling an animate statue. The heat of Mingan's body almost scorched the palms of Cathoair's hands, and his height and weight advantage meant nothing against the other's inhuman strength. He clutched the Wolf's wrists, pushed him back, tried to roll to pin him. But the Wolf held him up easily, laughing in his face with hot rank breath, and he knew how terribly he was in trouble.

Not since Astrid had begun teaching him to fight had he been so outclassed. Incapable of defending himself, like a battered child. Like the battered child he had been—

He panicked. He struck out wildly, fighting to get away now, to kill, maim, anything to avoid the strength of the predator that held him. But Mingan kept the grip, struck him across the mouth with an open hand, and pushed him back. The Grey Wolf was rising, both of them smeared in filth from the street, Cathoair beating at his face with gross futility, wondering where the hell Muire was—

Her voice rang out. Whatever she said was in a language he did not know, something that sounded archaic and mystical.

And then there was the reek of hot metal, competing with

the sharp musk of the Grey Wolf all over him, and the sting in his nose of his own blood. And a roar of machinery, loud as a helicopter, and—

He felt the hard shove, staggered back, fell against the stones. Pushed himself up, hands cut, arms shaking.

Turned to hurl himself at the enemy one more time, but . . .

The Grey Wolf was gone.

And where he had stood, an enormous metal statue loomed, a black stallion with two horned heads and mantling wings, the wet stones steaming around it. It pawed the ground and hissed like a giant teakettle, then turned its attention on Cathoair.

He ducked his head between his shoulders, and somehow made himself stand.

You could not have done more. It was a near thing, it said, as Cathoair put out a hand to steady himself against the wall. And then it turned, stared past him, and said, **Muire. Would you go after?**

Damp brick crumbled under Muire's gauntlet as she clutched at the wall. The smell of the Wolf was enough to trigger the harsh, atavistic memory of how brutally he'd bested her when last they met. But she dragged herself forward, sword trembling at guard, hands shaking cold and boots scraping the cobblestones. She had no idea what she *said,* exactly—but inside her head, she spoke a secret name.

Kasimir materialized like a shadow in the clear air above and plunged earthward, a thunderbolt, a mountainside falling. As he did, Mingan shrugged Cathoair off like an unwanted coat and slung him aside.

Cathoair knew how to fall. But by the time he rose again, Kasimir stood pawing at the stones where Mingan had vanished, and Muire managed to slip her sword into the sheath and go to Cathoair. She had not quite reached him when Kasimir looked at her and told her he could send her after the wolf.

Inside her gauntlet, her right hand ached. She tucked it under her arm, aware that she must look like a dog with a wounded paw. *Coward,* she cursed herself, and another voice whispered *Vengeance.*

Always vengeance.

If she could not get it for him, she would be hearing that whisper until the end of the world. "I would go after," she said. "Can you tell me how?"

Cathoair was close enough to turn and catch her shoulder. "If you go alone he'll kill you—"

Muire nodded, wondering if he could see the motion through her helm. "I fear he shall." She stepped back, so his hand dropped between them. And then she closed her eyes and shook her head. "I fear also that the risk of my death is no extenuation."

"We can hunt him together—"

"We have his trail now. If we let it go cold, who's to say we will ever catch him again?"

He stared at her, fists at his sides. And then snapped, as if he were spitting: "It's stupid!"

Then he stepped back as if he had shocked himself in his passion. "If you die, then what do we do about him? Is he just going to keep hunting the Technomancer's people?"

"Unless he can get to Thjierry herself? Yes," Muire said.

His eyebrows did something interesting at her casual use of the Technomancer's name. Muire bit her lip, too late, but he asked a better question. "And if he does, what happens then?"

"The end of the world," Muire answered, calmly and without hesitation. She'd had a great deal of time to think about it, lately. She stepped wide around Cathoair and walked toward Kasimir. "Th— the Technomancer is the thing that keeps Eiledon alive in the face of the Desolation. Her will. Her tremendously potent magic."

"That's true? It's not just stories?" By his tone, he would rather it were a tissue of lies.

"It's true," Muire said. "Every word of it. You know there was another city—"

"It fell," Cathoair said. It had been on the news channels.

"It didn't have someone like Thjierry."

"So when the wolf kills you? What then?"

She turned back. She looked over her shoulder. She smiled. "Keep fighting him," she said. "Find a way."

Kasimir? Where are we going?

Midgard.

Midgard is dead.

Aye. And so is Valdyrgard. Yet here we remain.

Point taken, Muire answered, and stepped up beside him. Kasimir poised like a giant wound spring. *How do we go there?*

Lay your hand on my mane.

She did, though it was hot enough to sweat her fingers inside the gauntlet. Before long the flesh would blister.

"Now," she said. And went forward with him, when he spread his wings and walked into the cold.

Dagaz (daylight)

In the cold and the dark, Muire thought of dying.

It hadn't been the first time. The first time, that promise of death—of surcease—sustained her through the long, brutal labor of excavating the frozen bodies of her brethren. Of chipping them free of the ice and each other, of dragging them to the location she had chosen for their cairn. The snow even proved a blessing; Muire's strength alone, no matter how much greater than mortal, would not have sufficed to the task without its slickness.

And it proved a blessing as well, because it was soft and cold and it reminded her of death. The death she anticipated, once this final task was complete. The silence and the peace. The end to bitter toil.

But first, she labored.

When the bodies were stacked, valraven among the children of the Light, tarnished among the unfallen, she found stones. With the blade of her lightless sword, she levered them up and piled them, course upon course over the dead. She built the barrow in a ring, packing snow into ramps—here, again, the snow was kind—and climbing each tier to set the next, knowing that when the blowflies arrived with summer—if there was a summer—they would find their way through sticky crevices to the bodies beneath. Then, as the maggots fatted themselves on angels (and in their own turn transformed and flew), the stones would fall and lie over whatever bones might linger.

Even the grave was but a temporary thing.

It would have to serve: she had no means of constructing a dome that might support its own weight.

She labored and carried, lifted and stacked. She grew thin with it, her hands cracked, her eyes near blinded by the weary sun. She chewed the kind snow from the battlefield for water, for thirst began to haunt her, and sometimes that snow was salt with the blood of the dead. She, who had never understood what it was to be cold, suffered with it—bleeding lips and dripping nose and chill to the bone. Still, it could not kill her, though she hoped it would. When her more-than-human strength failed her, and she—who had also never known sleep, except when wounded—collapsed into the snow and curled there, it would not freeze her.

She prayed for mortality. She received exhaustion.

Her punishment.

She had failed, and the Light had failed, and the Dweller Within had never risen from the sea at their backs to fight with them. As she covered Strifbjorn's gnawed face with stones and with the bodies of his brethren, she wondered if he had known that their flight north to the ocean was futile. She wondered if he had carried that terrible secret, so that they would not have to. If he had let them die in hope.

And she wondered if that had been better than letting them die in despair.

There was still Light, she learned. A fragment, a flicker. What she carried within her, only, and it gave her physical strength even while it wearied her heart. She could not reach outside herself and touch that larger thing, that certainty that had always buoyed her. She was, for always, alone.

The night the cairn was complete, it snowed, and Muire was again thankful. She did not wish to look up and see the sun, or the stars. She set the last stone across the top of her barrow, there on the cliff at the edge of the sea where her family had turned at bay and slaughtered one another. And she stood atop the grave and turned East, where the sky grew brighter.

Whatever she had promised herself at the end of her labors, she had earned. She picked her way down slick stones, her caution ironic in light of her purpose, and made her way to where the sea and the rocks awaited. The snow stopped during her descent, and the clouds wore thin and tore. By the time she reached the cliff-edge, sunrise painted the gray granite boulders with blood and time.

She reached over her shoulder and drew her black crystal blade. She had thought of leaving her there, to mark the barrow, but that now seemed indecent. The sun flamed, breathtaking, crimson and incarnadine and vermilion and hellebore and scarlet, and Muire drew breath as if that light could fill the hollow. The cold air only made her cough.

She had made herself a bargain. She thought of stepping into that sunrise. She pictured her fall, tumbling, and the wreck of her body on the sea-ripped boulders below. She imagined the brief sensation of flight and closed her eyes.

She spread her arms wide. A bitter sea breeze had tugged at her, almost lifting her up, and she took a deep and singing breath. This time, she did not choke on it.

She had stepped—

An echo arrested her.

Live.

She had opened her eyes. The sunrise was over: splinters of gold danced on the dark water far out to sea, and that was all. It looked like a path.

Live, the echo repeated.

A path. Not her path.

And so the moment passed.

And in the darkness of a murdered world, Kasimir creaking with the cold beside her, Muire stepped forward, as she had not, that other time.

That had been the first time. Not the last one.

There was a light, indistinct, like the light before dawn when the fog glides down hill slopes and smothers the valleys. "Hel," Muire said. "Is this not Hel's domain, Kasimir?"

On her left, he would not regard her. In this cold that conquered even the furnace within his iron body Kasimir was rimed white with ice, crystals frozen on the long wires of his lashes.

And after a moment, she too turned away. She could not bear to look at him, in the ghost of his lost whiteness. He looked as he had. Before.

She wondered if the Grey Wolf came here, to the mist and the memories, every time he vanished. If so, she could not wonder at his madness: only his survival.

Walk on, said Kasimir. Wings folded, eyes front, he stepped forward.

Sword dark, eyes front, through the mist she followed.

———

The Desolation spared nothing. Not pride, not love, not dignity. Not family, not friendships, and not hope.

Not Muire's fragile peace.

After the Thing refused Thjierry's counsel, the Technomancer disappeared for a time. Muire wondered, naturally, but she had found that the fewer questions she asked, the fewer others expected answered. In any case, Gunther was so busy being mysterious about it—"Fetching help," was all he would say— that Muire suspected he knew no more than she. And wherever the Technomancer had gone, there was enough work.

Dying is not hard. But it tends to consume all one's resources.

The Thing closed Eiledon's walls to the refugees driven out of the south. Still the displaced came, a multi-streamed river, people of all colors and nationalities and languages, a braid of folk of exotic origins and exotic modes of dress. But as time passed that river dried to a trickle, each refugee more ragged and hungrier than the last.

The only word out of the South now was the word that came with them. Cities, nations, entire continents were dead.

Muire, observing them on the remote cameras, understood that there was no aid to be sent. Truth, like a stone on her chest: this was not the first time she had watched a world die.

The world was wider now than it had been; its death throes were more protracted and terrible. And if she despaired, and longed for her own death, where was the blame?

There was no comfort in the knowledge that Eiledon was dying too. The wanderers they turned away might meet their end more quickly and more peacefully than the city that drew up its skirts against them, but taking them in would have done no good. There was already famine and plague within. Not just ordinary illness, but the engineered killers, the terror-weapons, the genetically delimited bioflus that had been designed to sweep through one's own troops—or civilians—and render them fitter, stronger, and more vicious. The citizens in the Arks were safe from those, more or less, with their enclosed biospheres and their filtered intercourse with the outside world. Those who lived in the city's apartments and streets, who died in its makeshift infirmaries and whose bodies were sterilized and committed to the tanks, they suffered it all.

The survivors were never considered exactly human again.

Eiledon was as doomed as the rest of Valdyrgard, and offering help would only exhaust them. More mouths would kill the city sooner.

She would be the last again. She was hardier than mortals, even now, even the engineered and augmented mortals of the new world. She would outlast, and she would watch each of them die, and she would in the end lie down beside the last of them and crumble, too.

Or so she prayed, though she also knew that there was no one to hear her. In her weaker moments, she thought of taking matters into her own hands, but wouldn't that be flight again? The same cowardice that had doomed her to be here, to bear witness? If she had had the courage to stand beside Strifbjorn, she could have died beside him too, and been spared this.

In weaker moments still, she feared she would endure forever, alone in a poisoned world, a haggard monster and a ragglad ghost. Still, Muire was among those who helped to raise the Defile. It exhausted every sorcerer and wizard in the city, and several died. But after that, there were fewer deaths from radiation and illness, and far more from starvation.

And then there were no more stragglers. No more refugees, and no more transmissions except the ones from Freimarc, a city to the far east that lay under ruthless martial law, but was somehow also holding on. The news was no better than the news in Eiledon. From everywhere else rose silence, or static.

Who climbs a mountain climbs alone, no matter who their comrades. Should disaster strike, no other has the resources to help; each needs all his strength for himself.

The world is such a mountain. From galling practice, Muire knew it was so.

Is dying easier or harder, when you do not have to do it alone?

Walk on, said Kasimir.

So Muire answered with her weary stride.

Muire had been many things in a long life, and one of those was a physician. When her skill with magic was no longer of use, at least she could tend the sick and wait beside the dying.

The last group of refugees was the worst. Five thousand strong or more, and they came not from the south, but from the north, returning along a path they had perhaps walked once already. When they reached the broad river valley below the mountain, they moved among the abandoned houses and shops of Eiledon's suburbs. They encircled the city, settled down along the broad once-green Boulevard that marked its processional entrance, and folded their arms.

"They're waiting to die," Gunther said, as Muire perched at his side. Muire, her workshop full of the ill and moribund, had given him her own bed when he fell sick. His hands and face were swollen with sores that leaked pus and lymph; his skin had the texture of boiled meat. He made as if to rise and she stayed him with a hand. "You're not getting out of that bed."

He *could* walk, but his feet left smears on the floor when he did. He settled back against the pillow and said, "If I'd known this was all I had to do to get into it, I would have tried this years ago."

She blushed and fed him soup so she wouldn't have to answer. They both knew he was dying. While he swallowed—painfully—she reached out to silence the news feed. Power—electricity—was one of the few resources Eiledon had in excess. The fusion plants and the orbiting solar arrays were entirely automated, entirely self-sufficient. And there was no competition for the energy now.

"No," he said, and made a paddling gesture with his hand, not quite willing to force his touch upon her. On the screen, the camera lingered on a woman, staring blindly over her cheekbones, with a child in a sling against her hip. Muire was not sure the child was breathing. "Something should be done, Muire."

She wondered if he thought he loved her. She wondered if he was right.

"There's too many of them."

"They're the last," he answered. "You know I'm right."

She tried to feed him more soup, but he turned his face away. His lips were numb and swollen, his voice slurred by the paralysis in his cheeks. The soup tended to drip over his seeping flesh. Muire had had to set small charms, tiny cousins of the massive wards of the Defile, to keep the flies away.

From below, she heard a sound. And then her name, called out in a familiar voice.

Gunther's eyes teared under puffy lids. "Thjierry."

Muire went to the top of the stair. "Thjierry," she answered. "And an army."

She set the soup aside and descended. The Technomancer stood among the injured and sick who lay on pallets in ranks on Muire's cold slate floor. Behind her were two figures in black armor, one a woman with the head of a cat and one a woman with the head of a hawk. There were others, but they walked among the casualties, offering such succor as they could.

It was a measure of the times that when a man with the head of a dog or a bull or a rat bent over another, few of the sick could rouse themselves to fear or wonder.

Thjierry—thinner, now, slack flesh drooping at the corners of her face—came to Muire with her hands extended. Muire descended the spiral stair and embraced her as a sister. They squeezed each other briefly. Muire stepped back first, trying to remember when last she had held someone in her arms.

She thought it must have been somebody who was dying.

"Gunther?" Thjierry asked, and Muire stepped aside without a word and gestured her up the stairs. Thjierry nodded and passed her, clinging to the banister as she climbed.

Muire went to put her armor on.

By the time the Technomancer returned, Muire was sliding Nathr into her sheath. She knew from Thjierry's face that it was over.

She raised her eyes as Thjierry came to her. "Did you see him?"

The Technomancer nodded. "I said good-bye. Thank you—"

Muire turned away. "He was my friend, too. What are these?" Her gesture went to the animal-headed creatures moving silently among the dying, crouching, examining, tending. One woman screamed, thrashing away, but the black-and-white-spotted rat beside her laid a hand on her forehead, and somehow stilled her panic.

"Unmans," Thjierry said. "I call them moreaux. My creation. Where are you going?"

"To do something Gunther wanted me to do," Muire said. She patted the hilt of her sword.

"I'm going to stage a coup," Thjierry said.

"Good. I'm going to bring those refugees through the Defile."

"Good." Thjierry had nodded, lips thinned. "We understand each other.

If you have to die, Muire had thought, her gauntlets bruising the soft joints of her fingers, better to go down fighting. Better to die in company.

Better not to be the last, and alone, weighed down with all that *knowing*.

Eihwaz (the tree)

ᛇ

Kasimir's hide rasped against her fingertips as he stepped forward: the creak of frozen metal on frozen metal. She paced three steps to his one, but he went slow. She could stay with him.

The ice flaked from his neck, his withers, his feathers. And that made no sense. She had thought the mist condensed and froze on him as if he was colder than the surroundings, but he was still hot to the touch—though now she could hold her armored hand against his shoulder without pain. In the savage cold, he ticked. Muire thought of a kiln, of a forge, of a smelter. Cooling.

Of course. The mist was attacking him.

And her. It rimed her armor as well, crusted the joints, cracked away when she moved and refroze so she walked with an arthritic shuffle. Its weight on her shoulders was enough to sense. She shrugged, and ice fell in showers and grew again.

"This is Niflheim. This is the land of Hel. Starvation her plate, and famine her knife."

The world is the land of Hel, said Kasimir. **All starve in the end.** *Walk on:*

She made herself do it, the stallion white beside her, his

wing against her back now pushing her on. She stumbled and he caught her, creaking, bracing her with his branching antlers until she steadied herself. The mist blinded and deluded, but Kasimir was confident, and so she followed.

Before them, the way darkened, that eerie ambient radiance growing less. Muire walked with her steed, pushing against the weight of the ice, Nathr dragging down her hand. Nothing was too heavy for her to bear. She was waelcyrge. She had borne up and carried and buried everyone she had ever cared for.

She might have run. But she had not lain down.

Kasimir's heads drooped. He moved like a windup automaton. But he moved, and buoyed by his example, Muire stepped forward, dragging her foot under a weight like the world. She planted it, shifted her weight, and stepped again. Again. Again. Again.

And found herself on a plain, knee-deep in discolored snow, the only light whatever trickled from the cold stars far above through the silhouetted branches of a great bare tree so vast she could not fathom it.

Still, she thought. *The stars.* And tilted her head back to see better, wondering if their light still sparked an answering glow in her eyes.

Kasimir—

She heard no answer.

She turned to him, and found him still as a statue, one hoof raised, wings half spread, the ice now vaporizing from his black steel skin on sizzling threads of steam.

"Shadows," she swore, and pushed against his shoulder.

No answer, though his heat again soaked through her glove. She passed her hand through one of the banners of steam rising from his hide, and it stayed disturbed, as if she had pushed through gelatin. "Frozen in time," she said, and thought of runes and mysteries and wizardry.

"Not he," said the wolf at her shoulder. "Thee."

When Muire spins on him, she leads with her blade: a whirl and thrust, a chance of making it good. Until the wolf slaps it aside, the light that flares in its crystal dulling against his palm as coals dull around splashed water. He braces his boot upon the blade, closes his fingers on her gauntlet, and—however she struggles—holds her there.

She hisses with rage. He hears it through her faceplate, and though she locks her left hand on his wrist, he lifts the helm from her hair and casts it away, revealing her features stark by swordlight.

She screws up her face and spits in his.

"Hush, sister," he says, wiping his cheek against his shoulder. "Peace. I shall not harm thee. Or this my brother," with a nod to Kasimir, who is not immobile, exactly, but might as well be.

Whatever the waelcyrge was about to say, that diverts her. "How can you be *his* brother?"

"My sire is his dam. He is my half-brother." Mingan had removed his gloves before he came to her. Now he lays his palm against her cheek, and though she shies away she cannot stop him. "The heraldry is complex. And art thou her creature?"

"Her?"

She conceals nothing. He has not the strength nor skill to seek deep, to look beyond the surface of her mind. He never has had, though it has cost him dearly: home, pack, family. But there it all is, roiled by the mists of Niflheim, the ghosts of all her memories. She is not allied with the Technomancer, and in fact knows nothing of that wizard's abominations.

Shadow, I have hunted thee.

"Foolish," he replies, bending close. He is not large, but she is tiny. He looms over her as Strifbjorn once loomed over him. "Futile. But a beautiful grim gesture nonetheless."

She was always fierce beyond her size. Indomitable in her will, and her honor. He thinks she never knew how she appeared to him, to the others: strange, fey, thoughtful, and wild.

He sees himself through her, the eyes in their caverns in his face, the cloak, the silver earring that swings against his cheek. Her fear is sweet. It is little effort at all to overmaster her. She cranes her head over her shoulder, leaning away from him, yearning toward her steed.

"Fear not," Mingan whispers. "I carry thee within me now, little one. I have taken thee out of time. That is all."

"Why?"

"For conversation," he says, and—because she is shaking, and not only with fury—he takes her out of the snow and ash of dead Midgard, and into a place he prepared among the roots of the Tree. When they appear, while she starts, he disarms her, and throws her sword far out over the snow. She'll find it again. But not before he's through with her.

She crowds away, back against the trunk—a trunk so vast its curve is largely imperceptible—her hands raised defensively. Her fingers brush the rune carved there, and she looks at it, startled. He does not think she recognizes it.

"So strip me of my armor and my weapons," she says. "I will not fear you."

But she does; he smells it on her. Over the scent of the flowers she crushes underfoot, the roses—red roses and white, hundreds of them—that he heaped around this bower. They have frozen. They crunch when she walks over them, and she stares down in horror.

"Flowers," she says.

"Roses," he offers. He holds out his hand, a supplicant. He does not remember how to speak to people. If ever he knew it. "A gesture of peace."

"Peace." Her fingers clench in their gauntlets. "The only peace between us is the peace of the grave."

"I thought thee in it," he whispers.

"You should be." She shakes her head, her laugh strained and murderous. "Are you courting me? As you courted *her*?"

In her voice is two thousand years of betrayal, the ghost of Mingan standing like a blood-soaked shadow at the right hand of a tyrant queen. He cannot deny the truth of that accusation. "Thou hast my parole that no harm will come to thee tonight."

"You have not mine," she answers. "Release my steed."

"Thy steed is not restrained," Mingan says.

She stoops, and hurls his own frozen roses at him, a fistful of them. They spin through the air. The stems and petals brush him. A few snag on his cloak. "Don't chop logic with me, you bastard. Either you brought me here to kill me, or—"

She shakes her head. Either her imagination or her voice has failed her.

Mingan shows her his teeth in a smile, to let her know that his has not. "I am my father's son, but that—I will not," he answers. He steps forward like a ripple in the starlight, and she would step back, but the Tree is behind her.

She is still within him, and he knows as he speaks that she will find him insolent. Still, he says: "Thou wilt sit, and thou wilt listen."

"Sit in the snow?"

"Art cold?" he mocked. "Or merely proper?"

"I am not fat on the souls of mortal men," she says. And folds her arms, and sits in the snow.

"No." He drops beside her and reaches to take her hand. The ridges of her gauntlet cut his palm. He raises a single finger in admonition. "Thou art weak, sister. Force not my hand, or it will go ill with thee."

"Do you think you are charming?" The scorn in her voice is her only weapon, and she wields it like a cutting torch. "Will you invite me to dine?"

"I have dined," he answers, softly, so she pales, to his eyes, even under starlight. But this is not that of which he wishes to speak. "Thou art the child of the Light who wrote the Book of Riddles."

She stares at his mouth; he has licked his lips. She lifts her chin and says, "I am."

"I wondered."

"But never enough to look for me."

"I thought," he says, so softly, "that it would not matter. That thou wouldst die with the world. No profit to murder or suicide, my dear, when we are all ruined."

"Two thousand years ago. You knew the world was dying then."

"Yes," he says. He does not elaborate, though he feels the howl of the Suneater under his skin. He contains multitudes, Mingan does, and if the Suneater had any physical form that mad wolf would be up and pacing. *Devour her,* it says, not words but a flare of hungry heat in his breast.

He's so inured to the pain, it cannot even make his eyes tear. He as good as feels fingers in his collar, twisting off his breath. He had been Heythe's lover, though she made the word filthy in his mouth. He had been her pawn, the object of her lust and sadism.

He knows more than Muire about what happened on the Last Day, and what it cost.

The light behind his sister's eyes flares until her irises seem transparent, window glass letting moonlight show. "So then why let me live?"

Comfortable in the snow, legs crossed and elbows on his knees, he chooses to answer. "Because thou art not precisely a child of the Light, anymore. Thou hast on thee a shadow, a touch of tarnish: I can see it in thy eyes, and I—" a hesitation, as of remembered luxury "—can taste it on thy breath. Thou art tainted, and thou dost ken, and thy Light has failed thee. Thou hast no reason to fight me, and many reasons to name me thy ally. And—" delicately "—I imagine we may have enemies in common."

"You are my enemy."

He still remembers how to smile. "And what of Heythe, of unkind memory? And what of Thjierry Thorvaldsdottir?"

Muire heard the words, understood them, comprehended them—and somehow still managed to blink dumbly at the wolf, as if he had entirely confounded her. "The Technomancer? She was a—"

—friend.

No, not exactly. Gunther had been a friend. Thjierry had been a friend of a friend, a professional acquaintance, an ally of convenience. But as Muire opened her mouth to say so, the Grey Wolf rose, fluidly, to a crouch. He rested on the balls of his feet, one knee, the fingers of one hand. He leaned in toward her, and widened his smile.

It was not his hunting smile. It was not terrible at all. That unsettled her more.

"And was it thee who taught her to work her abominations, then, little sister?"

"Abominations?"

"Her animal folk," he said. "Those poor beasts she's twisted into her service, given hands and made slaves. Was that thy magic, then?"

"As it was your magic that warped wolves into vile sdad-own?"

He flinched, as she had meant him to, but dared not hope. When he raised his eyes again, his smile was gone. The snow in his clenched fist creaked; slow water dripped between his fingers. "So," he said. "It was thee."

"No."

"Then how does she make them? She cannot sing life from a rock, as the waelcyrge can."

Trying to make it look casual, Muire stripped off her gauntlets, one and then the other, opening the clasps so they unfolded like clamshells around her hands. The right one ached in the cold; she rubbed it, and saw the Grey Wolf noticing the pale new scars. Yes, he should think on that, if there was any conscience in him. If there ever had been. She found she changed her mind every instant, as to whether there had.

She had walked among the einherjar and waelcyrge like a ghost, as pale and as unnoticed. Muire the scholar-gypsy, Muire the tower maiden: she had known lifetimes, and all of them bittersweet.

And among all her brethren, the Grey Wolf was the eldest,

and had been foreign even then. He wore grey when his brothers wore white and indigo, when they drank together in a lofty-beamed hall. He sat beside Strifbjorn at the top of the trestle, beneath the chair that was left empty by tradition, a single dark head bent toward that palest among the golden ones.

They had welcomed him at table on those rare occasions when he graced it, but he stayed always strange with the wilderness he haunted by preference. And Muire remembered him saying: *When we sang Men from the stones, little knew we how bright and brief a thing we were crafting.*

She closed her hands on rose stems, and pain drew her from that vivid memory. They were thorned, the frozen roses, and she clutched great handfuls and twisted them until the stems cracked and the petals shattered. Mingan reached out, catching at her wrists as if to prevent her from injuring herself, but he didn't hold tightly and she snatched her arms across her chest and overbalanced backwards in the snow, striking the gnarled roots of the Tree as she toppled, sliding against that unfamiliar rune.

She got an elbow down and pushed against it, kicking like a dog will to protect its belly. But he was over her, hands clenching on her arms until the bones creaked and she gasped in terror, his skin hot to the touch even though he had buried his hands in the snow, his breath rank on her face. All she could smell was him, as if she were wrapped in the hide of an animal. He pinned her in the snow, her armor bruising her back, his braid snaking over his shoulder, and his cloak fell all around them.

There was blood on her fingers, the blood she had sacrificed her gloves to put there, and she pulled the salty-slippery-sharp words of sorcery into her mouth and shaped them, worked them deep. One chance, she thought. He would not give her another.

The word for pain almost got away from her; it could have turned in her hand and cut her hard. But she juggled it, twisted it back, and formed her mouth around it. *Pain, lightning, freedom*— Her blood for an anchor.

He lowered his head, and though she arched back into the snow as much as possible, he bit her hard, diagonally across the mouth. Around the pressure of his lips and teeth, she only managed a yelp. The sorcery thrashed, all teeth and lashing tail, uncontrolled, and Muire braced herself for the agony of the backlash. But Mingan was there, beside her, delimiting, diffusing, pulling half the uncontrolled forces he'd unleashed off and filtering them through his own body.

The bite became a kiss.

Muire shoved hard against his pinioning hands, and bucked against him. Not enough, but enough to get his mouth off hers. He panted into the corner of her jaw.

And she heard him, as if his voice whispered into her heart. *Oh, so, candle-flicker?*

He brought his knee up sharply between her legs, driving her armor into her groin.

She tried to scream, but he was ready for her, his open mouth covering hers again in that obscene parody of a kiss. His thumbs drove between the tendons of her wrists. His chest swelled as he drew her breath in deep.

No, she thought, her mouth sealed under his. *No. No. I defy you.*

He pushed both her wrists into one hand and pinned them over her head, then covered her nose and eyes with the other palm. *Defy me as thou likest. I have more to show.*

She hung in time with him, attenuated, anchored by the pain in her wrists, her hands, her mouth, her groin. She waited for the rush, the pulse, the dizziness of her life flowing into him, of her soul feeding his strength. The snow under her back chilled the armor against her skin; the heat of his body made her chest prickle sweat. But this was not like the first time: she felt no confusion, no blurring of identities and lights and colors and pain. There was only the insupportable craving, the agony of a body near collapse from want of breath as she choked through an age.

And then, when she could wait no more, when the world spun black-edged around her and tears stung the corners of her covered eyes: *Thou wilt* like *this, little sister.*

And then he gave her back her breath, and all his merciless strength with it. It seared her throat and rolled into her lungs with all the wolf-heat of his immortal body, full of everything she had begged him to withhold the first time. Euphoria, rapture drowned her will, until she arched against him, pressing into the embrace. His palms slipped from her wrists and eyes, cradled her face and caressed her wet hair. She clutched at his shirt, tore the collar, flailed weakly at his head with fists that would not clench. Her blood streaked his hair, his face as he bent her head back between his palms and poured himself down her throat.

Thou shalt. Understand me.

And not only himself. She felt the other in him, the hunger that moved like a shark through calm water. The thing in his belly that pricked up its ears and laughed with bloody teeth, a furnace light glaring between its teeth. *Suneater.* It would burn her, she thought, as surely as Kasimir. Scorch her to cinders, until she flared and crisped from within.

All these years, all these lifetimes, she had saved this, un-willing to have anyone if she could not have Strifbjorn. And now the Grey Wolf broke the kiss, lying on his elbows over her, and drew back—and she groped after his mouth with her own.

His breath on her face smelled of sunlight. His voice, all sand and sea-salt and velvet, brushed the side of her throat. "Oh, thy little whore," he whispered. "Told he thee, I've had him? Spoke he of how he made sweet moan when I fucked his mouth, Muire the Historian? Sweetling, poet, scholar?"

"You loved him then," she said, gasping, sliding her hand along the cabled heat of his neck. "Why debase him now?"

"Because I loved him," the Grey Wolf answered, and pressed his face against her skin below the ear.

She'd ripped his shirt open. There was something about his throat; a slender band, flexible and tough as woven tita-nium, with a knot binding it together above a loose frayed end. It spilled light like the fire through a diamond in scattered droplets across his throat. Muire slipped a finger inside the necklace and heard him cry softly. A liquid sound, shattered, the sound that would seem to give voice to what heaved in her own heart. But he was the Grey Wolf, pitiless and immoral, hungry and aloof. She would not allow herself to believe he could mourn.

Hands shaking, disbelieving her own audacity—her own complicity—she reached up and knotted a hand around his silver-brindled plait, and pulled his mouth back to her own.

She did not lose consciousness, and she did not exactly lose control, for she knew every instant what it was she did. Her senses burned with unnatural lucidity: the animal scent of his skin, musky and bitter; the texture of callused fingers against her face; the copper-ocean flavor of blood; the fine wool of his waistcoat and the slippery silk of his shirt and his collar—and the coarse softness of his braid—knotted in her hands.

The weakness of ecstasy left her and she sucked at his mouth with the abandon of a nestling. She clutched at the devil: she dragged at his head as if pulling a lover's mouth to her own in the final spasm of passion. She tore his hair free and it tumbled around her face with the wild scent of a predatory beast.

She growled like a wolf as she lunged up off the snow against him, heard herself sobbing in fierceness as his hands lifted off her face and he tried to back away. She clung to him, and he had to take her wrists in his hands again and set her back against the trunk of the Tree until she stopped struggling.

He had no easy time of it. She was stronger than she had been, as strong as she was in her youth when she had built a cairn for all her brothers save this one, and she would not release her hold on his hair, or his collar. The rose-thorns cut her as they struggled, the frozen leaves and petals shattered through his hair. The Light that flared around them, pulsing with every pass back and forth of their breath, made the wet bark of the Tree gleam blackly, and cast in stark relief details that had blurred in dim starlight for millennia. He barely managed to hold her, and when she got her hand free once she grasped his head in clutching fingers and nearly brought his mouth back down.

Oh, brother, the hunger. . . . !

She expects him to laugh, in triumph and wrath, at her humiliation and desire. But she feels him through the places where their skin touches, and he is full of only sorrow and gratification and guilty, nauseated, satisfied need.

At last, he pins her against the Tree and holds her at arm's length, elbows locked, until she stops fighting. It pleases her savagely to make him struggle, to see effort clench his face. She curls her hand into a fist around the torn coarse strands of his hair and struggles to recollect her composure.

She cannot stop licking her lips, and all she can taste is blood. He bit her, and then she split her lips again upon his teeth, and his on hers. His hair, so sleek before, floats in a tangle like a halo around his face. It is smeared with blood from the small cuts on her hands.

She leans back against the Tree as he releases her, turning her face, unable to hold his gaze. Her fingers quiver; she could finish him in a few beats of their twinned hearts.

"In the old days," she says, "that was a wedding."

"Tomorrow," he answers, licking the blood from his mouth, "tomorrow this time, judge me again."

She sees it on his face, in the trembling of his hands, in the way he reaches to run a finger between that silken collar and the bruised welt she's left on his skin with her twisting. She knows it in her blood, with the knowledge that comes with the breath she's stolen from him. He apprehends how she feels.

She feels . . . strong.

12

Tíwaz (the sky)

There was no shimmer as Muire and the iron beast vanished. No rainbow light, no pulse of sound, no whisper, even, of disturbed air. Nothing. Just a flat plane of vanishment, as if they stepped forward through an invisible doorway, and then— nothing.

Cathoair reached forward instinctively, as if his hand could somehow snake across the yards between them and close on Muire's arm. *A vengeance specialist,* he thought numbly. *Yeah, I'll say. Cahey, there's dumb, and there's whatever you've caught.* His fingers closed on air, a futile pinching motion, and as he bounced on the balls of his feet to regain his balance, he let it fall to his side. A coil of twisted plastic that someone would soon salvage blew across the little courtyard, rattling on cobblestones. She was gone, every hair of her. Cathoair was alone and soaked-through-cold, bruises that would be black-and-blue by morning swelling on his cheek, his shin, his elbow.

He closed his eyes, dropped his chin, and squeezed his own arm. That hurt too, but not too badly.

He should have known: too good to last, too much to hope for. He should have known that nothing in the world ever worked out this well. And now, moreover, somebody was watching him. He felt the gaze on his neck, moving the fine hairs like a breeze. He flinched.

And opened his eyes, turning to survey the approaches with manufactured nonchalance. He needn't have gone to the trouble, as his observer was going to none to conceal herself.

It was her eyes he noticed first, because they gathered the dim available light and reflected it back at him in a metallic green shimmer. The second thing he noticed was that she was a she. Although her body was angular and alien under the black leather and ceramic armor, lean and breastless, her cloudy milk-and-pewter pelt peering through everywhere the armor did not cover, she stepped forward, and the cant of her pelvis, the angle of her femur were ineluctably feminine, though her stride, long and assured, fell on the border of swagger.

A flechette pistol hung on one hip, a coiled shape he recognized after a moment as a monofilament whip on the other. Not a weapon Cathoair would have chosen to try to handle, or to face.

An insignia of rank glimmering on her chest below the collarbone—he couldn't call it a breastplate, when her armor was all segmented overlapping bands—marked her Black Silk. The Technomancer's elite.

Cathoair swallowed half in relief and half in renewed worry. Here was help. And here was also the glove and boot of the law he survived on the fringes of. No one who lives by his wits enjoys talking to the cops.

"Name," she demanded.

They were supposed to be able to smell lies. "Cathoair. Officer."

She closed the distance between them, leaving clawed prints in the mud. There was enough light from the floatlamp to see her clearly, once she emerged from shadow. She made not a whisper of sound, her silence reminding him of the Grey Wolf's.

She wrinkled her nose, whiskers laid back against velvet-furred cheeks, and whuffed delicately. "He was here," she said, and even though he knew better Cathoair was startled by the sweet painstaking voice from an animal's fanged mouth. All he knew of animals—or moreaux—was holo and vii. And even though the machinimated imitations spoke quite clearly, if not quite in human tones, it was somehow different to find himself standing a meter from an unman, hearing her voice come out with extraordinary crispness. She sniffed again, leaning close. "You touched him."

"I fought him," Cathoair said. "He got away."

"And the woman, too?"

"She . . . chased." He drove his nails into his palms, scraping crescents of dead cells and sweat off the skin. He should have run—.

And then she would have chased him down. Unlike Muire, he could not vanish into the night as if he had never been.

"You were with her."

"Yes," he said. "I work for her."

"Not him." Her face was almost expressionless, but creases deepened between her eyes and her ears flicked forward. Not a frown, but something he could tell himself was intensity, focus. Her tail lashed: angry? Or did cats lash their tails when they were on the hunt?

"No."

"And what is her relationship to him?"

Damned if I know, Cahey thought, but didn't have the gall to say it. "She is chasing him."

"They are not allies."

"They are not allies," he answered, letting his breath flow out in relief. The tightness across his chest eased. "And you?"

The Black Silk settled back a little, weight on her heels, knees flexed. She did not look as if she meant to spring. "It is not my purpose to answer your questions. You'll come with me willingly?"

Unspoken in the request was the threat. "Where?" he asked, although his answer wouldn't change with hers.

"To Her," the officer said. "She is personally interested in this case."

Cathoair folded his arms. Before that moment, he hadn't noticed the cold.

Selene brought the human up the easy way, out of pity. It might be circuitous, but he was young and wobbly and slightly injured, and she thought he was probably slipping into shock. Which had the benefit of making him docile, but also made him stupid and prone to falling over.

At least he did not actually collapse. And he was biddable, or at least cooperative, which might prove as inconvenient as it was useful, because it tended to indicate he would not be able to provide much assistance in locating the quarry. Or—and here she felt half hopeful—perhaps he was simply clever enough to pretend, and more would emerge under interrogation.

But as she studied him staggering up the stair to the lift, clutching the handrail, she was doubtful. "Am I being arrested?" he asked halfway up, pausing and turning, craning his neck to look down at her. He was *very* young.

"No." She shook her head, the human way, or as close as she could come. From the way his eyes widened, it didn't look as he'd expected. "You are being brought in for questioning. That is all."

"Oh." But he turned away from her again—human arrogance, or exhaustion?—and hauled himself up another step. Three others, each more laborious than the last, and he reached the landing. Selene was two and a half steps behind.

The lift came to her thumbprint. No one used it unless admitted by an unman. The operator, waiting on the landing, was a silky-eared spaniel named Mnemosyne, but she was low-ranked and effaced herself in Selene's presence. The human nevertheless smiled at her nervously, and she wagged her tail in hesitant response.

Selene squeezed her eyes at the dog. Not everyone was created a warrior; a task for each, and each suited to the task.

That was Her law, and a good one.

The lift descended silently between its cables, rocking in the motion of air displaced by the falls. Selene could manage the complex currents around the Tower on a hoverboard, but others needed assistance. Or the security of the lift, no matter that sometimes it swayed like a pendulum.

It was swaying now. Selene affected inscrutability, scratching the palms of her hands against her armor, but the human's attempts to project calm amused her. He stood with his hands on the railing, fingers relaxed, face tilted upward and soft around the stiff vine of his scar. His throat worked, though, and his sweat was souring. When the lift clicked against the platform, he flinched.

Selene, still pretending incognizance, stepped past. As she brushed by she caught his arm, mindful of her talons. It would be less than helpful if she rent his flesh an inch deep. Human flesh was soft, as the damage to his face testified.

If he worked for Her, that injury could have been repaired.

The human came with Selene without resisting, so she led him gently through the steel blue light of daybreak. As they paused within the open cage, he turned and stroked the grille, which clacked shut in response. He jerked his hand back and pressed the fingers against his lips, but still stared about.

That it was technomancy did not mean it must be unlovely. Even to Selene's aesthetic, the lift was beautiful. The cornerposts of the cage were worked like tree trunks, the lesser bars between them wrought into vines covered in twisted leaves and ornate flowers. There were paste jewels set in the iron blossoms, gray and dull now but backed with foil mirrors. When the cage rose into the Defile-dimmed sunlight that already painted the reaches of Tower and Ark, they would catch it and erupt into brilliance.

Selene did not know where She had salvaged it from. She was certain She had not made it, but perhaps She had had it commissioned. There were ironworkers in the city still.

In any case, the tall young human reached out before the lift lurched into motion and steadied himself against the waist-high rail provided for that purpose. One hand only, though the fingers on the other twitched. "How long will you hold me?"

Selene's tailtip twitched. "That is Hers to decide," she said. And then, because she could still smell his sweat souring, she touched him lightly with the palms of her hands, fingers bent back for fear of scratching, and said: "If you have done no wrong, you have nothing to fear. Whatever you have heard, She does not take prisoners for the sake of holding them."

"Oh," he said.

The lift, once started, ascended more smoothly, though it

did twist between the parallel cables it rode. He managed the sway very well, for a human, though his balance was not as deft as Selene's. He cocked his head as if to study the sound of the ratchets, rhythmic and comforting. Selene's ears pricked this way and that, chasing it, but it came from all sides. "You have employment?" she asked. "We can send a messenger."

He looked down. His lids drooped. He had long lashes for a human, as long as a mare's. "My mother," he said. "She's pretty much dying."

He wouldn't look at her. Instead he craned his neck, staring out over the city as they rose above the rooftops as if he expected to somehow catch a glimpse through or above the Defile. There was nothing beyond but crumbled suburbia, but he could not be expected to know, and Selene could not think why she felt the urge to tell him.

She glanced around. The lift was a hundred meters above the ground already, and rising. Below, Mnemosyne stared up through the grayness, one hand resting lightly on the control stand, alert to the remote chance of emergency.

Selene sheathed her claws, carefully, and watched to make sure that they did not reflexively reemerge when she patted the human on the hand. His skin was moist against her pads; when she withdrew, she could detect his scent on her fingers. Her palms itched; she rubbed them together. She had no more than slight comfort to offer, but he appeared startled and grateful to receive it.

Not as startled as she, though, when she opened her mouth and said, "I am sorry your mother is dying." Personal comments to suspects were not protocol. It was not only inappropriate for her to say that; it should have been impossible. And neither was it protocol, when he stared at her—mouth open wide enough to show the several missing teeth at the side with the scar—to continue, "But in a complete analysis, I suppose we all are. Dying. Not sorry."

He shut his mouth. He smiled, just as they rose to meet the rays of sunlight descending to meet him. The strike of light across his face made him wince and squint and shield his eyes with his hand, but not before Selene saw they were a cracked, surprising hazel. As if she had been seeking permission, he rolled his shoulders back and said, "It's okay to be sorry, too."

Cathoair had never in his life been this high above the ground. Unsurprising, given that he'd spent most of his life in the Well, sheltered by the very earth-berg he now rose beside, hoisted on creaking cables. It must be safe; the Black Silk officer beside him seemed at ease and even a little amused by his discomfort.

Still, the motion of the lift and the slide of air between the bars was not a comfort. He locked his right hand on the rail—not that even a death grip would save him if a cable snapped—and distracted himself with breathing and the view.

The city's unkempt walls were visible in three directions, blocked to the northeast by the bulk of the Tower itself and the spires of Ark behind. Rising mist obscured the surface of the river, so Cahey could imagine the water beneath as a chasm, a gulf. Bottomless, except where it rose in midair to flow through the Tower, and morning light shone through. He wished Astrid were here to see this. She would adore it.

And he wanted her there, for strength and calm.

She would be frantic when he wasn't back at the Ash & Thorn by lunchtime.

When the sun grew higher, the mist would burn through. But not yet. Now, it sent creeping fingers through the narrow streets of the old city across the river, lapped the slate rooftops, coiled copper railings and wreathed goblin wings. It flowed down the slope into the Well and obscured the makeshift buildings there—and there, it would linger, shielded from the sun's rays by the Tower.

Out here, beneath all that sky, Cathoair was anything but comfortable. That was worse than the unsteady swaying of the cage beneath his feet, honestly. What was a little motion, a little height? The vast unboxed sky, however, made his heart sting, his mouth dry. It was bigger than him. Bigger than anything. And even up as far above the ground as this, he wasn't any closer.

If it wasn't for the green shimmer of the Defile bounding his horizons, even paling now as the light soaked through it, Cahey thought he might have sunk down on the floor and buried his face between his knees.

Still, they rose without disaster into the docking cradle. The lift latched into its clasps with a harsh, carrying sound, and the opening grille rasped. As the moreau led him out onto an exposed landing patio tiled in yellow sandstone, Cahey thought that was likely by design. It made enough noise to be thoroughly useless for sneaking.

He rubbed his hands on his trouser legs to dry them, and tried to seem at ease as he glanced around.

Despite the early hour, the broad yard before them was crisscrossed by pedestrians. Yawning students, most no older than Cathoair and some several years younger, slouched from what must have been dormitories to assemble before a building from which drifted cooking smells. Unmans, some armored like his officer and some clad in robes or loose trousers, moved among them but seemingly at cross-purposes. *They* did not seem sleepy, nor in a hurry to eat.

"Do—" He wasn't sure of a polite term, honestly. What did they call themselves? "—your people have their own cafeteria?"

"We eat first," the officer said. "Humans sleep. Unmans do not. And She says as we work harder, and it is no inconvenience to us to rise for meals before sunup, we take precedence."

Cathoair watched her sidelong as she spoke, but no trace of irony tainted her face or voice. "You don't sleep at all?"

"We have never needed to." Her tail swayed lazily, ears alert and polite when she glanced at him.

She padded forward across the stones, and he followed. And, unwilling to relinquish the conversation, asked, "So the Grey Wolf made you miss breakfast?"

He wasn't sure unmans had a sense of humor. They never did, on vii. But she glanced at him, whiskers slicked back against an inhuman face, and said, quite dryly, "We all make sacrifices."

Something chirped on her chest before Cahey could think of a clever comeback. She glanced at a screen on her wrist, a habitual motion. "She is expecting us," she said, and stepped back, rubbing her hands across her upper arms. She pointed with her chin, across the yard, toward a corridor between two buildings. "You are summoned."

He stopped dead, keeping his balance despite an uneven stone that rocked under his foot. It was obvious from her gesture that she did not intend to come with him. "I expected the armed escort to continue."

"Selene," she said, which did not follow. He stared at her dumbly, and she dropped her hands to her thighs, the claws peeking out of her fingertips. They caught the light with a gemstone glitter so he wondered what they were made of, and decided not to find out the hard way. "My name," she said, when he had blinked at her enough to transmit his confusion. "Selene. If you become lost, or disoriented, or are unsure what to do in a circumstance, ask for me. Even if you seem alone, Gunther will hear you. And someone will fetch me."

"I'm on my own?"

"You're never alone in the Tower," she said. One hand rested casually on the handle of her whip: an implied threat, or mere habit. He didn't care to find that out either.

And yet. He licked his lips. Astrid and Hrothgar—powerful, tough, physical—were not flukes, but rather indicative. Cathoair knew it was damage, that the people he found attractive were the ones who could at least match him blow for blow, and even more so those who could make a run at beating him. He understood the psychology behind it. He even knew where the kink came from.

And so while many people might be shocked to discover that he found this wiry, lithe unperson sexy, he wasn't surprised that the candid, predatory expression in her gray-gold eyes sent chills and heat rippling up his spine. *Slut,* he chided—not in his own voice, but in tones of remembered disparagement.

But then he thought, she hadn't had to give him her name. Or touch him on the arm.

Selene's directions were both concise and accurate, and Cahey never quite shook the sensation of being watched as he found his way alone across the yard, through a corridor between two buildings, through a garden and across another yard, this one enclosed on four sides by buildings. He guessed you would call it a quadrangle.

It was quieter here: fewer students, less movement. The ones he saw were mostly older, with two and a half decades, or three. Their robes—dark red, emerald, violet, gold, black, or combinations—fluttered with their movements. A few stood near him in a cluster, under the shade of their mortarboards, notebooks and viscreens clutched to their chests.

One turned toward him, frowning, but he would barely have noticed except for the sensation of her gaze. Because beyond her, beyond the far wall of the garden, was something he had seen only in pictures, in images from the before.

Trees.

Seven of them. He counted. Five green, in various shades, one a reddish violet with leaves like outspread hands, and the third with leaves splotched brown and green and yellow. Well, all of them had spots of yellow, here and there, but the one on the far left was mostly that color. Cathoair held his breath, and couldn't make himself walk forward.

For now, actually, he didn't want to. If he got under them, he thought he wouldn't be able to see them clearly. They were too big, too overwhelming. He and Astrid and Hrothgar and Aislinn together might just have been able to link hands around the largest, but it was as good a chance they might not, either. And they were easily six or seven times taller than he, tall enough that the Defile reflected green-gray light on their topmost branches.

The leaves turned in the wind, rustling, a sound almost like voices. Some kind of fruit swayed heavy in the branches of one, but he didn't know the name for it. He knew those things used to grow on trees, though, before they were vat-ripened. Things you could eat, and some things that were poisonous.

The bark looked rough. He wondered what it would feel

like to touch it, but there were barrier marks around each tree, showing the line of a force field. He wouldn't brave that for mere curiosity.

Well, all right, he might have. But not in the Technomancer's garden.

"Trees," he breathed. Someone in the nearest group of students giggled, something about new meat, and then got a square look at him on his scarred side and shut up. He didn't bother to turn and smile at her. Trees were better than teasing spoiled students.

By Selene's directions, he had to cross the quadrangle anyway. He reasoned that he might as well cross into the shade of the trees.

The funny thing was, he thought the gravity here was a little unstable. Each step felt slightly different from the last, as if he were somehow walking uphill or downhill on a perfectly flat surface. It might be some effect of the Technomancer's magic, the same spells that kept the Tower afloat over the city. He certainly wasn't about to stop one of the scornful students and ask them.

He saw his goal clearly. It was the only door guarded by unmans—a dog and a bull—and the wood was lacquered poppy-red and set with leaded glass windows that glittered in the light of the rising sun. It looked like the door to a palace. Well, the back door, anyway. Set absurdly in a plain gray stone building, over a little granite lintel, with a crystal knocker and no knob.

He presented himself before the bull. Wordlessly, it blinked at him, lowering a massive black head crowned with bronze-sheathed horns. Either one of them was the length of his forearm; taken together, he could have stood within the circle.

"Selene said I was expected," he said, hoping it was the right thing.

The bull regarded him for fifteen seconds, blinking soulful brown eyes, and ducked his head. Cathoair braced for the charge, wondering if he could grasp the horns and so vault over, or use the moreau's own weight to throw it to the ground.

But the lowering became a bow, and the unman swept aside, clearing the way to the door.

Cathoair mounted the steps. Selene had said knock, and so he raised his fist to do so, but at the last moment remembered the knocker. He lifted it; it was cool to the touch, still slick with dew. He was first to pass this way this morning.

He let the clapper fall. It struck the plate with a sound as transparent as a glass bell—it went right through his aching head—and the door swung open.

Whatever he expected within, it wasn't a perfectly institutional beige corridor with perfectly institutional speckled tiles. He glanced over his shoulder, frowning, but the unmans showed no sign of accompanying him. He squared his shoulders and glanced up at the trees, at their boles rising gnarled and curious to either side. The wind stirred their leaves and tried to unpick his ponytail, but whatever it might have been whispering, he couldn't make out the words. A warning, some part of his brain suggested, and he told that part to quit being so damned theatrical and go work on something useful.

He did not doubt this was a test. He was not unsupervised; rather, the Technomancer was seeing how he would behave when left to his own devices. Would he act like a citizen, responsible and concerned? Or like a criminal, with something to hide?

He wondered if the unmans really could smell lies. At least, he comforted himself, he hadn't told any. Also, this was the home of a hero. A potential ally. Something he suspected he would need, if Muire didn't return. And possibly even if she did.

Alone, Cathoair entered the Technomancer's tower.

Within, all was still and quiet except for his footsteps, which echoed strangely from the hard surfaces of the empty corridor. There were wooden doors on each side, plain, set with frosted glass windows. He walked between them, hands at his sides, trying to step squarely and lightly so his boots would not leave smudges on the floor.

He stuffed his fists in his pockets while he walked to hide the shaking. When he came to the end of the corridor, the final door lay before him. He looked left and right, but found no guidance, and he could not have seen more than a shadow through the frosted pane. There was a light beyond, so he tapped lightly.

When there was no answer, he pushed the door partly open with his fingertips and slipped through. Counterweighted, it swung silently closed behind him.

This must be the building's lobby. The tile here was some powdery-looking stone, silver-black and studded with red-black globs. Two staircases with treacherous-looking white marble steps curved up to a landing; beyond the rail he could see that another flight continued. And as if in conscious contradiction of the bland beigeness of the corridor, here fluted whitewashed pillars supported an elaborately medallioned plaster vault, and a dusty chandelier dominated the center of the ceiling.

His footsteps still echoed.

Several dark red auto-adapting chairs perked up when he entered the room, and the closest scampered toward him, full of hope. At first, Cathoair sidestepped it, meaning to continue on. But he realized after a few moments that there were too many exits and that he had not the slightest clue which of them he was meant to be using. He glanced around, wondering if there was a servant or guard somewhere, but the only sound in the great empty chamber was his breathing and the click of the chair's disk-shaped metal feet.

After he had spent a few moments in staring and in straining his ears for a sound or any sign of habitation, the chair caught up. Insistently, it nudged his thighs.

"Oh, all *right*," he said, and sat down, drawing his feet up so he could hug his knees, hunching his ears between his shoulders to wait.

The chair was a little more comfortable than he had planned for, and he was far more tired. It cupped him companionably, seeming aware of all the bruises and sore places, exuding a soothing heat, purring softly as if it enjoyed being put to use. Cathoair, raised to hardship, found he didn't mind comfort.

Before long he relaxed against the wingback, arm supporting his head and eyelids heavy. He jerked himself upright. The chair obliged. "Thank you," he said, ridiculously, and then grimaced, but it rubbed its arm against his hand and he felt comforted. He scratched it lightly, as he'd scratch a friend's scalp, and when his fingernails snagged on the threads of a mended place it shivered and made a low happy noise, the purring redoubled.

At least he could make a chair happy.

He was concentrating on that when a chime—like the pealing of the door knocker, but softer—almost made him knee himself in the face. Adrenaline flushed his system; his heart thumped and his head slammed into the back of the chair as he flinched away from the noise.

"I'm sorry," said a pleasant voice, male, with the kind of precision of speech Cathoair associated with University scholars. "I hadn't realized your startle response was so developed. Your pupils are quite dilated. I believe you would have hit me if I were standing beside you."

"I don't usually hit things I don't mean to hit," Cathoair answered. He slid his feet cautiously to the floor. When he grasped the chair arms and began to lever himself to his feet, it arched up, as if in disappointment. "You have pushy furniture."

"The chairs are a little domineering," the voice admitted. "Please, don't get up. I can't, and She probably won't."

It wasn't the Technomancer; she was a woman, and anyway Cathoair had heard her voice—on broadcasts and in historical records. It might turn out to be another unman, though. The way it said *She* made him suspect it was.

"Okay," he said, and settled back. "Selene sent me here to wait for the Technomancer."

"She's on her way," said the voice. Cathoair imagined a young man somewhere in a room, a room full of vii and holotanks, overseeing the entire complex. "She doesn't move as fast as She used to. I'm Gunther."

"Gunther—"

"Just Gunther. I used to have a last name, but things changed. Now I'm the computer."

He used to be a truman, in other words. Like the students here. Like Cathoair's mother. And he'd somehow—Cathoair guessed he knew how—become a part of the Technomancer's machine. A constructed servant. Which led Cahey to wonder about the unmans, where they had come from, and how they had been made.

"You're a fylgja. A fetch."

Inevitably, he also started to wonder about the chairs. And then he couldn't stay seated, no matter how sore he was or how much the furniture pouted.

As he rose, Gunther cleared his throat exactly as if he had one, and completely ignored Cathoair's comment. Was it rude to call the bound dead what they were?

The fylgja said, "I understand you're a friend of Muire's?"

"Yes," Cathoair said, hoping his reinforced caution wasn't too apparent. "I'm Cathoair."

"Hello, Cathoair," a new voice answered. This one, he knew; it was the one he had expected to hear all along.

He turned, and found himself face-to-face with an old woman on a hoverchair. She was skinny and haggard and gray, wearing two heavy sweaters over her robes, one with the collar turned up around her stringy throat.

"Cathoair—?" she asked, with her own voice, unamplified and unaugmented. Ancient as she might seem, her speech was firm, not tremulous.

"Just Cathoair," he said, face heating.

The Technomancer glided closer, the chair cornering smoothly on its stabilizers. It made no sound except a soft cushiony hiss. Cathoair's friendly chair withdrew discreetly, clicking softly. Maybe furniture had a pecking order?

"I see," the Technomancer answered. She was close enough now that he could see that her gray pallor was caused by a network of silver- and steel- and copper-colored lines that braided together with eye-defeating complexity. "Pity. I was going to ask how you were not one of mine. I wondered if you preferred to avoid an education."

"The Mongrels wouldn't take me," he said, quite proud of how level he kept his tone.

"I'd like to educate everyone, but the Ark and the Thing would not permit it," she said, and he believed the regret in her voice. "I'm sorry. They're afraid of all you new folk."

Holding her hand out, as if in evidence of her own decayed humanity, she glided up before him. Old and frail, completely helpless. Except, of course, for whatever he could not see.

"You're the Technomancer. You do as you please."

"Alas. You would think so." Thin shoulders rose and fell under the sweaters. She reached out and touched his hand, her fingers warm and papery on his skin. He expected the wires to somehow alter how she felt, but she was just an old woman, and her hands felt like his mother's hands.

"You're not truman either, though."

"Not anymore. But I'm the Technomancer. It would go ill for them if I permitted myself to succumb to the ravages of age. And so, what they cannot survive without, they are forced to endure." And then she changed the subject with a wave of her gray-skinned hand. "I interrupted. Gunther was asking about Muire. And the enemy she's hunting, who is also an enemy of mine."

"You know her?"

"We knew her," Gunther said. "Long ago. Before the Desolation."

"But—"

At least he had the sense to stop himself before he went any further. And the Technomancer nodded, as if she understood his distress. "Did you assume she was mortal? Truman?"

"No," Cathoair said. He closed his eyes. "Of course not. Any fool can see she's something else."

13

Raidho (the wagon)

R

Muire brushed at the spots of scarlet on her armor, expecting them to smear—but they were only rose-petals, adhered by melting snow. Her lacerated hands didn't sting. She supported herself against the trunk of the enormous tree with the other hand, panting, and expected when she stood on her own her palm would leave smears of blood to freeze upon the bark. But the only dark wetness, illuminated to her preternatural eyesight by the starshine, was the melted snow.

Her hands were healed. And more—the scars on the one Mingan had crushed remained, but they were old and white, and the bone-deep ache had faded.

"You healed me." Her hair fell across her eyes when she lifted her head. She did not trouble herself to shake it back. Her grimace—she couldn't call it a smile—felt on her mouth like an animal's snarl. Light surged from her mouth and from her eyes, dazzling beams that cast Mingan in stark brilliance so his shadow stretched long on the trammeled snow behind him.

"You healed yourself," he said. "As in the old days. How does it feel to be strong again, angel?"

"I hate thee," she said, and then her perfect, unblemished hand flew to her mouth.

He was not touching her. He could not actually speak into her mind. But she heard him, close and tender as if his breath warmed her ear. *Then in this we are united.*

Of course it wasn't really Mingan. It was merely the splinter of him she carried—would always carry—a shadowy, complex, and twisted thing she did not begin to apprehend. She wondered, if she had married, if she would be better prepared to confront the soul-shard of an immortal. Or if what Mingan had given her—what Mingan *was*—was as unlike the breath of a child of the Light as it was unlike the clear pale mortal simplicity of Ingraham Fasoltsen's memory.

But whatever, he was in her; she could taste him on her lips as plainly as vomit. Such a small word. So inoffensive.

Thee.

She pawed at her lips as if she could stuff it back down her throat. The Light that seared from her—the Light that he, tarnished, had returned to her with all her lost strength—flickered and paled.

"Carry me under thy heart, sister," he whispered. And the Grey Wolf smiled upon her, and vanished.

Judge me again.

Oh, but she did not *care* to understand him. He was an enemy. It should be enough.

One of his side steps into shadow, the faint rill of Light along his tangled hair, and then where he had stood, nothing. The moment after he was gone, there was Kasimir, ankle-deep in the snow, wings fanned, necks arched as he surveyed the battlefield. *Yes,* she thought, *battlefield,* selecting the word with a poet's care. "Nathr," she said. "Is she there by you?"

You are well?

"Not exactly. *Do you see my sword?*"

She is here. Muire—

This time, the note of repressed panic in his not-voice pierced her own fear and disorientation. She waded through the snow to him, knowing he watched her, that he noted her tangled hair and the light shifting through her irises as if through water, her ungloved hands and bitten mouth—no, that was healed as well—knowing that he *knew.*

And somehow she endured, stumbling through drifts until she could retrieve her blade. The sword blazed in her hand as it had in the dawn of the world, bright as a battle cry, wild as a shout. And Kasimir watched her, and did not judge. There was no need—this sin, she could judge on her own. Was duress an excuse?

Surely not for an angel.

Muire dried the sword with care, blade and hilt, but did not sheathe her. She couldn't bear, just yet, to be parted from the Light, even though it flowed from a polluted spring, sourced in all the lives the wolf had stolen.

Oh, yes. She knew now why silver might tarnish. And Kasimir, watching her, resting softly in her mind, knew also.

She thought of sending him away again, and going after the wolf alone, a tainted hunter in pursuit of tainted prey. She thought of remonstrating with Kasimir, of showing him what she had fallen to. Each time she thought there was no more bottom, somehow she wound up demonstrating the descent.

He snorted his answer. And she looked at him, her sword burning in her hand with an unclean light, and said, "I don't understand this."

You are not tarnished.

"How do you know?"

Your blade knows.

Against that, she had no argument. But she weighed it in her hand a moment, and looked at the way the light fell, the stark blue light and the black tree-trunk and the snow-white snow and the red roses crushed like blood in the pattern of the their struggle. And then she went to him anyway.

She held her hand to his fire, pressed naked flesh tight to withering metal, and felt only warm strength. And then the weight of his head as he reached over her, and pressed his cheek to hers.

I shall not lose you.

Another time, Muire might have waited until they were out of the snow to interrogate Ingraham on his silence. But not today—if days could be said to have any meaning here. Nor was she in a mood to argue with this mortal scrap, not here, calf-deep in the drifts of a dead world. She was healed now, fatted on poisoned strength, and she had Mingan. Though the memories he had left her were fragmentary and confusing, she was determined that they would be enough. One hand on Kasimir for support, Nathr an anchor in her hand, Muire turned herself within.

It was unlike meditation, and also unlike searching one's own memories. More like searching the fragments of a dozen mirrors heaped in a pile. She had fragments, unreconstructed glimpses and imaginings. Too much of it was random, unreadable. Sheer chaos. But there were things both ghosts had found important, which were recent to each memory.

It had gone beyond simply avenging the dead, and—no matter how she sought to deny it—into some deeper mystery.

Ingraham remembered how he had died. And Mingan

remembered how he had done murder. And—though neither of them was happy to share with her—that was a place to start, while she sorted through shatterling histories.

She knew at once when she found the right moment in Ingraham's memory. The scent and texture of the air, the echo of his footsteps, the cold patter of rain on his hair—all conspired to remind her of the night he died. She walked with him, felt the raw chill of the night and the long, soaked cloth package in his hand. That was the delivery. The important thing. The thing Ingraham Fasoltsen had died for touching.

An unman met him at the foot of the stair he had died upon, and Muire saw her with a shock. A shock that Kasimir echoed, because under the fur and armor, the inhuman proportions and the lanky outline, both he and Muire knew her as soon as Ingraham looked into her eyes.

In Ingraham's memory, the Black Silk extended her hand to take the bundle, and Muire reached out with her own left hand as if to lay Nathr across her palm. Then she jerked back, staggering in the snow, slipping against Kasimir's obdurate shoulder. She bruised herself falling, but she was beyond burning now, and it didn't interrupt the memory. Inside her head, Ingraham extended his arm, and slid the bundle into the unman's grasp.

As if it were a real dream, a nightmare, Muire hauled herself free only with effort. She leaned on her steed's shoulder, thickheaded and disoriented, and tried to shake the rag-tatters of phantasm from her psyche but only made her own head spin. If she had stayed with the memory a few minutes longer, she would have lived Ingraham's death with him again. And she could have lived it through the Grey Wolf also, but she did not care to experience that particular luxury again.

Instead, she considered the unman. Muire had seen her the first time and thought nothing of her. But now she had the wolf in her, and the wolf knew—

Selene. Her name was Selene, and Muire knew it because Ingraham knew it. But that had not always been her name.

Herfjotur.

Kasimir blew a massive breath, snow melting before both his noses. With great sweeps of his antlered head, he swept aside drifts, as if he meant to crop the grass beneath. But instead, he sighed more softly and said of the slave soldier who had, in another life, been his rider: **Have we all returned?**

Two is not all. "And if we have? What for?"

And what good does it serve if they know not what they were? If they do not recollect what was, they might have stayed dead, and saved us the pain of remembrance.

"Kasimir—"

He waited, alert to her following question.

"The wolf said you were half-siblings. That his sire was your dam. How is that possible?"

It is not, said Kasimir. **I have no forebears. I was made as I am.** And then a pause, while he shook the snow from his antlers. **That is to say, only paler.**

Whether he had meant her to or not, she laughed. From the smug expression he twisted over his shoulder, it was no accident, but his next question after she controlled herself was serious. **And what sword was that, that Ingraham brought to the moreau?**

If he would not call her Herfjotur, then neither would Muire. And if ever Muire had wondered if the Light was all an illusion, if there were in plain truth any world-girdling, world-guiding hand, she doubted no longer. Strifbjorn *or*

Herfjotur might have been a coincidence. But both of them, reborn and unknowing? No mere trick of fate could be so spectacularly cruel.

Taken in that light, the answer to his question was obvious. "I know what sword it is," she said. "And if you think a moment, so will you."

Svanvitr, he said.

"Of course," she answered. "All you have to do is think about who showed up to claim it."

And failed.

"Well, yes." Muire stepped away from Kasimir's shoulder, half confident she could stand on her own, at last. She slipped Nathr into its sheath across her back, using both hands to steady. "Failure is his habit, after all."

Kasimir lifted both heads to stare at her, as if disbelieving she had said what she had said. She had never heard bitterness enter his tone, but she thought if she would have, it would have been now. **They are**, he opined, **very dramatic failures. As a rule.**

That made it her turn to snort and kick at the snow, so she obliged him. "Saddle, please."

He made her one in a whirl of light, while she found her helm and gauntlets and pulled them on. As she stretched up to the stirrup, her left hand fisted in his near side mane, she said, "Oh, you know another thing?"

Perhaps.

And useless to point out that it was a rhetorical question. "The Wolf accused me of complicity with Thjierry. Of some blasphemous conspiracy. Now that we know what we know . . ."

It has to do with the swords.

"It must. But I don't know what use they would be to any-one not waelcyrge or einherjar."

Kasimir went silent and still, motionless as the statue he resembled. The only sign that we were not frozen in time all over again was the rhythmic drift of steam from his nostrils, a plume for every exhalation.

"Kasimir?"

His diction grew as ponderous as the timbre of his voice. She had never heard him speak this way, as if choosing his words with great care, and the emphasis made her fist her gauntleted hands together.

I think . . . I must take you to see Cristokos.

(D)uire had never flown very much. She'd preferred to avoid mechanical transportation when she could. There had been the brief jaunt astride Kasimir when she was shock-sickly and out of her mind with pain, but that was both transient and delimited within the walls of the nighttime city. Other than that—aircars, rarely, a few short plane flights, twice a semi-ballistic. Oh, and she'd stood on the moon, once, when there were still tourist flights. It was only money, and she hadn't been able to resist that.

This was different. Kasimir's wings rowed the air with long, indefatigable strokes—like a heron's or a raven's, rather than a raptor's hover—and to Muire, crouched along his neck, it seemed as if his body rose and fell between them, rather than the other way around. He took them into the air while they were still by the roots of the tree, spiraling up through branches that made a seeming two-dimensional composition in matte-black against the bottomless indigo of the starlit night.

Does the sun ever rise here?

There is no sun here, said Kasimir. **It was destroyed.**

Muire's eyesight was better in the dark than any human's, and now, though it was restored to what it had been before the Last Day, she still found herself hoping Kasimir's was much better than her own.

The branches they swung between were enormous. *This is what a tree is to a sparrow,* she thought, though there were neither trees nor sparrows anymore. *Is the tree alive?*

Without light, there is no need for leaves. Kasimir couldn't shrug in flight. **But can such a thing die, I wonder?**

We did, she answered. Which was true, and useless, and she closed her gloved hands in his mane and let his furnace heart warm her, though the frigid wind of his ascent stung her eyes. She cast her head back, and for a moment allowed herself the illusion that they could climb as far as the stars, that there was escape and the chance of homecoming.

Foolish, of course. You could never go back. Only forward. And sometimes, there was nothing to go forward into except the ice.

This old world had ended in war and famine and chill. What arrogance was it, for her to imagine that she could save the new one? Wounded as it was, burned to the heart and scarred irretrievably, wasn't it better to let it die and hope something clean rose from the ashes? To tear it down, and start over again?

Wolf, she told the voice in her head, *I do not heed you.*

But neither could she silence him, and all his insinuations.

Niflheim was as it had been, season of mist and shadows and painful memories. She knew when they shifted home, because the transition from darkness to predawn was as abrupt as if someone had lifted the shade from a cage. The rich translucent silk of the dead world's firmament vanished into mist and was then replaced by a thinner sky, pewter with morning light and sere. Air that had been thin and cold choked Muire with the next breath, and she tugged the faceplate of her helm down. The filtered air was better.

Below, she saw the glow of the Defile and the lights of Eiledon flickering fitfully, no more bright than the stars. She thought they would descend, but instead Kasimir spiraled higher and began beating East, toward morning.

The sun's rays struck Kasimir, at his height, before they reached the ground below. Without her polarizing faceplate, Muire would have been dazzled; as it was, she trained her eyes on the ground and watched its slow unveiling until the moment when shadows appeared, cast by the direct rays of the sun. They were not high enough to really see the terminator, but just knowing night still gave way to day was a relief. She had not realized, until it slipped away, what a pall Mingan's graveyard world had cast over her.

Valdyrgard stretched below, and she watched it skim beneath the racing shadow of Kasimir's wings. So much devastation: everything might have been a desert, that was not ruins. She could tell hill from valley, but the slopes were eroded in deep badland runnels, and farm from forest was beyond her. Even the soil was dead; bones—white, or stained ocher—should have long crumbled, but where there was nothing to decompose them they lay heaped or peeking through the cuts of dry washes, glinting here and there like mica chips in granite.

They passed over a silent ocean, where no gulls wheeled, and its beaches were heaped with bones. All the life the sea had cast up to molder, worn by the water and buried in the sand, but still piled high.

Which is better, a world of ice, or a world of bones?

Kasimir did not answer. Instead, he asked, **How is it that you have not flown over this land before?**

"I didn't like flying." With the helm closed, she could speak and hope to hear herself.

Kasimir interrogated her statement, although not really in words. She seemed to him to adapt to flying very well.

"You are not an aircraft," she said. "It's different."

Aircraft? Helicopters? How did you travel?

"I walked," she answered. "There almost always seemed to be plenty of time."

Gebo (gifts)

X

It was rising noon by the time Kasimir turned sharply toward the mountains on the left, and Muire—who had been lost in her own bitter reflections—whooped and grabbed at the pommel. He wouldn't throw her. She never doubted him. But intellectual surety did little to silence the thunder of her blood.

The valraven climbed hard, straining, the rattle of his wings deafening as he pumped for altitude. Clouds obscured Muire's sight for a time, and when Kasimir broke clear she saw a pass, a stark saddleback ridge between two peaks. The air thinned and cleared again as they rose, and she opened her faceplate to feel its sting.

When Kasimir crested the ridge, his hooves so low over the stone she thought they might strike sparks—she shouted.

She had been wrong about the trees and the sparrows, and that at last—after all the long weary hours—silenced the Grey Wolf's nihilistic cynicism. Because below Kasimir's wings, a long steep valley—practically a canyon—bounded in pink granite cliffs stretched into the distance. The base of every slope was thick with pines, and where the pines gave way, wildflowers grew in rank profusion. At the far end of the gorge, a stream tumbled rock to rock, bouncing down natural terraces from its source on the shoulder of that peak, splashing rainbows up the face of each escarpment.

The cold wind brought Muire the smell of pine trees. Her hands knotted in Kasimir's manes, she fought for calm, but her composure cracked, and tears streaked her cheeks until they froze there. *It's real?*

Kasimir, descending on taut wings, answered, **Yes.**

He touched down lightly on a rocky part of the streambed, hooves sizzling in the water, feathertips flicking a spray of crystals into the sun before he settled them. He edged to the bank, careful of the tree branches, and paused beside a ragged boulder of convenient height. Muire swung her leg over his necks—easier than the wings—and slid down his shoulder, aiming her feet to avoid the protruding bits of a logjam. When she was grounded, she patted Kasimir's shoulder and hopped down the rock to the mossy bank below. Kasimir, meanwhile, splashed away into the deepest part of the stream and lowered his heads to drink.

Muire turned back, under the feather-needled bower of the pines, damselflies dancing sequined by the water, and called out, "Where do I find Cristokos?"

Follow the path. He awaits.

And that would be the only answer she would get. He'd been playing coy with her for the entire journey, neither willing to identify Cristokos, nor tell her much about him—except that he was a mage, and a friend. The wolf in her might have been suspicious, but then the real wolf had tried to lead her to be suspicious of her mount. And unlike einherjar, the tarnished were perfectly capable liars.

So Muire, choosing to trust the stallion, allowed herself to be led. If he wanted to play surprise-games, so be it. She could give him that pleasure.

In the back of her head, she felt him snort.

There was indeed a trail, a quite clear one that led diagonally down and away from the streambed. It had been worn by many feet, she thought, or a few feet over a long time, the roots that crisscrossed between the sponge of needles polished like the bones she'd flown over. The understory was clear of deadfall for a long way on either side, and she could see places, gaps in the canopy and divots in the earth, where big trees had come down and must have been sawn up and dragged away. Small trees sprouted in those sunny intervals, racing toward the light, and Muire knew that in each case either two or three would grow together, or the one to climb highest would soon shade the others out. In each sunny patch the saplings had been weeded thin, only the strongest contenders left to make their own fate.

All the evidence confirmed that someone lived here, and managed this wood.

She found herself stopping at random intervals to stare at flickering birds—chickadees, a cardinal—and once crouching to exclaim over a clutch of small toadstools. They grew up among the pine needles, ocher at their tips and jade-colored around the rims, with cream-orange gills and stems shading to peridot at the top. The caps and stems were sticky with some excretion, and as glossy as if they had been glazed and fired in a kiln. They smelled faintly sweet, faintly earthy, and she bent close to detect the aroma but did not touch.

They were so lovely, growing undisturbed and unhusbanded in the shade of those carefully tended trees, that Muire found herself undone. Unmade completely, by a little plant a couple of centimeters across.

She dropped a knee to the path to steady herself against the nausea of grief. It was too much, barbed and bitter under her rib cage and up her throat, so she hung her head between her shoulders and curled her armored hands into the loam while tears and mucus dripped from her eyes and nose. She wished she dared howl, throw back her head and wail, for that might chase the knives from her breast. But she was caged in her heart, as if a bruising collar twisted off her air, and all she gave voice was an ashen whimper squeezed between her lips and the back of the gauntlet she stuffed against her mouth.

So much nothing. It was bottomless, and when she rose each day and did what she found before her to do, she coped simply by not thinking of it. But there was the wolf, as if he stood before her, all that void and emptiness given tongue and eyes.

This time tomorrow, she repeated, *judge me again.*

She could not. No longer. There could be no judgment.

But as she stood, and wiped her mouth and nose on the corner of her much-abused cloak, she determined: there *could* be a reckoning.

She pulled her helm off so the wind could stir her sweat-lank hair. Then she turned, moved through the trees, let the light fall upon her, around her. Songbirds flickered through that same light; she paused to hear the drum of a woodpecker. That could have brought fresh tears, but this time she was ready; set them aside. Bundled and labeled for later.

The path crossed a rill, a tributary to the stream Kasimir had shown her, at which Muire ducked to rinse her face. When she stood, water trickling under her armor to dampen her shirt, she cast her head back and breathed deep, through her nose, as if to clear the lingering stuffiness of her moment of hysterics. This air rode down from mountain heights. It carried the scent of snow laced with alpine flowers, herbs and sunwarmed grasses, the creosote of pines. And no trace of the one she sought.

Downwind, she thought, and only then realized that she was scenting the air like a wolf.

More down, a long walk alone, and she began to appreciate Kasimir's wisdom. She had needed this, the peace, the time in isolation during which to detach, examine, and collect herself. There was a great deal to fathom: the wolf and what he had done; this place; the appalling truth of hope.

There was no chance of coping with any of it. The most she could manage was to put it away for a time.

Which was, after all, what she had been doing since before the Last Day. Fold it up, fold up the lavender within it, and seal it neatly away. No matter what it was; no matter how terrible. That had kept her alive. After a fashion.

The trees began to thin, the pines giving way to mixed growth, and more sun and warmth filtered through. Muire thought she must be reaching the valley floor. She came to another brook, the slope slight enough here that it pooled among the roots of beech and oak and she must follow the trail around. It led her to a bridge of peeled lashed logs over the outflow. By the scorch marks on the wood, she deduced who might have dragged them there. When she crossed, her footsteps made a hollow sound, reflecting off water. At some point in her descent she had stopped limping.

Below the confluence, she caught a glimpse of something black and massive, the whiff of machine oil and char. "Oh, if he made me walk this and then beat me down here—"

In the echo of her mind, there was no answer. And when she stepped out of the trees into a broad clearing, there was no Kasimir.

Rather, she confronted something she had never expected

to see again outside of archived images: a steam locomotive, mulched halfway up its driving wheels in loam and leaf litter, hulking antique, derelict, and enormous in the afternoon light. Behind it was a coal car and three passenger cars, and at the back, a peeling green-painted caboose.

Muire paused, hands hooked inside her helmet, at waist level, and regarded the thing. "You didn't fly this entire train up here."

There is a rail under the soil.

Of course. Things get buried in a forest. "It's been here since the Desolation? Why isn't it rusted?"

She heard the crunch of footsteps approaching, and that warned her enough that she was not surprised when a voice that was not Kasimir's answered. "Cristokos is fixing," it said, and the diction and phrasing were odd enough that when the speaker hove into view around the sweep of the locomotive, Muire was not surprised to find that he was not human.

"You're Cristokos?" She thought she knew the answer, but it seemed polite to ask. "I am Muire."

His nose twitched at the tip of his parti-colored snout. "This one is Cristokos." Then he shocked Muire by leaning forward at a precarious angle, extending his hand, and waiting for her to respond.

She'd never shaken hands with an unman before. She'd never, honestly, thought of one as an individual. But she unlatched her gauntlet, wiggled it off, and reached to make the clasp.

The crooked collection of bones and sinews that made up his hand was stronger than she'd expected, his grip firm and warm. She shook it once and stepped back, reestablishing the distance between them, hiding her shock of recognition. *It's all of them,* she thought, and wondered how it was that she had not noticed before. But Mingan had. And now she carried the Wolf within her. He had known about Cathoair before she had, too.

Cristokos straightened, permitted his hands to fall to his sides, concealed by the draping sleeves of his striped homespun robe. The waist was cinched by a braided leather belt, and a flute in a case hung from it. But it would not be the *right* flute, and Muire forced her attention back to the present, and her eyes away. "You've been restoring the locomotive."

"It is something to do," he said, turning his body away, but glancing invitingly—or warily—over his shoulder. "And the work was waiting."

She took it as an invitation to follow. "It will never move again."

"It is so," he agreed. As soon as she fell in beside him, his gaze fixed on the ground. "Does that one wish refreshment?"

"Don't let me take your food. I don't require it." Glutted on the Grey Wolf's spirit, she suspected she would not feel hunger for a long while.

But Cristokos shrugged and said, "More grows than is needed, and jars for canning are precious. There are strawberries. What is not eaten will only go to compost." He paused, and shot her a sly sideways glance. "Or into the pony."

His delivery was both dry and perfect; in her fragile state, it made her laugh out loud. When she glanced back at him to share the joke, though, he seemed to be studying her, and she realized that his comment had been a test of some sort. "The pony can have as many strawberries as he wants."

"Hmp," said Cristokos. "Here, that one may sit on the steps and rest. This one will fetch what there is."

The steps he indicated were the steep narrow swinging steps to the first of the three passenger cars, and Muire sank onto them with relief. Cristokos bustled off toward the tree line. She laid her helm and gauntlets aside and busied herself loosening the straps of her armor. She paused halfway up the first greave, however, and thought of Kasimir.

Is this safe?

I would have told you, were it otherwise.

She let a sigh escape and continued running her hands up the clasps, which opened to her fingerprint.

And Cristokos. Does he know your name?

She had, she told herself, no cause for jealousy. She had abandoned Kasimir, had left him in isolation for centuries.

He is not my rider, Kasimir answered.

But he is Yrenbend.

Yes. Unhesitating, but in what would have been a hush, had he but spoken aloud.

Kasimir. Are they all back?

I know not. I should not have asked *you*, if I did.

Kasimir.

I know not! And then, soft as the wind. **Ask Cristokos about the swords.**

She pressed him, but he would not answer. And so she stripped her armor off in silence and piled it beside the train, then resheathed Nathr across her back. She stood, arms wide, letting the wind dry the sweat from her garments, and examined her surroundings.

There were fields not far downsteam. She identified nodding grain, still too green for harvest, and the broad leaves of bean plants. From here down, the valley did widen, descending in rock-walled terraces. Cristokos must keep quite busy.

She wondered what purpose all his industry served, when he was here alone and could no doubt have subsisted by foraging. Nevertheless, when he returned carrying a dripping basket, she was happy to sit down across from him on the blanket he spread on the grass.

In the basket were strawberries, protected by cheesecloth and kept cold, apparently, in the glacial stream. There was also soft bland un-aged cheese packed in a glass jar with a screw-on lid and a loaf of bread wrapped up in a towel. That latter must have been placed in the basket after it was removed from the stream, however, because when Cristokos produced it and broke off a piece for Muire, it wasn't soggy at all and the center was still warm.

The only drink was water, and it was yet the best meal she had tasted in ages. The strawberries were no bigger than the caps of the glossy toadstools, and each one had a slightly different flavor from all the others—sweet, tart, viny—so there was adventure in eating them. There were eggs in the bread, and the cheese was *cheese,* not a tank-farmed substitute.

Muire licked a dab off her dirty forefinger and asked, wincing at the faint aftertaste of her own salt.

"This one keeps goats," he answered, and stroked his homespun garment. "Cloth and milk are thus provided. There are no cattle in the valley."

The blade across her back kept Muire sitting straight. She reached for the cold mountain water and did not drink, but cradled the pottery cup between her palms. Had the wolf been walking through the world all this time, seeing the faces of those he had slain worn like masks by random strangers? No wonder he was mad, if what Muire saw wasn't merely evidence of his madness infecting her.

It is not.

If I were crazy, you would say that also. She was met by silence; if he had a rejoinder, he kept it to himself.

She had found Strifbjorn once, centuries before, and wondered if it were a sort of doom that had befallen him, to be reborn endlessly in ignorance, to play out a tragedy time and again. But then there was Cathoair, who was the antithesis of tragedy, and there was the cat-faced moreau Selene, and there was Cristokos with his bizarre dissociating circumlocutions.

Muire wondered if he were damaged. Maybe the urge to serve was so deep-wired into the moreaux that they could only attain self-direction with an injured mind. It was a terrible thought, and it brought with it a wellspring of discomfort with Thjierry, with what she might have done to secure the future of Eiledon.

And then she thought, *But I was also created to serve. And is it so different?*

Muire looked at the unman and gnawed her lips.

"Cristokos," she said, "my steed brought me here to speak with you. About the Technomancer and the wolf. The Grey Wolf."

It wasn't easy to read his face, the jet-bead eyes and the piebald splotches obscuring any expression more subtle than a cringe or a snarl. But it was easy enough to understand the way he glanced down, attention fixed on the bread in his hand and the cheese he spread over it.

Muire thought of taking his wrist, demanding attention, but she thought that unlikely to garner what she needed. Instead, she rocked up onto her knees, reached over her shoulder, and grasped Nathr's hilt. The blade slid free of her sheath with a sound like a stream of water ringing into a bowl. Most things that were not immortal would have flinched from it.

Cristokos sat straight, glanced up, leaned forward. Muire laid the blade across the picnic blanket, and—though her fingers were reluctant to release the hilt—sat back. "My blade," she said. "Nathr. She's not the first such you have seen."

The unman's broad throat worked. He glanced away. "Those are Her tools," he said.

"They're not. Not unless she has appropriated them."

"She has many." The bread in his hand must have gone forgotten; he looked at it in surprise and covered his distress by taking a bite. Strong gnawing teeth made short work.

When he swallowed, Muire leaned forward again. "Cristokos, please."

That *was* a snarl. Just a flicker of one, wrinkles on each side of the long snout, quickly smoothed.

"Does that one say please when she commands her steed?"

If his briefly bared teeth could not make her pull away, the tone of his voice was sufficient. "It is more that we serve the same ideal, than that either of us serves the other."

Cristokos's long fingers could move quickly, a deft dismissive flick beside his face. "But that one accepted his service."

"I did not wish it. And I have a feeling there's no winning this argument with you. Either I did not resist him strongly enough, or I abandoned him when I should have been there to protect him. Is it so?"

He looked up at her, a glance through lashes that could have been coquettish, but she thought was rather mulish now. She nudged the sword toward him with the backs of her fingertips, nails clicking softly on the hilt. "Thjierry took yours, didn't she? She didn't ask. She created you her animal, and she bound you to her will. It was written on your bones when she made you. She carved the runes deep."

The moreau flinched. He set aside his supper and covered his face with his hands. "She did what She thought needful."

And how it hurt him to defend Thjierry, Muire would never, she thought, comprehend. But still, even now, even here in his hard-won freedom, Cristokos could not sit and listen to Muire speak ill of her who had been his mistress.

Yes. She *had* been created to serve. And though she had failed her service, she understood now with terrible clarity that it meant something, to be allowed the option to fail.

"How many swords are there, Cristokos?"

He shrugged. "An approximation, four hundred." Not even half of the swords; not even half of the children, who had never been many. "Her unmans are forbidden to touch them."

"And how many moreaux?"

He looked longingly at Nathr, laid across the blanket between them. Muire made her hands very still and looked away: tacit permission. "An approximation? Four hundred."

Muire closed her eyes. But she did not hear the whisper of cloth that would mean he reached forward to touch her sword.

He cleared his throat. "This one touched such a blade by accident."

"And then you escaped," Muire said. Not damaged, then. Just unbound, only partially, under uncontrolled circumstances. He still carried the Technomancer's bond. But he had externalized it, made it other.

And there had been a price.

Cristokos shrugged. She could hear the cramped spaces and fearful hiding in his tone when he said, "This one is a rat. Rats are for sneaking."

She turned back to him. He reached out softly and laid his fingertips against the black crystal of Nathr's blade. And deep within, barely visible in the strong afternoon sun, an eddy of starlight answered.

15

Fehu (possessions)

ᚠ

"She's at least five hundred years old," the Technomancer said. "I suspect she's much older, but that was as far back as I could trace her."

"She's from before the Desolation." From the vantage of Cathoair's nineteen years, it was a span beyond bewildering, into incomprehensible.

"Well." The tilt of the Technomancer's head was an old woman's mockery of a young woman's simpering. It charmed him. "So are a few of us. But not all of us are quite so well preserved. I presume, from your startlement, that she had not taken you into her confidence, Cathoair?"

He shook his head.

She sighed, her hoverchair scooting backwards in response to a command he did not catch, and beckoned him to follow. "It was too much to hope for," she said, as he walked alongside. "She never trusted Gunther either, did she?"

"Not with that," the disembodied voice answered.

It did not take a great deal of native genius for Cathoair to figure out that they wanted something from him. He thought of Muire quoting poetry in the darkness, his own flip dismissal of the religion behind it, her pursuit of the Grey Wolf. He thought of the sword in her hand, and shook his head and snorted through his nose. Ridiculous. Ridiculous to imagine. The more ridiculous because he suspected he was right.

He'd been harboring designs on *that*?

"Something?"

Cahey, startled back into himself, almost jumped. "I'm not certain," he said. "I think you know her better than me. We only just met. We're not friends; she pays me."

"Pity," the Technomancer said. "I know she's not mortal. But there are so many possibilities. Do you think she might be an alf, the last alf?"

She sounded wistful, actually. And she looked it, eyes dreamy and hands relaxed on the control bars of her chair.

"It's a reasonable theory," Cathoair said, choosing his words with great care. He could have agreed unequivocally, but somehow the lie troubled him. And he couldn't very well say, *Oh no, she's an angel. She's been hunting her enemy for thousands of years, and it's just your luck she caught up with him about when he decided you needed killing. Aren't you fortunate?*

There was a pause. They traveled down another beige corridor, the doors swinging open before them without a touch and sealing behind.

That must be Gunther's doing. In any case, Cathoair had to stride out to keep up with the chair.

The last door opened onto sunlight. Midmorning now, and class must be in session. Cathoair could hear voices through open windows, but the only person in sight was a young woman propped on her elbows in the grass, her hair falling around her book and her bare feet kicked up from the knee so her full skirt puddled over her thighs. She might have been his own age.

His palm pressed his scar. He pulled it away, and stuffed his hand into his pocket again.

The Technomancer seemed oblivious. "It seems like there used to be so much more magic in the world," she said. And then she shook herself and looked up at him, smiling. "My Selene said you fought the Grey Wolf. And forgive me for saying, but you look like you got the worse end of that fight. How is it you lived?"

Cathoair thought about that very carefully before he answered. Somehow, his memory for things concerning the Wolf—and Muire, for that matter—seemed very crisp. Vivid, as if only they were real and the rest of his life had been a dream.

He remembered hard hands turned generous, and shuddered. "It wasn't what he wanted," he said. "He didn't want to kill me."

"Or Muire?"

"I don't know." That, Cathoair could answer without dissembling. "He vanished. She went after him. I don't know—"

"She's very old," the Technomancer said, and Cahey thought she meant it to be comforting.

"You haven't met him," was all he could say.

Her chair moved over the gravel and grass silently, the footprint of its repulsor field pressing the blades flat. When she had moved on, they sprang up again without harm. When they passed the girl on the grass, she hid her face behind her hair, but she seemed more awed than afraid. Nevertheless, Cahey caught himself scratching at his face again.

He couldn't hide the scar, though, and he didn't need to be ashamed. Other than his mother, who had been there when it happened, only Astrid and Aethelred had any idea what it meant, and they would never tell.

To cover the gesture, he held the hand out and caught sunshine cupped in the hollow. The Technomancer craned her neck curiously. "This is the sunlight that doesn't fall where I live."

"You were born in the Well?"

"We're not allowed in the Ark." He shrugged, and turned his hand as if he could let the light spill from its hollow like water. "It's protected."

"You're afraid of the sky, is what it is. I never intended for people to move down there."

"But you had to know they would. The city is crammed to bursting. And we have nothing. A little extra protection—what if there was radiation, whatever, something the Defile couldn't handle? So you get all *this* earth overhead and hope."

She looked at him, cannily, eyelids half lowered. "You're not stupid," she said. "What can you learn?"

He shrugged. "I can't read. What *can* I learn?"

"I'm sorry," she said. And she seemed to mean it. "That's my failing. If I were what I should be . . ."

"Ma'am. No one can carry every burden." He meant it, too. She seemed as if she believed she had failed him personally.

Her mouth worked for long moments before settling on a smile. "We must choose what we weep for, Cathoair?"

"If you like." But he nodded.

The Technomancer lifted her chin and looked away. "Gunther, fetch Selene please. Or Borje, if she is busy."

"As you wish, Thjierry."

Cahey sort of wished there was a sense of presence when Gunther appeared and vanished, but—nothing. He wasn't used to being surprised; one of his knacks was knowing where people were. Always—in a crowd, in a dark room, around a corner. Gunther made him nervous. Jumpy. More than a little.

"Cathoair." The Technomancer's formality of tone commanded his attention. He turned to face her. She continued, "You must be in pain and if I were you, I would want food and sleep and a bath quite badly. One of my moreaux will take you to a room where you may refresh yourself. I will wish to speak with you further."

He opened his mouth, about to plead his case on behalf of his mother. *She's dying. She doesn't have anyone else.* The Technomancer was a kind old woman, and every word she had said to him was the deep-dyed truth as she believed it. She would surely take steps to aid him.

The dying had the gift of ruthlessness. He knew that by hard experience. And there was something in her expression as she looked up at him that stopped his voice completely.

"Thank you," he said. The last words to part his lips until Selene arrived to lead him away.

Selene's palms would not stop itching.

If she had touched some unfamiliar plant, made contact with an unidentified substance, she could have understood it. However, there was nothing. Nothing.

And it was a maddening sort of itch. Not one Selene could shrug off, put out of her mind. This was like the nagging of her sex when her heat had used to come upon her, before she was changed: compelling, compulsive . . . *mandatory.*

But unlike a heat, she did not know what to do about *this.*

She was on her way to the infirmary for a lotion when the summons came. Not much time would have been lost if she continued—it was only a slight detour—but She was accustomed to a prompt response, and Selene took a great pride in exceeding expectations.

She rubbed her palms against her thighs in a manner that was becoming something of a nervous tic, and gave Gunther an ETA, measured in seconds.

She beat it, too.

When Selene arrived in the Quadrangle, She was still with the nearman, who did not—by Selene's understanding of human scent and facial cues—seem happy. It must be awkward wearing one's whole interior life on display, for anyone to read. Something to do with primate hierarchy and band structure, team hunting behavior predicated on being able to see where a comrade was looking and what he was feeling. But that was how the monkeys cooperated, by direction of gaze and expression and verbal signals. Selene guessed it wasn't really an obvious set of signs unless you had the keys. Even the monkeys seemed to make a lot of mistakes, and one would expect it to be hardwired into them what each set of wrinkles and grimaces conveyed.

She looked up as Selene came within view, but waited until she was quite close before speaking. The nearman—Cathoair—followed her line of sight, and Selene thought his expression brightened. This was not a response she was accustomed to, from humans—trumans, nearmans, halfmans were generally unhappy to notice the arrival of one of Her representatives.

"Selene," She said, "please take Cathoair to a dormitory, and see that he is fed and made comfortable."

An easy enough request, and Selene also understood that it was given to her not as something beneath a Black Silk, a punishment for failing to take the Grey Wolf—She did not punish Her servants—but because She thought there might still be more to learn from Cathoair. And that was a delicate task, un-suited to any but the first rank.

"It will be my pleasure," Selene said, and gestured for the nearman to follow.

Which he did, without complaining, with only a nod to Her to excuse himself from Her presence. Not that She minded informality; Her power was a fact, no frail construct that must be buttressed with ceremony.

But Selene had gone barely four steps when Her voice arrested her stride. "Selene?"

"Yes?"

"Are you well?"

Selene paused, considering. Considering what in her behavior might have made Her ask, considering the itch in her palms and the frustrations of recent failures. Not her fault, no, and She would never hold Selene accountable. She would say it was Her own responsibility, that She had not prepared Selene adequately, nor created her adequate to the task.

For the first time that she could recall, Selene did not care to hear that reassurance now.

"Fine," she said, and—nodding her excuses—beckoned the nearman on.

It was an effort, but Cathoair remained silent as Selene led him down graveled paths and through acres of gardens, things he had never seen—flowers that seemed to exist for the sake of being flowers only, and trees that gave shade and scent and clean oxygen but served no other evident purpose. Everything was sunlit here, and the air was clean, cleaner than anything he'd ever smelled, so he could pick out what must be the distinct aromas of different flowers. A truman with a push-mower cut the grass; the sunwarmed scent was dizzying. They came to the river and crossed it on an arched stone bridge, and when he stared down into the water, he half expected to see fish.

It was as if he had somehow been transported back in time, to another world. And through it all, Selene walked a few steps diagonally ahead of him, tail flicking lightly against her calves, as if this were perfectly ordinary, perfectly everyday.

To his own surprise, Cathoair grew angry. "By what right?" he asked, only half aware he spoke aloud. And then Selene glanced over her shoulder at him, incurious eyes in her broad feline face, and he stammered his embarrassment. "Sorry."

"What is your question?" Her ears flicked forward. She hadn't a mane, precisely, not like a lion's. But her face was surrounded by a thick ruff of variegated pewters, smokes, silvers, and pearls, and his fingers ached to touch it.

Oh, what the Hel. "By what right do you have all this," he asked, "when we have . . . darkness? By what right does your world cast mine in shadow? What gives you the right to plenty?"

She stopped short and turned to him, and he tensed himself for a blow that never fell. A low rumble vibrated the air between them, and he thought at first it was a growl, but just as he was about to step back, he realized that it was a different sound entirely.

Her eyes were squeezed in what must have been her smile, and the sound she made was *purring*. It sounded nothing at all like the simulations of cats he had seen and heard on vii.

"If you think this is plenty," she said, "you should see how they live in Ark."

Cathoair found himself staring at her, flabbergasted. By the way Selene shook her head, though, he could sense her frustration. "This is a trust," she continued. Her hand swept out. "Someone has to keep it. So when the world has had time to heal, there will be something to repopulate it."

"Us. *You?*"

"Moreaux are sterile." She said it defensively. If she were human, he would have guessed the lifted chin was defiance, but he was musing too much about unman body language already, and he knew it could play him spectacularly wrong.

"I'm sorry," he said, hoping she would understand what was he felt the need to apologize for. Not her sterility, exactly, or his own ignorance, but—

"It is nothing. We do not die. And I had kittens in the before—"

She shrugged. If she meant, as he thought she meant, that they had been born when she was just an animal, before the Technomancer uplifted her, then those kittens were long dust, and any potential descendents with them. Nothing survived outside the walls of Eiledon, now that its lone sister-survivor had fallen. The outside world was a poisoned ruin, and those who went there to salvage—which was what Cathoair's father had done—went into danger.

She still stared at him, and he wished he could read her face. "Me too," he blurted, because the weight of her regard was such that he had to say something, and that was the only thing he could think to say that wasn't insensitive or condescending.

She stared harder, tail lashing. "Do not mock me."

"No—" He held up a hand. "Me, too. I'm sterile, too. I'm nearman because of an engineered flu. Supersoldier bug."

"And it rendered you infertile. Of course. They loved that trick in the old days; render the troops barren, and maybe if you fought hard for them, *they* would give back your future children after the war."

"And now *they* are gone. And here we are." Cathoair started walking forward again, in the direction Selene had been leading him, because it was easier than looking at her face. "It's not so bad. My partner doesn't want babies, and she's not the only one who likes not having to worry."

Selene caught up effortlessly. "Come on," she said, and if she changed the subject out of pity for his babbling, he wasn't offended. "I'll show you the rose garden."

Selene had not expected to like the nearman. She didn't like humans as a rule; they were too self-conscious, too enmeshed in their ego-reinforcement games. And Cathoair had that. It wasn't that he was unlike other humans, because he was—egocentric, confused, scrabbling.

But he was also something else. He watched her with awareness. He did not mock her service, even by implication, even when he did not condone the means by which she served. And so she found herself picturing him as a peer, a companion. His polished skin and bound-back hair made her think of a stallion, nervy and long-necked and proud, and Selene wished for a bitter moment that he could have been one of Hers.

But he was not. And so all Selene could do in her own right to reward him for approximating worthiness was to let him stay for a while in the sun.

The rose garden lay behind the old Botany building, appropriately. It was over an acre square, bordered by high briar thickets, and one of Selene's brethren sat crosslegged on the grass before the gate, weeding out the bed.

Even after the end of the world, there was weeding.

"Hello, Orpheus."

"Hello, Selene." He was a mockingbird, gray-feathered and white-barred. For a joke, he mimicked her voice so perfectly that Cathoair turned to look at her when Orpheus spoke.

Selene squeezed her eyes to show she appreciated the humor. "This is Cathoair. One of Her guests. I am here to show him the garden."

"Let me move," he said, and scooted aside so they would not have to walk over him. And so they entered the garden.

It was very fine in the sun, full of warmth and scent and the rustle of leaves, the hum of insects.

"What are those?"

Selene had to push Cathoair's pointing hand aside with the back of her own to keep him from poking a honeybee. The insect buzzed away, frosted with pollen like flakes of gold leaf, and Cathoair glowered at her.

"It's a bee," Selene said. "Don't touch. If you scare it, it stings you, and it dies." She took a deep breath as he sheepishly withdrew his hand. "And some people have a fatal anaphylactic reaction to the venom. Even if you don't, it smarts."

He nodded, accepting her correction, unhumiliated. "Thank you." He leaned forward, though for a better look. "Where do they come from?"

"They're the last bees in the world. She salvaged the hives."

"Oh." She noticed he kept his hands laced one inside the other, behind his rear. She approved. Right up until the moment when he turned, arms still locked behind his back, and kissed her human-style, full on the mouth.

Warm, musty, richly man-scented breath flowed across her face. His lips were weird, muscular, flexible, and they moved in complicated fashions. His cheek brushed her whiskers; they slicked back automatically, as if she had been rubbing her face against him to claim him with her scent glands. It was bizarre, a bizarre behavior, and for a moment she thought about apes and mating behaviors and their monkey germs and how *strange* everything humans did was.

But what shocked her most was that she did not pull away.

She let him do it, rather, and then when he pulled slightly away she rubbed her cheek quickly on his chin and then licked the tip of his nose.

"Ow!" He jerked back, one hand touching where her tongue, like a rasp, had left a raw place. The salt and blood of him filled her mouth, and now her flews were tingling, itching too. She leaned in, purring, and he backed away a step. "You bit me."

"Licked," she said, working her tongue against her palate to explore the flavor of his skin. "If I had bitten, you would not be talking." And then she yawned, so he could inspect her mouth, the finger-thick canines, premolars like shearing chisels, and the reverse-barbed surface of her tongue, adapted for smoothing fur and shredding meat off bones.

"Oh," he said, as he had said about the bees. "So that wasn't such a good idea?"

She blinked, and considered, and slicked her whiskers against her face in contemplation. "It's what humans do to friends."

"Yes."

"And grooming is what cats do to friends. So you may assume that if I found it strange, I did not—too much—object to it." And then, because she felt wicked and whimsical, which were not emotions she was accustomed to, she added, "So what *have* you got, besides pretty?"

"Try me and find out," he said. He smiled widely, cheek twisting around his scar.

Selene, in sudden cowardice, shook her head and backed away. "I'll show you your room," she said, wondering if this was why the cryptic immortal had taken him into her company.

Seemingly cowed, he let her lead him to the dormitory and show him the small suite he would inhabit. But when she left him there and locked the door between them, she was perfectly aware that his gaze remained on her until the narrowing crack was sealed. And once it was, Selene leaned against the wall beside it and licked her chops and tried to get the taste—and the itch—out of her mouth.

"Gunther?"

"See what?" he answered, without hesitation.

She laughed, a cat's soundless amusement, and nodded thanks.

She liked Gunther a lot.

It developed that Cristokos did not live on the train, or even particularly near it. He inhabited a house—a log home, too spacious for Muire to be quite comfortable calling it a cabin, even if it was one in every technical detail. But in Muire's head, at least, cabins were still what they had been five or six hundred years before, on a more eastern continent. One room, rough-hewn, and if one were lucky enough to have a plank floor instead of rammed earth, one spent a fair fraction of one's time sweeping out the sawdust from the borer beetles that inevitably inhabited one's walls under the bark.

This was a structure with two rooms and a loft, a mortared fieldstone fireplace, a laid stone floor. It was a cabin the way Cristokos was a rodent. Yes, surely, that was a description. But it was not even remotely the whole story.

And now Muire stood on its porch and watched the sun go down, something she had not seen undimmed by the Defile in centuries. The sun slid behind mountains while it was still high in the sky, leaving indirect light to reflect down into the valley. Twilight lingered long, but this did not lessen the drama of the colors.

This sunset flamed vermilion and incarnadine, fluorescent oranges, unreal colors that Muire could barely believe existed outside of the forge. So she barely noticed when Kasimir materialized in a gravel patch provided for his use to the left of the porch, rustled folded wings, and stared at her.

She waited until the sky had grayed before she spoke.

"I could stay here forever."

You could.

"No one could ask more of me than I have done." It was hard to get that out without glancing at him for a reaction, but she managed.

No one with a modicum of compassion.

Muire snorted and dusted her hands by slapping them against her hips. "Well, that lets *me* out, then. You're taking this very well."

Because you're not sincere.

"You question my resolution?" But now she was teasing, and she knew it had gotten into her voice.

Not at all. Thus it is that I know you will return to Eiledon. The slap of steel wires against steel hide as he swished his tail. **What calls you home, Muire?**

You're making fun of me.

With you so brave? Nay, never. Both his heads stretched long on their necks, and his ears wobbled. She rolled her eyes and looked away.

She expected some word from the splinters that threaded her soul: Fasoltsen, or the wolf. But they were voiceless. "Why now? Why have so many of us returned? Were we assembled to fight the Desolation and failed?"

And why do you know them now, when you did not before?

"I knew Cathoair."

Gravel rattled under Kasimir's hooves. He bit off mouthfuls of grass with a ripping sound, and chewed slowly. He said nothing, and he didn't need to. She had known Cathoair because she was pathetic; because she looked for Strifbjorn in every passing face. But Kasimir's questions had been rhetorical, and she already had the answer: Mingan would have known them, and so now so did she. She was restored to strength, brought back from the edge of the shadows.

That was all.

It shocked her to realize how frail—how human—she'd grown.

"It's simple, isn't it? Once you have all the evidence. Thjierry somehow collected a number of my brethren's swords, and she's using them to summon back the dead. She's using their souls to animate her constructs, and their swords to control and enslave them. And the wolf does not approve, and intervened too late, and so managed to kill the messenger but not retrieve the blade."

Your understanding matches mine. And moreover.

"Moreover," she said, "the wolf sees no reason to salvage this world, when it is already so ruined. He'd rather tear it down. It would not, after all, be the first time. And the Techno-mancer and her constructs are the only thing between Eiledon and the wolf, and Eiledon and the Waste." She reached out and rested one palm flat on the porch-pillar, rubbing the smooth peeled wood. "So what are we going to do about it?"

Simple, Kasimir informed her, **does not mean easy. Are you ready?**

She rubbed futilely at her nape. "Let's say good-bye to your friend the rat before we go."

Berkano (family)

After another long flight, Kasimir returned Muire to Eiledon in the middle of the night. The trickiest part of the journey was passing through the Defile unnoticed. Muire was certain, given what she now understood, that she did not wish to come to Thjierry's notice any more than she already had. But Muire, along with the Technomancer and a handful of other magicians, had raised the thing; if she could not pass through it undetected, no one could. And so they came in under cover of darkness, Muire whistling a spell of concealment until they were down.

She went home first, leading Kasimir in to her foundry through the glass courtyard doors, wondering if they had managed to sneak past Sig or if she would have some explaining to do. The stallion settled down in the corner by the forge like a giant dog, wings furled tightly and one chin resting beside his hooves. The far neck craned over the crest of the near one, head propped on his own mane, as he observed her sleepily. She wondered for a moment how his brain worked; was his consciousness divided, or a gestalt? Was one head dominant, or did they serve different functions? It was obvious at least that one could keep watch while the other slept . . . but how did it *work*?

Magic, he said.

Which was, she supposed, a good enough answer. She stumped upstairs to shower, change, and charge her vii so she could check messages. The poor thing had gone dead seeking signal in the otherworld, and she owed Cathoair an explanation. In his place, she would be frantic.

She placed it in the induction field and powered it on. As she had expected, once the *happy birthday* was over with, the message chime dinged fast and frequently enough that she lost count. She scrolled through the list once while she was stripping for the shower and did not find Cathoair's code tag. Astrid's and Aethelred's, however, each appeared more than a dozen times.

"Shadows," she said, and checked the first and last couple of messages in the queue.

And then she was flying down the stairs, pulling a clean shirt over her head so fast she tore it along a seam, hopping on one flour-white leg after the other to pull her trousers on. Kasimir did not need to ask what the problem was; she showed him, and he started to heave himself to his feet.

"No," she said. "Stay here. You're conspicuous—" an understatement "—and I can call you if I need you."

What shall I do if someone enters?

No one was likely to, except Sig.

Muire found socks and boots and slung Nathr's baldric over her shoulder. "Pretend you're a work in progress," she answered, and ran still-barefoot for the door.

Perhaps it would have been wise to have called ahead, but Muire had left her vii sitting in the charger, and even if its battery were not flat, by the time she remembered it was too late by far to go home and fetch it. She actually considered calling a cab, but thought she could run the distance in less time than it would take for transportation to arrive.

And so she ran.

Flat out, dodging the street traffic, her feet slapping a rhythm for her breathing. Running now, as if it made a difference. Running as if the time for haste were not already irretrievably lost.

Nathr banged her spine, her shirt flapping in the wind of her passage, one sock twisted inside a hurried boot. And people cleared a path for her, as if her haste obliged passage. They stepped aside, or she sidestepped, and once someone who saw her coming across the bridge shouted *Make a hole* and miraculously, the hole appeared.

She cleared the descent into the Well in a controlled avalanche, down the steps in two bounds, and plunged into the crowds of streetlit merrymakers, cutpurses, and whores. A Mongrel might have detained her, curious where she was bound with such dispatch, but he never so much as brushed her sleeve.

She hit the doorway of the Ash & Thorn still trotting, and almost got clotheslined by the bouncer. But she managed to stop before tumbling into his embrace, which she had to assume was good luck, given his expression.

"You have some nerve," he said, and latched onto her wrist with a grip she could have broken without effort.

Instead, she let him hold her, though he squeezed hard enough to creak a mortal woman's bones. "Has Cathoair come back?"

"They've been calling you, trying to find him," the man answered, taken aback enough by her directness to slip a little.

Hrothgar, that was his name. The one with the blue hair, whom Cathoair had kissed in the ring.

Just Muire's luck.

Yrenbend's remembered voice mocked: *There are seen hands and unseen hands, little sister. Angels do not believe in coincidence.*

"I'm not the one who ended up a rat," she muttered.

"Excuse me?"

Oh, shadows, she'd said it out loud. The wolf-sherd laughed in her heart. She shook her head, wondering if the jangle of voices was already driving her mad.

In any case, the hand on her wrist was plain enough for all to see.

"That's why I'm here," she said. "I hadn't been home to check messages. I came as soon as I heard—" She stepped back a pace, so her arm leashed between them.

Hrothgar gave a small tug. Not hard. "Come on. I think we'd better talk to Astrid."

He led her downstairs without releasing her, and that he left the front door unguarded reinforced Muire's deductions about how seriously Cathoair's friends took his disappearance. Hrothgar brought her through the crowd—thinned, now that the fighting was done for the evening—and into a back room she should have suspected the existence of if she had ever taken a moment to wonder.

And there he left her. The latch clicked as he pulled the door shut.

Astrid would doubtless be along in a moment, so Muire took advantage of that moment to straighten her blouse and appraise her situation. Hrothgar hadn't tried to relieve her of her blade, which was for the best—both for his own safety and for what it revealed about the circumstances of her custody. Also, the room in which she had been left was a failure as a prison cell. Most mortals would have been able to break the door or the lock, and the hinges were on the inside. Even if they had taken her sword, this place was full of potential weapons: the weights on the exercise bench; the chain from which a kick bag depended; the bottles of alcohol; the table and the chairs.

Muire slipped out of her baldric, hung Nathr over one post of a ladder-back chair, and sat to wait.

No more than five minutes later, the door swung open again and Astrid and Aethelred entered. The chrome-skulled bartender breathed like a bellows in the dim room, which made Muire suspect he must have been hauling his metal armature up and down stairs at speed, and Astrid's hair was unbraided and had left a long wet semi-transparency down the shoulder and front of her misbuttoned blouse. She had a bowl of water in her hand, and reached out gingerly to set it on the table-edge within Muire's reach. "Hrothgar said you had been running."

"Thank you," Muire said. She cupped it in one hand and let the water touch her lips, as much to hide her face for a moment as to quench her thirst, and waited for Astrid to play her next card while Aethelred leaned against the wall beside the door.

Astrid, no disappointment, cleared her throat. "What exactly is it you've gotten Cahey into?"

"I don't know where he is," Muire answered. "I haven't spoken with him in over a day. Tell me what I can do to help."

She put all her conviction into it, sitting back in the chair, doing her absolute best to appear relaxed. Astrid just eyed her, fingers tapping on the opposite forearm. "So you don't have any idea why the Technomancer has arrested him?"

There was *someone* in Astrid too. The intensity in her expression bordered on a flash of light, and Muire, full of the Grey Wolf's strength, could no more have missed it than she could have missed her fingers on the end of her own arm. *As if her name wasn't enough of a clue, you idiot?*

The folded arms, the arch expression, were such that Muire could almost see the outline of her long-lost sister, as if Astrid wore a waelcyrge's ghost as a cloak. And Muire wasn't sure if it was herself or the wolf-sherd that quailed most when she realized who it was that stood before her, wrapped in mortal flesh and innocent of her own existence.

Sigrdrifa.

For a moment, Muire feared she'd said the name aloud.

Was it a doom then, that they would be betrayed from within by the same hands as before? The wolf-sherd bristled in her bosom, all bared teeth and lust after blood. Muire, with effort, gentled it, though it cost her. It was not yet time to make such judgments. If it would ever be her place to do so.

If not yours, then whose?

Muire could not answer him. Nor Astrid, neither. But it was a relief to bare her teeth, and so she did, and said, "I can't be certain. But I know how to win him back."

The threat of death is not what baffles the wolf. Death cannot dismay him. But the possibility that his death could thwart his purpose—*that* binds him in the shadows, keeps him from stepping through the Technomancer's wards into her Tower.

It would be easy to enter. A single short step out of shadows, and he would be among her creatures like a fox among chickens. Like a wolf among sheep.

Once, he would have taken that single, short step. Out of the half-world and into the fire. Strange to think on it now, when he is old and moth-eaten, but he had been impulsive once. Quick to love, quick to lunge.

He has learned a great deal about trickery since. The Technomancer has survived her enemies in this fortress for more than three hundred years. None of those enemies are—were—the Grey Wolf, it is true. But Mingan is not fool enough to think that makes them unformidable.

There was a time when he knew himself unbreakable, unrivalled. Unmatched in hunger and strength. There was a time when he knew a great many things. And he has learned that he had been wrong about most of them.

Now, he has the rage of the sun-eater and the sorrow he drank down with Muire's breath, and he is certain of nothing. So he lingers between spaces, liminal, indeterminate, watching for a glimpse of his enemy's face or the face that never was his lover's, and waiting.

He has also learned to wait.

Perthro (casting lots)

ᚹ

Rescuing Cathoair did present a series of somewhat intractable technical challenges. The first of these was that of gaining access to the Tower. It was a floating island; the approaches were controlled; it was a sorcerer's holdfast. The obvious solution would be Kasimir, but Muire preferred to hold him in reserve.

Especially as he was their most reliable means of escape.

Kasimir suggested the possibility that Mingan's kiss might have left Muire with the ability to pass through shadows, but the technique was not intuitively obvious, and the wolf-sherd at least superficially unforthcoming. Muire thought she might have successfully interrogated it, given time . . . but time was in extremely short supply. And there was the other issue. The one that informed her options and made Muire's eventual decision a foregone choice before she knew it herself.

Muire had business with Thjierry, had had it since she took Cristokos's hand and understood who he used to be, and how he had come to return in that form. Whatever her goal, what Thjierry had done—perverting sacred weapons to enslave sentient beings—was more than obscene. It was blasphemous. Anathema.

So there was a single real possibility. Muire would present herself, plainly and in her own person, at the gate to the tower.

In the interests of combining alacrity with symbolism, Muire made the approach at sunrise. Alone, over Astrid's objections.

"I know you don't trust me," Muire had said. "And honestly you have no reason to. But if I can't bargain with—with the Technomancer, then we'd be stupid to give her more leverage than she already has."

And Astrid had answered, "I can take care of myself." She lifted her chin, staring Muire down across her height advantage. "He's my partner. I've known him since we were kids."

Muire opened her mouth to retort, *You're still children,* and couldn't, quite. Cathoair wasn't yet twenty, unless Muire was seriously underestimating his age, and she didn't think Astrid was more than five years older. They were irresponsible, carefree, living hand to mouth, and if either of them ever was likely to settle down to responsibility, Muire would be very surprised. But it wasn't glimpsing the ghost of Sigrdrifa in Astrid's eyes that silenced Muire.

It was the realization that no matter how feckless and young they were, they never had been children. No more than Muire herself had. Less so, even; Muire might have walked out of the starlit sea a woman grown, but she had been centuries old before anyone had expected her to make a hard decision or, once she had made it, defend it. And when she had, it hadn't gone so well.

While she'd had to fight for her life, and her supper, she'd never had to whore for it. She looked down. "I'm sorry. I can't take you."

"I can take myself."

Muire had spread her arms wide in exasperation. "I can only get two away safely!" she said, sharper than she had intended.

And Astrid had taken a step back. "Oh," she'd said. "Why didn't you say so?"

So it was that Muire waited alone—except for the unman operator—and unarmored—because she was maintaining the pretense that she came as a guest—on the intentionally rickety lift platform, staring up at the bright gray morning while the cage descended. Muire did not think there would be sun today, or rain either, but clouds had come in the night. She squinted against their unhealthy luminescence. The glow did not come entirely from either the day-faded Defile nor the occluded sun, and she was glad not to be in the open, unprotected beneath such a sky.

The unman beside her worked the lift controls silently, and Muire made an effort to treat him as etiquette demanded—as no more than a part of the furniture. But every time he caught on her peripheral vision she started, and had to look away quickly so she would not stare. Because under his skin, he was one of her brothers, too.

The wolf is mad, you know. You have no guarantee that this is anything but contagious delusion.

It told her something, though—that he was seeing the unmans as avatars of the Light, and had chosen only to slay Thjierry's human servants under his vendetta.

Not that a human life should mean less than an angelic one.

He was tarnished. He had taken that first guiltless life, and all those after, and he would never be clean again. But if he were unwilling to murder his brethren— Oh, she didn't know what she was hoping for. Hoping for a reason to believe he could be saved, and that was daft.

The cage clanked on the edge of the platform, and she stepped forward. She hadn't expected it to be empty; unmans, surely? An honor guard, or just a guard? But there was nothing, and she glanced over her shoulder once, just to make sure the operator intended her to proceed.

But he nodded, and she stepped in. Alone.

The grille rolled shut, and she rested one hand on the grab bar, pretending it was for balance only. And then with a creak of cables, the lift started upward, and Muire forced herself to relax. The wind whipped her skirt around her calves, and she reached around her hip with her free hand to catch the pierced-work eagle chape at the bottom of Nathr's cherry-leather scabbard and steady the blade.

If she died here, now, well—she wouldn't have to keep fighting, then, would she? And if that happened, Cathoair would be safer in Thjierry's tower than where Mingan could get to him.

Oh, yes, defeatism, and she didn't really mean it. But then, she wasn't really scared of the cable snapping, either.

And then a masculine voice, one she thought she should recognize, spoke in her ear, and said, "Happy birthday, Muire," and she was glad she'd taken a grip, because it prevented her from spraining an ankle when she spun and her foot caught on the barred floor.

"Who are you?" Microspeakers, probably, but that didn't make the disembodied voice less unsettling. Nor did the fact that she *nearly* knew it.

"She's forgotten me already," he said, and sighed windily. "You don't look a day over a hundred and fifty, you so know."

The lift cage rocked hard in the wind; she balanced over the bump without really noticing. "Gunther."

"In the—voice. I've missed you," he said, his enthusiasm ringing bright and hysterical. "Did you get my messages?"

"The happy birthdays." There was grit on the grab rail, a little rust showing through the chrome, that bit into her palm when her fingers tightened. The sky was growing brighter as the sun rose. The crawling light that shimmered along the cloud-base did not so much dim as it was washed away. Muire thought of semiprecious moonstone, and the way its blue adularescence dulled in hard light. Any of a dozen things could be lurking up there: rogue nanotech, undispersed battle-magic, some ancient and hovering summoned malevolence. Or it could be nothing at all, just a sickly glow. That quality of light sucked all saturation from colors, made her burgundy skirt dull brown and the ocher-and-blue slate roof of the building she was rising past seem as drab as its granite gutterspout gargoyles.

"Yeah," the voice that said it was Gunther replied. "Thjierry said I couldn't call anyone. But she didn't say I couldn't send a card."

Muire squeezed her eyes shut and said, "I buried you."

"You buried worm-meat," he answered. "I wasn't there anymore. I died in Thjierry's arms, Muire. What does she do for a living again?"

Muire's other hand still clutched her bronze eagle scabbard chape. She thought about swords, about the kiss of angels, about drawing Ingraham Fasoltsen's last breath into her own lungs to seek vengeance for his murdered soul. She thought about the tarnished, and how they stole every breath, except that final one, and so avoided the geas.

She thought about using the weapons of dead angels to

draw the souls of dead angels back from their rest, and incorporate them in salvaged flesh. *Created to serve,* she thought. And *there was no one else. She did what she thought she had to do.*

She turned Gunther into a fylgja.

Muire knew she would have done differently. But she did not know if she would have been right to do so.

And so she forced her fingers to uncurl. From the sting, she'd probably imprinted the pattern of the filigree into her flesh. "I am so sorry," she said, wondering as she did if any words that passed her lips had ever been more inadequate. She could have done something.

She could have *noticed* when Thjierry walked into her own home, and stole her friend's *soul.*

Inanely, she said, "Has it been very bad?"

He laughed, a touch frantic, and said, "You have got *no idea.* Ones and zeroes, ones and zeroes, and never a damned cup of tea. Whups. We're almost to the top. Hang on. There's a bump."

Thjierry was not waiting at the landing, but two unmans were—a lion and Selene. They led Muire through a grape arbor and into a relict gazebo, hung with firm green unripe fruit and broad-leaved vines that softened the uncomfortable light.

And there, in a cane chair, was Thjierry.

Muire had come in with ideas of what both best- and worst-case scenarios might look like. Neither was quite adequate to the truth. The Technomancer was neither a hulk, immobile and decrepit, nor remade entirely a gleaming machine. But neither was she spry and limber. She was just an old woman alone in a chair, her hair wispy and tousled, the corners of her mouth drawn down to delineate her jowls. Her hands folded over the knob on a steel-headed cane, liver spots thick on slack gray skin marked with channels like the solder-tracks in a solid-state device. She raised one of those hands and beckoned Muire with a crook of tidy-nailed fingers, but Muire found herself frozen with indecision just at the edge of the shady space.

"Are you shocked?" Thjierry asked, when Muire had been silent some seconds. "It is shocking, isn't it? But it's what all flesh is heir to."

Muire thinned her lips, and had sense enough not to respond. Not when the words on her lips were: *I am not flesh.*

Thjierry looked around, furtively, as if to see if anyone except Muire and the unmans were in earshot, and whispered the next sentence conspiratorially: "Except yours, apparently. Tell me the secret isn't your moisturizer."

Most terrible, that it *was* funny. Thjierry's timing was perfect—it had always been good, and practice had not harmed her delivery—but there was something so desperate about the defusing joke, a match struck in terror of the dark, that Muire flinched even as she began to laugh. And then she came to Thjierry, leaving the unmans behind as she crossed the wooden floor, and dropped to a crouch before her.

"I missed you," she said.

"I missed you, too," Thjierry answered.

Muire wondered how much she was dissembling. They had been allies, never close, mostly linked through Gunther. And then Muire thought, *Uncharitable, angel. Perhaps she's missed you exactly as much as you have missed her. Which is to say . . . somewhat.*

"Did you avoid me because you are immortal?" Thjierry asked.

Muire shrugged. "Did you avoid me because of what happened to Gunther?"

"Oh, that." Thjierry reached out with a papery hand and touched Muire's throat above the baldric, above the collarbone. "I wasn't sure you would understand."

"Then," Muire said, "I wouldn't have."

"We couldn't afford to fight, you know. You and me."

"No," Muire said. "We couldn't have." She folded Thjierry's hand in her own, and Thjierry closed her eyes as Muire squeezed.

"We still can't. Can't afford to fight. You know, Muire, it was your sword that gave me the idea." The hilt protruded over Muire's shoulder, and—after disengaging from Muire's grip—Thjierry brushed it, then drew her hand back languidly, rubbing the fingertips as if they stung. "Is that your secret?"

"*My* sword?"

"When I came to visit you. It was hanging on the wall, and the same magic was in you both. That's what's kept you young. I can make it work for the unmans, but—" She knotted her old hands together in frustration. "Only a little for me."

"Two hundred years—"

"Only a little. Look in a mirror, woman."

Muire smiled. "I try not to. You know, those swords are the reason the wolf is hunting you."

She nodded. "They're also the only thing keeping the Desolation outside. Do you have a better answer?"

"Not yet." Muire dropped a knee on the floor for better balance. "Thjierry, you're holding a friend of mine—"

Thjierry smiled. Her breath, when she spoke, was not precisely evil, but it smelled musty, like a long-closed-up room. Yes. Cathoair. I hoped he'd bring you to me, and he has. Would you like to see him? I could have his scars erased, you know. Ask him to talk to me about it. For a friend of a friend—"

"I would like to see him."

"Well then you shall," Thjierry said. And as Muire stood, waiting to be dismissed, added, "—and after you have seen that he is well? Come back and talk to me some more?"

"About the swords?"

"About what we are going to do, to protect Eiledon. I'm dying, you realize."

"Yes," Muire said, her hands cold and clenching. "I had guessed."

uire had expected both unmans to escort her from the Technomancer's wind-stirred bower, but the lion stayed behind, leaving Muire in the charge of Selene, the leopard. It might be uncourteous to speak with an unman uninvited, but Muire found she was wearied with rules.

She turned to Selene as they walked and said, "How did you come to know Ingraham Fasoltsen?"

Vengeance, he murmured, as though his name were a trigger. Muire pinched her temples with one hand, trying to massage the headache away.

For Selene's part, she seemed neither confused nor discomfited by Muire speaking to her. Certainly, she was less uncomfortable overall than Muire, who saw Herfjotur every time she looked at the unman.

Her ears slicked back, and she seemed to consider. "Not long," she said. "Perhaps fifteen years? He was not old by human standards. How long have you known your . . . friend?"

For the love of all that was holy, he was already making

passes at the catgirls. Muire would have happily covered her eyes with the raised hand, but the bricks of the path were cracked and heaved up unlevel, and she needed to see where she was putting her feet. "We just met, after a fashion. But sometimes it feels as if I've known him forever."

An odd rumbling noise emerged from Selene, as she squinted in feline laughter. Muire tried to remember how long it had been since she'd heard a cat purr. She'd never seen an unman laugh, hadn't known they were capable. Thought on that, shaking her head and wondering what else she didn't know about unmans, as she followed Selene into a black brick dormitory that might have been red once, or yellow. It looked old enough to have acquired its patina during Eiledon's industrial era, when the streets had been thick with the smoke of factories and motorcars, and must be absolutely sweltering in high summer. Muire remembered it from her tenure at the university, but she had never been inside.

"He's on the fourth floor," Selene said. "Would you like to take the lift?"

"The lift is out of order." Gunther interjected himself into the conversation as smoothly as if he had been there all along. Which he had been, in his own fashion, Muire supposed. If he inhabited a nanotech fog, she was breathing bits of him in and out with every draught of air. "It will have to be the stairs. Shall I take her up, Selene?"

Muire wasn't sure what relief looked like on a snow leopard, but she was willing to make a guess. Cathoair was, indeed, already making friends. "Thank you," Selene said.

So they ascended the stair together, Muire and Gunther—if Gunther could really be said to ascend—and as Muire had suspected he might, Gunther took advantage of the moment alone.

His voice half hesitant, half wistful as she'd heard it once before, he asked, "Will you help her?"

Muire paused to rest on the second landing, for extended privacy rather than from weariness. There was a window, and she went to it, pressing her face to tepid glass to expand her field of view. "Will you tell her everything I say?"

"If she makes me."

It was an honest answer. And one that told Muire a great deal about what Thjierry had become, as Gunther had no doubt intended. "What's going on here, Gunther? What's she concealing from me?"

It might have been a breeze in some open window that riffled Muire's hair, though this window was not open. Or it might have been the caress of an invisible machine. She did not ask. She said, "I know about the swords—"

"*What* do you know about the swords?" he interrupted. Intent and forceful, as when they had argued literature and history until all hours of the morning. And he had tried to kiss her. Just the once.

She wondered if he remembered. She wondered why she said no.

Self-mortification.

Adding insult to injury, the wolf-sherd yawned complacent assent.

"I know she's using them to control the moreaux," Muire said. Down below, on some inaudible signal, the students had begun to trickle across the campus. There were so few of them: clumps of two and four, where she remembered rivers. "To keep herself alive. To keep you alive."

"And?"

"Of course there's an *and*." Muire muttered. "I don't know the and. Will you tell me?"

"To keep Eiledon alive."

"Well, by implication—"

"No. Directly. All the hamarr, the vitality, that supports the city's survival is drawn through the swords and focused through Thjierry. She's turned herself into a prism, with the blades as the source of the light. Metaphorically speaking . . ."

Not metaphorical at all. Except—

She didn't turn away from the window to say, "The blades aren't source of *anything*. They're just a conduit."

"So where," he asked with rhetorical weight, "is the hamarr coming from?"

Muire frowned across the hazy skyline to the Defile, at the city walls and the crumbling suburbs beyond—all visible from this height. She made her hands release the windowsill, but they promptly knotted themselves in her skirt. "Oh, Light," she said. "I know what you're not saying."

"She's cannibalizing the rest of the planet," Gunther said, merciless. "Draining its hamarr to support Eiledon. And has been for two hundred years. Freimarc—she's responsible for all those deaths, Muire. And now that that's gone, she has to find something else, or—" He imitated a brief sharp exhalation.

"And you and I helped her do it."

"Well," he said, "it seemed mean to bring that up."

Cathoair wasn't sure what he expected when he heard footsteps approaching the locked door of the suite where the Technomancer had warehoused him, but a crisp polite knock was not it. "I'd say come in," he called, without rising from the stiff-seated chair beside the window. "But the door is locked."

The voice that followed did not precisely come in answer, because what it said was, "Gunther?" But it jerked him to his feet anyway, hands twitching at hip-level.

"Muire?"

"Just a moment," she said. "Are you decent?"

"I can get you references and affidavits, if you like—oh, am I glad to see you."

She stood framed in the doorway staring at him for a moment, cleanly dressed in a skirt and tunic, her hair insipid from humidity. "Glad to see you too, kid. And what did you do to get yourself locked up?"

"Why are you blaming me?" He was already crossing the room, grabbing his discarded jacket off the foot of the unused bed. Softer, when they were face to face, he asked, "Did you get him?"

"No," she said, standing aside. "And I blame you because it's always your fault. Come on—"

"Are we getting out of here?" There were so many other questions he wanted to ask her: *Who are you really; how old; what are you doing here, now; why me?* Those were questions for when they were safe somewhere that wasn't atop a floating earth-berg.

"Does this look like a rescue?" She smiled. And winked at him, ever so slightly, just a droop of lashes across her cheek. "I have to have another talk with Thjierry before we go. But I thought I would take you to breakfast in the dining hall first. If it's anything like it used to be, you'll hate it."

———

When Muire said *I have to have another talk with Thjierry before we leave*, she didn't expect Cathoair to pick up on the subtext. But he frowned at her and blinked and said, "I think I understand," in a voice that suggested, just possibly, he did.

She fed him—and, as if to prove her wrong, he didn't complain—and then took him on a comprehensive tour of the university grounds. She was fortunate to have Gunther's assistance where progress or entropy had overtaken her knowledge.

They all knew they were killing time until Thjierry sent for Muire again, but it was almost fun, for a little, although Muire could not forget herself under the glow of that toxic sky. The overcast wasn't unusual. But she did not choose to grow accustomed.

When the summons came, they were in the sciences quarter between Engineering and Oneiromancy, and Muire was trying to remember the way to a particular stone bench she had been fond of. Gunther's teasing was interrupted by a chime and Thjierry's voice. "Muire. Will you join me in the pavilion, please? Your friend, too, if he likes."

This was not a conversation Muire cared to have in front of witnesses. She suspected she would only escape diminished in her own eyes. She did not care to be as diminished in Cathoair's.

"Wait for me," she told him, and walked away.

Running from or running to. There wasn't so much difference in the end.

Thjierry was where Muire had left her, attended by the same pair of unmans. They must be her best, her personal favorites. *The house-pets,* Muire thought, her mouth sticky and dry. If she had ever envisaged a reunion, this would not have been it.

But her sword was at her back, and Kasimir only a whisper of his name away. She was as well-defended as anyone might be who strode into the lion's den. *Literally,* she thought, eyeing Selene's sleepy-eyed compatriot. His hands—paws—were like great soft gloves with razorblades peeking from the fingertips. She didn't care to test his reflexes or his resolve.

"Hello, Thjierry," Muire said, as if she did not see the moreaux at all. There was a chair for her this time, a small table set between the two. She sank onto the edge of the wicker rather than crouching like a cat at the Technomancer's feet. Whatever happened now, the hour for theatrics was done.

"Hello, Muire." Thjierry didn't gesture, but on the moment, another unman appeared with a tray and tea service. His long golden-furred ears partially obscured his face as he bent down to pour. He withdrew before Thjierry reached out with gray fingertips and nudged one bowl closer to Muire.

Muire took it up and touched it to her lips without drinking. The liquor was pale amber, and bits of leaves drifted across the bottom. A jasmine petal floated by the lip, and Muire thought how long it had been since she smelled blooming jasmine. "I need to know what you wish of me," she said. "Before I can decide—"

"Cooperation," Thjierry answered. "Simply put. There is no other option. We have so little, so very little to sustain us. And you can give us more."

"I don't understand," Muire said, though she had an uneasy sense she might. Someone else might say the old woman was mad, but Muire did not think that was the right word. *Obsessed,* rather, and terrifying with it. "I won't give you my sword—"

"The sword wouldn't be enough." Thjierry drank, and must have finished her tea, because she reached for more. And the plate of lemon cookies. "Do you remember when you saved the children, Muire? You were always soft of heart."

"The refugees. Yes. When we went against the Thing."

"We saved a lot of lives." A pause, while a cookie was dunked and consumed. Muire, in the hesitation, collected one for herself and balanced it on the edge of her bowl. It smelled crisp, sweet, citrusy, and her mouth watered. "So many lives."

"You still do."

Thjierry smiled, if you could call it that. "So you *will* help me."

"Tell me," Muire said in soft patience, "what it is that you want?"

"Oh, but that means laying all my cards out for you—which, you are right, is as it should be. If we are to be allies again." She sighed. "Drink you tea, Muire. You used to like strong drink. Do you still?"

"Bourbon," Muire said. "That's not something that can be had in the city any longer. Bathtub gin, I can find you—"

Thjierry nodded. "We get a little. I can send—"

"No."

From the way her head jerked back, Muire suspected it had been a long time indeed since anyone interrupted the Technomancer.

"Just please answer my question?"

"You must have known," the Technomancer began, slowly, "that you could not send your creature back and forth across the Defile willy-nilly, without drawing my attention. He is very large, after all, and a sorcerous machine. And not precisely subtle."

Muire could not remember the first time adrenaline made her blood sing in her veins in response to a threat. She nodded, and kept her suddenly cold hands folded in her lap. "Of course not," she said.

"You might *not* have been aware that there are still a few operational satellites. And you probably could not have had any way to know that we would use one to follow you, the last time you left the city with your beast."

"Gunther," Muire said, disappointed.

"Sorry," he said, miserably. And it wasn't fair to hold him accountable. It wasn't as if he had options. "How did you cast the perception cloak over that valley, though, if you don't mind my asking? It took me most of a day to get through it, even when I saw *exactly* where you'd vanished."

"I'd prefer not to answer that at this time." Not a lie. In fact, close to the truest thing she'd ever said. *Perception cloak?*

Cristokos is a mage.

Of course he was. The unmans were turning out full of surprises. "You want the valley."

"For experiment only," Thjierry said, one hand upraised. "It endures. Somehow. The soil is alive. Somehow. Your doing?"

Muire shook her head. She ate the damned cookie, and drank the damned tea. Even waelcyrge have their limits.

"I want to find out why it was not destroyed. And duplicate it. And likewise your creature. And then—"

"And what if you destroy it?"

"Excuse me?"

"In the process," Muire said. "What if you destroy it?"

Thjierry lifted her bowl to her lips and sipped, but Muire could see that it was empty. "We won't."

Her stare was calm and challenging; a weight of absolute conviction settled across her face. Muire turned her head away and glanced at the unmans as if nervous. The lion stood impassive, arms folded, as if he heard nothing. But Selene—

The leopard's gray-gold eyes rested inscrutably on Muire, and when Muire met that gaze, the leopard stared hard for a moment and then glanced away. *Thank you,* Muire thought. It was nice to have one's judgment of a lie confirmed.

Cathoair also says she is lying.

Uh. How does Cathoair know?

Gunther is letting him watch the feed. Her displeasure— oh, go ahead and call it fury—must have been evident, because she had a distinct impression of Kasimir ducking his heads, ears wobbling as he shook out his manes. **He *said* he was invited.**

And so he had been. Hoping her face had not given too much away, Muire nodded. "Can I have a day?"

"Twelve hours, how's that? It shouldn't be too hard a decision. Agree and the world lives; demur, and the world dies."

"And Cathoair? Now that you have me, may I stand surety for his freedom? Surely, my parole—"

Thjierry, Muire thought, did not have to take quite such transparent delight in interrupting her, in turn. "You have it backwards," she said. "You're not surety for his cooperation. He is surety for yours."

Uruz (tenacity)

ᚢ

This time, Thjierry was not so eager to release Muire on her own nominal recognizance. When Muire left the pavilion, Selene came with her. She would not have been alone even without the moreau, though, for Kasimir counseled her silently.

This changes nothing.

I had only thought myself too old for heartbreak.

We are never too old for that.

Walking beside Thjierry's noble abomination, Muire scrubbed her face across her hands. *Was she a good woman once? That is how I want to remember her.*

Any hero might have bent under that weight, Kasimir said slowly. **If we are not too old for heartbreak, neither is she.**

Muire must have been moving like the shambling dead, because as they climbed a broad stair into a garden of pansies, Selene put out a hand to steady her. She used the back of her fingers only, and said, "Are you unwell?"

"Overwrought," Muire said. "That's all."

Still, Selene stayed close beside her, though what she meant to do about it with those talons if Muire fell was unclear. Not so different, Kasimir and Selene. The legacy of war had made of each of them something that could not touch.

"Why do you carry the whip?" Muire asked when they had ascended to the level of the garden. It was something to say. "I would think you were more than adequate in your own person—"

As if Muire's question had made Selene herself wonder, her hand rose to her belt and unhooked the coil. She stroked it softly and then fitted the butt into her palm. The static field that held it harmless released with a static hiss. "The white one. On the left."

And then her hand moved and there was a sound like tearing paper, and a flower that had been twenty feet away lay at Muire's feet.

"A creature's reach should exceed her grasp, don't you think?" Selene said, and coiled the whip away.

Muire bent to retrieve the pansy. It was velvet-purple at the heart, more the ghost of lavender than truly white. Its stem might have been severed with a knife. "I see," Muire said, and tucked the bloom into her neckline.

Selene was already moving forward again.

They rejoined Cathoair on the steps of the campus museum. Despite the overcast, he'd stripped off his shirt and was stretched out on the dished marble steps close by an ancient magnolia tree whose twisted branches were supported by wires and mortar pillars. It was past bloom for the year, but the withered once-white petals remained scattered on the steps like letters scribbled in sepia. Cathoair seemed to have nothing more on his mind than watching the boys and girls go by.

But he rose when Muire and Selene approached, letting his shirt and jacket dangle from his hand; they offered no assistance as she tried not to be distracted by the muscles of his stomach and the fine line of hair disappearing behind his waist-band. He glanced warily from one to the other. "Everything good?"

Muire shrugged. He stuffed his hands into the frayed pockets of dark grey trousers.

"We need to talk," Muire said, and looked at Selene.

"I can request a room. Gunther?"

"Don't say Hi or anything, Muire."

"Hello, Gunther."

"Yes," he continued. "The conference room on the sixth floor of the library is available. Will that serve?"

"Thank you," Muire said. "I know the way."

They trooped up the stairs single file, Muire in the lead and Selene trailing. Muire doubted not that the unman was prepared for violent action if Muire made her think it necessary.

The core of the library was as ancient as any in the world, a converted chapel that had housed the books of the Thane of Eiledon since the city was no more than a stone-and-thatch settlement huddled on the banks of a river only bridged within living memory.

The modern building had risen up beside the ancient chapel, dwarfing it, but the university's collections were too vast even to be held here. In this structure, they walked past polycarbonate cases in which hung racks and racks of real books, the rolls of paper weathered at the edges, the scroll dowels yellowed or blackened, nicked and gouged. Some were gilt, some silvered—the silvering black with tarnish now—some of vermicular wood so friable Muire thought it would shatter at a touch. She despaired of the scrolls of those books, and passed them by.

In the reflections, Selene seemed unmoved. Cathoair stared

about himself uncomprehendingly, and finally reached out left-handed to touch a protective case. "These are all books."

"Books," Muire said. "Or nostalgia. All the research data are digital, holographically stored in nearly indestructible crystals. Like monks in an age of oblivion, hoarding whatever history they can find."

"Did that happen?"

"It's happening now." She turned and looked over her shoulder at them both. "You won't find many ages darker than this. And here's the conference room."

Turning aside, she entered as if it were a foregone conclusion they would follow. They did, and Selene shut the door behind them.

"No chance of privacy?" Muire asked, and Selene shrugged. "Sorry."

"So what's going on?" Rather than flopping into a seat, Cathoair leaned one buttock on the table edge, dropped his shirt across the surface, and folded his arms. "I've never felt quite so like a conspirator as since I met you."

There was water in a carafe, and Muire poured herself a glass and drank it while she organized her thoughts. It gave her an excuse to glance out the window; the prospect could not have been better for her purposes if Gunther had selected it on purpose. When she drew aside the curtains, Muire faced the Arcology and all its mirrored gleaming windows.

Ideal.

Excellent. Is there any reason why we can't just jump back to Midgard to make our escape, as Mingan does?

The Grey Wolf would seem to be able to look between the worlds before he moves from one to the other.

I cannot.

For a moment, Muire thought about walls and buildings and tree-grown mountainsides. *I see your point. That's why you took us so high before you brought us back, the first time.*

I thought it safe to dog his steps, and pass through Niflheim where he had. Also, Midgard is empty. So it is safer going than coming. But distances there do not compare to distances here. So consider it an option to be undertaken only in desperation.

But you could use it to pass through the Defile without ever crossing the field.

Yes, Kasimir said. **That is what we shall do.**

What about the mist?

The mist is a gift. It can only serve to conceal us.

And if it eats us? Melts our faces off?

She could imagine his tail swishing. **Then we need not fight tomorrow.**

And when she was finished biting back laughter, she changed the subject and asked: *Kasimir,* Muire said, *I don't need an answer now. But do you suppose it's significant that the site of Eiledon in Valdyrgard corresponds roughly to the site of the world-tree in Midgard?*

Yes, he said.

Good. Because I do, too. And do you know what that rune carved in the world-tree's root might be?

The eighteenth rune. The secret one.

But what does it mean?

No one knows. Except the All-Father.

And he's dead. Muire turned back to the room. Selene stood stolid in the corner, arms folded, eyes downcast, and Muire pretended for a moment that she was the statue she pretended. She would like to sculpt her, those perfect sinews and the sleek elastic muscle. But it was to Cathoair that Muire spoke.

"I'm not sure I'm going to do what Thjierry wants me to do," she said. "If I don't, that puts you in a very awkward position. Put your shirt on, would you?"

Muscles in his throat rippled as he swallowed. But he picked up the shirt and started threading his arms into the sleeves, and then—without being told—put on the jacket, too. Though he left them both open down the front, Muire let it rest. "She's going to keep us prisoner," Cathoair said, looking at her directly.

Muire nodded.

Gunther said, "Muire, I can tell by the expression on your face that you're thinking of some audacious plan. And I feel constrained to inform you that it's not in my program, currently, to allow you off university grounds. Or to commit any acts of sabotage to university property."

Muire sighed. "That's that, then. Gunther, before I give the Technomancer my decision . . ."

"Yes?"

"May I view where the swords are kept?"

A pause. "Thjierry says yes. And says she hopes it will help you understand the desperation of the circumstances. Her laboratory is on the top floor of this building; she will meet you there in ten minutes." And then a deeper pause, as if to indicate that he was speaking on his own behalf, now. "You should know that my core consciousness is also housed in that laboratory. And I will not permit you to leave this facility while I am at the helm of its defense."

———

He *just asked me to kill him,* Muire said later, climbing the stair.

Yes.

It complicated her plan enormously, but Muire still envied the orrery. It dominated the penthouse level of the library, glistening and turning and whirring softly, no louder than a pocketwatch. The arms were steel, the fixtures brass and copper and soft-hued gold, rubies and garnets glinting in the works. From the heart of it, barely visible, came the shine of light through vacuum tubes and solid-state crystals. The stars were tremulous lights in the nested crystal domes surrounding the works, the planets filigree, shining from within. Muire wished desperately she could see it at night, in all its glory, revealed by its own lights. It must have weighed tens of tons, but the whole of it appeared as light and perfectly balanced as a spinning gyroscope.

It made her uneasy to look at. It was lovely, exact, fantastically precise. But it left her dizzy and weak if she stared for more than a moment.

Still she paused in the doorway for a moment and watched the grand machine spin. Comets swept around the edges; the great worlds of the middle system swung in stately progression; at the center, by the light of the yellow sun, the little messenger worlds spun vertiginously, carving bright runes in the air.

The rest of the penthouse, incongruously, looked exactly like a wealthy sorcerer's living quarters should look. A half-partitioned laboratory, with slate floors and slate-topped steel tables, occupied the side of the room with the northern light. Opposite, a pleasant living space, grass-floored, with ferns both as borders and in pots, on stands before broad windows. It was furnished in airy, simple slat-sided wood, the sort of benches and tables one would expect in a gentleman farmer's home.

Despite the wonder of the orrery, Muire found herself staring at the curtains, their black-white-and-rose pattern of stylized calla lilies somehow deeply unsettling.

"Very few have seen what you are looking at," Thjierry said, shuffling around the base of the thing on two canes, barefoot on the verdant grass. "Take your shoes off, if you don't mind?"

Muire complied, standing on each foot in turn. Selene was already barefoot, of course. And Cathoair seemed frankly glad to be rid of his, and left them tumbled by the door. *If we live, I'll buy him boots,* Muire promised herself, and thought after the fact that it was the nearest thing she'd uttered to a prayer in twenty-five hundred years.

Barefoot, she came down the stairs, and felt the grass under her feet. Thjierry offered her a hand; Muire accepted the clasp. "The orrery is beautiful."

"And functional," Thjierry answered. "It draws up the hamarr, and processes it so it can be used to sustain our tank agriculture, the medical and conception programs, the Defile itself—everything."

Muire bit her lip and turned to look at it again. She was not a technomancer, but even she could sense the pulse of power in the giant anachronistic machine. *We must not destroy this.*

Must we not?

Muire took a breath that smelled of grease and metal, and stared at the spinning worlds and moons that made up the thing. Was this what Gunther had meant? Was he in here, too, linked to this clockwork heaven? Would he show her what to attack?

"The swords?" she asked, when she could bear to hold the eyeless machine gaze of the orrery no more.

This time, Thjierry gestured. "Gunther, please."

In silence the gleaming brass base of the dome split open and trays like map drawers slid out in staggered ranks, as if they had been stacked into a pyramid. Each one was sealed with crystal, and under the crystal of each lay the swords, neatly side-by-side on velvet, hilt by point by hilt by point. Too many to count conveniently, but there were at least thirty drawers, and twenty blades in each, though not all drawers seemed full.

You are standing in a wizard's Tower, Muire reminded herself, as she took the seven or ten steps necessary to see clearly into the topmost of the nearest bank of drawers. "You're not using the blades as a computational matrix? Or merely as a power source?"

"They're crystal," Thjierry answered. "They can be written to with a laser."

I should have thrown them each into the sea.

She named each blade as she passed it. *Dragvandill. Solbiort. Aettartangi. Droplaugar. Skathi.*

But Svanvitr was not there. Muire would have known its wire-wound hilt anywhere.

"Which is the most recent? The one Ingraham Fasoltsen died to bring?" Mercifully, that worthy remained silent, and the wolf-sherd too.

"Here," Thjierry said, stumping toward the laboratory. "I haven't written it yet. I can show you the process tonight; I know you'll find it interesting, and I wonder what input you might have—"

Muire followed, half wrapped-up in Thjierry's scientific enthusiasm until she thought, *she is so far out of touch with reality that it's a foregone conclusion to her that I will help.* Even then, it was hard not to take the contagion.

The sword rested on silk draped over a black iron rack upon the farthest table. Muire glanced over her shoulder to make sure Cathoair was still shadowing her—bare feet made him stealthier still—and beckoned him to follow before she advanced.

Here. Here was where she would summon Kasimir. Beside this vast window, safely far from the orrery that had become Eiledon's clockwork vampire heart, ticking, ticking. Here, where a rack of computational crystals hung on the wall behind the sword, shielded by yet another pane of polycarbonate.

When Muire looked at it, the status lights flickered in an unmistakable wink.

Snakerot. She had hoped—

She had hoped, that was all.

She glanced at Thjierry for permission to pick up the sword. Thjierry nodded, and Muire noticed that Selene had interposed herself between Cathoair and Muire, hand on the butt of her whip. Absolutely expecting trouble.

Svanvitr slips into her left hand as if waiting. A longer and heavier blade than her own, but for now the hilt suits her palm. She hefts the sword, as if to peer down the blade for straightness.

—ecstatically, the crystal flares to light.

Selene moves, lunges for her, the hand on her whip pulling it from her belt. Another flick and she'll have it in play. The air thickens around Muire's arm. Gunther, following his program, against all desire.

But Muire is waelcyrge. Least of her sisters. Least of them all. But herself again, after twenty-five centuries in abeyance. She moves through the thickened air; Svanvitr is Light, and slices free as if through water. The blade drags. The blade cuts. The wound seals up behind.

Not so when she plunges it into the crystal racks of the computer. *That* is a wound that won't heal. Muire slashes, and the stiff air loosens. And where is the whip? *Where is the whip?* She moves freely again, and the light that blazes from her might be blinding. Must be blinding: Thjierry's face is screwed up around her eyes; she's let one crutch fall to shield her vision with a lifted arm. Selene's pupils are contracted to pinpricks in velvet, dark instead of showing light, and she struggles—Cathoair has her arms, from behind, his big hands on her biceps.

In a moment, she will twist free and shred him. No human flesh can withstand those claws.

Muire steps into Selene's reach and—thinking of Cristokos and his accidental freedom—kisses her on the mouth, breathes hard down her throat.

Shock, recoil. Her lips part, her eyes fly wide, both hands tense and splay, displaying diamond-sharp claws as the whip thumps to the floor. Her fine-pointed teeth slash Muire's mouth. Her whiskers prickle-scratch Muire's face.

The unman spasms, convulsing as if it were electric current Muire applied to her skin, and not lips. The Light flows into her. Muire flows into her—

She knows not what she does. Neither to what this will give rise, nor how to control it; but the wolf-sherd does. Selene trembles in her hands, claws raking and missing skin and then connecting, slicing down through muscle on Muire's neck and shoulders as she stops struggling and lunges into Muire's arms. Her tongue darts, barbed like a cat's, rasping flesh from lip and gum. Her eyes close; she strains against Muire, fur and muscle beneath the armor, cable strength. A rough purr . . .

Muire thrust her away, tasting blood, broke the kiss, sucked in air and pushed Selene, away, *hard*. The unman sprawled against the nearest table and slid into a crouch. *"Pony."* Now *would be good.*

And Kasimir was there, beside her, Cathoair's wrist in her hand as she threw herself across the saddle and hauled him after, the sharp scent of burning cloth and hair and skin as he banged the stallion's hide, and then the downbeat of mighty wings—

And then cold. And Niflheim. And the smell of the crushed pansy warming between her breasts.

And all her ghosts come round again.

Sowílo (sun)

When Muire came to tell Cahey they were ready to go back to the city, she was carrying a map drawn by Cristokos, one of the odder creatures Cahey had ever met. The unman was a parti-colored rat who seemed a friend of Muire and her giant teleporting metal beast, though Cahey had been somewhat distracted and disoriented when they met, after being detained, rescued, burned, vanished, flown across unknown hundreds of miles, and brought down in a landscape he hadn't even known the word for until Muire told it to him.

Forest.

A week ago, he'd never seen a tree with his own eyes. Now, he was sitting under one while a rat-mage smeared salve on his stinging leg and said, "Rats have ways in and out. This one will make those ones a map." And who seemed pleased, in a rodent-like manner, when Muire told him of kissing Selene.

I kissed her first, Cathoair wanted to say, but sensed it wouldn't be smart.

The other thing Cristokos had done was touch once, lightly, the sword Muire stole from the Technomancer. Then he had wrapped it tightly in linen over silk, and bound and sealed it with colored cords and wax. "That might hide it," he said. "From him and from Her. Might not. These ones must hide those, also. For going in, as this one was hidden going out."

So there were more bustlings, while Cathoair sat on a streamside boulder in sight of the metal horse and soaked his leg in the icy water until they were ready to leave. With a hand up from Muire and a boost from that selfsame rock, he managed to mount the stallion without reburning himself, and the sweep of wings lifted them like a carrier bag caught up in a wind.

There was this about flying behind Muire, clasping her waist: she wanted him. He could *not* have missed it.

They returned to the city more furtively than they had left it, creeping through vaults and booby-trapped medieval sewers while concealed by Muire's spells of ward and camouflage. This involved her whistling a weird atonal fall of a melody that echoed eerily all around them and made Cahey dizzy and confused, with a tendency to wander off in random directions if she didn't lead him. He couldn't follow her explanation. It was all *skaldr* and *harmonics* and *sidereality,* and he gave up after thirty seconds and just nodded.

When they came back to the surface, it was in the claustrophobic back passages where the Badwater district bordered on the Narrows, hard up against Eiledon's southwestern wall. This was one of the oldest precincts, and had never been opened out for vehicles wider than a hand cart. The alleys and lanes, paved with heaved slate blocks, were so narrow Cathoair could have reached out and laid a hand flat on each opposing wall.

He'd never been in this part of the city before, and said as much, limping barefoot over the oblong cobbles.

Muire looked at him, her small features almost washed off her face by the oblique and shadowless light. "You didn't tell Thjierry who I am."

"No," he said. "Well, I don't know who you are, exactly—"

"—Muire," she interrupted, and seemed to find it funny.

"—but I think I know *what* you are."

She touched her sword. The second one hung beside it, swaddled until it looked like a bundled loaf. "She hasn't figured it out?"

He shrugged. "She's a scientist. Who wants to believe in angels?"

"Waelcyrge."

"Which are angels."

Her jaw was locked too tight for the sound she made to be a laugh, but it was as close as he thought he was going to get. "Angels imply the existence of god," she said. And then checked herself and put up her hands. "You know what? Fair enough. I'm the only one left." They strode side-by-side, him checking his step to make it easier for her to keep up. She drifted right, opening a little space between them, and turned to look at the oft-repaired wall of whatever block of buildings they were passing. The wall had started off stone—pink and gray granite—and over more years than Cahey could comfortably imagine had been patched with limestone, red brick, yellow brick, and great crumbly swaths of mortar. Salvage, all, and some of it no doubt from long before the Desolation. There had never been autos in this corner of the city, but it was year-blackened from centuries of coal fires and motorcycles.

It came to him with mouth-drying exactitude that the

reed-boned blonde on his right hand was older than the wall, older than the street, older than everything he had ever seen except the river Naglfar. "You like it here."

"This is medieval Eiledon. The city I knew a thousand years ago." And then she paused, and did put her hand out and let it trail along the filthy wall. "It's like the Desolation had never happened. And the world went ever on."

"As long as you never look at the sky."

"I try not to," she said, and gave him a shy sideways smile. "For a lot of reasons."

And for a lot of reasons, that seemed like the end of that conversation, so he went looking for a new one. "I realize we're probably on the down low, but—"

"Astrid," she said. "You can send her a message when we get where we're going. No screen calls. Paper and a messenger. Can she read?"

He checked hard, and then realized she asked because she needed an honest answer. "Sort of. I didn't give the Technomancer her name, or Aethelred's address. Though they were pretty slick about trying to get it out of me."

"For once," Muire said, "the complete breakdown of record-keeping works in our favor."

"Where are we going?"

"I have a place." She turned left across him, guiding him down the narrowest lane so far.

Her place was a fourth-story walkup. She must have had it magicked somehow, because he walked past the stair door until she called him back and physically placed his hand on the knob. He kept a straight face somehow when she touched his wrist, but it wasn't easy, and he turned away a little to hide his reaction.

On the other hand, if he could kiss an unman, what was to say he couldn't kiss an angel?

They stepped inside, into a room that looked as if it had been closed up for the winter, sheets thrown over the furniture and the windows draped heavily. Muire crossed to them and flung the curtains wide so light streaked through dingy glass. Cahey moved around the space, pulling sheets off things, wincing on behalf of his bruised feet but stubborn.

If Muire wasn't going to complain about hiking through sewers and over cobbles barefoot, neither was he.

"Wait," she said. "Not that one—"

But he'd already dragged the drape off whatever it was, and then stood staring at the shimmer of patinaed bronze.

A statue, life-sized, of a small woman in medieval clothing, with long wrist-thick braids framing a face as sad and stern as the moon's. He stared at it for half a minute before he realized that it was Muire.

"Your face is on backwards," he said, because it was the only thing he could think to say, and without turning away from the window, her knuckles white on the held-wide draperies, she said, "I sculpted it in a mirror. A kind of compulsion. I put it here so I wouldn't have to look at it," and that was that.

He let the sheet fall from his hand. No point in covering up what you'd already laid plain. "There's not a lot of dust. Do you come here often?"

"Stasis spell," she said. "Junior cousin of the one that keeps the Tower in the air. I haven't been in here in a hundred years, so it should be safe." She let the curtain slide from between her fingers, and turned to study them in the light through the filthy window. "We are corpse-maggots."

Flat. Toneless. Her shoulders curved in defeat, and he

thought her eyes were closed. He said, "I don't understand you."

"Corpse-maggots. We are. What do you know about coffins?"

He shrugged, realized she couldn't see him, and put a hand on her shoulder. "People used to bury their dead."

"Generations," she said. "Generations of flies can breed and feed and mate and die inside a coffin, until the body within is bones. But they are still breeding in a coffin. And one day they will gnaw the last sinew from the last bone, and there will be nothing left for them to eat."

She put her back to the window. He had not known her face could arrange itself into such sorrow. He nodded to show he understood. "Except each other."

"Sooner or later, not even that." She folded her arms, but it seemed more as if she meant to keep herself in than keep him out. He stepped closer, and she gave him no ground.

"Angels with no god," he said, bent enough that his breath stirred the hair beside her ear. "So what do you serve?"

She closed her eyes. "We thought we served the Light."

And he leaned across her folded arms and kissed her.

And she let him.

At first, just permission, as if that was all she could manage. And then her lips parted, and her arms opened, and she rested her hands on his shoulders, face tilted up so he could better reach. He waited a moment, still, before he touched her with his hands—until she made a small noise of inquiry, and then he rested the palm of one hand against her cheek, fingers spidering lightly around her ear. He touched the collar of her tunic, and she didn't push his hand away. He was holding his breath, and she was staring up at him, an indistinct sort of foxfire rippling through her clear gray irises as light ripples on the bottom of a disturbed pool.

And then he laughed, leaned back far enough to get a breath that wasn't full of the scent of her, and said, "When I thought about this, I thought about taking your armor off."

Her pupils dilated, the radiance under her corneas flickering dim in a manner he would have dismissed as a trick of the light, if he had not known what she was. "You thought about this?"

He kissed her again, soft and quick. "Don't be ridiculous. You didn't know?"

"I'm not—" she lifted her hand from his shoulder to make a hopeless gesture "—good at things."

"You're fabulous at everything I've ever seen you try."

"I've never done this before."

Whatever he had been expecting her to say, it wasn't that. "Never."

"It wasn't a priority," she said, but it was feeble and he thought it would only make things worse if he pretended to laugh.

So he moved his hand against her face and said, "Snakerot. What were you waiting for?"

"You weren't here," she said. And that might have been romantic, in an over-the-top kind of way, if she hadn't sounded so damned much like she meant it.

Still, nervous as she seemed, he had to respect her for trying. He caught her hand in his, lifted her fingers to his mouth, and bit her knuckles softly, as he might his own if he were thinking.

"Come on," he said. "Let's go lie down. I have all kinds of things to show you."

In the evening, they argued. It started when he told her he had to leave, and she would not consent until he told her why. He might have pushed past her anyway, but without her help he couldn't find the door. And so he had to bargain.

"It's a personal errand," he said. He knew where the door was. *Exactly* where it was. They'd come in through it, after all, and he didn't forget spaces. But he couldn't find it; his eye slid past as if from ice. "I have to pay a bill."

"Urgently. Today."

"Yes," he said. And then, because her jaw was set and her arms were folded, he said, "And I have to visit my mother."

"Cathoair, we're *hiding*."

"I know," he said. And then, because he had to, and because it wasn't like it was a secret, exactly, he told her. About the hospice and the cancer and why he really did have to go, and she couldn't come with him.

And she blinked at him and unstubborned all at once. And said, "You should have told me you needed money—"

"I did." He smiled. He meant to smile, anyway, but from the stretch of his face it might have been more like an smirk.

She didn't look down, though. "You didn't say why."

"Was it any of your business, then?" He shook his head. "Look, I don't want charity because we're sleeping together—"

"I don't sleep," she said, which cracked him up and defused the tension a little, at least, so when he said, "I don't want the money and the sex getting tangled up for us, okay?" she was able to just nod and say, "All right. Do what you have to do."

"I always do."

She grabbed his collar and pulled him down to her level. Then she kissed him on the cheek and let go. "And be careful."

He winked. But didn't answer.

Cathoair walked in past the private rooms to his mother's crowded ward in the back. He could see from the doorway that she was failing. But at least the hospice could medicate her, and dull the worst of the pain. He tried not to dwell on what an irony that was, that it seemed not even death could rescue her from suffering and humiliation. And for another irony, what was killing her was just cancer, the old-fashioned kind, the kind that had been cured before the Desolation and was still treatable, if you had money. There were new diseases, engineered, that killed more quickly.

There was no such thing as a good death. But Cathoair wished the world might have shown her some chip of mercy.

She was tough. It kept her clinging to life far longer than Cathoair had hoped. In honesty, longer than he had prayed, not that he believed in the efficacy of prayer. And less so now, having met Muire, than ever.

She was sleeping when he arrived, and he hated to wake her to change the sheets, so he sat for a while holding her hand, listening to her breathe. When she was young, she used to be so beautiful. Cathoair wished he had a picture, but all that was long gone. No data from his childhood.

Just as well.

His fingers must have tightened on hers, because—without opening her eyes—she said his name. He kissed her on the forehead because her lips were ulcerated. "Hi, Mom."

Her voice was breathless, and he wondered how long it would be before she lost it. "And me without . . . my lipstick on."

She squeezed his hand hard while he pretended he was laughing. "Don't wear yourself out talking, okay? We can just sit, once I get your bed fixed."

Her eyes cracked open. "I want to talk."

"You know you're everything to me." No matter how gently he touched her, her hair brushed off when he smoothed it.

Her tongue flicked across her lips and he rushed to pour her water. Awkward, when she would not release his hand. "I want you to do something."

"Let me change your sheets. Let me help you roll over."

He stood, and twisted his hand gently to make her let go. He steadied the glass for her while she sipped, and then set the glass aside. She spoke more easily after, though he wished she wouldn't. "I want to go to the river. I want you to help me cross the river now, Cathoair."

He started pulling out the hospital corners on the right side of the bed. "Hey there, edge over."

She closed her eyes. "Not fair to ask."

I killed for you once already. But he couldn't say that. Not here. And it wasn't just for her that he'd done the killing.

Brick dust bruising hands and choking the scrape of concrete against his face the smell of garbage please.

Please don't.

And too much pain. . . .

Not just for her. No. But she didn't need to know that.

"I know," she said, though he could barely hear the words through her breath. "If you just tell them to stop the IVs it wouldn't take long. I don't have to take food."

"Mom. Please . . ."

"Please." She said, "Cathoair, honey, let me do this for you. I know you can't afford to keep me here. I *know.*"

Her tone left no doubt as to what, and how much, she knew. He looked down at his hands, the scarred knuckles going pale as his fingers knotted on the sheets, and wondered what else she knew. Not that he'd killed her husband; that was no secret between them, though they had never spoken of it. But maybe more of why than she'd ever admitted.

He didn't want to think about that, because then he would have to think about why she let it happen, and that was as useless as covering his scar. He said, "I still need you to roll over, okay? I'm going to change the sheets on this side."

When he left, he wasn't thinking clearly. He trotted, almost running, working through the sting of his bruised feet and blistered calf. He hopped over the drunks who hadn't managed to crawl back to their squats. But other than the human sweepings, anything that could be salvaged, was. There was garbage— night soil, whatever could neither be eaten not composted, whatever the rats left—but no litter.

He would not weep. He would not show weakness. And he would not let the grief that wanted to swell up his throat choke him, leave him reeling, easy prey. Because he already knew that he would speak to the staff the next time he visited. He had never been able to tell her no for long.

It affected him, of course it distracted him. But it was not an excuse for his failure to notice the Grey Wolf until Mingan's hands closed on his collar and swung him against a nearby wall. Effortlessly, like a man swinging a puppy. Except a puppy—

Cathoair's idea of a puppy: he had never seen one—could bite. Threads snapped; the shirt cut into his underarms. Air burst from his lungs, so he was all but silent, wheezing, though he would have screamed shamefully if he'd had an ounce of breath.

Mingan smiled and set Cathoair down, deceptively gentle. The Wolf leaned him against the wall, barely upright . . . and grabbed his chin in one hand, and the nape of his neck in the other.

Dry hands, hot, callused. Eyes dripping silver light, so it pooled and ran down the Wolf's creased cheeks like tears. But the look on his face wasn't sorrow.

He stank of something bitter and sharp. His thumb moved across the scar on Cathoair's cheek, a sickening caress, and Cahey somehow got his hands up, on Mingan's shoulders, and shoved. Mingan kneed him in the solar plexus, so if not for the Wolf's grip on his neck, Cathoair would have gone to the ground.

Mingan might have meant to purr, but his voice was a vicious rasp. "Who would wish to mark such a pretty face? I know a way to find out—"

Cathoair jerked against his hands, eyes streaming, but he might as well have fought an iron shackle. "Bastard—"

"Oh, sweeting. Thou scorned not my money before. Whyso now?" The Wolf wore leather gloves, and still the heat of his body soaked through, so hot Cathoair thought he would surely have burns wherever the wolf had touched him.

Cathoair pulled against it, and did not answer.

And the Wolf laughed at him. "Perfidious candle-flicker," he said, in a hush. "Remember me."

And kissed Cathoair.

Cathoair, as an adult, had met very few people who could match his strength. But when he was a boy . . . he had been the next thing to a street kid, and that was another story. Now, he grabbed Mingan's wrist with both hands and it was like trying to bend stone. He couldn't fight: a dozen things—panic, anticipation, the rush of catastrophic memories—locked him in place.

Paralyzed by history.

The Wolf's voice had gone even stranger: still rough, almost gentle now. "My rival," he whispered, his lips moving against Cathoair's own as Cathoair tried not to understand. "My sister has excellent taste. What a fragile, beautiful boy thou art."

Cathoair couldn't breathe, couldn't run. Couldn't even straighten himself against the wall. He wondered if Mingan had cracked his ribs, and thought it wouldn't be bothering him long if so. *He's going to eat me. Like Ingraham Fasoltsen.*

And then the Wolf's slick, hard tongue prised his lips apart, flicked his teeth, and when Cathoair tried to gasp a breath, to keep fighting, his left hand tensed on the back of Cathoair's neck and dragged him close, so the breath went across Mingan's face, through Mingan's lips.

Cathoair . . . lost. Lost, and could not have cared less. Nerves, muscles, tendons relaxed, surrendered. Life fled every limb like water running down to the sea through all the rivers in the world.

Bliss. Bliss, and dying.

Cathoair reached out with both hands, his last measure of strength, and yanked Mingan's body against his own, pressed his mouth down, broke both their lips between their teeth so the bright taste of blood flavored the kiss. Shared breath brought tumbling memories, salty bittersweet jewels. Things he, himself, had cared not to remember. The taste of someone else's spit. The bruises left by fingerprints.

And things he could not say how he remembered, because they were not *his,* memories of ice and hope and desperation and someone—*Mingan,* Mingan younger and smiling—kissing him like this, just like this, and his heart leaping up like a salmon—

And then the memory Mingan scoured him for.

It has been years since he had thought of his father's death as anything but *the murder.* And there it is, the terrible pinch around Cathoair's throat of the woven belt the old man looped there to control him, once he got too big to be held down one-handed—*don fight me Mouse I don wanna hurt you*—and of course Mouse's what the old man called Cahey's mother Miriam, too, and isn't that just sick and perfect—and the blade in Cathoair's hand, an old armor-cutter, small enough to conceal in his palm and the shopkeeper he'd fucked to get it said it could cut through steel plate, never mind the old man's belly, and it does, slice and effortless and all that blood and the stink of the opened guts, but he's not dead, not so quickly, and Cathoair didn't think about this part, the old man's got the blade in his hand and Cathoair mostly gets his upper arm in front of his face, he thinks, but he staggers back out of arm's length, the old man can't chase him, not with his guts all over the floor like that, tangling up his feet when he takes a step.

Oh, Cahey, Astrid said when she saw him. *Who did that to you? What happened?*

He had been so in shock he told her.

Then she—and Aethelred—helped him cover it up, make it look as though both he and the old man had been attacked by a cutthroat. They never spoke of it again.

But that was past. So long past, and so long ignored that when it came before him he felt as if he could put a hand out and let the history run through his fingers. Someone else's rape. Someone else's murder. Someone else's pain.

But in the now-time, someone whimpered, someone cried out, muffled by another's mouth, and Cathoair—some detached fragment that was drawn back, observing, impassive to his own ravishment or death—did not recognize the voice as his own.

Mingan. Weeping into the kiss, weeping as he killed him.

Crying for me? Light, why?

Because I have failed thee, the Grey Wolf answered, and then he blew Cathoair's breath back into him. And then it was like Mingan was inside him, wearing his body and soul like a coat. Looking through his eyes, blinking, stretching into his skin. Brilliance flared about them, so bright it burned its afterimage on Cathoair's eyes despite closed lids.

Dying seemed a tiny price to pay for such a kiss, and now he knew why Selene had fallen away from Muire so disconsolate.

Cathoair was still choking after the taste of it as Mingan threw him on the stones and he slid ten feet. The Wolf stood over him, panting, disheveled, running a red tongue over a bloody mouth. Five seconds, ten, they stared like circling fighters.

Until the Grey Wolf collected himself: flicked his cloak about his shoulders, shook his queue down his back, and dusted gloved hands. He lifted his chin and smiled. And then he *winked,* like it was their little secret, and his cloak swirled heavily against the tops of his boots as he turned and strode away.

Nauthiz (want)

ᚾ

Selene picked up the nearman's trail in Dockside, close by the old cloister at Britomart and Barber that had become some kind of hospital now. He might have been injured in the escape, but if that was the case, not too badly: he smelled of liniment and antiseptic, but he was alone and moving under his own power. And quickly, away from the hospital. Toward Citadel, into the old quarter of the city.

His scent was fresh, and strengthened by a falling dew. Even without a canine, Selene could track him almost as fast as he could run. She was a little surprised when she *caught* him, though, halfway through Hangman, not far from the old gibbet in the marketplace from which the precinct took its name.

Once she had located him, she didn't know what to do next. Bring him in, of course, no question. Her instructions were perfectly clear. But then here he was, sitting splay-legged against a wall with his palms fallen open on his thighs and his head lolled forward. The air stank of blood and the Grey Wolf, and she thought for a moment his neck had been snapped.

But no. The areaway he lay in echoed with the rasp of rough breathing, and when Selene padded close he lifted his head as though the motion hurt him. His hair had come free of the usual ponytail, so fleecy locks protruded in every direction; his expression was slack and unchanging. Clots of blood drooled down his chin and streaked his cheeks, as if he had been struck in the mouth. His eyes caught the light as he moved, flashing blue-silver like an unman's. Dark-adapted, Selene thought, in addition to the speed and strength that she had learned first-hand.

But he was incapacitated now, or very near it. She squatted beside him, weight on the balls of her feet, carelessly allowing her claws to furrow stone. "Cathoair."

If he had seemed less injured, she never would have come so close. Nor would she have offered him her wrist, claws loosely folded inside her hand, as a prop by which to lever himself to his feet. And she was not unwary. If he had been only so fast as when they wrestled before, what next transpired would not have.

He lunged into her arms, moving as fast as Diana, bowled her onto her back, crushed her body under his own. She yowled, arms spread wide against the reflex to eviscerate, and his mouth covered hers.

She *would* have bitten him for that. But some unfamiliar reflex twisted in her breast as the taste of his blood and the Grey Wolf's filled her mouth, and instead when he breathed her screech in, she kept breathing it out, and accepted what he gave back a moment later.

What Muire had done. The same thing, irksome and terrible and sweet. So simple. So sweet, filling her until she was nothing but breath and light and will—

He recoiled, rolled to the side, and measured his length on the stones. "Snakerot," he said, staring up at the sky. "I'm sorry. I'm— I thought—" A deep breath. He pressed his hands over his eyes, and Selene, dazed, imagined she saw a ripple of light around his fingers. "I thought you were someone else."

"You were distraught."

"I am *so* sorry."

"It's nothing." She touched her mouth. To wipe the blood away. And pushed herself upright and glowered at him, not that he could see her with his hands like that. "If I give you a hand up, are you going to molest me again?"

"No." He planted a hand on the ground and levered himself maladroitly upright without assistance. "How did you find me?"

"You can't hide from Black Silk," she said. "Not for long. Not in Eiledon."

"You're here to arrest me."

Selene shook her head, although he was correct. But when she opened her mouth to say the words, what she heard her own crystal sweet voice say was, "Actually, I've come here to defect."

When Muire returned to the Ash & Thorn, she carried crumpled paper in her left hand and a lifetime's cold fear in her heart. The bar was quiet in chill sunrise, and things had changed: Hrothgar met her at the top of the stairs and held the door.

Are none of them even the faintest bit jealous? she wondered. She had grown old.

The future was an alien world.

At least taverns were familiar. And this one was growing into a sort of home. "If I don't stop coming here, you're going to start charging me rent," she said to the bartender, a flat attempt at humor.

It was terrible, but Aethelred smiled anyway. It had to be a professional skill. "Thank you for bringing him home," he said.

"Sorry it took so long," she said, and waited for him to tell her where to go. As she had suspected he would, he gestured her toward the door to the private room Astrid had introduced her to. But as she walked past him, he laid a hand on her arm.

"You're too old for him," he said.

She looked him in the eye. "Light. Does everybody know?"

"I haven't told anyone. And I wasn't sure until just now. You've gotten unused to people, haven't you, Menglad Brightwing?"

"I have been a long time alone." She reached out lightly with the hand he had been touching, and pressed the fingers to the chromed side of Aethelred's face. "And you're wrong."

"Wrong?"

"Cathoair knows. He figured it out. And I'm not Menglad. She was my sister, and she's dead. I've always been Muire, and you haven't heard my name because it isn't in the histories."

He pressed his own hand over hers; warmth and comfort returned. The bowed and rebowed serpent flashed in the collar of his shirt. Muire couldn't regard it without irony. "Why not?"

"Because I was the historian."

Astrid, Selene, and Cathoair waited for Muire in the dusty storage room. Selene curled patently asleep on a bench, Astrid had thrust her boots up on the rickety table, and Cathoair paced a winding path around the clutter. The two awake both looked up at Muire when she entered, and with a gasp that caught like a bubble behind her breastbone, Muire saw the shimmer of silver across Cathoair's eyes.

"Strifbjorn?"

He flinched, and hard, wincing like a cat who's had water flicked in its face. And then looked her in the eye and frowned and said, "*What* about bears?" while Astrid stared thoughtfully.

"Never mind," Muire answered, and made sure the door latched. "The Wolf—"

"It's in the note," Cathoair said. On her bench, Selene yawned elaborately. Muire did not think unmans slept.

"Tell me in your own words, again." She dragged a chair around, Selene and Cathoair both wincing at the noise, and perched on the very edge the better to listen while he went over it in detail. Which he did, restless, hands describing complicated arcs, somehow entranced and enraged by his own story.

When he was done, Muire leaned forward without standing, and looked from Cathoair to Selene. "Is she telling the truth?"

"Yes." Without even a trace of hesitation. "I believe her."

"All right," Muire said, thinking of finding herself here, again, and arrayed beside these ancient allies and enemies. *There are seen hands and unseen hands. And nothing ever changes.* "You're in. What are we going to do about it?"

With her eyes, she tried to ask Cathoair *How are you?* And though he met her stare and quirked head directly, his expression was like a mannequin's.

Muire. Before you make any decisions. There is one more angel you should include in your councils.

Cristokos.

We are underway.

Who's in charge of this operation? But Muire cleared her throat, and explained. "So there's another coming."

"His name?" Selene asked. The first words she'd spoken since Muire entered the room.

"Cristokos."

"Oh." Selene's ears went up, her whiskers forward. "It will be good to see him. I'm glad he isn't dead."

"You know him?"

"There are only a few hundred of us," she said. And Muire nodded, remembering how it had been before the Last Day. She had, indeed, known every one who died on that battlefield, and many on both sides had been friends.

"All right," she said. She didn't know if she would sleep any more than Selene did. She had not, since the second time the wolf kissed her, and she hadn't missed it. "Then I think we should get some rest, all of us."

Cathoair stood up. "I'm going to find Muire and Selene a place to rest," he said. Which was all the hint Muire needed that he didn't expect to be sleeping with her. And then he turned to Astrid and said, "Would you ask Aethelred to put me on the card for tomorrow?"

"Cahey—"

"Look," he said. "I'm not hurt. My leg's fine. I have honestly never felt better. And I need the fight."

Astrid frowned at him for a painful ten seconds before glancing at Muire for support. Muire almost shook her head; that easily, and she was co-opted into the Cathoair Preservation League. Astrid didn't trust him to take care of himself, but she certainly trusted his judgment when it came to people. Muire caught the glance, lobbed it back, and smiled.

"Cathoair," she said, "I can pay it—"

"So can I." *He* wouldn't meet her gaze, the subtext clear in his avoidance. He might whore. He might do all sorts of things. But he wouldn't put himself in that position to people he *liked*.

If but one aspect of Strifbjorn might survive, must it have

been the stubborn, stupid pride? "Even the end of the world couldn't make you listen—"

But he cut her off with a slicing hand, and seemed—oh, please, Light, please—to have missed her damning slip. "I have to fight," he said, slowly pushing his fists into his trousers. "Because I need to hit someone. And if I do it in the ring, I don't have to do it the rest of the time."

His voice came plainly, matter-of-fact. Muire felt her foot lifting before she even realized her body meant to drag her back a step. She put it down in the same spot she had lifted it from, but she knew her face was white and still. She opened her mouth and had nothing to say.

"The wolf—"

"I don't want to talk about it." He was looking at Astrid, not at her. "You made me go over it once. Once was enough, don't you think?"

Sometimes, the best thing you could do was take the defeat and regroup. And some people were prone to moral cowardice. Muire had no idea how this would seem to another.

"All right," Astrid said. "But you're not fighting anyone but me. Deal?"

"Star," he said, "I love you."

Cristokos reached the Ash & Thorn under cover of darkness the following night, seeming frightened. Muire did not blame him.

Kasimir had left the rat-mage off outside the city, and Cristokos had entered in the same manner as Muire and Cathoair. Muire and the valraven had agreed; he was not to dare the Defile until he was needed.

Aethelred took the robe-swathed rat-mage better than Muire expected, smuggling him in through the delivery hatch without comment. But then, his bar was into the late night rush, and his back room was already brimming with livestock and angels. And Muire was beginning to understand something about the burn-scarred old cyborg with the serpent medallion dangling against his chest, and the dozen or so street kids and hustlers that used his bar as a base of operations.

Aethelred was doing what he could.

Selene had returned with nightfall. She had risked a return to the Tower and—Muire devoutly hoped—a false report, so she would not seem to have become rogue, and she awaited them in the back room. After an affectionate greeting that seemed to involve a good deal of sniffing—though Muire averted her eyes from the details—Cristokos pushed his hood back from his long face with both hands and crouched in an unhappy lump on his chair. Muire brought him a bowl of wine, which he took in long fingers.

"The valley wine is better," he pronounced, after dipping his nose in it. But he licked the droplets from his whiskers and drank, shivering.

Muire bit her lip softly. Yes, Cristokos's wine *was* better. It was real grapes, for one thing, not tank-grown. And if he assigned its goodness to where those grapes grew, that was only part of the story.

But he was shivering as he drank, so Muire sat down across from him, and Selene stood behind his chair, her hands upturned, the backs resting on his shoulders. What was it, to go through life always aware that one's very touch was a weapon?

Cristokos seemed to take comfort in it. His long, ropelike

tail curled tightly around one leg of his chair, as if clinging for security. "This one missed the city," he admitted, in such a small voice that Muire winced. *City rat, country rat.*

"I need your help."

"This one ran away," he said. Whatever happened to Muire's face, it brought his ears forward, and Selene's, too. He continued, "That one knew."

"I knew," she said, and gritted her teeth. "I ran away, too."

He made a brushing-away gesture with his hand. "Moreaux are not that one's people."

"No." She should have said, *I don't mean that I ran away from your people.* She should have confessed.

Cathoair had asked, obliquely, never knowing how important it could be. What was an angel with nothing to serve?

"Are you ready to face the Technomancer again?"

"This one will never be ready," he said, and finished the wine. "But this one will do what must be done."

He seemed unwilling to lean out from under Selene's touch to set the bowl down, so Muire took it from him, trying not to notice how his eyes closed with relief when her hand brushed his. Rats lived in tumultuous colonies, warm squabbling families and warm close-pressed bodies.

He had been as alone as Muire ever had, without the thin comfort of knowing why. Was it some punishment for opposing Heythe? Had they been meant to do other than they had done? Or was it just that the world was full of woe, and the world kept calling them back again?

"The stallion said you had news."

"Ill news." His throat worked. "Something is happening in the valley."

He startled, and Muire was halfway through turning to see

why when she realized that she was on her feet, fists clenched, and it was from her that he was flinching. "Sorry," she said. She picked up his bowl, cupped it in her hand. "Thjierry is using the valley up."

"Yes," he said, and Muire's hands whitened on the bowl.

"We led her there," she said. "I am sorry."

The rat-mage nodded as if he believed her, but it was Selene who spoke. "So we fight?"

"It seems she's leaving us no options." Muire looked down at the bowl in her hand and slowly relaxed her grip. A little harder and it would have shattered in her hand. "More wine, Cristokos?"

He nodded. Muire looked at Selene, whose nose scrunched in distaste. Very well, two bowls. Muire wanted alcohol herself.

When she emerged into the bar, it was the quiet between fights. Aethelred was engaged in making book, but he tore himself away when Muire caught his eyes. "All right, we won't start until we have everybody—half a minute here. More wine?"

She slid the borrowed bowl for Cristokos across the counter, and with a bit of rummaging came up with her own. "Who's next in the ring?"

"Cahey," he said, and looked at her under the half-burnished ridge of his brows. "And Astrid. Tell me you tried to talk him out of this."

Muire spread her hands.

"I know. Might as well argue with a battle shoggoth. It's going where it's going, and all you can do is get what's breakable out of the way."

Past the tips of her fingers, Muire said, "He's good." But what she meant was, *He'll get hurt someday.*

Blue and green neon rippled in reflected bands across chrome when Aethelred shook his head. His voice wasn't low—even in a lull, the Ash & Thorn was hardly quiet—but nobody more than three feet away would have overheard for the noise. Another occupational proficiency. "That's not what this is about."

"No." She picked up the bowls, but didn't step away from the bar yet. "Why won't he let me help him?"

"With *money*?"

"I have more than I will ever need." Oddly offended. "I don't want to *buy* him."

"No, he only rents," Aethelred said, which struck Muire as unfair. But then he continued, "He's not for sale. You and I, we have to talk. *He* needs to talk to you, too."

"Wish me luck—"

"No," he said. "You know what? I'll tell you. It's—you know about his mom?"

"I know she's dying."

Aethelred puffed air between his teeth, cheekflesh pouching around his breath on the meaty side of his face. "Ask him, sometime, where he got the scar."

"I did. A duel, he said." Something cold and hard was accreting in the pit of Muire's stomach.

"Well," Aethelred answered, "That's true, as far as it goes. But he's got reasons not to let himself get beholden to people he cares about. And he cares about you, trust me on that one."

"I'll have to," she said drily.

"He ever mention his father?"

Muire, the wine balanced in either hand like a statue of undecided Justice, waited him out. He stared at her unremittingly for several seconds, but she was more patient by centuries.

He turned his head and spat on the floor. "Should have killed the son of a bitch myself, saved Cahey the trouble."

Muire drew one deep, painful breath. "I'll do what I can."

He slapped her on the shoulder lightly, like a man shaking off the news of an old friend's death. "That's you and me both," he replied, and then: "Add it to your list—snakerot, Muire, I have to get back to these—"

Across the bar, Cathoair and Astrid were testing the ropes before climbing into the ring, and Aethelred's would-be bettors were growing restless. "Go," Muire said, and picked her way back to the access door. By the time she made it through the press, she heard a cheer. Tables near the wall had no view, and were mostly clear; she set the wine on one and stepped up on a stool for a look.

Astrid and Cathoair were still teasing, she thought. Playing. Cheerful. This wasn't a serious fight yet, if it ever would be. But it was a good performance: as much fun to watch as it might have been to put on.

Astrid bounced off the ropes, where Cathoair had knocked her, and delivered a left-footed roundhouse to his chest. It staggered him, but he came back swinging while onlookers roared. Astrid sidestepped him, ferocious, laughing, fists and torso weaving like snakes. He grinned at her and whirled so as not to give her his flank, veins bulging in embossed relief across his lean, gleaming body.

Muire wondered if they were so fierce in bed together.

The door clicked behind her as she went back to Cristokos. She was shaking almost too hard to hand him his bowl. Gallantly, he pretended he didn't notice.

He was trembling a little himself.

"How does that one plan to end Her without destroying the

city?" Cristokos gestured with the bowl, chittering as wine slopped across his knuckles. He transferred the bowl to the other hand and tongued the fluid off.

Muire sat down. "That's possible. I think . . . if problematic. Do you happen to know how she maintains the levitation on the Institute? I know there's a stasis. But you were her lab assistant—"

"If She falls, does the Tower fall?"

"That's how it works in novels," Muire said, apologetic.

Cristokos sipped the wine. "A combination of effects—engineering, technomancy. Levitation, augmented by a motion-stasis that affects the foundation, as that one has surmised."

"Nothing else? What about the orrery?"

"The orrery is discrete from the levitation spell. But the levitation does rely on gyroscopic stabilizers," he said. "It resets against them. Technomancy, but as far as this one is aware they are fail-safe."

"So if we were to *stop* the orrery . . ."

Muire had never before seen a rat smirk. "This one thinks it *might* work."

The sounds from the bar filtered through the door, and Muire had been tuning them out without realizing it. But another roar—the loudest yet—was followed by silence. And her head came up. And she rose.

Selene had turned too, hand on her whip, when Muire glanced aside to see if she was imagining the oppressive quality of the quiet. She nodded, and Muire moved past her, toward the door, leaving the unmans in the room. Protected.

She was not thinking enough to pray. Just moving. Into a silent room that smelled of blood and strong drink.

Aethelred was not at his post. He had crossed to the corner, near the ring but not in it, hunkered over someone on the floor. Muire thought she should be moving faster, shoving bystanders aside—she was a doctor, for all the good it had ever done her, for all the good it would do her now—but she just kept pacing, slowly, methodically, unable to get a clear look through the crowd. *Well,* she thought with terrible lucidity, *that makes everything much simpler, doesn't it?*

Until she saw Cathoair squatting inside the ring, back against a padded cornerpost, arms draped over his knees and long fingers dangling. And *then* she began to run.

Aethelred was trying to breathe for Astrid. He was doing everything he could, but from the loose way her head rolled on her neck when he started the chest compressions, Muire knew. Astrid's eyes were glistening slits, whites purpling with the leakage from burst capillaries, and Muire stopped beside her body for longer than she should have, to nerve herself before she stepped into the ring.

Coward.

She expected Kasimir to contradict her, but he was silent inside her, a deep and audient void. Muire stepped forward, touched the rope, closed her hand around it, swung into the ring. Cathoair lifted his face, blood and sweat streaked across his cheeks, an awful hope bright in its corners.

Muire shook her head.

The only reaction was a stilling. If she had not known him, she would have seen nothing but an impassive face remain impassive. But her hand went to her throat, for a brief second before she made it extend toward him.

Silently, he took it.

She pulled his slack weight up, helping him balance on his bare feet. He was limping on the right, and left bloody footprints. The sole was split. He wasn't feeling the pain yet. When she released his hand to put her arm around him, it hung like a withered leaf on his arm.

Muire turned him from the body, but his head kept swiveling, craning on the long, elegant neck. "Come on, Cahey. Come on. Upstairs."

He let her lead him. "She stepped into it," he said.

Muire sat beside him, close but not quite touching, in his plain little room with the mattress on the wooden floor. They leaned shoulder to shoulder against the wall, while hours straggled by and Cathoair did not speak.

The mirrors reflected enough light to gray the world under the Tower by the time the rhythm of his breathing changed. "I can't do this anymore."

"Do you need to?"

"I have responsibilities." His voice was cracked and dry.

Quietly, with all the assurance that had never worked to convince her, either, Muire said, "You do not have to carry the world alone."

He drew and held a shallow breath. "I think I hate you right now."

But when she reached for his hand, he let her take it. "I wouldn't blame you. Was this my fault?"

"The wolf was. What he—" And then he stopped, swallowed, and did tug his hand free, so he could knuckle at his eyes.

Muire stood, fetched a bowl of water. He had not moved when she returned. She helped him hold it while he drank, as his hands still didn't seem to work properly. He didn't protest when she dampened a handkerchief and wiped the blood from his face, washed his foot, improvised a bandage—but he also didn't help. When she sat back, he said, "I'm kidding myself. You're not the reason he came looking for me."

"No," she said. "You are."

"Why?"

A hell of a question to answer, but he had asked, and now she had to find a way. "You used to be somebody we both knew," she said. "Back when the world was beginning."

"You're talking about reincarnation."

"Yes."

"Oh." He stretched against the wall.

He was still naked, except for his fighting silks, and the sweat had dried on his skin. Muire couldn't understand how he wasn't freezing. She anticipated the next questions with dread— who was he, what was he to you—but he surprised her.

"Is that why *you* found me?"

"No. I found you because I was looking for him."

He breathed out, shuddering, and put the bowl down between his knees so he could lay his forehead on crossed arms. "Well, that's something, then. I can still hear him in my head."

"I know," she said.

"Is that what you did to Selene?"

"Yes."

It was strange, sitting there in the cold dark with him, both silhouetted by the faint light filtering through the window. Strange, and very quiet.

He said, "This is—really hard."

"She saved your life," Muire prompted.

Passionless: "So I could kill her."

Kasimir, what do I do?

If I knew that, he answered, **I would have done it for you centuries ago.**

"Cathoair," she said, "I'm sorry."

She shouldn't have been startled when he turned and bit. But as Aethelred had observed, she wasn't very good at people. Still, the venom lacing his voice took her aback. "What do *you* know about it?"

"Why? Because I could never have done something so terrible that I knew I could never make amends for it? No matter how long I try, or how desperately I wish I had done something different?"

"You're an *angel*."

"I have had," she said, pulling away, turning to face him, "a great deal of time to make mistakes."

He stared up at her. She crouched before him, resting on one knee. She said, "That girl was your friend."

"Astrid," he corrected, tonelessly.

"You screwed up, kid."

He had not expected her to say that. His eyes focused, and he looked at Muire as if trying to remember who she was. And she grabbed him by the biceps and the chin and hauled him up. He flinched when the weight came down on his split foot. *Good.* A reaction. Something was getting through.

He leaned over her, tottering, and she held him up by main strength. "You did something terrible. You were distracted, and you went into the ring, and you got your friend killed."

He cringed as if struck, and shook his head, *no.*

There's a ruthless utility in self-loathing. Hatred can keep you alive, keep you bound until time has a chance to turn weeping wounds to puckered scars.

He strained against her grip, but she held him. She spat the words in his face, every one a jagged knife to cut them both. "You killed her. You have to carry that. It was your fault."

"No," he said, and then, very quietly: "Yes. Oh, Light. I'll do anything. Just—"

But you can't bargain, and you can't trade, and he knew it even as he said it. He wanted to go limp, and she hit him. She cursed him. She slapped him as hard as she dared, and she called him a coward and a fool and a hundred other things she had called herself over the long, long weary years.

He took it all, as if he were one of her statues, and she shook him harder and pushed him up against the wall. "No," she said. "You don't get to give up. You don't deserve self-pity. You don't deserve to rest. You have something to atone for now, and you're going to live up to everything she wanted you to be."

The silence was broken only by the unsteady rasp of his breathing. Muire grabbed him around the back of his neck, knotted the fingers of her other hand in his hair. "You are going to live long enough to make it up to her, you son of a bitch."

He grabbed her by the shoulders and tried to throw her across the room. She held on. They both went down, scrambling, pulling hair, gouging. She tried to pin his wrists and he got in a good backhanded smack that split the inside of her cheek against her teeth. She swore again, grabbed his hand, tore at his hair, pulled his face around and kissed him as hard as she could.

He—convulsed. Shoved, both hands flat against her collarbones. And then he wrapped his arms around her and hauled, squeezed, face buried in her shoulder, wrenching out animal sobs.

She thought he would never stop weeping. She held him,

said his name, muttered nonsense. She told him she loved him, and he flinched, and she told him the truth: that the wound would never heal, but someday it would be just a bitter scar.

Eventually he collapsed against her, breathing like a rattling engine, and she held him down against her shoulder and stroked his hair, pushing the wet locks aside. She said, "I'm going to tell you something that might make sense to you in ten years, or never. You won't want to hear it right now, but you need to remember."

He backed away against the wall before he nodded, very carefully, as if he'd suddenly realized how much his head and neck hurt. Her eyes must have filled up with light, for she could see him clearly now. He smelled of tears and sweat, and his expression was too thoughtful, too measured; a look Muire associated with the worst of news.

It's not a question of if you will lose him. It is only a question of when.

Not if he loses me first. Oh, but how would that be better?

She had sent Kasimir away.

There are times when you just can't stand to be loved.

He drew the tips of his long dark sweet-smelling fingers across her lips. She closed her eyes, the better to memorize his scent. It took him so long to frame the words that she did not at first understand. "I'll understand if you can't forgive me."

Not a denial. Not sending her away. *"Forgive* you?"

"For . . ." He sounded as if his throat were closing around the words. He wrapped his arms around his knees, drawing them against his chest. "You shouldn't—ever—forgive somebody who hits you. They don't stop. You should go."

"Oh." She tried to smooth his hair, but his hair was not a smoothable sort. "I hit you first."

He stared at her. His lips twitched. He started to laugh, brutally, and then he started to choke. Muire thought he was going to vomit, but he didn't, quite.

When he had quieted and was breathing again, in tortured gasps, she stroked his cheek and said what she had to say with all the force of will she could put behind it. "It's not my forgiveness you need. It's your own."

He rocked back and forth, slowly, shaking his head. Muire couldn't tell if he was listening, but his eyes were on her.

"But in the meantime, Cathoair, you use whatever you have to. No matter how dark it is. No matter how it cuts you up, if it lets you feel *anything,* if it lets you keep fighting—use it. Live. Get through."

He thought about it, and then he nodded.

"You're right. I don't want to hear that." He reached for her, kissed her blindly. "I need—"

"Tell me."

"He won't leave me alone," Cathoair said, softly. "He won't get out of my head."

"He won't," she said. "That's one of the things we get to live with too."

He closed his eyes. He averted his face, and covered hers with his spider-stretched fingers. "Will you . . . ?"

"Kiss you like that." Cold understanding. Sharp and reckless. Ice on the edge of a knife.

"Do it."

Muire looked between his fingers, felt his hand slide down her face. Drew a breath that couldn't steady. "Take off your silks," she said, reaching to unbutton her own collar. "I want to feel your skin."

Cathoair was trembling, this time, and Muire was the strong one. Strange how quickly roles can change. Fragile turquoise sparks flashed over and between them when they kissed; when she breathed him in and gave him back, over and over again; when she pushed him down on his back and took him inside of her. Glowing droplets beaded his skin like a dew of sweat, smearing against her hands and forearms when she hooked them under his shoulders and pulled him up, covering his open mouth with her own. Dark poetry surged her veins—branding, cauterizing. They were netted over, bound by viscous, slender strands of light that slid and stretched between their skins, their mouths, their loins, their fingertips. It tangled between like sweat, like saliva, like semen, like hope.

His eyes were so bruised in the glow of her own that the hazel seemed indigo. The healed marks on the backs of his fingers caught her lip when he brushed his hand across her mouth, and he wept again, hot against her throat.

When they were done, he did not sleep. And only the gray reflected radiance of morning washed the old wild sheen of starlight from his skin.

She was old, and too worn thin to wonder. But oh, what a beautiful boy he was then.

Ingwaz (growth inward)

◆

Because he did not sleep, he could not say he'd awakened. But, lying in the darkness, Cathoair made his plan. Nothing messy, violent, or horrifying. Nothing that would inconvenience anyone, except in the blunt necessary inconvenience of death. Nothing that could hurt a bystander, or whoever found him. He couldn't help hurting Muire, but there was no remedy for that. What she had thought was comfort, he knew for a farewell.

He discovered in the planning that he did not care how much pain he caused himself.

He thought about leaving a note, but it would shame him to be remembered as an illiterate scrawl. Aethelred would know what to do. Aethelred knew where to find his mother. And if she wanted to give up her life without a struggle—well, so did he. Aeth could give those instructions as well as Cathoair ever could.

He'd be waiting to meet her on the other side of the river. She would have to forgive him there.

Poison would be best. And poison was easy to find. Aethelred used strychnine to keep the rats out of the bar. The cabinet was locked, but Cathoair had duplicates of Aethelred's keys.

Cathoair would arise in a little, when he had lain here long enough to seem convincing, and he would clean himself up and go downstairs and see about the strychnine.

He was going after Astrid. Aethelred would know what to do.

$\mathcal{M}$uire found him seizing, because she had been sitting at the bar with Selene, drinking Aethelred's burned mock-coffee and trying to come up with a plan. They both heard the crash from the stairs, and as Selene swung wide to flank her, Muire headed straight for the door. It was locked, but she broke the lock with her hand, a sharp inelegant twist that pulled the knob apart.

The door burst open to her yank, revealing Cathoair sprawled against the steps, spine arching uncontrollably, blood streaked across his face from where he'd struck it falling. For a moment she paused, considering, and then she was climbing past him, sliding her thigh under his head, just trying to steady him and keep him from dashing his brains out against the steps.

Selene appeared in the door as Cathoair seized again, driving his skull into Muire's abdomen so she retched. She braced her hands on the wall of the stairwell and said "Get Aethelred."

The moreau vanished, while Muire endured unwitting blows. *Never stay with anybody who hits you.* Oh, Cathoair.

It wasn't more than ninety seconds. Ninety seconds like time buried alive, while Muire crouched cramped and fearful in the dark stairwell. It smelled of mildew, as everything in the Well smelled of mildew, and she wondered if this was how Cristokos had felt, wedged shivering into crevices, using his new freedom of mind to crawl away from home and creator and guardian and everything he knew.

"Strychnine," Aethelred said, coming across the bar at a trot that creaked his chassis and rattled the building. "Somebody's been in the cabinet where I keep the rat poison. What did you *say* to him?"

"Only what I thought would help," Muire snarled back. "Barbiturates. Have you got any?"

Aethelred hesitated, glanced at Selene. "I'd just assumed, a bar like this—" Selene said. And, "If you tell me where, I'll find them."

He did, and told her where to find a hypodermic, and gave her the key. "If we can get him into a dark quiet room and keep him warm, get him to stop convulsing, he might live," Muire said. "Depends on the dose. Death comes from exhaustion. You suffocate because you're too tired to breathe. We need to move him."

They had him on the stone floor of the bar by the time Selene returned, Muire still cushioning his head with her body. "Give me the needle."

"You're busy," Selene said, and knelt beside Cathoair, feeling along his arm. The injection she administered was quick and professional, and it triggered another seizure. It was short-lived, though; as the barbiturates took effect, Cathoair's body slackened, his jaw unclenching. But his breathing grew shallow, and Muire could hear it slowing. She groped for a pulse. "Shadows. Out of the frying pan—"

She closed her eyes. They could move him, try to rush him through the streets to a clinic. She could pay for care—

Muire, he is leaving.

No. She pressed harder, seeking the faint flutter against her fingertips. "Damn it. Damn it. *Damn it.*"

Kasimir. Talk to him. And come here, please.

I hear. As softly as a manifesting ghost, he stood in the center of the bar, heads ducked and wings furled tight, his caparison shining white and azure and silver against the soot of his hide. Selene recoiled, her whip in her hand and her back to a corner like a frightened cat, all her fur on end and poking between the straps of her armor.

"Help me get Cathoair up," she said to Selene. "I have to take him to help."

Selene stared at her, obviously measuring Muire's stature against Cathoair's and finding it wanting.

"Just do it," she said. Aethelred was already reaching for him. "Careful," Muire warned. "Don't burn yourself on the horse. Kasimir, lie down."

He obeyed, and they managed to get Cathoair draped across his neck, protected by the saddle and the blanket. Muire slung a leg over behind him, and then Aethelred said, "How are you getting that thing out of here?"

"Oh." *Can we—*

We're underground.

"We can take him out the delivery bay," Aethelred said, snapping his fingers so metal clanked on metal. "Follow me."

And then they stood in the back alley under a floating streetlight, bright moonlight seeping all around the edges of the Well, and Kasimir cautiously spread his wings, so as not to bump either of the fragile creatures standing near him. "We'll be back when we can," Muire said, steadying Cathoair across her knees and trying to arrange him so the pommel wasn't likely to break his ribs on takeoff. She wedged his limp body as best she could, and knotted both hands in his shirt.

"Go."

His wings swept down and he kicked up, and they were airborne, sailing over the heads of Selene and Aethelred, who ducked even though Kasimir's high-tucked hooves cleared them by inches. **And where are we going?**

You said there was a chance you and I and Mingan were not the only ones left.

I said he was still alive when the Last Day fell. I do not know further.

It's worth a gamble when the alternative is losing.

As it was the last time you asked for a miracle?

Just take me to the ocean, horse.

Selene watched them rise and envisioned her life gone with them, torn away on the horse's iron wings, shredding behind him like a wedding veil. As if with his passing, he had torn away her illusions, and she was only beginning to understand what she had lost. Certainty. Service. Devotion. Love and community, a home, brothers and sisters, someone else who took responsibility and guarded and warded and kept one safe from everything hard in life. Because fighting wasn't hard; patrolling wasn't hard; protecting people from predators wasn't hard at all.

What was hard was making decisions, choices. Taking responsibility. Knowing that when you caught one you let another fall, and living with that choice.

Selene did not think she wanted it.

A coil of air too dank to be called a breeze brought scent. Cristokos has slipped outside, staying within the shadows of the doorway. She was about to gently reprimand him for carelessness, but then she realized it didn't matter if he were seen. Unless one of them who was not a traitor to Her saw him, he was just another unman, and a rat at that. Who could tell them apart?

You feared me.

"Horse?" she said. She looked around, feeling like an idiot when Aethelred and Cristokos both turned to stare. But she didn't know what else it could be. It was a sound that wasn't sound, the memory of someone with a vast deep quiet voice having just a moment ago spoken.

It is I. You feared me, in the bar. Do not fear me.

There was something in the voice, some passionate emotion. It was deep and cold and lonely, and Selene ducked her head, only mouthing the words she said next. It must have been enough. "You are frightening," she said. "And the first time you appeared was the beginning of the end of my life."

You are free now.

"And do you like freedom?"

A pause. **I choose service.** And then a longer pause. **But it is service *I* choose.**

Ineffectually, she tried to stroke her fur flat where it had tufted through the armor. She gave up, after a moment, and curled her own claws into the unarmored part of her upper arm. Warm blood welled around the claw-roots. but she did not drag and tear, only flexed. The pain was wonderfully focusing. "I'm alone," she said, and turned to face the wall. "Like Cristokos."

Like everyone.

"Oh, everyone who?"

Everyone you stand among. Everyone who has just left your presence. All alone. Each of us.

Oh, she thought.

And he said, **Think about it.**

Ten miles downriver from Eiledon, the sea was terrible to behold. Kasimir set down with his hooves clear of the tide, wings held high and daintily like a gull's.

It didn't smell like an ocean. Muire had been born from the sea, named for the sea, had spent the first six hundred years of her life at its very verge. She knew its scent in her bones, like the ache of a long-lost love.

This was not that.

The waves that moved against the shore seemed oily, heavy in the moonlight. Stiff foam floated on them like clots in milk. The beach was barren—no weed tossed up in clots of seawrack, no shells nor fish-bones. Nothing but the skeleton of some immense creature beached on its back a half-mile west, below a bluff, gleaming in the moonlight like sculptured stone.

Kasimir dropped to his knees, and Muire clambered down his side, using his foreleg as a step ladder. Her boot smoked, but she didn't feel the heat. She pulled Cathoair down after her and cushioned his fall as best she could. He was limp; she could feel no heartbeat; she could not tell if he was breathing.

"You left me here once, you craven bastard. Don't you *dare* die on me again."

He cannot hear you. Kasimir's breath came painfully, for no reason Muire could detect. Slow, and heavy, and with a pause between as if each one left him almost unable to draw another.

"Kasimir—"

I breathe for him. Call the snake.

Cathoair's skin was chill. Muire laid him on his back on the sand, below the tideline but above the poisoned waves, and hoped she was not doing him more harm. She composed his hands and feet, and knew it for nervousness, for stalling.

She made her way down the beach and stood where the waves could hiss by the toes of her boots, tugging at the sand. There was no stability anywhere in the world, but here it was made manifest. She took a breath and raised her voice, let it ring out as it had when she had been a poet, and declaimed. "By moonlight, by earth and by ocean, bearer of Burdens, I summon You."

For long moments, while she waited, nothing at all. Muire doubled over, hands on her knees, the astringent cleaning-fluid smell of the waves overcoming her. *And what if he doesn't come?*

Then the world is truly dead. And there will be no renascence.

Muire straightened. She rubbed at her fingers, as if the tips kept stinging from where she'd struck Cathoair. He lay still on the beach, so still, his palms upturned and open as if to catch the moonlight.

Muire went and sat beside him, on the stand, and slipped her fingers through his own. "He's gone," she said, meaning the one they had come to beg for assistance. Kasimir was still breathing like a man in a press, and she hoped he would stop before he followed Cathoair all the way down. But it would be futile to remonstrate. She could tell him nothing of which he was unaware, and he was fighting each breath like a battle in a losing war.

She should have kept the barricades high, manned the battlements of herself a little better. It had come to nothing; she had accomplished nothing. Nothing, except more death. And having let them touch her, Kasimir and Cathoair, she would only lose them after all.

And the world lost with them.

Muire laid her cheek against her free hand and murmured something she had never thought to hear an angel say.

"It isn't fair."

No, sister. Not fair, not bright. Not now, nor never will be.

At first the light was hard to see. It could have been the reflected radiance of the setting moon or the rising brilliance of the sun shimmering across the ocean. Cautious tentative fingers of light spread through clotted water, until slowly the sea began to shine. Music echoed in her ears—faint, unearthly, chiming: song swept down from all the windwracked stars above. Arpeggios and falls, teasing Muire's hair like a breeze, a distant and almost forgotten chorale.

The Snake rose from shallows that could not have held its bulk, a long lean coil of pearly light, tattered golden tendrils surrounding a narrow, thoughtful face. A serpent of incomprehensible size, dwarfing the wreck of the carcass down-strand. Great wounds and sores putrefied along the length of body vanishing back into the deeps, and it swam toward her, coiling and uncoiling, moonlight trapped within the writhing translucence of its bulk. And she understood, with awful clarity, just how it was that the Light had failed, that the Dweller Within had failed to come to their aid in the last battle. He had cut them off, silenced himself, drawn wide . . . so they would not live his pain along with him.

No abandonment, nor forsaking. Rather, a sacrifice.

I was a long way off, small sister, and have come back a long way in answer to your plea. Speak, that I may know your need, for I have long left the world behind. The Wyrm bowed its scarred head over Muire's. The snout swung to and fro, stately as a massive pendulum. It seemed to sweep its gaze along the beach, but only empty sockets marked where eyes had been. THEY'VE MADE RATHER A MESS OF IT WHILE I WAS AWAY.

Muire could have stood, but she would have had to release Cathoair's hand. And what did a snake care if you met it standing? She clutched tighter and asked, "Elder brother, who hurt you so sore?"

IT IS A POISONED WOUND FROM LONG AGO. AND IT IS TIME. I AM THE BEARER OF BURDENS, AND THE WORLD HAS GROWN SICK AND OLD. There was nothing of self-pity in its voice, despite black tiredness. Rather, it mocked. It opened its mouth as it spoke, and Muire saw the ropelike tongue rolling a small shining object among rotting teeth. BUT I ENDURE. YOU HAVE BROUGHT ME A BROKEN ANGEL.

"Is he an angel?"

ON THE VERGE OF IT. AND ON THE VERGE OF BEING NOTHING AT ALL. I COULD ENVY HIM THE LATTER.

Muire closed her eyes, but forced them open again, and wondered if what she was about to offer was just more selfishness, again. Because yes. The Snake had only spoken something she felt herself.

She supposed he knew it. But she still said, "I wish an intervention."

THE PRICE IS A LIFE.

"I wish to take his place."

YOU OFFER YOUR DEATH FOR HIS LIFE?

"I should have died for him in the snow."

The great Serpent coiled, and considered. NOT MUCH OF A BARGAIN. I'VE ONE WOULD PLEASE ME BETTER.

She knew better than to trust gods when they grew mocking.

But Cathoair's hand grew cold in her own, and she could barely hear Kasimir's breathing, when it had been like a steam engine moments before.

"Tell me."

YOUR DEATH FOR HIS LIFE, THAT IS NOT EQUITABLE. SOMETHING YOU CRAVE FOR WHAT YOU ACCOUNT AT NOTHING? Its forked-lightning tongue flickered briefly, offering another glimpse of its toy. Amber, she thought. A nugget of amber. YOUR LIFE FOR HIS LIFE, THAT'S A FAIR BARGAIN.

"I have always served you."

YES.

"Then how can you—"

TAKE MY PLACE, it said. BEAR MY BURDENS. AND HE WILL BE HEALED.

Rotting flesh, sores and gangrene. Kasimir rattled out a breath. The Snake dropped its head, and Muire smelled the death on it, rotten meat and the befouled sea. Its tongue flickered out to taste the hollow of her throat, a touch as light as a featherfall.

"No," she said. *Coward. Coward. Did you ever pretend you were anything more?*

THERE ARE THINGS THAT ARE BROKEN BEYOND MENDING, MUIRE THE SCHOLAR. THERE ARE THINGS THAT CANNOT BE SET RIGHT. FOR THOSE THINGS, ALL WE CAN DO IS BREAK THEM AND FORGE THEM ANEW, LIKE SHATTERED SWORDS AND RUINED WHEELS. ARE YOU THAT THING, SMALL SISTER? IS THE WORLD ALSO?

Muire imagined Kasimir white and shattered in the snow, and Gunther wasted on his deathbed, and Strifbjorn eaten alive, reaching out his hand as he fell, as she turned and ran. She saw a city ripped by lightnings, and a great battle raging in the sky overhead. She saw poisoned earth and sorrow, and the rotten wounds in a great Wyrm's side, and she recoiled. *It is not* all *my doing, this evil!*

None of it was your doing. It was my evil to bear. I ask again.

Dying, all dying—Eiledon, the world, falling into Shadow and red light: the pain of the world, the black knife cutting, the wound at its heart. The Snake, twenty-five hundred years dying. And so close to the end.

She could give him surcease. She could save Cathoair.

She looked at the pus dripping and turned away, cheek pressed to her shoulder. The hardest thing. Not to die, but to live. **Live!**, with Kasimir's heart, through iron and fire. What she had said to Cathoair was true. It were cowardice to lie down. "And you, Snake? Are you that thing?"

I am old.

"So is the wolf." Thunder rumbled over the water, the first fringes of cloud fingering the moon. Somewhere far out, Muire could hear the hiss of dead rain. "And if I could heal you? If *we* could heal you? Would you tolerate the pain of healing? Or are you a thing that can only be reforged?"

You cannot.

"Are you even willing to let us try?"

A life for a life. Not a death for a life. No, no easy bargains here. *Coward,* Muire told herself, as the first drops hissed into the water and against her stallion's hide. To ask of another what one would not oneself do—

The water falling from the dark sky was freezing cold, and not a start-of-summer rain at all. And well . . . they were all cowards under this rain, then. Except Kasimir.

"You said he was on the verge of being an angel. Einherjar. So make him one. His life for his life. Isn't *that* a fair bargain?"

He stared at her. And then if snakes can smile, he smiled, and if snakes can wink, he lidded his eyes. IT IS DONE, he said, and vanished into the water.

THOU LOVEST THE WORLD FOR THOU ART THE WORLD. THOU ART BLASTED AND BLACK, THERE ARE CORPSES AND BONES UNDER THY SKIN, BUT THOU ART LONGING TO BE HEALED. THOU ART FEARFULLY ALIVE, SMALL SISTER, AND FEARFULLY WEAPONED, AND FEARFULLY WOUNDED—AND THE SOUL IN THEE IS AS CRIPPLED AS THE EARTH UNDER THY FEET. BUT THOU HAST TAKEN THIS LAND AS THY WARD. NOW UNDERTAKE TO SET HER ARIGHT. LOOK TO THE EDGE OF THE SEA.

Something glinted there when the lightning flashed, and then it shone between flashes—brighter and more, as the rain washed the sand away. Now Muire laid down Cathoair's hand. Now she stood up from the wet sand and crossed the beach, and now she crouched and brushed the clinging sand aside.

She knew this blade, even more so than she knew Svanvitr. She knew its plain round pommel and its straight, broad blade, so much heavier than Nathr that it seemed ridiculous that the same word meant both weapons. Sand clung to her palm, and she rubbed her fingers against her palm to dust it away. And then she reached down and lifted it free of the strand.

It glowed softly in response to her touch, and the rain that washed lingering sand from its blade dripped from the point like burning candlewax, glowing with its own contagion of light. Kasimir breathed easily now, picking his way toward Cathoair with all the delicacy of a giant, pensive cat, while the rain steamed off his sides.

He breathes.

His eyes opened as Muire came up to him, the hazel washed away in a ghost of silver light. He sat up, drawing up his knees, arms wrapped tight around them. Silently, Muire extended the sword, pommel-first. "It's name is Alvitr," she said. "Does that mean anything to you?"

He raised his gaze to hers, and his face was terrible, impassive, stern behind the scar. The face of a warrior. The face of an einherjar. He unwound one hand from his knees and laid it on the hilt.

"Who gave you the right to choose for me?" he asked.

She looked at his face, and made hers the same. "Who gave you the right to leave me behind?"

Laguz (the sea)

Open air. Open rain. The slip and twist of sand under bare feet, scouring uncalloused arches. The wind on his neck.

The lightning. The hiss of the waves.

Cathoair left the massive sword Muire had thrust upon him shoved point-first into the sand beside her stallion. It shed an eerie blue light, shimmering through the glass beads of the rain. His head was full of poetry, music, light, the sound of an entirely different sea.

Muire walked beside him and would not return his side-long glances. The fey light made her look inscrutable. Inconsolable. And Cathoair found himself thinking that there should be a word for the way the hair sticks in curls to the neck of somebody you ought to have learned to love but didn't, when you are walking with them at night, down a beach in the rain.

But because that word didn't exist, what he said instead was "I've never seen the ocean before."

She seemed to study the sand. It was perfectly trackless before them; there was nothing alive here to leave a trail until they had wandered over it. Behind, two sets of footsteps stretched back toward the light, hers shod and his naked.

"This isn't really an ocean," she answered. "Oceans aren't dead."

"It's the only ocean I'll ever see." He turned into the rain. It slapped his face, smarting, leaving a faint smell of camphor behind. "What would happen if I walked into it?

Then, she looked at him, her face made all crooked and peculiar by the inconsistent light. Or perhaps that was just her expression.

"Nothing much, now, most likely. You're immortal now. Unless something kills you—"

"And what can kill me?"

"A sword through the heart," she said. "A bullet through the brain. Are you going to try it?"

He rubbed his neck, the back of his skull through the hair. It seemed like it should hurt. He remembered the convulsions, and how Muire had held him up. He'd known that strychnine was a painful death. But no one had ever told him that it left the victim in perfect wakefulness throughout.

He wondered if he would have chosen something different if he'd known, and remembered a woman in his mother's neighborhood who had killed herself by climbing atop the fire in her grate. If you wanted oblivion badly enough—

"No," he said. "I think the moment's passed."

She rolled her shoulders to ease her back. He heard the crackle of vertebrae. "Cathoair, why didn't you tell me about your father?"

"I'm going to smack that son of a bitch." And having said it, he bit his lip at the unthinking violence of the words, wishing he could repudiate them. Wishing they were not windowglass into the buried truth of who he was.

A killer. A brute. No different from his father.

She shook her head, and the wet hair blew into her eyes. She growled at it and scraped it back with stiff fingers. He wondered if maybe he did love her a little after all. "He assumed I knew."

"There are things people don't talk about. Because nobody wants to hear them, and nobody wants to be the broken thing that gets left behind after they happen, all right?"

He wouldn't have pushed against himself, in this mood. But then, he was newer at the angel game than she was. She said, "Do you . . . would it help? To talk?"

"Done some. Probably done some forgetting. If you want to know, I'll tell you. It won't help me, and you won't like it."

The quiet hung there in between them for a little, being the noisiest silence he'd ever heard. She coughed. "I thought . . ."

"You thought?"

"I misjudged you," she said, in tones of apology. "I thought you were . . . fast. Reckless. A footloose greedy narcissistic kid."

"I know," he said. "I like it when people don't get me. It's like being three steps to the right of where they think I am. They'll never hit me in a million years."

She grunted—did angels grunt?—and they walked in silence for another kilometer until she bent down suddenly and fumbled up a flat stone. "Alvitr. The sword. You know you're keeping her."

"They're for killing people."

"Aethelred told me something about that, too. Anyway, that one is for more than just killing people."

His hair dripped cold water down his neck. He half raised his hand, and then shrugged. He couldn't get any wetter.

"Alvitr," she said. "It means 'all-white.' You'll take her."

"Why so pushy about it?"

"Because I promised the Snake we'd try to heal the planet," she said. "And that's why he made you live."

"So what are we going to do?"

"The four of us—" and he knew she meant Selene and Cristokos "—and Kasimir are going to steal all of the swords from the Technomancer, and use them to free all her unmans and turn them back into einherjar and waelcyrge, too."

"That's ballsy—wait. *Back* into angels?"

"Where did you think their souls came from?" she asked, arch but smiling. "And when we have four hundred angels, we're going to go looking for the rest of the swords. And see who else we can find. I think everybody's come back, Cathoair. I think all of us are back, and this is our time, and we can put things right. Heal it. Start the process at least, so it can mend itself." Her chin came up; her face brightened with passion.

"You really mean to save the world," he said.

"I really do."

He bounced a half step and kicked air, shadowboxing, his fingers curled loosely, his jaw locked against nausea. But he could do it. If he had to. If he envisioned every blow as murderous, and went in swinging with his eyes afire. He looked at Muire and said, "I don't think I can hit someone again unless I mean to kill them. You need to know that."

"Take the sword, einherjar."

Light, what a word. Archaic, stupid word. He wished she'd just say angel. She did sometimes, spoke sloppily. It wouldn't kill her.

But she was still looking at him, not blinking, the light from her eyes staining their sockets.

Cathoair drew a breath. "I'll need to figure out some kind of a sheath."

"Thank you." She still hefted that stone. He watched, curious, as she turned it in her hand twice before curving a forefinger around the edge.

"What are you doing?"

"Watch." She stooped and whirled, arm extended, and launched the rock out over the ocean. It left her hand glowing brightly, wheeling through the rain sheeting light, and spun across the water. Cathoair held his breath, waiting for the double plunk—stone into water and then displaced water into itself again—but there was no sound loud enough to carry over the rain. Instead, the stone just touched the water, brushed it, and lifted up again. And again, and then another time, until it had left a diminishing chain of circles on the surface, illuminated from below by its own sinking light until that light went out.

He watched, entranced for moments after, and only when thunder broke the spell did he turn and say, "Show me how?"

"It's not magic," she said. "Except the light part. And it's not hard. Of course I'll show you."

And she did.

She was right; it wasn't hard at all once you mastered the wrist motion. He got five skips on his sixth try, and after that Muire stood back and watched him try to repeat it for half an hour. The rain stopped during his practice. The squall blew past, and the moonlight glazed the beach.

"It's all about picking the right stone," Muire said, and after that he did better. It wasn't as good as hitting the heavy bag, but it took concentration and focus and precision and tightly controlled violent motion, and since the thought of clenching a fist made his gorge rise it would have to do for now. The split across the ball of his foot had healed along with everything else. He hated it for not bleeding.

The sky was going grey, the pale light of the blade washing out in the pale light of dawn. "Are you ready to go back yet?" Muire asked.

"I just want to watch the sunrise," he said, amazed that it was suddenly so important. He crouched down and found a disc-shaped rock, gray and grainless, with a white band of cloudy crystal across the middle. The gray part was almost silky, but the band had a different texture, and for a moment he weighed it in his hand, contemplating sending it after the others. But his hand found its way into his pocket, and when it emerged it had left the stone behind. "Then we can go home."

Cathoair lives.

That was all. Just the stallion's voice-that-wasn't, murmuring in Selene's ear, before the return of silence. She wondered why he chose to speak to her, but relayed the information dutifully. Cristokos made a small chittering noise; he knew Selene cared. Aethelred closed his eyes, laid his rag on the bar, and let his head fall back on the stumpy pillar of his neck, as if exposing his throat to god.

What the stallion said did not prepare Selene to see Cathoair walk in unsupported, however, filthy and damp and lithe and straight-spined and as if he had never known a day's pain in the world. Nor had she expected the bastard sword at his hip, or the awkward way he kept a hand on it, startling every time it rattled against something—the doorframe, a bar stool.

"Cathoair—"

He looked at Selene as if he was looking back from the top of a thousand-mile climb. "Apparently, we're angels," he said, and walked past her, and past Aethelred, and into the stairwell where he had nearly died.

She heard him rising.

Muire had stood in the doorway, watching, a frown on her face. She entered the room as Cathoair left, stopping next to Selene just in time to watch the door click shut. "I try not to be jealous," she said, apologetically, her tones low enough that Aethelred could pretend he hadn't heard.

Selene sneezed. "It's not your most engaging trait."

"No," Muire said. "It never has been."

"I can't use him for what you want him for, you know."

Muire just looked at her. "Selene—" She swallowed. "If you talk to Thjierry like that, she'll never believe you're the same creature."

"I'm not," Selene said, her tail lashing. "I can't. I can't be her again."

"You want to?"

"It was easy."

"Yes," Muire said, and Selene did not think she was talking about Selene. "It was." She looked down and scraped her boot across the floor. Sand fell from her trouser cuffs and scattered the stone. "I'm going to ask you to confront her. And to intervene to win freedom for the other moreaux."

"Freedom," Selene said. "What's that?"

Muire shrugged. "Mostly unpleasant, from what I'm learning. Was that a yes?"

"It's a yes," answered Selene. "But only because your stallion convinced me of something."

"What's that?" Muire looked up then, tilted her chin and looked Selene in the eyes over the bridge of her china-doll nose. Who would have expected a warrior angel to look like a child's plaything, with freckles on milk-white skin, and grey-glass eyes?

"That choosing what you serve is different than being owned."

"Hey," Muire said. "Enjoy choosing. Let me know what that's like, would you? I need to go pick up another sword. And my fiddle—"

Selene shook out her ruff, pricked her ears. "It's safer for me to be on the street than you. I'll go. Tell me where."

Safer for Selene to be on the street, and probably also not safe for Muire to be on the rooftop. But she climbed anyway, up the rickety outside stair, noting that it needed—in places—to be repaired. And she sat down on the tar paper, laid the sword that was not Nathr down beside her, and folded up her legs. "I owe you an apology, Bright one."

You owe me nothing. She imagined him swishing his tail, slapping at imaginary flies. Not that a real fly could pierce his hide. **What do you owe yourself?**

You've caught me out. I was unjust. I left you alone.

Do you desire forgiveness?

Just your attention. If he were standing over her, both giant heads would have swiveled just then so he could watch her side-long, as horses will, with the full attention of a single wise eye in each. *I have tried to be sorry you chose me. I can't.*

An alarm bell rang somewhere in the distance. In her mind's eye, his ears worked, twisting forward and back. Muire breathed deeply, as if she meant to put what she had to say into real spoken words. *I think you saved me. I think*—and no mercy, there, because the voice of the mind could not catch in your throat and spare you—*I think if I had left you in the snow I would have been tarnished. And I may be diminished. But I do not think I am damned.*

He said nothing, but she felt the motion as one giant head dipped before he shook it up again, tossing his forelock back. **We are what we are,** he said, **and that which we are shall be sufficient.**

"I wish I had your faith." She covered her mouth with her hand. *What have I done to Cathoair?*

Saved him.

He did not want to be saved.

Then he can make that decision for himself, again. He does not want for courage.

She pressed her face into her hands. "No, just sense." The words were a mumble against her fingers, but Kasimir would hear them.

Kasimir?

He listened. She could sense his listening.

Tell the wolf I want him to come talk to me.

I can ask, the warhorse answered, **but I cannot say if he will answer.**

Muire was still sitting in the shadows on the roof of the Ash & Thorn when he came up behind her. She didn't turn. She could smell him, musk and bitterness and beneath it all, the clean scent of the ocean that Cathoair would never see.

"Speak."

His voice was soft, and very close. And Muire thought she heard a trace of her own tones on it. She felt him in her belly. "Did you ever love him?"

"Even as I love you," he answered. *You.*

Muire the Historian spoke the first lie of her life. "You want me, you mean."

Her fingers worried at the knotted brass pommel and wire-wrapped hilt of the sword laid across her lap. Silence. The heat of his breath warmed her throat, the back of her ear.

"I gave him up," she said. "I might even have won him, but as soon as I saw he might want somebody else, I walked away. I was too afraid of what he would choose, and so I made the choice for him."

"Walking away," he said. "We have that in common."

Still she did not turn, though she could feel him over her shoulder.

"This war will be the death of thee," he said. "Thee, and thy steed as well."

"So what? I should come away with you?" Now, she had to see him. She craned over her shoulder at his tired profile, leaning away. And he turned and looked her in full in the face, and touched her cheek with gloved fingertips.

"Leave me no more alone. Let the world end; the world is ending. If you crave living over letting go, we can go elsewhere, as others have."

And Muire smiled, and oh, the sudden light in his eyes. He was perfect: predator, avenger, hunter in the twilight. He crouched beside her, the Angel of Death—dark as a lodestone, and shining as a knife—and begged her not to die.

"Is that a knowing you have on you?"

"No," the wolf said. "There is no seeing and no seithr. The days of prophecy and heroes are ended. But I know it as I know the taste of blood; ascend, tonight, and thou wilt not come down again the same as thou art now."

"I owe her vengeance."

"Damn vengeance," he said.

"I am waelcyrge," she answered, holding his gaze. She rolled to the side, put a knee down, and stood with the sword hanging cloth-bundled in her hand, only the hilts peeking free. She closed her hand over them, but he didn't step back, only rose to face her. "I am *for* vengeance."

"Then you owe me vengeance before her." He spread his arms, the cloak rippling, baring his breast. "Did you call me here to take it? To pay back her servant's life and be free of his whispering, always the whispering? *Vengeance, vengeance, vengeance.*"

It was an eerily accurate mockery of Ingraham Fasoltsen's litany. But then, of course, Mingan had swallowed his soul.

And Muire shook her head. "I have chosen my vengeance for Ingraham Fasoltsen. He will have to content himself with the death of his employer. Probably," a small smile, "in the fullness of time, because I have no plans to kill her."

Mingan raised an eyebrow. Muire raised her right hand—the left one on the sword—and touched his cheek. "The children of the Light did not decide. We acted. We were the Snake's hands and teeth. Decisions . . . decisions are a divine prerogative, or a human one. Angels are not *deciders*."

He gazed at her, his face as still as water.

"When we chose something other than our destiny—when we chose something other than dying in the snow, under the weight of the tarnished—we both debased and elevated ourselves—"

"*Now* you believe in free will?" Rich, cold, his voice rang with irony.

"There comes a time when you have to decide for yourself,

and damn the voice of authority. And tonight, if I ascend not, there is no one but me to answer for the truth: that our world will pass from beneath us and be gone."

"Let it happen. Let it die."

"I know why you hunted her," Muire said. "The Technomancer. I know what the outrage was—"

"And you watched, two hundred years, and did nothing."

"I did not know."

"You did not care to know."

Muire closed her eyes and nodded.

His voice grew soft and distant, as if he spoke more to himself than to Muire. "But do not attribute to me a morality beyond what I contain. I am old, and the world has worn thin on me. I welcomed the Desolation. I *craved* it."

"Where were you," she asked him, "when the Desolation fell?"

He paused. "Freimarc."

Muire laughed. Deep and sure, ringing, while Mingan frowned at her like a cat whose sense of social niceties has been offended. She shook her head. "And your presence preserved it, as surely as my presence preserved Eiledon. And Kasimir's kept his valley. Because we were there, and what we were, and full of the life the world was losing. Ironic, isn't it?"

He stared at her. And then he closed his gleaming eyes, tilted his head back, and laughed in agony, fell and sorrowful.

She reached to touch him, let her hand fall as he raised gloved, iron-hard hands and scrubbed tears away. When he stopped, swallowing, his plait bouncing on his shoulder as he ducked his head, he would not meet her eyes. "So," he said. "I will live in your new world, candle-flicker, and I will continue alone."

"No, little darkness. Not alone."

She drew the sword from its bundle, leveled it at his chest, and he stared. He stood perfectly still, eyes on the point, making no move to defend himself or to flee. And then a wild sorrowful light flared into his eyes, and he looked past the blade, into Muire's. "I threw her into the sea."

"The sea gave her back."

"And you retrieved her from the wizard. Why?"

Muire reversed Svanvitr in her hand and extended her to him, pommel first. And Mingan—he stood as if frozen, watching the hilt of the sword as if it were the head of a snake.

"I came to kill you if you would not listen," he said. He made no move to take Svanvítr from her hand. "I have been watching the world wind down, and it is restful."

"It is not what you are made for." She stretched the sword further.

"I am fallen," he said. "There can be no answer for what I have done. I am everything the tarnished were, and more."

"Mingan, you were meant to be here, and yours is the hardest road of all. You dress in shadows, brother, but there is starlight in your eyes."

He gasped, his hands flexing at his sides. His eyes clenched shut again, and his head jerked once, sharply. "Strifbjorn might have lived. They all might have lived, without me."

"And they all might have died."

"No!" he cried, and then, "No," he whispered.

"You are forgiven," she said, usurping another divine prerogative, and he cringed. Cringed away, recoiled—as if whatever he felt had shocked him, and spun back toward her, hands outstretched. He snatched the crystal sword, blade slicing her fingers as he pulled it free. She let go, blood scattering from her hand.

"Decide," she said, and spread her arms out as he had, earlier. "My sword is in the kitchen. Yours is in your hand."

He raised Svanvitr as if to plunge her through Muire's breast, into her heart. The blade was dark, dark, dark.

Muire.

Muire took a step toward the point. Mingan drew her back another inch, lofted her above and behind his head like a javelin. Like the hand that held it, the tip of the shadowy blade shivered.

Muire!

"Decide," she said, as calm as if she had never run for her life from anything.

Svanvítr flared savagely into incandescence.

And it was the wolf who hissed once, turned on his heel in a whirl of cloak, and ran, unable to vanish into the shadows when the shadows streamed away on all sides from the brand of light in his hand. Footsteps, from he who was usually so silent, pounded the stairs. Muire heard a board crack, heard the hesitation and then the thump as he leaped the last flight to the ground.

She closed her eyes and breathed out, long and quietly. "Well," she said, hugging herself, wondering when she would begin trembling, "one redemption down."

Six million and twenty to go.

The wolf runs.

But what he runs from is in his heart, it is in his hand. He is no ghost now; his bootnails ring on stone. Shopkeepers and urchins turn to watch as he pelts past, his cloak aswirl about him, Svanvitr singing in his head with joy to be reunited. His intangibility, his anonymity, are stripped from him in a blaze of light, as surely as the sun at dawn strips the mist and mystery from a river. He is in the world now, and there is no escaping it. Pinned by the sword in his hand—

—at least until he pauses to think. And then he realizes, he has a cloak. The light can be swaddled away. He cannot stop it burning him—burning not his hand, his eyes, but his spirit and mind—but he can hide it, and perhaps find the shadows and the otherworld again.

He darts into a yard and tears his cloak over his head. The thick wool is soft, unwieldy. It clings to his hands and swings with heavy drape, but he manages the sword. Svanvitr is muffled.

He leans against the wall, panting, his face streaked with light. The song still burns through his mind, scourging, polishing. Stripping him clean.

Madness is nothing. Madness is an old friend, a comfort to him. He is the son of a god and a giantess. He is a god-monster. He is the Sun-eater. He was born to destruction, to mayhem, to wrath. The world is full of things that want destroying, and also full of those who do not covet destruction. So he was chained to the end of the world. There was a poem that was also a prophecy, and he lived it. *The wolf, till world's end.*

And now he is a wolf driven by the goad and the hunt, crazed by the cage and the chain. He is the wolf run mad—

Someone giggles.

He opens his eyes and looks, this way and that, expecting a child. The scent is not a child's, though, and the giggle is . . . unsettling. He sees a woman, a human—a halfman, he guesses they'd say, with their arbitrary unconsidered rankings—dressed in blue like a waelcyrge. But her blue is dingy, the hem torn, food stains on the breast of her dress. She's grown, older than Muire's pretty toy, and she holds a heavy bucket dangling from her hand. She looks right at him, though one of her eyes doesn't seem to focus. And she giggles. And says, in strangely accented words, "Ma, there's a man in the yard."

Like some wolves, some humans are simple. This is one. She steps toward him, and he edges back, the sword in his hand. He could take her, swallow her. Make her serve a purpose. Sustain him, darken him, layer him in stain. With his other hand, he touches the blood-warm silver swinging heavy in his ear.

She drops the bucket at the base of the kitchen steps with a thud. She reaches for him, one-handed, as if she means to stroke the plait fallen over his shoulder. He twists his head to the side, and his collar tightens against the tendons.

He is only a wolf. And a wolf without a pack is nothing.

And his pack's leader has reclaimed him.

He is the Grey Wolf, and no matter how the collar at his throat still chokes, it never could bind him for all time. Only until the end of the world.

The end of the world is upon them.

Betimes an old tree must fall, for a new one to find the Light.

Muffled sword in his hand, he steps into the shadows.

23

Algíz (shelter)

ᚠ

Maybe it wasn't a very good plan, but it was the only one Muire had. Considering her resources—two magical swords that weren't much use for anything practical except cutting through anything in their path; a spell-casting, mechanically inclined rodent; a catgirl with a whip; a retired cyborg tavern-keeper; an animate steam engine; and a deeply depressed nineteen-year-old—she thought she had done as well as could be expected.

Strifbjorn might have done better. But Strifbjorn was a war-leader, and she would never have his help again.

And after all, it might work. Because Muire suspected Thji-erry would never allow herself to be placed in a position where she was not the primary opponent. And so she would never expect Muire to play the distraction in her own plan.

Selene had already retrieved Muire's armor, along with Svanvitr—now disposed of—and Muire's fiddle. Cathoair and Cristokos helped her dress, and though she didn't need the help she permitted them to perform the service as befitted their sense of ceremony.

When Cathoair kissed her on the forehead, she even managed him a smile.

Kasimir came for her a little before sunset, and Muire walked out into the Riverside market square to meet him. No slinking in alleys tonight. They went to Thjierry openly, as befitted angels.

While Muire mounted, a crowd began to form, ringing Kasimir at what they perceived as a safe distance. The attention made him restive. Not nervy, as a horse might have been, but Muire could read in the set of his tail and the arch of his necks that he was basking in their fascination. She tapped him on the crest with her knuckles. "Stop posing for your statue. We've a long way yet to go."

I thought you might like to see it now, given the odds against us living long enough to see it cast.

Thanks. But she straightened the wires of his mane so they all fell down the same side of each neck, and settled herself in the saddle. *Ready when you are, beloved.*

He preened under the pet-name far more than under the grooming, and with a flick of his tail was airborne as effortlessly as if he cantered around a paddock. Heavy wingbeats bore them upwards, the air groaning under the weight of his massive steel form. Muire felt the wind in her face, sliding between the joints of her armor, and let herself laugh.

Kasimir's answering whinny had something of a stallion's shriek of challenge in it, as they climbed into the sky.

The last thing Muire had said to Cathoair was, "Do what Selene tells you," and he was damned if he was going to let her down. He wore the sword she'd given him awkwardly across his back. They hadn't found a scabbard to fit it, but Aethelred had sewn two steel rings to either end of a length of webbing, and slipped through those, with the baldric run across his chest, it stayed well enough.

If all went as planned, he would have to draw it before long. He thought of that, and tried very hard not to anticipate disaster.

Selene followed, like a guard; Cristokos and Cathoair walked ahead of her, side by side. She held her whip in her hand, uncoiled, and Cathoair had a moment to consider that if he were not the person—the unperson—he was, he might be having a hard time trusting her. But Selene was as honest and uncomplicated as a drink of water, and he found he appreciated that. Especially when she was at his back with a weapon, walking with him into a fight.

They came to the Broken Stair, and Cristokos stood aside so Cathoair could be the first to climb it. As he came to the top, he saw that there was an unman sentry posted, just as Selene has said there would be, and Cathoair—Selene and Cristokos behind him—walked forward slowly, his hands in plain sight.

"Achilles," Selene said. "Look what I found."

"He's armed," said Achilles, and Selene made a noise of agreement. "I have the weapon with reach," she said. "It was just as easy to let him carry it this far. Would you summon us three hoverboards, please, and then disarm him? Prisoner, spread your arms wider."

The golden-eared dog called for rides as Selene requested, while she said, very calmly, "While we are in the air, your board will be slaved to mine. Your duty is to stand very still and not fall. If you try to escape, my whip can reach you. Do you understand?"

"Perfectly," Cathoair said, and bit his lip.

Then Achilles came back to him, and hesitated. "Who is

this?" he asked, looking at Cristokos, who stood with his hood raised.

"Cristokos," Selene said. "There was something wrong with him, but now he's better. He turned in the nearman."

"I should call it in—"

"Please do." Cathoair tried not to stare at her tail, lashing. "That would be convenient. But first his sword, Achilles?"

"Bend down, please, sir."

Cathoair did as ordered, and heard the sword blade ring like a glass bell as Achilles pulled it free. The web baldric fell to the ground as the unman backed away, getting himself and the blade away from Cathoair's greater reach. And then he jerked, as if shocked or startled, and looked down at the thing in his hand, and dropped it to the stones. "Selene—"

He went to his knees, and Cristokos was instantly beside him, the striped hood thrown back and his black hand and his pink hand wrapped tight on Achille's wrists as the canine curled into a ball. "Shh," he said. "Shh. That one will endure. It is a promise."

Cathoair drew a deep breath and went to retrieve Alvitr. From above came the hum of the hoverboards descending.

The rattle of a helicopter greeted Muire before they had halfway ascended. She wasn't surprised; Thjierry had to be expecting them, given what she was doing to Kasimir's valley. But she did lean over his necks and urge him to climb harder, higher, faster. She didn't think Thjierry would shoot at them. But she hadn't thought Thjierry would sacrifice an entire world to save one city, either.

As the helicopter swung into view, Kasimir beat for altitude.

It was a glossy glass and metal bubble, spider-black, long mantis legs folded tight under the cabin. When Muire turned to look, she glimpsed the machine gun and rocket ports. "Go!" she shouted at Kasimir. "Go! Go!"

I do not fear that machine, he said, but he heeded her demands and fled it, putting himself between the helicopter and the glass and brick walls of the university so the pilot dare not take a shot.

I don't want to have to kill the pilot.

Oh, said the warhorse. **Of course not.**

He turned on a feathertip, a spiral as tight as a bedspring, and Muire felt the bend of his spine through her seatbones. Down now, down plunging, whizzing between buildings and, when he pulled out, over the heads of shrieking students. The helicopter roared after, electing a more conservative height, and Muire locked both hands on the pommel of the saddle and let the wind pull her arms out straight. Mouth open, whooping with joy as Kasimir ruptured the air.

And then there was Thjierry.

Kasimir backwinged like a peregrine, the snap shattering windows to both sides, and brought himself into an elegant stall. The helicopter overshot spectacularly.

The Technomancer stood in the center of a red brick path bordered by lilies, body canted at a sharp angle forward over her crutches, her hair shocked every which way by the wind. She stood impassive as Muire and the valraven descended, settling light as a dandelion seed to the walk before her.

Or so it seemed until his hooves touched brick and the brick powdered, the ground shuddering under his weight.

Muire drew Nathr but did not brandish the blade. Instead she lay it across her armored thighs. A touch of her heels sent

Kasimir forward, exactly as if he could feel her. "This time, I come to you in my strength, Thjierry."

The Technomancer pushed heavily at her props, and for a moment, Muire saw the scene as anyone else would. The heroic old woman in her frayed brown sweater, indomitable, uncowed before the armored witch on her iron beast of Hel.

"What do you want?" Thjierry asked. "I offered you allegiance. I *begged* you for help. And you destroyed my ally—your *friend*—Gunther, and assaulted me, and you come now why? To destroy me? Is Eiledon not dying fast enough to please you?"

It was a very pretty speech, and Muire wondered for how long Thjierry had rehearsed it. She was playing to the audience. And that audience was rapt. Thjierry might be the only one on the pathway—small and frail before Kasimir's might—but students clustered three deep behind every overlooking window (the shattered ones as well)—and Muire was sure that moreaux in force lurked just out of sight, and beyond every door.

"Oh, yes," Muire said, resigned to playing her role. It didn't matter. All that mattered was that Thjierry kept looking at *her*. "Let's talk about Eiledon and its death, *Technomancer*. Let's speak of how you have kept it alive all these years, not by your own strength, but by stealing hamarr. Let's speak of your *engine,* my lady magician, and how it is that the orrery draws hamarr from all the world to keep fresh what should be rotten. Let us speak of the souls you've enslaved, the minds you've bewitched. If you live by feasting on corpses, what is life?"

"Life," Thjierry answered, with profound dignity. "That's all it is. All there is. Life."

They faced one another across fifteen feet of brick, a scant five meters between the banks of white and bronze and burgundy lilies, and Muire thought she had never in her life seen someone who looked less afraid. One by one, the campus lights were flickering to life, white washing away iron twilight, and Kasimir and Thjierry each cast two long shadows from the lamps.

"So have you come to slay me, then? I warn you: I stand in my holdfast, on ground consecrated to Tyr, and it will not go easily for you."

"No," Muire said, as Kasimir lowered one head to lip weeds insolently from between the bricks. "I've come to do what one does with corrupt sorcerers. I've come to challenge you to a duel."

W here the hoverboards let them off, they separated. Cathoair came with Selene, but Cristokos went his own way, shoulders hunched and hands dry-washing, into the underground. Selene, who had been watching for it, did not even see him vanish.

The remaining two continued into the campus, businesslike but with concealed haste. Selene's presence precluded casual challenge. Even for the dinner hour, shortly after sundown, the pathways seemed deserted, and from somewhere not too far away Selene heard the brief thunder of steel hooves powdering stone.

"She's doing it," Cathoair said, and Selene folded her ears down tight against her skull.

They entered the library without incident. After his last visit, Cathoair knew the way as well as she did, and his long legs hurtled him up the stairs faster than she could manage unless she dropped to all fours and bounded like a cat. She caught him on the turns, however, and they stayed within two strides the whole way up.

She didn't like the unfamiliar web harness under her armor.

It chafed, and she would have stopped to pull at it, but there was no time now, and they were at the door.

The doorkeeper was Borje, though, and the heavy swing of his stone-black head and armspan horns brought Cathoair up short. The bull snorted, wet nose twitching, and lifted his chin to squint over the human at Selene. "What is this?" he asked.

"Show him," Selene said.

Cathoair hit him with the flat of the sword. Hard, maybe harder than he had to, and the bull blinked and then bellowed, "Hey!" and grabbed for the human with mammoth three-fingered hands. Cathoair sidestepped—fast, faster than any human Selene had ever seen—and whacked the bull again when he went by.

Selene cringed, thinking of torture sports and matadors, but again, the human drew no blood. And this time, the bull pulled up, confused, and turned to Selene blinking. "He hurt me," he said, and then sat down on the floor, doubled his fists in front of his belly, and curled around them as if to keep them safe.

"This is sickening," Cathoair said, and Selene pressed her thumb against the door.

Selene gave him a steadying look, and saw him swallow. "You should try it from the inside."

And then they were in the Technomancer's quarters, under the span of her airy brass engine, and Selene shut the door and with Cathoair's help dragged the sofa over and wedged it under the handle. "I can't open the drawers."

"That's the other thing the sword is for," Cathoair said, and strode grimly forward.

He went after the map drawers with the no-nonsense swing of a construction worker wielding a wrecking bar. No finesse, no technique, just heft and muscle and the sound of the blade cutting metal like the sound of peacocks screaming. And cut metal it did; like slicing paper with a trimming machine. Selene, from farther back, wielded her whip. Its monofilament tip cut much less dramatically: she moved her hand, and a section of drawer facing fell away.

But she was curious about the sword. "What is that made of? Diamond?"

"I don't know," Cathoair said, and looked along the blade. It blazed in his hand with a merry blue-white light. He frowned at it, and slung it back over his shoulder. Muire could sheath hers in a single automatic motion. Cathoair's technique involved some groping for the bottom ring.

Selene moved toward the ruined drawers so he would not notice her amusement. She coiled her whip and began drawing out swords, eminently respectful of the points and cutting edges.

They had three little piles of blades on the floor already when there was a click audible even over the ticking of the great machine, and inside the crystal domes of the orrery, a trap door swung up from the floor. Selene stepped back; Cathoair turned toward the noise. And within, Cristokos drew his narrow body out of the crawlspace and flattened himself against the floor, below the path of the wheeling planets. He began to inch forward, belly-crawling, almost slithering like a snake.

He did not look at them. They might have been invisible. But Selene and Cathoair shared a glance with one another and went silently back to work. Until Selene's hand brushed something in a drawer, and she stopped, frozen, as if she had touched a live electric wire. Her fingers closed on it; she drew it out without daring to look, and held it in her hand.

Solbiort.

"I don't understand."

Her name is Solbiort, the stallion repeated. **She is your sword.**

On the south end of the cricket pitch where she would do battle, Muire stood over the abyss and tuned her fiddle. The field was a little less than thirty yards of close-clipped grass, mown recently enough that the sharp, slightly musty scent of chlorophyll colored every drawn breath. The skies had darkened to indigo now, the light in them only visible where the trees were silhouetted, but the pitch was so brilliantly floodlit that the putrescent light from the Defile could not stain the world sickly green. Twenty yards north, Thjierry waited, leaning between her crutches with ill grace. Muire thought if it were not for those, and the lawn, she would be pacing.

Kasimir was not on the pitch, according to both plan and the rules of combat. He stood back and to the side, before the bleachers, with a clear line of sight and six of Thjierry's faculty sorcerers and three handpicked unmans to prevent him from interfering. If anyone were laying odds, Muire would have put her money on Kasimir.

I am quite certain she intends to claim me as a spoil.

If she defeats me, you still have a mission.

He snorted.

And that job is not *killing her.*

Fasoltsen murmured *Vengeance.* Muire bowed her head. *Sometimes justice is more complicated than an eye for an eye,* she told him. He wasn't interested in her excuses, though, so she rosined her bow, checked the fiddle's four melody and four drone strings one final, compulsive time, and composed herself for war.

Muire had no doubt Thjierry was the better sorcerer. She had never been much more than a dabbler, more interested in the music and the metallurgy and the bend of nib against paper than the magery any of those implied. And blacksmithing was not a battle-art, except in the preparation.

In its evolved form, neither was technomancy. But the skill it had developed from, the runamal—the craft and carving of letters and sigils of power—*that* had some virtue in combat. And because of Cristokos and Gunther, Muire knew that Thjierry was well acquainted with the antecedents of her art.

Rune-making and galdr, spell-singing, were not so different. Both were the sorceries of words, and instrumental music was just a different language. Muire might be older and of broader experience, but Thjierry was a professional.

Muire's advantage was that she did not have to win. She only needed to hold Thjierry's attention. And if she was careful not to consider too carefully the cost of losing, all was well.

There were no judges or referees in a wizard's holmgang. There was only one rule: the field of combat was sealed with the warriors within, and only the death of one of the duelists could unwork the spell of binding.

Muire let her bow and fiddle hang by her thighs, one in each hand, and nodded to Thjierry. And Thjierry nodded back, shifting restlessly on feet that seemed to pain her. A brown-haired wizard, tawny-skinned by contrast to his cream-white academic robes and mortarboard, stepped to the edge of the pitch. He spoke in a carrying tone. "Do you both agree that all other methods of settling your quarrel have been voided?"

"I do," said Muire. She could not make out Thjierry's answer, but the Technomancer's lips moved, and what she said seemed to satisfy the presider.

"Do you both agree to abide by the law of the holmgang? You will fight on an island, upon which one of you must die."

"I do," said Muire, and perhaps the wind had shifted, for this time Thjierry's answer carried.

"Have you any reason I should not seal the island now?"

"I do not," said Muire. She had left her helm and gauntlets strapped to Kasimir's saddle. Now she braced her fiddle beneath her chin and set the bow against it.

Some preparation had been made in advance. The presider only crouched and scratched a bindrune in the dirt with the tip of a yew twig.

Muire felt it take, a stillness and parity of air, and drew her bow sharply down.

Whatever work Cristokos was at inside the orrery, it was *hard* work, and Cathoair struggled not to fidget. He figured that he and Selene had bundled half a ton of swords—"More than four hundred at about three pounds a piece? At *least* half a ton," she said—and piled them before the long window, roped together with an intricate series of knots, and the rat-mage was still at it. He had a series of delicate tools, which he withdrew from inside his robe and replaced there until Cathoair wondered if he were wearing some sort of vest lined with elastic loops and tiny narrow pockets, and he had an access hatch open in the base of the machine and the upper half of his body inside.

Cathoair paced, trying not to listen to the sounds that filtered in from outside. They intruded anyway: the high wail of a fiddle, the roar of a crowd. And the flashing lights—green, gold, blue-silver.

He knew what the silver was. But it seemed buried under the green and gold.

Even Selene seemed to be getting nervous. "Cristokos, how much longer?" It was the first thing either of them had said to him since he began work. She had to pitch her voice loud to give it a chance of carrying through the crystal spheres, and Cristokos's protruding tail didn't even twitch in answer. Cathoair wondered how loud the clockwork was when you were inside it.

He bounced on his toes, swinging his arms, trying to find something to do with the restless energy. Spoiling for a fight, to be honest; it had all been far too easy so far.

And just as he was thinking that, someone started pounding on the door.

The first passage of magic was easy. Muire defended; Thjierry attacked. Muire's bow slipped and skidded along the strings, her fingers flying, the drone strings buzzing as the music rose. Songs of defense, songs of warding. No need to fight yet, when she could let Thjierry exhaust herself pummeling Muire's defenses.

The Technomancer was stronger, an adept and crafty with it. Muire had all the time and stamina in the world. *Let the other do your work for you*, Yrenbend would have said, and Muire, fingers flying, was grateful to his ghost. The first attack splashed against her defenses and rolled back like turbid water.

But frontal assault, death-magic, was not Thjierry's only weapon. The next one came subtler, a fingering at the edge of the music like the touch of elegant, intrusive hands. Thjierry chanted, not discord but harmony, and though her voice was dry and cracked over the rising wail of Muire's fiddle, somehow it changed the music, tangled through it. A spell to bleed; a spell to draw off power and hamarr and make it the spell-singer's.

Necromancy indeed. Necromancy worked upon the living.

Muire could have let it happen. She was immortal, ageless; she held all the hamarr she needed. Enough for cities of mortal men. But then that strength would be Thjierry's as well, and Muire could not permit that. She held herself tight, tuned her energies in a spiral. She became a vortex and let Thjierry's attack grope fruitlessly at the slick whirling edges of her power.

It wasn't entirely successful. Thjierry got hold of a thread, unraveled it like drawing cotton candy off the spool, like a dark companion winding off a giant star's photosphere. Muire could see the light, the spiral gyre, the flare of blue-silver fading to incandescent green. Green and gold, solstice colors, and Muire was a creature of brief chill summers when the sun never set, of the endless nights of winter.

Maybe it was, after all, she who was the monster. Perhaps it was Thjierry who was right—

The insinuating thoughts, another attack. Thjierry touched her hamarr, and sent poison back along it.

Muire gritted her teeth and counterattacked. She knew songs of combat, songs to lay warfetter and snap warriors' limbs. She used them now, the music wailing from her fiddle. The music was the sound; the sound was the word; the word was the rune; the rune was the power.

And a rune could freeze flesh, let blood, tear sinew. They were not the fort of her strength, but Muire knew the seventeen. And she did not think even Thjierry knew the eighteenth.

She leaned into the music and fought back, hard. The fiddle wailed, and Thjierry fell back a step, dragging her crutches. And then she rallied, raising her voice, thready and age-worn and shot with power, and the rise and fall of what Muire played seemed to echo, empty, across a vast and uncaring plain. She could barely hear the sound of her own music, just Thjierry's voice mounting higher, louder, drowning out everything that was not her words and her song.

The fiddle was no magical instrument, just a gift from a dying mortal man, but Muire treasured it. She played louder, faster, filling up the darkness, a manic reel that rose and rose and rose until—

The eight strings smoked and snapped.

The human started and spun at the clamor. Selene laid the back of her hand against his arm. "We're not going out that way," she said. "It's all right."

He didn't relax, exactly, but his hands dropped from the guard position. "We won't have long." His scent peaked; he slapped his palms together like a man about to get down to work.

A thump from inside the crystal dome drew Selene's attention. She turned to look in time to see Cristokos backing out of the access hatch, rubbing his head. He turned, saw them, and gave her a spidery thumbs-up.

Selene looked at Cathoair. Cathoair nodded.

Stallion? We're ready.

As Muire went to her knees, Kasimir spread his wings, scattering unmans and sorcerers like infantry before a charge. The ones before him fell back, turning, and he felt the immaterial bonds they meant to hang on him clutch at all his limbs. He knew nothing but contempt for their shackles. He was already rising.

Muire was sealed within the bounds of the holmgang, and he could not reach her. And reaching her was not the task she had set. So he beat higher, higher, and let his wings carry him away from another rider in mortal peril, while someone on the ground found the sense to reach for a machine pistol and bullets splashed against Kasimir's hide.

He would have remembered the window from last time even if Muire had not reminded him of it. He could have come in through the wall—he was Kasimir, and bricks and mortar could no more withstand him than could a paper bird-cage. But it was safer for those within if he could see and avoid them.

Bullets shattered on his haunches and wings, the impacts growing less with distance. It should still be possible to evacuate the others, frail as they were, until the enemy had time to close distance and the organization to mass their fire.

He must hurry.

Kasimir came up even with the top floor of the library and plunged through the plate glass window as if he meant to come out the other side of the building. Selene and Cathoair had warning. They should be under cover, away from the flying glass.

Yes. And here they came running, until he hissed at Selene to stop her skittering barefoot among the shards. It was a good hiss, somewhere between a steam locomotive and an angry adder, and it drew her up. A sword hung at her hip, lashed on a length of rope, and her hand fell to it in a gesture that could have broken even an iron-banded heart under the weight of memory. **Stand aside.**

They stood, and Kasimir advanced upon the crystal domes. He expected a stout blow of a wing should shatter them, but instead they rang like a bell, and he snorted and kicked out. The vibration was terrible; within the dome, Cristokos flinched and covered his ears.

I'll go out the way I came in, the rat said. *I'll meet you on the ground.* He slithered through the trap door and was gone.

Kasimir turned back to the window. Cathoair and Selene draped the bundled swords over his withers and around his necks until they hung against his chest and shoulders like bunches of grapes, distributed so his caparison would protect the ropes from the heat. They rattled when they moved.

They were not heavy.

Come. Be ready.

Cathoair and Selene picked across glass to stand in the frame of the broken window, Cathoair kicking glass splinters out of the frame until the lower edge, at least, was clear of daggers. Selene drew a strap of her harness free of the collar, and threaded a rope through the loop, making it secure with a series of careful knots. Cathoair mirrored her, checking each of his knots against hers. She glanced at his rope and nodded, and then they turned to Kasimir. "Ready," Selene said, and gave him the ropes.

He took one in each mouth. **Trust the harness. Don't hold the ropes. You will burn your hands if you try.**

When he flew out of the window, it was slow and controlled, his wings moving on long gentle sweeps. He did not spiral down to the city, but rose, traveling away and afar.

Muire heard Kasimir break free as she fell, as the neck of her fiddle snapped in her hand, and breathed a prayer of thanks she knew would go unheard. The grass was wet under her knuckles. Her armor bit into her knees. She whimpered.

The fiddle was ruined. She left it where it had fallen. Got one foot under her and then the other. Rose painfully, as shuffling steps dragged close.

She stood and looked Thjierry in the eye.

The Technomancer stopped three meters away and waited. Her crutches dangled from her elbows; she stood wobbling wide-legged as a foal, unsteadily. One palm was held upraised and a bindrune blazed on it, carved with the short knife she still held in her left hand.

Muire almost imagined she could see the wires behind the blood. "Oh, Thjierry. Don't you see it's over? They have a *chance*."

"If I could not do it, it could not be done." Her fingers tightened on the knife. "I wish you could have helped me try, instead of ruining everything."

"I wish your answer had been something I could have borne." Muire drew Nathr and let it sway in the air like the snake it was named for. It wasn't much defense against the warfetter—blindness, deafness, and incapacity—that burned on Thjierry's hand, waiting to be sent to her—but it was better than nothing at all.

"I'm sorry," Thjierry said, and turned her hand to blow across it as if she were blowing a kiss.

Her gesture might have been to slit the flap of an envelope holding him, for with it the Grey Wolf stepped out of the shadows at her side. "Mingan—" Muire shouted, raising her blade.

"Vengeance for your passenger, sister," he said, and swept Thjierry into his arms, knocking her crutches aside. She struggled against him, kicking, and he pressed his mouth down over her shout. Muire plunged forward, hand locked on her blade, but before she had covered half the meager distance, Thjierry's knife-hand came up and sank the blade hilt-deep in Mingan's throat. She tore, a savage gesture, and blood spilled over her hand, but the knife did not move far. It stopped on something, and by then, though her hand groped at the hilt, she had no strength to wield it.

The blow seemed not to discomfort the wolf at all. And Muire had stopped, arrested as if by magic herself, and pressed the knuckles of her sword-hand to her mouth. She willed herself forward, but her feet would not step. Powerless.

There was strength in the old woman yet. She took a long time dying, while the blood dripped across Mingan's collar. Too long, too long. Something was wrong, more wrong than Mingan committing his murder. Because Thjierry hung limp in his arms, and the holmgang island flickered and went out, and the Grey Wolf seemed to swell and crest and crash and shimmer full of light and energy—

It was not only her he was drinking, but the Serpent, and the city, and all the hamarr she had drawn into herself to keep Eiledon vital.

He was drinking down the world.

"Mingan! Enough! Enough! Mingan, *hear me!*" Whatever emotion had held her, horror released her now, and Muire darted forward, tugging his arm, hauling Thjierry's corpse out of his arms.

"Wolf, I charge thee *stop*." She dashed him across the face with Nathr's hilt.

He jerked back, hand to the wound, and stared at her, his eyes bottomless and full of gleams of light. Then he dropped his hand and the split cheek and the bruise were as if they had never been. He tugged the knife from his throat, looked at it incuriously, tipped his head like a wolf, and slid it into his sleeve.

"As you bid," he said, and went away.

24

Kenaz (the pyre)

〈

When Muire left the holmgang, none of the sorcerers stood against her. She walked among them, stripping off her armor, letting it fall. She was too tired to carry it. The sword she kept, though she returned her to her scabbard. She kicked away her boots before she climbed the library's portico stair.

She found Cristokos in the atrium, beneath the glass towers of books. He had been shot and had fallen crumpled, a tiny fragile thing underneath his voluminous robes. Still warm, when she composed his limbs and drew the hood down over his eyes, when she stroked the hand-woven cloth, sticky with his clotting blood, and she wished—strangely, sadly—that she had had a chance to return his sword. That they had had a chance to play music together just once.

Or just once more.

But wasn't that unfair? He was not Yrenbend, no matter how she recollected him. Once more, to her, was once only to him. That she saw in him someone who had been a friend should not be his burden to bear, but hers. Like the Dweller Within, it was her pain alone, and perhaps unkind to burden another with it.

It isn't fair. No. It was not; not fair at all.

It was only history, in the weight of all its injustice.

Too late for that revelation to spare Cathoair. He had asked her what gave her the right to choose for him; she might have said, the All-Father. But the All-Father had long abandoned them.

Left *her*. And so only she remained, to assign herself that right, and the responsibilities that went with it.

Like cleaning and composing poor Cristokos as best she could, and kissing him on the cheek, so her nose ruffled his fur. He smelled of clean animal and blood.

"Don't take this the wrong way," she whispered in his ear. "But I hope you don't have to come back again."

She took his flute. She did not think he would miss it.

There was another moreau at the top of the stair, and she thought at first that he was dead also. But as she drew close, she saw him trembling, and crouched beside him, one hand resting on his broad neck, below and behind his mighty horns. They were bull's horns.

She didn't flinch when he lifted his head.

"Who are you?"

"Borje," he answered, and she bent down and kissed him on his great slimy nose.

"Go rest, Borje," she said. "It's going to be all right. All is well."

Her second lie, she thought, as she watched him descend.

Ah well, it didn't matter now.

She had to cut the door open with her sword, but that also didn't matter. Because when she let herself into the Technomancer's tower, it was empty except for the wreckage of the drawers, and a shattered window.

The orrery had wound down.

When Kasimir returned, well into the following morning, he found her still waiting there.

This time, they flew toward the ocean again. He'd left Selene and Cathoair in his valley, along with all the swords.

The trees die. It is a kindness that Cristokos will not see.

Muire touched the flute and didn't say a word.

The moon was up; the beach glowed bright below them. Kasimir landed almost in his footsteps from the night previous. And Muire slid down his shoulder and ran to the water's edge, to call forth the Dweller Within.

She was not as surprised as she would have liked to go unanswered. She looked at Kasimir, who stepped across the tideline toward her. His ears came up, and he said, **I have nothing more**, as if asking forgiveness.

"Thjierry fed the Serpent to the wolf," Muire said. "She had all that energy twisted up in herself and her Tower and her orrery, and she used it to beat me, and she tried to use it to keep Mingan from swallowing her soul."

Yes. I think so.

"We lost."

We die in peace, he said. **That's something.**

Muire slapped his shoulder with the flat of her left hand. "Come on," she said. "Let's fetch Selene and Cathoair, and go and die at home."

When Kasimir returned them to the city, Selene and Cathoair were not—exactly—as she had last seen them. But they didn't speak of it that night, and not until a day or so after, when they had retrieved Cristokos's body and given it to the river, and attended Thjierry's state funeral—after which Selene went to each of the unmans in attendance in turn and kissed them on the mouth.

Muire could not help but catalogue their reactions when they pulled away and licked their lips, staring at her. Some shaken, some avid, some wincing. As many responses as there were unmans, and there were a great many unmans indeed.

Selene came and stood beside her, after. "I wish I could say thank you."

Muire closed her eyes, because they stung less when she did. "I understand. Your response to what I did was not . . . uncomplicated."

"The Grey Wolf was looking for death," Selene said, when she'd been still long enough that Muire thought she might be dozing in the afternoon sunlight. "So were you, and so was I. A pack of would-be suicides."

"I found something else," Muire answered unhappily.

Selene rumbled, leaning her shoulder against Muire's shoulder. It was a moment before Muire realized she was purring in pain. "It's broken," she said, and Muire did not ask what *it* she meant.

As for Muire, she didn't weep until she got home and turned on her vii, and no-one wished her a happy birthday.

Before midsummer, what babies were born, were born dead. Aethelred, Cathoair, and Selene came and went, went and came, never staying long. They were busy with a city in need of hospice care, and with the fall of the Technomancer, whatever peace was kept in Eiledon was kept by Cathoair or the moreaux.

Muire was no help, and Kasimir did not leave his valley. She could not bring herself to trouble him, though she ached in his absence. How easy it was, to grow accustomed to having a friend. But he had his vigil, and she had hers.

And so she watched the world ending.

She was, she knew, poor company, brief and cold. She could have gone out and doctored the sick, but she only managed the work briefly, when Sig was felled by that winter's influenza. He lived, though Muire knew it was only a stopgap. Aethelred came and lectured once or twice. She didn't yell back. She was too tired, through the autumn and into the cold, and something was stirring in her belly, making her hips ache and filling her with sleep.

It will never quicken, she thought, and indeed, if it lived in her womb it grew more slowly than any mortal babe.

And then it kicked, and Muire feared for it.

In the deep of winter she stood at her window and watched the river flow its icy channel. She laid a hand against her belly and said, *Kasimir.*

I hear you.

Are you well, beloved?

I am in my valley. I miss Cristokos.

I miss him, too, she said. She pressed her hands against her mouth. It was becoming a nervous habit. She frowned and forced them down. *Kasimir, I want to come home with you to die. I want to leave this place. Will you come and fetch me?*

In a little, he said. **Give me a few more days alone.**

————

The last time Cathoair came to Muire, he came alone, very early. She was wrapped in her robe, sitting at the table and drinking the tea Sig had brought, or at least rolling the bowl between her palms. He came barefoot in the snow—he was always barefoot, now that the cold no longer troubled him—and barechested, wearing nothing but a pair of loose white trousers covered in patch-pockets and a swordbelt with a sword. Muire rose to let him in when he knocked. The river was at his back. She smiled at him across the snow.

"You look good," she said, although his eyes were dark. She tugged her robe tighter over her collarbones, wondering if it would hide what little belly she showed.

"You look awful," he replied. "I came to talk."

"I'd like to listen," she answered. "Come inside."

She led him into the foundry, which was quiet and dark, the drapes closed. He hauled them open and looked around. "Dusty."

"I haven't been using it much." She waved at the pot, the steaming bowl. "Tea?"

"No, thank you." He crossed the dark slate floor, spattered with droplets of metal bright as stars, and caught her under the chin with long, scarred fingers. "You loved him."

"Yes?" She hadn't meant it to sound like a question, but it insisted on becoming one in her mouth.

"Who I used to be." He looked to the left, mouth working. "Useless language."

"I helped invent it," she said. "Thanks a lot." And when he smiled, abashed, she found the strength to say, "I loved him. I loved you. After a fashion."

His eyes gleamed softly, with a blue-white Light she recognized. "I wouldn't have hurt you for the world."

"Oh, Cahey." She brushed his hand aside. "It's the world that hurts us, you idiot."

He snorted. "But we hurt each other too. I didn't want this. I didn't *ask* for this."

"What?"

"Immortality," he said. "Futility. Dying for a cause."

"It's not the cause that's killing you." She touched his scarred cheek with her fingertips. "If I were strong, I would have done it alone. I could have spared you and Selene."

"We'll be the last—"

"I know. I'm sorry. I'm sorry. I'm a coward and weak, and I couldn't—" She turned, but he came around her. Escape was not so easy. "I couldn't—"

"You couldn't be the last one twice."

"No," she said. "I am not strong."

"Oh Muire." He looked away, and she flinched from it. But then he looked back and said, "You are the strongest thing in the world. It's just that there is some stuff nothing can withstand. Not flesh and blood. Not angels. Not the whole damned mortal universe. That's all."

"Oh," she said.

And they were silent for a while, until he touched her arm. "My love is not water in a bucket, you know. It's not as if someone else can drink it all up and leave none left for you."

Oh, little boy, when did you get so wise? She didn't have an answer. She was selfish, and she always had been, and all she could have said was, *I can't stand not being first in your heart a second time.* And that was wrong: he was not Strifbjorn, and it was not fair to try to make him be.

Not fair, not fair. But then, she had never seen fair in a thousand years. Why should the world alter, now that it was over? She changed the subject, to sting him free. "Your mother?"

He stepped back and half turned. "Gone."

"How?"

"Easily," he said. He closed his eyes. Bowing his head, he pinched the bridge of his nose between his fingers. "In the end. Gone upon a kiss."

"I would have . . ."

He opened his eyes and cocked his head, and gave her one last smile full of bitterness and glory. He spiraled back to her like a sooty-winged moth orbiting a candle, so she pressed one hand flat against his chest to stop him coming too close. If he embraced her, he'd know; he'd feel the doomed life moving inside her. Better, far better he went away in ignorance. *What the eye witnesseth not, the heart never grieves.*

His heart beat evenly against her palm. "Muire. Are you sure you want to die alone?"

"I'm sure," she lied, for the third time. *Kasimir, come and get me.* "There's nothing I want from you. Cathoair—"

"Don't say it."

"I just wanted to say—" She had her dignity. "—I'm sorry."

His eyes tight, he jerked away. His hair stuck out like a horse's docked tail. It was getting longer.

"Fuck me," he said. "This is the happy ending." And kissed her forehead across the distance between them before he went away.

———

Mingan was waiting, wearing his crystal sword, when she came up the snowy iron stair to the roof, where she had heard him moving. His eyes glittered like faceted stones, and not merely with reflected light. He said, "I noticed your lovely child leaving. From the riverbank."

She did not ask what he had been doing, standing under her window in the dawn.

He ducked his head. His nostrils flared, and he touched her stomach. "Muire—"

"It will never be born alive," she said. "There's no life left in the world to feed it."

"His."

"Mine," she answered, and pushed his fingers away.

"I came to ask your hand one final time."

She touched his arm through the cloak and shirt. He did not seem to notice. "Three times pleaded, and three times refused. Like Jenet in the history of Black Jenet—"

"She accepted the fourth offer," he answered.

"That was a ballad, wolf."

"And this is the world. I need you. I'm changing."

She moved her hand and touched his chest. His heart beat slowly, unalterably, too close to bear. "Let me see your eyes."

He turned to her, and his eyes were blind with Light. His hand came up to brush his collar, under the open neck of his shirt. She could see the welt it had worn, cutting into soft flesh. His brow wrinkled vertically and he cocked his head to the side. And Muire almost laughed: he really *did* look like a wolf when he did that. A worried wolf.

"Let us go," he said. "Leave this world. Let us find another. Your child might be born alive—"

She smelled him, felt the heat of his hand as he laid it on

her arm. A fat, wonderful moon hung overhead, low in the sky near the Tower, clear in the night and undimmed by the faded, still-fading, Defile. Near it, Muire made out the reflected light from two antique satellites, barely visible as disks.

"Refuse a duty? Oh, wolf. Surely you know better. You know what is in you, Mingan. You know what you swallowed."

"I am the Sun-eater," he said. "But that was in another lifetime, and the world that was is dead."

She shook her head. "I mean the Serpent, not the sun."

Silence. But by the wolf-sherd within her, she guessed what he was thinking. "Thjierry stuffed a god down your throat."

No laugh, but his eyebrows twitched with the flicker of his eyes. "It's not the first time. Nor even the third."

She *did* laugh, and that was fine. She needed it. "You know what you must do."

"I don't want it," he said. "I can't bear my own burdens. How can I carry anyone else's?"

Mountains, she thought. *You can't get anyone else up them. It doesn't stop us trying, though.*

She smiled. She knew now what was expected, what the end would be. "Neither do I. But I'll take it from you."

"You—?"

"Kiss me."

He stared. "Muire—"

Her heart was a razored fragment in her chest. She didn't want it either. *But then, what has wanting to do with anything?* "Shut up. You said you didn't want it. You're fighting it with everything that you've in you. So pass the burden to me. I'm asking for it."

"It's not complete."

"I know how to mend it." And she did, too—and he had

showed it to her, all unwitting. The eighteenth rune, carved in the root of the world-tree. The thing that brought them back, again and again. The thing that should have brought back the All-Father too, had his death not been so determinedly final.

"Your child—"

"It's her chance to be born at all, you old bastard. Give *in*."

He stared at her, but she was adamant. She took his plait in her hand and tugged it, demanding. And so he bent down, softly, and softly kissed her on the mouth. She breathed in, and he breathed out, and her senses filled with the scent of cut grass, the scent of ylang-ylang, the sound of wings and of the ocean.

The pain began, and with it came the glory. Something rang from her—a ripple through water, a peal through still air. Where it passed, the light flickered for an instant brighter.

When he drew back, his mouth was trembling. "I knew the world wouldn't end yet," the wolf said. "I just hoped I was wrong."

"How did you think you knew?"

"Heythe promised me she'd come back." His smile showed teeth, and Muire almost choked on it.

"You put a great deal of store in the word of a traitor."

"A goddess," he said. "The *threat* of a goddess."

"Oh," she said. And nodded. "Yes. Are you wearing a knife, Mingan?"

"I have," he said drily, "the one the Technomancer stuck into my neck."

"Give it here."

He did. And she bared her arms, and into each one, carved a rune. The eighteenth rune, the secret one, that she now knew.

When she was done, she gave him back his knife. "Mingan? Come and walk by the river? I think it might be my last time."

They walked in the moonlight, on the snowy stones, beneath the stars and the shining lights high in Eiledon's towers. Muire threw a shiny coin—a copper coin, a very old one—halfway across the Naglfar, and thought of too many names to name them all in one blessing.

Mingan, watching, laughed bitterly.

"Mingan."

He looked up as if his name were a caress, and then as if what he looked upon were a source of wonder. "It hurts you."

She remembered the ancient, eyeless, wounded Wyrm and bile rose in her throat. But she remembered also Kasimir's valley, and Cristokos feeding her strawberries that each, individually, tasted of summer and of themselves. And it was too late to change her mind now anyway.

She said, "There will be more pain than that."

The light in the wolf's eyes dimmed—grief, or something darker. "Why did you forgive me? After all the darkness, and the blood on my hands?"

She shrugged. "Do you think you have to die to be reborn?"

"Don't be ridiculous—"

But she touched his sword-hilt, and silenced him. "You know what the eighteenth rune was? The secret one?"

"Rebirth," he said. "Resurrection. When the old world went down, the All-Father carved that rune in the root of the world-tree. And so what died did not die forever."

"It's in the swords too," Muire said. "And now it's in me. We're all stuck. All of us. And the others don't know *anything,* because those that die before they're born again forget. They're not the same person anymore, and no matter what we do to them, how much we hate them for it—"

"I know," he said.

"Cathoair and Selene. They'll never know what we know. You. And me. And the valraven. It's only the ones who live through the transformation who remember. And somebody has to tell the others."

"Oh," he said. He squared his shoulders under the gray cloak, and Muire laughed at him. "Yes, Historian."

The first thing you may explain, said a great iron voice that rang between them, **is what you meant, exactly, when you said that we were brothers.**

Kasimir!

He spiraled out of the sky, gleaming in the starlight like a stallion blown from glass. And Muire laughed out loud when she saw him. Each feather on his wings was perfect and alabaster, and his hide shone so clean in the moonlight that the shadows on him were as blue and glowing as shadows on the snow.

He landed and folded his wings with a precise flip-and-settle, brushing Muire's cheek with the softest of feathers.

She threw her arms around his nearest neck.

His muscle was warm and firm under her hands, his hide strong and taut as silk. Flawless.

Your doing, he said. **Your miracle, again. The world renewed.** And then, ears flickered flat: **If any of my brethren lived, they would say I was careless of riders.**

She kissed his noses and rubbed his ears; he sighed and stretched with pleasure. "You've been a long time without your ears scratched, beloved."

His eyes were dark liquid amber, appraising, sorrowful as

the eyes of warhorses become. **No such courage in all the world**, he said slowly, nosing her breast over her heart.

Mingan stood and watched for a moment, and then turned to go. And Kasimir said, **Do not.**

The stallion bowed one head over Muire's shoulder and leaned his porcelain muzzle against the small of her back. His horns shone ivory and gold, reflecting in the river along with the streetlights. The wolf turned and looked over his shoulder. "You have tasks," he said quietly.

You are not to be alone.

Mingan shook his head. "She's made her choice," he said, and tried to smile.

I know, the warhorse replied, shaking out his gorgeous manes. **I am Kasimir.**

Muire stepped back to see him more clearly. "Not Selene?" Mingan's jaw just worked, soundlessly.

And Kasimir tossed his heads, speaking in familiar, exasperated tones. **This one made me wait two thousand years for her. Will you do the same?**

"You will do this," Muire said to the wolf.

"I'm not worthy," he said at last, and Muire laughed out loud and skipped back a step, pulling him closer to her horse.

"He would not choose one unworthy," she said, still laughing, and laid the wolf's hand on his nose. They regarded one another—Kasimir placid, waiting, and Mingan like the victim of an arranged marriage.

"Shadows!" Muire swore. A sort of translucence was shivering through her, as if she were somehow becoming a thing of light and cloudy glass. She had to hurry; there was no time. The child kicked in her, stronger. Determined. "If I'm to suffer all the ills of the world, you two *are* going to keep yourselves busy making sure that it's as pleasant a place as possible. And that starts with you, wolfling, not making your steed unhappy."

"Lady," the wolf said, and laid his hand on the hilt of his sword, "we are but four. You lay a task before us."

"Wolf," she answered, stepping away from that darkest of warrior angels and his shining, shining stallion, "at least *you* don't have to do it by *yourself.*"

"You grieve me, Bright one." The light in his eyes was at war with tears and shadows.

I GRIEVE *for* YOU, came the answer. And, spreading white, sudden wings, what had been Muire knew that it was time to go.